SCOTSMAN'S KISS

Connor lifted his right hand and slowly unwrapped a bloodied lady's handkerchief from around his knuckles. He held it up for Charlotte's inspection. "Sorry, about the condition."

Astonished and touched, she stared at the lace-trimmed good luck token she'd given Erik in the draper's shop. "You carried my handkerchief into the ring?"

"Wrapped around my hand, just as you saw," Connor said, a grin spreading across his battered face at last. "You know, I think it brought me luck."

His pleasure coaxed a smile to Charlotte's lips. "I'm glad you won, Connor, truly I am."

"Then give the victor a kiss."

She laughed, immensely relieved to know he was well enough to devil her. He deserved a victor's prize. She stretched up to brush a kiss along his cheek, but he caught her shoulders and pressed his lips firmly against hers.

His grasp tightened on her. Charlotte tilted her face up to his, too eager to know the taste of him once more to resist. When he took her mouth again, she opened up to him like a flower, inviting him to deepen the kiss . . .

Books by Linda Madl

BAYOU ROSE

A WHISPER OF VIOLETS

THE SCOTSMAN'S LADY

Published by Zebra Books

THE
SCOTSMAN'S
LADY

LINDA MADL

Zebra Books
Kensington Publishing Corp.
http://www.zebrabooks.com

ZEBRA BOOKS are published by

Kensington Publishing Corp.
850 Third Avenue
New York, NY 10022

First Printing: September, 1998
10 9 8 7 6 5 4 3 2 1

Printed in the United States of America

To my sister, Lisa, who is not my twin,
but my dear sister nonetheless

Acknowledgments

Thanks to all who helped so generously in the preparation of this book in many and varied ways: Janette and Betty Kenny, Kayla Westra, Heather Heath-Frank, Margaret Ohmes, Kas Randolph, Leann Shoaf, Kristine Hughes, Evan Marshall, and John Scognamiglio.

The Kiss

The greatest bliss
Is in a kiss—
A kiss of love refin'd,
When springs the soul
Without control,
And blends the bliss with mind.

Ye fleet too fast—
Sweet moments, last
A little longer mine!
Like Heaven's bow
Ye fade—ye go;
Too tremulously fine!

—Charlotte Dacre
From *Hours of Solitude*

ONE

Outskirts of London, 1828

Enthralled, Charlotte St. John stared at the prizefighter's naked beauty. She could but marvel at the poetry of his every bare-chested move. Shoulders surging. Huge. Powerful. Dark head held high. Golden eyes flashing. The very sight of him made her face grow warm.

Vanished was her vow to avert her eyes from the violence in the boxing ring. Charlotte had never attended a prizefight before, though her twin sister Cassie had. Charlotte had known from the outset that she would hate the fighting. Nothing had changed. She still hated the violence.

But the moment the dark-haired boxer stepped onto the canvas and swung at his opponent, he held her transfixed. Even as a droplet of perspiration trickled down between her breasts she could not look away. *He was the most gorgeous creature she'd ever laid eyes on.*

"That's him, the Scots boxer we're going to meet," quipped Tony Derrington, Charlotte's cousin who sat across from her in the open carriage. He'd already pulled off his hat and begun to cheer along with the rest of the crowd. "I say, he is a fit fellow, is he not?"

Charlotte snapped open her fan, flapping it frantically in a vain attempt to cool her flushed cheeks. "Yes, indeed he is."

The coachman had wisely parked the landau in a spot that

gave them an unhindered view of the boxing ring roped off in the meadow below. The May sun bore down on them as they watched the victorious boxer stroll around the ring and the odds-makers pay off the wagers on his match.

"Yes, by Jove," agreed one of the young men leaning against the Derrington landau. "The Brawlin' Scot is a fine fighter."

The prizefighter had just defeated another boxer with a knock-out punch to the jaw. The defeated fighter, sporting a swollen-shut eye and a bloody nose, was being helped from the ring.

"What a thundering good bout!" Tony added. "I see why he has set all of London to talking. What say you, cousin?"

Despite her dismay with the other man's injuries, Charlotte could hardly make her breathing return to normal as she watched the victor accept the crowd's adulation.

A self-assured grin lit the Scotsman's handsome face. Arms raised and urging his audience to cheer louder, he paced along the ropes. His short, dark hair glistened in the sunlight and hard muscles rippled beneath the gleaming perspiration on his chest. Even the three long, white, parallel scars that slashed down his ribs and across his back could do nothing to diminish his naked magnificence.

"Cousin?" Tony prompted, peering across the landau at Charlotte. He'd been concerned about her professed dislike for the sport. "What do you think?"

"Yes, I can see why he might inspire comment," Charlotte allowed, her voice as casual as possible. Yet strange feelings fluttered within her. She never would have dreamed that the sight of a half-naked brute who made his living bloodying peo-ple's noses could send shivers through her. She was mortified.

"Brawlin' Scot" the crowd chanted. "Brawlin' Scot." At the sound of their renewed roar, the Scots boxer threw back his head and laughed. He loved them as much as they loved him. Despite her condemnation of the sport, as much as Charlotte wanted to diapprove, she found herself caught up in his pleasure.

She could not bring herself to look away from his naked muscular chest, sprinkled with dark ringlets. Or from his kilt swinging easily about his long legs, giving a glimpse of shapely knees dusted with dark hair.

Was it silky or coarse? Charlotte wondered, then blushed as she squinted to get a closer look. Suddenly aware of the impropriety of her thoughts, Charlotte waved her fan nervously in her face. Forcing herself to look away, she took a shaky breath. She had never contemplated such intimate questions about a man before—not even about Edward to whom she was nearly affianced. What was happening to her?

"You're not feeling unwell, are you?" Tony asked, leaning toward her.

"What?" Charlotte stared at her cousin. "Unwell, no, I'm fine."

"Good," Tony said, obviously reassured. "We'll make our way over to Nigel Eldwick's coach as soon as the crowd clears. He always hosts drinks for any of the fighters who care to meet Society and we always join his party. The Scotsman should be there too." Tony turned away to speak to the other young men gathered around their landau.

They were expected? Charlotte drew a deep breath. Tony and Cassie were expected. Not her, but today she was Cassie and she would have to go.

Annoyed with her foolish reaction to the prizefighter, Charlotte frowned at the rabble. She'd only come with Tony today as a favor to her twin sister Cassandra and her fiancé, Dudley. They wanted a respectable alibi for the day and they seemed to think that Cassie being seen at a boxing match would suffice.

Charlotte had worn an oversized hat to help with her disguise—not that she needed it. She and Cassandra were identical in every way, from their striking red hair to the slant of their delft blue, kittenish eyes. Only a few people could tell them apart. Mother and Nana, of course. Tony and Tony's mother, Aunt Dorian. Except for when Papa was angry, he knew them apart. Otherwise, servants and friends saw whom they expected to see.

Cassandra had often used their identical likeness to her advantage. She loved the unconventional—the more outrageous the adventure, all the better to Cassie's way of thinking.

Until today, Charlotte had willingly aided and abetted her sister. Sometimes it had been more fun to impersonate Cassie than to be Charlotte—though she would admit that to no one.

But she wished she did not have to accompany Tony to Eldwicks' little ringside gathering. Charlotte spied ladies in several of the open carriages. But on the whole it was riffraff that surged across the heath and around their carriage. The crowd smelled of unwashed bodies, stale cigar smoke, and ripe ale. Their talk was full of irreverent boxing cant and harsh oddsmaking. How on earth could Cassie, Dudley, and Tony enjoy such base entertainments among the lower classes? Charlotte sniffed at the thought.

Gorgeous as the boxer in the ring was, Charlotte was sorry she'd ever agreed to this masquerade.

"I'm glad you're enjoying the outing," Tony commented, nodding in the direction of the ring. "His name is Connor McKensie. Can you credit it? He's a member of the aristocracy."

Aristocracy indeed, thought Charlotte, shoving thoughts of his beauty aside. The man in the ring was brawny, bare-legged, and completely unrefined. A boxer. Beautiful, perhaps, in a Greek athlete sort of way, but definitely unrefined. Hardly aristocracy. Yet, once she glimpsed him again, she could not drag her gaze from his dazzling good looks.

"Spectacular bull, ain't he?" said one of the other young men loitering around their carriage. "He's from one of the old Highland clans. I hear there ain't nothing to do in them hills but drink, steal each other's sheep, brawl and breed. They say he's one of the best."

Tony frowned at the young man, who instantly straightened and touched his hat. "Pardon me, Miss St. John. One of the best at brawling, I meant to say, of course. He's good at the brawling."

"And what sort of recommendation is that?" Charlotte snapped, as her wayward mind noted how nicely the Scotsman's laced leather footwear clung to his muscular calf.

"Did you hear about his fight last month?" began another of Cassandra and Tony's friends who was leaning against the carriage. "He beat that bully of a fighter in Cambridge. That's when I first heard the tale about the scars. You've heard it, haven't you, Derrington?"

What about the scars? wondered Charlotte, remembering the white scars on the Scotsman's back. When Tony, who was still watching the fighter, didn't reply immediately, she nudged his foot with hers. "Tony, the scars?"

"The scars? Right, I heard it happened in the Highland cliffs," Tony said finally. "He actually killed a wild Scottish lion with his bare hands."

Charlotte's breath caught in her throat. *Bare hands*. Her gaze fixed on the boxer's *beautiful, bare hands*. As if on cue, the man Tony had called Connor McKensie waved large, powerful hands over his head once more. The crowd sent up another cheer.

What would it feel like to be touched by those hands? A chill raced down Charlotte's spine despite the mysterious melting heat that trickled along her limbs and flooded into her face.

"Are you well, cousin?" Tony asked again, sliding her an uneasy look.

"Yes, of course." Charlotte nodded her assurance quickly. "Didn't I just tell you I'm fine."

But her heart sank as she realized she had failed to mask her mysterious reaction to the dark-haired man in the ring. She and Tony were partners in crime and she did not want to fail him. If Aunt Dorian knew what they were up to, Tony would suffer as much as she and Cassandra. With determination she forced a Cassandra-like smile to her lips.

"Then, shall we go make McKensie's acquaintance?" Tony asked, as he climbed out of the landau.

Charlotte hesitated. At the moment she longed for the cloistered safety of her quiet study where she could examine the new translation of Homer that she'd found in the bookstore last week.

"I say. Tony Derrington? Cassandra St. John?" A slender man in a tall hat and a bright green waistcoat stood up in his landau on the far side of the meadow and waved his gold-headed cane at them. "Do come over for something cool to drink. The Scots fellow will be here soon."

"Hello, Eldwick. We're on our way." Tony waved in return.

Bewildering panic spiraled through Charlotte, leaving her weak and unnerved. She simply could not bring herself to think of coming face-to-face with the gorgeous man she'd just seen in the ring. Cassie could do it with her usual aplomb. But Charlotte knew she would be tongue-tied. She tugged on Tony's sleeve. "No, let's leave, now, Tony. Say I'm unwell."

"But you just said—" Tony cast her a glance of confusion. "We can't snub Eldwick. He's seen us and he'd take it dashed badly if we left without stopping by. Besides, cousin, you like Eldwick and he likes you."

"I like Eldwick?" Charlotte exclaimed.

Tony grinned and nodded. "You know your sister has a penchant for originals."

"Botheration!" Charlotte toyed with her fan, desperately searching for some excuse to escape from Eldwick's invitation. If the Scot's presence in the ring unnerved her from across the green, how would his immediate presence affect her? She almost choked on the thought. The alarming heat in her cheeks and the jelly in her knees didn't bear contemplation.

"Please reconsider, cousin," Tony pleaded, his dark gray eyes sad as a pup's. "You and I, Cassie, have been ever so keen to meet the prizefighters. But, if you truly feel unwell . . ."

Charlotte sighed. She'd always had a soft spot for her young cousin. She could hang Cassie's keenness, but Tony's obvious disappointment tugged at her conscience.

Resignedly she sighed and feigned disinterest. "Then promise me we won't stay long. Pay your addresses to Mc-something and I'll chat with Eldwick. Then we'll leave."

"Capital." A grin brightened his eager face as Tony jumped from the landau step and reached back for Charlotte's hand.

The crowd around Eldwick's carriage was a sample of the larger audience that had cheered for the prizefighters earlier. Off to the side sat a wagon bearing refreshments for Eldwick's guests.

Charlotte fixed Cassie's gay, dauntless smile on her own lips. But her fingers clutched nervously at Tony's arm as they made their way across the soft ground and through the crowd around the Eldwick equipage.

Eldwick, his sister, and her companion greeted them cordially. Charlotte and Cassandra were acquainted with both ladies and most of the gentlemen present. Everyone was animatedly dissecting the last bout. Charlotte nodded to their host and flashed Cassandra's famous smile at the entire party. With little effort she fell easily into the role of her sister, a role she had played so often.

"I say, Cassandra, where is Dudley, that dashing fiancé of yours?" Eldwick touched his hat in greeting. "Is he so sure of himself that he can let you go gadding about with only your cousin as an escort?"

"Dudley is off in the country on business for his father," Charlotte explained. She and Cassie had rehearsed the story only last night. "Tony has been kind enough to entertain me while Dudley is away."

She smiled at Tony and he returned the affectionate expression. He was an able partner in any adventure. " 'Tis my pleasure to escort my cousin."

"And your sister, Charlotte?" Eldwick leaned closer to Charlotte's ear as if to share a confidence. "I hear she still trails after that poet fellow. Sir Edward Simon, is it?"

"Seymour," Charlotte corrected, tensing at the reference to the man who had captured her heart. "His name is Sir Edward Seymour and I daresay you should make note of it, sirrah. He will be quite famous someday: one of Britain's great literary legends."

"Cousin?" Tony warned with a subtle but pointed lift of his brow.

Charlotte realized her Cassandra smile had faded and her voice had grown harsh.

Unwittingly, Eldwick had hit a nerve. His reference to Edward had been so unexpected and so tinged with disapproval that it rattled her. It also served to remind her that if Edward ever discovered she'd attended this disreputable prizefight, he'd most likely turn his back on her forever. He thoroughly and militantly disapproved of pugilistic endeavors.

With effort Charlotte summoned Cassie's captivating expression to her lips once more. "And yes, Mr. Eldwick, in reply to your kind inquiry, Charlotte is still quite fond of her poet."

Without waiting to see Eldwick's reaction, she turned to speak to one of the ladies.

"And does he return her affections?" Eldwick persisted.

Had the man no sense of propriety? Charlotte fumed, slowly turning back to Eldwick.

"I'm not privy to Sir Edward's heart." Charlotte smiled tightly. If only Eldwick knew how much she longed to know Edward's secret feelings. "Perhaps you should ask him."

"Well, of course, Nigel meant no offense," Miss Eldwick, his sister, interjected with a nervous laugh. "Forgive my brother, Miss St. John. It's just that your sister Charlotte is so intelligent and those artistic types are so unconventional. One never knows what they might do next."

"Unconventional?" Charlotte repeated, taken by surprise. People thought her unconventional? Cassie was the one who was always the center of attention because of her escapades. Surely everyone knew she and Cassandra were equally intelligent. Cassandra just refused to acknowledge her abilities.

But Eldwick had already forgotten their conversation and was gazing over their heads. "Here comes our triumphant prizefighter now. McKensie, over here."

Eldwick's sister and her companion whirled around. With coos and squeals they rushed toward the handsome pugilist.

Repelled by the ladies' enthusiasm for a brute of a man, Charlotte's Cassandra-like smile dipped into a frown. Women's demeaning behavior toward an attractive man always disgusted and embarrassed her. Perhaps his countenance was appealing to the eye and his body—broad and long, dark and tanned— shouted masculinity, virility, *but really.* He was, after all, only a man. A prizefighter.

Charlotte turned to see the boxer striding toward them, his kilt flapping about his knees and a loose white shirt covering his broad chest. Her heart began to pound a little faster. She drew a long, shuddering breath and tried to ignore the growing weakness in her knees—*he was only a very beautiful man.*

TWO

"Smile, cousin?" Tony spoke softly into her ear. "Smile. Remember you're supposed to want to meet the victorious Scotsman. You must speak to him. If you don't, what are you going to tell your sister?"

"That she should have come herself," Charlotte snapped feeling petulant and childish and short of breath. She had absolutely no desire to be presented to Connor McKensie. At the moment she couldn't remember why on earth she'd agreed to do this impersonation for Cassandra.

Suddenly Connor McKensie was standing before them, his body blocking the sun, the shadow falling over Charlotte and Tony. Charlotte stared, completely unprepared for the Scotsman's overwhelming size. Fighting back the urge to escape, she stood her ground. She had to. Cassandra never retreated.

"So who do I have the honor of introducing myself to?" the Scot boomed as he smiled down at Charlotte. His voice rumbled from deep inside. The soft, distinguished burr of his homeland accented his words. "I'm Connor McKensie."

Droplets of water gleamed in his short, dark hair, proving he'd just come from his post-fight sponging off. The faint scent of pine reached Charlotte.

For the most part he appeared unscathed by the fight. His aquiline nose remained straight and his sensitively formed lips bore no splits. The small cut over his right brow would be healed in a few days. Other than that, no bruises marred his masculine jaw. No scars flowered his ears. No chipped teeth betrayed him as a fighter when he grinned.

She continued to stare only partially aware of the social gaffe the prizefighter had just made. A gentleman always waited to be presented to a lady first. He never introduced himself. It wasn't done.

Eldwick's sister and her companion fluttered at his side, seeming to take no notice of the *faux pas*. Nor did they make any effort to redeem the situation.

Tony, who seemed to be the only one to keep his head about him, stepped forward. "I'm Tony Derrington and this is my cousin, Miss Cassandra St. John."

"Miss St. John. So few ladies have the courage to attend a prizefight that I make it my business to meet them all," McKensie explained, that beautiful, joyous grin spreading across his face. Then he spoke as if addressing all the men present. " 'Tis an easy sacrifice to make, gentlemen, meeting all the ladies. Especially when all are as lovely as those here today."

Miss Eldwick tittered and her companion simpered.

His glibness sharpened Charlotte's reeling senses. She drew in a deep breath. So the man was as fluent with his tongue as he was powerful with his fists.

"What say you to the earl?" Tony asked, clearly reminding Charlotte of the fighter's status.

"Of course, I offer congratulations to the victor," Charlotte said without conviction. She bobbed a hasty curtsy and prayed McKensie did not hear the insincerity in her voice. *Earl indeed?* What overblown names these bullies of the boxing ring got up for themselves.

Eldwick waved in Charlotte's direction. "Miss St. John has been eager to meet you."

"Yes, indeed, I have," Charlotte agreed, sputtering over her own hypocrisy. She was at a complete loss as to what more to say to the lout.

"But, how she frowns at me, gentlemen." McKensie laughed

heartily. "I fear if all ladies were so delighted to make my acquaintance, I'd be destitute of feminine company."

His ability to mock himself brought a reluctant smile to Charlotte's lips. Eldwick and Tony laughed at the absurdity of his claim.

"I'm sorry, sir," Charlotte said, ashamed of her lack of graciousness. As much as she wanted to find fault with him, Connor McKensie seemed likeable. Egotistical, perhaps, arrogant, but without a trace of malice. No chip on his shoulder. Nothing bully-like about him—quite the opposite, in fact. He seemed to be enjoying himself in a good-natured way.

"But 'twould never happen, my lord," vowed Miss Eldwick and her companion agreed. They nodded furiously. "You without a lady on your arm, never, never."

"Cousin, where are your manners?" Tony murmured in her ear. "Offer McKensie your hand."

"I'm sorry, I forget myself," Charlotte stammered, offering her hand at last. She was making a muddle of the whole thing.

" 'Tis my pleasure to meet you, Miss Cassandra St. John," McKensie said, lightly taking her fingers in his. His touch was warm and light, his skin smooth though tough. He performed a quick, graceful bow over her hand. Charlotte knew despite his rustic appearance, he'd greeted ladies often in his life.

"Uh, thank you, sir," Charlotte said still without a clue about what Cassie would say to a boxer. "Your reputation precedes you."

"Is that so?" The Scotsman seemed skeptical. "How so?"

"Uh, well . . ." Charlotte inwardly cursed her speechlessness. She could only think to ask the obvious. "Is it true that you killed a lion with your bare hands?"

"So, that's the part of my reputation that precedes me?" quipped the Scot, chuckling again. "And I had hoped it would be my legendary charm."

The men laughed. The ladies giggled. But Charlotte truly wanted to hear his answer.

" 'Tis an absolutely biblical feat," she said, thinking instantly of the story of David and the lion. "Surely you have some comment to make on the experience? Wouldn't it have been safer to shoot the beast than use your hands?"

He laughed once more, a low joyous rumble of amusement that Charlotte found soothing—and contagious.

"The lion stalked the sheep, then the shepherds, then me. Aye, 'twould have been easier to kill him with a gun if he'd allowed me the advantage. The cat preferred the close combat of an ambush. Leaped upon me from a rock."

A devilish grin split the Scotsman's face again. His white teeth flashed in the sunlight as he reached for the hem of his shirt. "Would you like to see the scars?"

"No, that's quite all right." Hastily Charlotte spread her hands before her to forestall any more baring of skin. She'd seen as much nakedness as she dared for the day. "But were you not frightened?"

" 'Twas frightening when I thought about it later," McKensie agreed, sobering for a moment. "I drained a bottle of whisky that night, afterward."

He smiled softly this time, almost an indulgent expression. "When you fight for your life, lass, there is no time to be frightened. You just fight. 'Tis never like the sport we play in the boxing ring where no one is going to die on the canvas."

"But that's not true," Charlotte countered. "Sometimes fighters die."

"But 'tis rare under Broughton's rules," the Scot said, a hint of regret crossing his face. He studied her a moment longer.

"The Brawlin' Scot is of no mind to kill anyone," Eldwick interjected.

"Yes, of course, I understand that," Charlotte said, helplessly enthralled by McKensie's golden eyes.

"Does fighting trouble you, Miss Cassandra?" he asked with a lazy, knowing smile.

"What is there to trouble anyone?" Eldwick interrupted again. "Boxing is more than just prizefighting."

"It is the gentleman's art of self defense," Tony chimed in. "A quarrel need not turn into a duel or murder."

"Murder no, just a bloody fight," Charlotte snapped before she realized the words had fallen from her lips.

McKensie tossed back his head and laughed. " 'Tis the science of fisticuffs, Miss Cassandra. And once in a wee while there is a split lip. But enough of this discussion."

McKensie turned his full attention on her and repeated her sister's name softly, the sound sending shivers down Charlotte's spine. "Cassandra? Your mythical namesake was beloved by Apollo. You know that, of course. If she was as lovely as you, 'tis no wonder she snared a Greek god. Fiery Cassandra, King Priam's daughter."

The classical reference startled Charlotte, rendering her mute once more. The Brawlin' Scot knew his Homer. To free herself of his powerful gaze she inclined her head in acknowledgment of his compliment.

She suddenly knew who he was in her mind's eye. If she was Priam's daughter, he was Lord Byron's god, Apollo—dark-haired and golden-eyed. She recited silently to herself, *The Sun, in human limbs arrayed, and brow all radiant from his triumph in the fight* . . .

Charlotte shivered once more in the heat of the day. She clutched at Tony's arm. "We must go now. So nice to see you again, Miss Eldwick. Mr. Eldwick. We must be on our way, Tony."

Tony said his farewells and dutifully led her away.

"You met the Brawlin' Scot. Satisfied?" she muttered as they made their way back to the Derrington landau.

"Well enough," Tony said, handing her up into the open carriage. "Now we can answer all of Cassandra's questions and she will have her alibi."

"Yes, and I shall never have to meet Connor McKensie again," Charlotte said, settling herself into the carriage seat. But her senses continued to lurch every time the image of the prize-fighter flashed across her mind. Now that she was out of his looming presence, she was beginning to feel quite pleased with her effort.

She'd seen her first boxing match and survived being presented to the Brawlin' Scot. And Edward was none the wiser. And the experience had been absolutely exhilarating. Definitely something to note in her journal.

But she was still unnerved by the potent feelings McKensie had stirred in her—emotions that Charlotte had never experienced before. Her hand still tingled from the heat of his touch and her ears still rang with the deep resonance of his voice.

Yet she sensed that some finale was at hand. She and Cassie were becoming too old for this childish nonsense. The masquerading would have to end, and soon. From now on, Cassandra could meet her own prizefighters. Charlotte would never have to suffer another encounter such as she'd just had with Connor McKensie.

Her life would drift back to its normal, placid routine.

Pleased with the prospect, Charlotte settled back against the carriage seat and wondered why she felt so unaccountably disappointed.

THREE

"Damnation!" Connor yanked the short end of his lopsided cravat, then glared at it in the mirror once more. He could have sworn he'd gone through the exact motions the tailor's shop assistant had taught him. "Tell me what merit there be in having a bloody piece of cloth tied around your neck just so? Seems to impress the gentlemen more than the ladies."

"To be sure." Erik looked up from the book he was studying on the table. "But there will be both lords and ladies to impress at the Earl and Countess of Seacombe's *soirée* tonight. Tie it well."

Connor turned back to the mirror of their low-ceilinged, sparsely furnished, hired lodgings. "Aye, I'll try again."

They'd taken up residence on the unfashionable east side of London the first day in the city, partly because the accommodations suited his finances. In the month since their arrival they had pursued every opportunity and taken advantage of every society reference and letter of introduction that Connor had managed to acquire since they'd left Kinleith.

With each winning purse Connor had gained, they'd paid off their expenses and acquired more gentlemanly trappings. New shirts filled the clothespress and new footwear littered the floor. Mrs. Needham, the landlady, refused to carry a bath up for them and she would agree to do laundry only once a week. But the lodgings suited both Connor and Erik well enough for the present.

Connor knew he could not accomplish his goal without investing in a certain level of appearances. For the most part, the accessories that society forced on a gentleman troubled him little. Things were only objects to be used when convenient and shed when useless. He glared closer at his cravat and purposely dismissed his frustration. "No glorified neckerchief is going to defeat me."

"I didna think so," Erik said after glancing at the object of Connor's annoyance, then turned back to his book. Moving a lighted candle closer to the pages, but not so close as to allow the wax to drip on it, Erik went on, " 'Tis your kilt the ladies are going to be minding if you ask me—not the fancy knot tied under yer chin."

"Aye, the tartan makes the ladies stare and the men frown." Connor couldn't stifle a grin. He'd not missed how the ladies' gazes drifted in the direction of his knees. Miss Cassandra St. John's eyes, those clear-blue, wary eyes, had wandered as frequently as most.

He turned to his distant cousin, the man more an older brother than a family retainer. Erik's dark, curly head was bent over the book once more. "What else do you find in that text of gentlemen's deportment that we should be knowing?"

"Yer no heathen—I don't know why yer so concerned about deportment," Erik said with the easy frankness of an honest man. Connor's burly second cousin was as much a part of his life as a true sibling. For reasons Connor had never fully understood nor troubled to discover, Erik had come into the family to be fostered when Connor could but toddle the length of the great hall. Erik had been eight years old then and they'd grown up together, Connor's only male ally in a family of three daughters and a son. The boys had even studied at St. Andrews University together. They were more than lord and retainer, or even cousins. They were like brothers. Connor considered himself fortunate to be the only heir to a title who had a big brother with whom to share the burden.

"Ye know most of this, but here's something," Erik said. " 'If ye meet a lady acquaintance in the street or park, ye must turn and walk with her if ye wish to talk.' Says here it is poor manners to make her stand still to talk in the street."

Connor nodded and turned to tug on his cravat once more. "What else?"

Erik chuckled. "Here's an odd one. 'When going up a flight of stairs ye must precede the lady and in going down, ye follow.' Nary a word about what a gentleman is to do if he catches the lady casting a leer up his kilt."

"I'll accommodate the ladies with a free peek," Connor said, amused by the rules Society had drawn between English gentlemen and ladies. "Far be it from me to say anything to embarrass a curious lady. Any conversation pointers?"

"Ye never seem to be lacking for words so I wouldna worry about that," Erik said as he continued to page through the tome. After a moment of silence while Connor worked with his cravat, Erik added, "She will be there tonight, ye know."

"Lady Dorian, of course. She's our hostess."

"Nay, I mean the St. John girl. She is Lady Dorian's niece." Erik looked up from the book and caught Connor's gaze in the mirror. Connor disliked the flinty hint of practicality in Erik's eyes. "Cassandra St. John, the bonny red-haired girl ye met at the last mill."

"I remember who the St. John girl is and it is of little consequence to me." Connor turned back to his cravat and the dissatisfactory knot. He'd already speculated that Cassandra St. John would be at her aunt's house this evening. He needed no reminder.

The pretty, blue-eyed redhead's image had haunted him during the days since their meeting. She'd been like a lithe, porcelain doll standing in the meadow among the rabble—in pink and white rosebud muslin, her face framed with the silkiest, flaming-red hair he'd ever seen the likes of. He'd never even met a Scots lass who could match that fiery color.

His canniest instincts, which he was known for, told him that Miss St. John had faced him steadfast and determined when, for some reason he couldn't fathom, she had wanted to run. One cross word from him and she would have bolted like a doe before a hunter. Ladies seldom ran from Connor McKensie. A retreating female intrigued him, especially such a mysterious one.

He smiled at his dark good looks in the mirror. There were certain things he knew about himself. The ladies liked him and people, men or women, seldom deceived him. Miss St. John's courageous pretense had puzzled—and amused—him. What would she say if he told her he'd seen through her brave front? She'd be horrified, no doubt. A pretty blush of embarrassment would spread across her smooth complexion and that expressive mouth would purse in dismay. He couldn't keep himself from wondering what it would be like to kiss those delicate, vulnerable lips.

"Well, the fact that Cassandra St. John's father owns Glen Gray should give it a bit of consequence," Erik said, still casually leafing through the book. Connor did not miss the significant change in his cousin's tone of voice. "Cassandra St. John is affianced already, but her twin is not—at least not officially. And if I know what that gleam in your eyes means, you might find Miss Charlotte equally bonny."

"One sister is as good as the other, you think?" Annoyed and startled by Erik's cheeky suggestion, Connor frowned at his image in the mirror. Erik was always willing to talk things over, but he seldom offered counsel about Connor's romantic interests. Dissatisfied with the knot that only a moment before he had thought passing acceptable, Connor tugged viciously at the neckcloth, yanking out the knot and beginning for a third time.

With a bland smile, Erik went on. "All I'm suggesting is ye make yerself agreeable to Davis St. John, to his sister, Lady Dorian, the Countess of Seacombe, and St. John's family, especially his daughters. The girls' goodwill canna hurt our cause."

"I know what you're getting at, Erik, but I shall not be tied down to a pale, helpless London lass. If she's anything like her

sister, this Charlotte could never survive a winter in the Highlands, let alone be of any service to me or the clan. I'll wed a
hearty Scottish lass. I have my eye on several good prospects.
All of them pretty, capable, and competent to be the Countess
of Kinleith."

"Good prospects?" Erik's mouth twisted into an unaccount-
able smile. "I'll wager not a one of them could bring money
and British influence into the clan."

"That won't ever signify." Connor finished tying the cravat
knot to his satisfaction at last. "Because I can win Glen Gray
in my own time, by the labor of my own two hands, my own
way—not because I marry the daughter of the English owner.

Connor flexed his bruised knuckles and studied them. They
were healing. The purple splotches had yellowed around the
edges and the ache in the bones had faded already. He'd be fit
for the next fight when the time came. "We only need a few
more fights, maybe a challenge for the championship to fatten
the purse. Then I'll have enough to make Davis St. John a fitting
offer for the glen. Where are my dress gloves for tonight?"

"Here, gentleman's gloves." Erik gestured to white handware
on the table. "Are ye ready for yer coat?"

"Aye." Connor allowed Erik to help him slip on the new,
tailor-made, black velvet garment cut expertly to flatter his
broad shoulders and narrow waist.

"I thought the tailor was going to bust a gut when ye refused
trousers to match," Erik said with a chuckle.

"I was right, was I not?" Connor asked, admiring himself in
the mirror. The effect was exactly the one he wanted—from the
stylish cut of his dark hair to the tail of his finely tailored coat.
From the waist up he was all society gentleman. From the waist
down, his kilt declared with an undeniable flourish that he was
a Scotsman.

"Ye were right about the coat, Connor," Erik agreed with a
grin. "But about Glen Gray. Ye be capable of winning it, I know.
I'm no saying you're not. And I'm no talking of marriage to a
lass who doesna stir yer heart or at least yer pizzel. But think

on it this way, Connor. Why put all yer eggs in one basket? There be a lot at stake."

"I know what's at stake," Connor said, unwilling to listen to his older, not-so-wiser best friend. No one knew better than he what the glen meant to the clan. He'd spent many a sleepless night plotting the necessary steps, reviewing figures, studying the surveyors' maps, assessing what was needed for survival—for victory over the Forbes Clan. "It's the lives and the future of the McKensies that are at risk, not my heart."

Erik brushed a bit of lint off the shoulder of Connor's coat. "Aye, but maybe think of cracking the doors of yer heart a bit to see what happens."

"I'm always at the females' mercy, Erik," Connor said, flashing a grin at his best friend. Erik meant well. "Anything to amuse the ladies. I'll even precede them upstairs so they can leer at my knees."

Erik laughed.

"But know this," Connor said, turning to catch Erik's gaze and strengthen the importance of his words. "I'll not wed a British lass for a parcel of land, McKensie Clan feud or no."

Edward Seymour placed his elbow against Aunt Dorian's marble fireplace mantel, clasped the lapel of his green frock coat in one hand, and leaned his cheek against the palm of his other. With his wild mane gleaming like a brown halo, he smiled wistfully at Charlotte. "It was kind of your aunt to invite me this evening."

Recognizing Edward's favorite poetic pose, Charlotte smiled appreciatively and fibbed, "Aunt Dorian was so pleased to have you come."

In that particular full-skirted frock coat, and with his long, loose hair, Edward did resemble his hero, the late infamous poet, Lord Byron. Charlotte was really quite proud of Edward. He looked so cultured and ethereal, she wondered how she could ever have allowed that brute of a boxer to capture her imagination—let alone invade her nightly dreams. She nudged Cassie next to her. "Doesn't Edward look handsome tonight?"

"Um, handsome." The smile on Cassie's lips was more derisive than appreciative. She and Charlotte, along with Edward and Dudley, had gathered in the drawing room. Dudley looked debonair and handsome as ever in an evening coat that Cassie had selected.

"Has Edward given the gift to you yet?" Cassie whispered in Charlotte's ear.

"No, he's given me nothing," Charlotte muttered between tight lips. She was sorry she'd told her twin anything about Edward's promise to her. Earlier that day he had sent a note promising a gift. With her heart in her throat, Charlotte could only think that this would be her heart's desire at last—a love token from Edward. He'd been calling on her for over a year now, since the beginning of last year's season. She expected him to declare himself any day. When she'd read his note, she'd been so excited she'd shared all her hopes with Cassie.

As the evening progressed, Edward had made no effort to give her anything and now Cassie wouldn't stop asking about it.

Charlotte flipped open her fan to cover her words. "Maybe if you'd leave us alone, sister, he'd feel more free to give me something."

"Very well," Cassie said, slipping her arm through her fiancé's. "Let's see who's here tonight, shall we, Dudley? But we'll be back soon, Charlotte."

As soon as Cassie was gone, Edward drew Charlotte closer to him. Her hopes brightened.

"May I say, my dear, how captivating you look tonight in your blue satin," Edward said "I'm almost inspired to compose a poem to your beauty."

"How kind of you, Edward," Charlotte said, flattered. *Please,* she prayed, *if not a gift at least let him declare his love.* She and Edward were perfect for each other. Even Papa must approve this match, she thought. Edward possessed both a title and an income. He would inherit the family barony at the beginning of the year. When she and Edward were wed, they could retire to the quaint but elegant farmhouse in Dorset and share a quiet intellectual life of study and poetry. Charlotte smiled at her poet. "Please, Edward, save your efforts for your truly great works."

"It's true, a poet must be careful not to squander his talents." Edward stepped away from the mantel, took Charlotte's hand, and kissed it. "You are so wise, my dear, and so very good for me. That's why I've brought this to share with you."

Charlotte held her breath, her gaze following Edward's every move as he reached into his coat pocket and pulled out a small trinket. Slowly he offered her the treasure in the palm of his hand, a gold miniature frame with a lock of mousy brown hair displayed in it.

Puzzled, Charlotte glanced at Edward uncertainly.

"It's a lock of Lord Byron's hair," Edward explained, his voice edgy as if he were disappointed that she hadn't instantly recognized the prize. "A special dealer brought it to me. Isn't it wonderful? It was snipped from his head and carried back from Greece. Such a find. Such a keepsake."

"Indeed, it is," Charlotte agreed, feeling a bit deflated and silently chiding herself for having dreamed of more.

"I thought you'd like to have it," Edward said, offering the miniature frame to Charlotte. "For a while, at least. Then I'd like to have it back. 'Tis valuable, you know."

"I understand." Charlotte took the framed lock of hair from Edward's hand, truly honored yet disappointed. A simple vow of undying affection from Edward's lips would have satisfied her. But she also understood that Edward was sharing what he valued most. She would not refuse the honor. "I shall cherish it, of course. It is so thoughtful of you to share this with me."

"I knew you'd like it," Edward said with a gratified grin and a puffed-out chest. "May I get you some punch?"

"Yes, please." As soon as Edward was gone, Charlotte carefully took a handkerchief from her reticule, wrapped the min-

iature in it, and tucked it safely away. The reprieve allowed her
to gather her disheartened wits.

The sudden movement of air fluttered the lace trim of her
blue satin gown. She looked up into Cassie's eager face.

"Well?" Cassie demanded. To Charlotte's relief, her sister
was alone. "I sent Dudley after punch. What is it? Let me see.
A book of poetry? A locket? A betrothal ring? What did he
say?"

Embarrassed by her own high hopes, Charlotte shook her
head. "It is a lock of Byron's hair."

"A lock of a dead poet's hair?" Cassie laughed until she
caught sight of Charlotte's face. She choked back her laughter.
"I'm sorry. We should have known that Edward would not con-
duct his courtship as other gentlemen do."

Charlotte smiled weakly, thankful that her sister had refrained
from saying anything more belittling. Cassie's opinions could
be incisive and altogether too accurate. "Yes, we should remember that."

"Well, here you are, the two of you together," sang a delight-
fully familiar voice.

Charlotte and Cassie turned to find Aunt Dorian, their hostess, bearing down on them.

"Cassie? Charlotte? The Earl of Kinleith, who is my guest
of honor tonight, has asked to renew your acquaintance," announced Aunt Dorian. She came to a stop in front of the girls,
the plumes in her hair dipping with the sudden movement. Several gentlemen followed her—Uncle Nicholas, Papa, and a third
man Charlotte did not recognize. "Lord Kinleith said he met
you at the fight last week, Cassie. And you, Charlotte, he asked
to be presented to you also."

Charlotte frowned. She didn't recall Tony presenting her to
an earl.

Only when the tall, dark man her aunt gestured to grinned,
did Charlotte place him. Before her stood a golden-eyed Apollo
in a black velvet evening coat. She blinked, then choked back
a gasp of surprise.

"Misses St. John," Kinleith said, offering them a slight bow and his handsome smile.

The Connor McKensie standing before Charlotte bore little resemblance to the prizefighter she'd met at the boxing match. Gone was the ragged hair. His dark curls lay neatly trimmed along the edge of his high coat collar. No wrinkled shirttail this evening. His tantalizing muscular build filled a well-tailored tail coat. His snowy white gentleman's cravat was perfectly tied beneath his strong jaw. His shirtfront stretched smooth and taut across his chest. Only his bare knees and kilt testified to his roughness.

Charlotte's knees began to quake as when she and Kinleith had first met. All the strange, elusive sensations that had flooded through her then surged over her once more. She touched Cassie's arm to steady herself. If the Brawlin' Scot flashed that devil-may-care smile at her again, she knew her frail composure would vanish.

"Now, don't have an attack of shyness," Dorian said, giving Charlotte's arm a comforting pat. "It's time you met some other men besides Sir Poet What's-his-name."

Charlotte cringed. Her aunt did not like Edward—his title and his literary ambitions notwithstanding. She'd made her feelings plain to Charlotte some time ago.

" 'Tis indeed a pleasure to make your acquaintance." The earl took Charlotte's cold hand and bowed over it. "I'd heard that Davis St. John was blessed with beautiful twin daughters."

"My lord." Charlotte curtsied and refused to meet his gaze.

"And I have a lovely wife, too," Papa said, unwittingly saving Charlotte from having to respond at length. Despite Papa's complimentary words, she sensed that he was displeased with Lord Kinleith's interest in her and Cassandra.

Kinleith moved toward Cassie and took her hand. "Miss Cassandra, how nice to see you again."

"Yes, likewise, my lord." Cassandra bobbed an appropriate curtsy and turned her famous charming smile on the man she'd never met.

Obviously beguiled, Kinleith bowed deeply. Though his manners were less polished and glib than a gentleman of the *ton,* his demeanor was passing respectable.

Charlotte glared at him. How dare he misrepresent himself that day at the boxing ring. He was truly titled and hardly the rustic he'd have had her and the others believe.

Still looking into Cassie's eyes and holding her hand, he added, "I insist, the pleasure is all mine."

Mysteriously miffed, Charlotte snapped open her fan and beat the air with it. For the first time in her life, she longed so to wipe the flirtatious simper off her sister's face.

FOUR

"Thunderation, Charlotte. He's gorgeous," Cassie whispered in Charlotte's ear.

"I told you that," Charlotte murmured behind her fan.

"But—but, boxers are usually—they lack a cert—I never thought you meant *truly gorgeous,*" Cassie whispered from behind her fan, sounding as breathless as Charlotte felt. "But we must get him to give up the kilt. It's just too provincial."

Fearful of being overheard, Charlotte thrust an elbow in her sister's side. She rather liked the provincial look of his kilt and decided he was at least as correctly dressed for the occasion as Edward was in his poet's coat.

Kinleith, who had yet to release Cassie's hand, bent closer. "I'm sorry, I did not hear you."

Unfazed, Cassie's smile broadened. "My sister was just confiding in me how handsome she thinks you are."

Charlotte gasped, embarrassment burning in her cheeks. Her fan beat the air rapidly. She refrained from a retort, knowing Cassie would just add something to make it worse.

When the prizefighter's tawny eyes settled upon Charlotte again, her pulse raced. To her dismay, the addition of evening clothes had not lessened his bare-chested, sensual appeal which had stirred her so during their first meeting. She stared back at Kinleith, catching a slight narrowing of his eyes as he studied her. He couldn't know, could he?

"How kind of you, Miss Charlotte," he said politely and

clearly without vanity. He released Cassie's hand at last. Though his smile never wavered as he scrutinized Charlotte, his golden eyes suddenly snapped dark and keen.

Helpless to turn away, Charlotte stood riveted by his gaze, as paralyzed as the prey of a wily predator. She took a deep breath against the chill that coursed through her. Impossible. But she'd seen it. The flash of recognition in the gold depths of McKensie's eyes. If she didn't know better, if she wasn't absolutely certain it was impossible, she would have sworn Connor McKensie recognized her.

"I found our first meeting quite unforgettable, Miss Cassandra," McKensie said, radiating his charm toward Cassie now. "One seldom has the privilege of meeting the fair and lovely Cassandra, daughter of King Priam."

Charlotte snapped her fan closed and bristled. How dare he.

Cassandra beamed, basking in the warmth of Kinleith's golden smile—and the compliment she'd never heard before.

Resentment ached in Charlotte's heart. The name was her sister's but those words of admiration were hers. The prize-fighter had said them to her first. She was King Priam's daughter. The compliment belonged to her, not Cassie.

Lord Kinleith's smile broadened with the pleasure of Cassandra's simpering response, but his gaze flickered over Charlotte once. Then he released her sister's hand.

Charlotte waited, hardly able to take a breath. Would Kinleith repeat the most treasured aspect of the compliment—the part about her being the beloved of Apollo?

When he did not, secret relief swept through her followed by an odd chilling conviction. Connor McKensie withheld those precious words because he recognized the difference between her and Cassie.

Nonsense, Charlotte almost spoke aloud and blinked. She was being silly. With narrowed eyes she turned to study the earl. No one but family could tell her and Cassie apart. No one.

"Charlotte?" Edward elbowed his way to the fore with punch cups in hand.

Aunt Dorian quickly made introductions.

In a voice dripping with censure, Edward looked Kinleith up and down. "So this is the gentleman pugilist."

"I'm sure we're all pleased to have Lord Kinleith bring some distinction back to the sport," Papa said. "Jem Ward throwing that fight a few years ago has left a bad taste in the mouth of many a boxing fan."

"You'll not find me throwing a fight," Kinleith said with a laugh. "I like to win too well."

"Well, one would expect nothing less from a pugilist," Edward said with a sneer. He took Charlotte's arm and began to lead her away.

"Charlotte, dear, don't let Edward take you away. I have something more to ask you," Aunt Dorian said, pulling Charlotte back into the group. She stood stretched between Aunt Dorian and Edward like a mismeasured drapery.

Aunt Dorian went on as though nothing was amiss. "As a Scotsman, Lord Kinleith has seen little of London after nearly a month in Town. You're always so well-informed about the sights and events. Why not act as his guide?"

Charlotte gulped down the lump in her throat and attempted to free herself from Edward and Aunt Dorian.

"I believe Charlotte is ill," Edward said. "She's turned pale."

"No. Really, I'm fine."

McKensie's gaze drifted lazily over Charlotte again, a cool, golden-eyed inspection that left her feeling as if he'd just fingered the wispy curls arranged over her ear. The breathtaking sensation confused her. "I'm not certain I could be of much assistance to Lord Kinleith."

"Dorian, I'm certain Lord Kinleith has no difficulty finding a guide when he needs one," Papa said, clearly indifferent to his sister's concern for the Scottish laird.

Silently, Charlotte thanked her father for attempting to rescue her.

"Say yes." Cassandra elbowed Charlotte and whispered behind her fan. "Say you'll be his guide. We can do this."

"Do what?" Charlotte whispered, mystified.

"We can be Lord Kinleith's guide and make him the most

sought-after member of the *ton* this season just as we did with
Dudley last year."

"Oh, no." Charlotte glared at her sister. The transformation
of Dudley from an unfashionable country viscount into a stylish
gentleman of quality had been Cassie's project, not hers. And
Cassie had been so successful that she'd decided to marry the
dashing new man she'd created. Delighted as Charlotte was for
her sister's success, she had no desire to take on any such project—especially not with the Scotsman, who hardly appeared as
malleable as Dudley. "I told you—no more changing places,
Cassie."

"I heard you, but we both know that was just your fear of
Edward's censure talking."

Charlotte gasped. "I am not afraid of Edward's censure!"

"Shh. Yes, you are. You're terrified that he will find out that
you like doing more than reading poetry and philosophy in front
of the fire."

"That is not true." Charlotte could not believe Cassie thought
Edward held such sway over her.

"Then prove it, and say yes," Cassandra pressed. "I can't be
Kinleith's guide as myself. I'm betrothed. But if you agree to
it, as Charlotte, I can do all that needs to be done. The coaching.
The teaching."

"Girls, what are you whispering about?" Aunt Dorian asked.

Before Charlotte could speak up, Edward stepped in. "Lady
Dorian and Lord Kinleith, please consider that Miss St. John
is entirely too occupied with her literary study to have time to
entertain a man of pugilistic tastes."

The possessive pressure of Edward's hand on the small of
Charlotte's back startled her. She stiffened. He'd never touched
her so before.

The poet went on. "No offense, Lord Kinleith, but Charlotte
knows nothing of the east end."

Behind her fan, Cassie rolled her eyes.

Edward's presumption vanquished Charlotte's confusion. She
definitely was not afraid of him, though winning his favor was
near to her heart. "Perhaps that is exactly the point, Edward. A

newcomer from the Highlands like Lord Kinleith, could benefit
from my literary tastes."

Kinleith grinned. "No offense taken, Seymour, but I agree
with Lady Dorian and Miss St. John. Her cultural knowledge
would be just the point, wouldn't it?"

"Splendid," Dorian said, clearly pleased. She turned to her
brother. "I sometimes fear that we Londoners don't show our
northern neighbors the kind of hospitality they deserve."

"I quite agree," Charlotte said, amazed at her own forward-
ness and wondering at what she'd just gotten herself into.

Edward glowered at her, but she pretended not to see his
disapproval. He'd declared no intention. He had no right to
speak for her, no claim on her time or her company.

"It's settled then," Aunt Dorian said. "You might begin with
a drive in the park. Don't you think that would be appropriate,
Davis?"

Papa agreed.

"Of course, I'd be delighted to enjoy a ride in the park with
Miss St. John and Sir Seymour, if he'd like to join us," Kinleith
said pleasantly, all good manners and propriety.

"I don't waste my daylight hours with inconsequential activities such as parading in the park," Edward snapped, glaring
at Charlotte.

"A drive in the park tomorrow it is, then," Dorian said, linking one arm with Charlotte and the other with Lord Kinleith
and leading them into the buffet. "So nice. Just the two of you."

"Perfect," Cassie whispered into Charlotte's ear.

Charlotte was glad that Cassie and Aunt Dorian were pleased.
But Edward was clearly disgruntled and probably wouldn't
speak to her for a week. And Kinleith—the satisfaction Charlotte glimpsed in the Scotsman's sparkling topaz eyes over the
top of Aunt Dorian's head as they walked into supper was
enough to give her pause. She was ever so glad that when the
time came for the drive in the park, Cassie would fill her place.

FIVE

"Don't be a pea-goose, Charlotte," Cassie exclaimed the next morning when Betsy, the maid, had finished dressing her hair and had been dismissed. Still sitting before the mirror, Cassie held up one earbob after another, measuring the effect against her reflection. "Lord Kinleith can't possibly tell the difference between us."

"I honestly think he might suspect," Charlotte insisted as she stood behind Cassie and handed her another pair of earbobs to consider.

"Fiddlesticks." Cassie laughed ruefully. "No one outside the family can tell us apart, not even Dudley or Edward."

"I know that." Charlotte frowned as she handed Cassie the pearl earrings. She did not care to be reminded that the love of her life could not tell the difference between them."

Truth was not always beautiful. It was often dashed disappointing. Edward and Dudley could not tell them apart even with a kiss. She and Cassie had tested the two men on more than one occasion and neither ever suspected that the girls were not who they claimed to be.

The realization had disappointed Charlotte, almost to tears; but Cassie had only shrugged philosophically. They were identical, after all, she had reminded Charlotte. Why should they expect anything more from their future husbands?

But Charlotte could not rid herself of a strange feeling about McKensie. "There's just something about the Scot that makes me think he might not be so easy to fool. Here, try this pair again. I know you like the rose quartz, but I favor the lapis. They show our eye color to advantage."

"I believe you're right." Cassie held a lapis earbob to her ear again and studied her image in the mirror. "Yes, it looks very you. I shall wear the lapis pair. But you do know why Lord Kinleith is interested in us, the daughters of Davis St. John, don't you?"

"No, why?"

"Oh, Charlotte, you must get your nose out of your books and your mind out of those lofty altitudes and listen," Cassie said, fastening the second earring in her lobe. "Lord Kinleith seeks Glen Gray."

"Who?"

"Not who. Where. Glen Gray, a famous Scottish glen that two clans, McKensie and Forbes, have been feuding over for three hundred years. And Papa owns it."

"Feuding is forbidden or against the law or something isn't it?"

Cassie heaved a long, suffering sigh. "Laws and facts are two different things, sister. Gossip has it that despite the law, the Forbes and McKensies are still at odds over this piece of property that lies in the hills between the Highlands and Lowlands."

"How did Papa come by it?"

"Some business arrangement he made a few years ago. The land had been confiscated by a British lord after Culloden. You do know about the Highlanders' defeat at Culloden?"

"Yes, of course I do. Edward is thinking about writing a poem about it."

"Glen Gray was part of a larger business deal that Papa negotiated a year or so ago."

"What are you saying?" Charlotte asked. "That Kinleith is interested in us because of Glen Gray? But Papa said we should follow our hearts as he and Mama did. He'd never marry us off as part of a business arrangement."

Cassie rearranged a curl just behind her ear. "Yes, follow your heart—as long as it fancies a titled gentleman."

"But Papa is so rich and he has many friends of the gentry and quality," Charlotte protested. "He merely wishes for us to marry well."

"But you know how he'd love to have a title in the family."

"But—" Charlotte stammered, having never considered how far Papa's social ambitions might extend. "Aunt Dorian is a countess. You are going to be a viscountess and I will be a baroness."

"Should Edward ever offer for your hand."

"That's not fair, Cassie." The painful reminder of Edward's slow courtship made Charlotte frown. It was just like Cassandra to twist the knife of her disappointment. "You have your future all settled. Must you torture me over mine?"

Cassie jumped up from the dressing-table chair and hugged her sister. "No, it isn't fair. And I'm sorry. It's just that I think you could do better than Edward and I think Aunt Dorian quite believes so, too."

"But that is my decision to make," Charlotte said. "Edward and I are perfectly suited. Just give Edward a chance. We love books and scholarly pursuits—"

Cassie moved away, waving her hands in the air as if to fend off an invisible attack. "You have listed Edward's sterling qualities for me before, sister. I still don't see them."

"What would I possibly have in common with a boxer?" Charlotte asked.

"We shall soon find out," Cassie said, turning to the mirror once more.

"Is that why you are doing this, taking my place? To match-make? If so, you can just—"

Cassie whirled to face her sister. "Don't flatter yourself. If you don't have something in common with Lord Kinleith perhaps one of my other friends does."

Betsy's rapid knock preceded the opening of the door. "Lord Kinleith is waiting in the drawing room, Miss Charlotte."

"Thank you, Betsy," Cassie said. "Is Mother with him?"

"She greeted him, miss, but then she had to be on her way to the Hellenic lecture she was attending this morning. So he is quite alone."

"Good. Please tell him I'll be right down."

"Yes, miss."

"See, this is working out perfectly," Cassandra said as soon as the maid had disappeared. "Mother's gone so we need not worry about any interference from her. Nana is still in the country with her niece and Papa is at his business office."

"Just what were you saying about why you want to do this?"

"I'm doing this, Charlotte, because I've always thought it would be fun to meet a gentleman boxer and now we have one on our doorstep. I think we might just give him a little bit of polish and a little something for all of Town to talk about."

"Oh," groaned Charlotte. "Remember, you are doing this in my name."

"Never fear, sister," Cassie said, an airy bounce in her step as she headed for the door. "I shall not forget."

Connor watched the pretty redhead in blue-flowered muslin pause in the drawing-room doorway before she entered. Instantly he wondered why he had ever agreed to this ridiculous social charade. Because he liked Lady Dorian, he reminded himself. And because he'd reconsidered Erik's advice. No need to put all his eggs—the acquisition of Glen Gray—into one prizefighting basket. Just how much of his interest was based on the appeal of the lady in question?

More than he cared to admit, he suspected as he watched a tremulous smile soften Miss St. John's face. She walked toward him, offering her hand in greeting. The fabric of her gown clung to her body, hinting at small, firm breasts, a narrow waist, and tantalizingly long legs. The blue earrings swung from her lobes accenting the vivid blue of her eyes. She made a pretty picture.

It was really remarkable how much alike the two girls were, he mused.

"Have I the pleasure of greeting Miss Charlotte again?" he said, bowing over her hand.

"Indeed, my lord, it is my pleasure," she replied with a curtsy. "The weather has turned fine for our outing, has it not? It is a beautiful day for a drive in the park."

"So 'tis, miss."

"I am so glad that Aunt Dorian suggested we do this," she said, smiling up at him with confidence. "One always sees things anew when showing them to another, don't you believe? I will point out the sights and you must in turn tell me all about your boxing career and your Scotland home, too, of course. I've only traveled as far as Edinburgh."

"Then, of course, I must enlighten you as you endeavor to enlighten me."

"Betsy, have you brought my wrap?" Miss St. John turned to the maid, who stepped forward offering Connor Charlotte's pelisse.

Connor made no move to take it. "Will you excuse us for a moment, Betsy?"

The maid cast her mistress a questioning glance.

"Leave the wrap on the chair," Miss St. John said. As soon as the maid was gone, she turned back to Connor. "Is something amiss, my lord?"

"Nothing will be amiss as soon as you go back up those stairs and send Charlotte down."

Surprise flickered across Cassandra St. John's face. "What on earth are you saying? I am Charlotte."

"You are not. My appointment was with the lovely St. John miss whom I had the pleasure of meeting at my last fight and with whom I have my appointment today," Connor stated as evenly as he could. His sudden annoyance with the twins surprised even him and he could not keep himself from going on. "You may find it amusing to play this little trading-places game, but do not foist the sport off on me. Do I make myself clear?"

Once more, Cassie paused as if she were considering a protest, as if she were weighing the wisdom of contradicting him.

"Persist if you must, but I have the impression that your Aunt Dorian and your own fiancé would be most displeased to learn of this little game."

"Yes, perhaps they would be." Cassie's eyes widened in surprise—and in respect, he hoped. "You want me to send Charlotte down? But I must tell you I'm not certain she'll come."

"She has no choice, now does she?" Connor said, unwilling to accept anything less than what he'd been promised: a drive in the park with Charlotte St. John.

"No, I suppose she doesn't." Cassie shook her head and started for the door.

"And tell her I like your earrings." He gestured toward Cassandra's earbobs. "Those with the blue stones."

Cassie studied him for a long, tense moment. The alertness of her stance and the narrowing of her eyes told Connor she was taking serious measure of him for the first time. He leveled a forthright gaze at her fearless scrutiny. He had a fair idea of what Cassandra saw in him—danger and displeasure—and he intended it to convince her of the error of her ways. He was also immensely glad he was not affianced to this twin.

"Yes, I will tell her," she agreed at last and was gone.

Connor paced the well-appointed drawing room, hardly aware of the richness of his surroundings. He had not gone to all the trouble to call in a debt in the form of a showy black curricle and a prancing team of grey hackneys to be made a fool of by the St. John twins.

She might not come? Just what was that all about? he fumed amidst the Greek vases and Hellenic-style furniture. Charlotte was the one who had agreed to the appointment in the first place. She was the one who had shown up at the prize fight. He stopped, face-to-face with a marble bust of some Greek god. Aye, he'd met Charlotte on the heath, but she'd been using Cassie's name. And now she didn't want to see him? Was it possible had she not wanted to be there in the first place?

"My lord?"

Connor turned to find the St. John butler addressing him from just inside the drawing-room doorway. The cool aloofness of London servants annoyed Connor. "What is your name?"

The butler blinked. "I am Horton, my lord."

"Just what is it that you want, Horton?" Connor snapped.

"Miss St. John asked me to serve you tea," the butler stammered with less than his previous imperiousness.

"Tea?" Connor knew from the way the man winced that his temper was showing. Whatever the twins' game, he was not going to sip tea while they plotted their next move. "I do not want tea, Horton. Miss St. John went upstairs to change her dress and I don't care to be kept waiting. See what's keeping her."

"Ah, yes, my lord." The butler bowed and hastily backed from the room, nearly bumping his backside on the door.

The murmur of voices and the rapid padding of small feet on the carpeted floor above brought a wayward smile of satisfaction to Connor's lips.

A door slammed. More muffled conversation.

His smile broadened. So the sisters were at odds. Connor relaxed a bit and turned to stare out the window at the sunny day. Aside from putting eggs in different baskets as Erik had suggested and the twins' and their aunt's plans to remake him—they were hardly the first females to wish to reform Connor's ways—there might be something to this social convention of being seen in the park with a respectable lady at his side. Especially if that lady was the daughter of the man who owned Glen Gray. Word was sure to get back to Ramsay Forbes. The point was not to aggravate the marquis, but to let him know that the McKensies were still in the ring.

Footsteps on the threshold brought Connor around in time to see one of the twins stop there and eye him. "Lord Kinleith."

He smiled, immediately recognizing the softness in the depths of Charlotte's eyes that was absent from Cassandra's. Also evident was the gentle sweetness in the curve of her lips, even when she frowned. Though she walked with the grace and confidence of all the young ladies who had been presented at court, there was a vulnerability about Charlotte that Cassie lacked. He wondered what kind of prim young woman could convincingly play the part of her hoyden sister, then withdraw into herself, all coolness and restraint. The puzzle left Connor intrigued.

"Miss Charlotte." He bowed. "How lovely you look in blue and white stripes. The change suits you."

Without smiling, Charlotte curtsied and touched her earlobes. "Thank you, my lord. But I wear the earbobs upon your request."

"So I see." Connor reached for the pelisse that Betsy had left and draped it over Charlotte's shoulders. "Shall we go be seen in the park?"

The traffic in the park was heavy, for the sunshine had brought everyone out to soak up the spring warmth. Gentlemen and ladies on horseback and families in carriages clogged the paths, but no one seemed to mind the delays. Hats were tipped and greetings aplenty were exchanged.

Connor had no difficulty with the team or the curricle and found that he enjoyed the curious glances cast in his and Charlotte's direction.

He was pretty much a landlubber where horse and carriage were concerned. In the Highlands, or Edinburgh, for that matter, a man highborn or humble walked everywhere. But Connor liked the way the curricle and team handled. Nice sense of power to have a matched pair turn and move on at command.

Everywhere along the park paths they drove they saw perfectly matched, fine blooded animals, brushed to a gloss, turned out in shiny harnesses, pulling fine vehicles, and attended by liveried grooms.

" 'Tis a spectacle," he said, admiring the elegant habits of the ladies on horseback and making note of the gentlemen's fine coats, usually of blue with gleaming brass buttons.

"But not nearly as much of a show as it once was. When King George was only the Prince of Wales," Charlotte said, "Mama said when she was younger, the grooms all wore powdered wigs and the coaches had richer ornamentation."

"Hard to believe it was grander than this." Connor liked the spectacle. It certainly was an interesting way of getting to know who was who. And for the right people to see him—with Davis St. John's daughter. At first their conversation was general and interrupted by responding to salutations from numerous passersby.

"I do not see Sir Seymour here today," Connor said finally, knowing full well the topic of Charlotte's beloved poet was bound to be a delicate one.

Charlotte frowned and drew her pelisse closer about her shoulders. "Sir Seymour writes late into the night, so he sleeps quite late into the morning. An artist cannot always keep the same hours as society."

"Or as the rest of us mere mortals," Connor added for her, then laughed.

"I realize it might be difficult for a man of your interests to understand the artistic temperament," Charlotte said, studying the path ahead of them.

"Tactfully put, Miss St, John." Connor attempted to bring his amusement under control. "But honestly said, I believe. So while we are being truthful with each other, let me ask you exactly why you agreed to this arrangement suggested by your aunt?"

"Honestly?"

Connor nodded.

"Because Cassie wanted to get to know a prizefighter."

That answer displeased him, but he would not comment. "And what else?"

"Well, she and Aunt Dorian think they can reform you."

"Reform me? From what into what?"

"If you must know, Cassie turned Dudley from a countrified viscount into one of the most sought-after gentlemen guests at balls and *soirées*." Charlotte said, staring straight ahead. After a pause she added, "I understand you might have designs of your own."

"Designs? Me?" Connor mostly kept his attention on the horses. "And what might those be?"

She cast him a sidelong glance. "Acquiring Glen Gray."

"Guilty." Connor waited for her to express her indignation, but only silence followed his statement. "But what chance have I? Your sister wears the Moncreff betrothal ring, does she not? Sir Edward is quite possessive of you. Am I mistaken?"

"No, you're not mistaken," she said, continuing to stare at the path ahead of them.

"So all I can do is entertain you and your sister and remain in your father's good graces," Connor pointed out. "And why are you here? Did you agree to this drive because of your aunt Dorian, your sister, or Seymour?"

She turned on him, her blue eyes blazing with indignation. "Would it disappoint you terribly to find that I make my own decisions?"

Connor grinned. "Not at all."

"I would not have said yes to Aunt Dorian's suggestion unless I meant yes," she asserted, her back getting stiffer and her lips becoming thinner by the minute.

"Good, I'm glad to hear it," he managed to say without chuckling, gratified with her spirited reaction. "I'm pleased to have a guide to all the proper sights of London."

"I think we should begin with the Tower of London," Charlotte said.

"I've been there."

"Then Westminister Cathedral," she suggested without pausing.

"Done that, too."

"Pall Mall?" she offered.

"Driven along there several times."

"Well, then there is the theater district and the opera," she said.

"You have me there," Connor admitted. "I've not been to that part of London. But I'm not overly fond of opera and all that singing."

"But it's so much more than singing," Charlotte asserted. "You must go to the opera at least once."

"But, you know, fair is fair," Connor said. "I would ask one thing of you."

"What's that?"

"That you agree to allow me to show you the parts of London that *I'm* familiar with."

SIX

Connor could feel Charlotte studying him for a long moment. When he slid a glance in her direction, he saw tense skepticism in her face. But curiosity gleamed in her eyes.

"Just what parts of London do you speak of?" she asked.

"I suspect there is a lot of London that you haven't seen, Miss Charlotte," Connor said, deftly turning the team into the London street. "This could be a mutually beneficial educational process for us—this idea of your Aunt Dorian's."

It did no harm to remind her that they were both trying to please Lady Derrington. "This way I get to know your London and you get to know mine. You know, a sort of a *Life in London* adventure."

"You mean a tour of polite London and of the low life, too?" she asked without deigning to look in his direction. "Not that I've ever read that disreputable *Life in London* penny press drivel."

"A tour of the two worlds is precisely what I mean."

"And you have read Eagan's *Life in London?*" she asked, turning toward him once more, her blue eyes wide and curious.

"Aye, 'twas entertaining. What did you think of it?"

"I said I read very little of it." She faced forward again with a self-righteous tilt to her chin.

"Which chapters appealed the most?" Connor asked, unfazed. "Polite society or the street adventures?"

"I don't recall," she replied, seeming more interested in a carriage they had just passed. "Cassie brought it into the house. I only paged through it out of curiosity. 'Tis very popular, you know."

" 'Tis popular indeed." Connor admitted. "But it only seems fair. If I'm going to submit myself to your educational efforts, should you not accept mine?"

She made no immediate reply. When she finally spoke, she regarded him with those wide, innocent eyes. "If I agree, must I watch *you* fight?"

So it was the fighting that distressed her. He should have known, Connor thought. She'd made no secret of it when they first met.

"No, of course not, if my fighting disturbs you," he said, surprised by his disappointment. But victory in this matter loomed too close to allow petty feelings to distract him.

He pulled the curricle up to the front door of the St. John townhouse. Though he wanted this lady on his arm for Ramsay Forbes to see and he wanted her in the crowd cheering for him, he would take it one step at a time. One glance at Charlotte's earnest blue eyes convinced him that there was only so much he could maneuver her into.

Charlotte St. John might appear soft and amenable on the surface, but there was a steely core in her that would not bend to just anyone's will. "I don't believe being in a prizefight audience is what your Aunt Dorian intended."

"Good, then I agree to your proposed adventure." A small smile of excitement formed on her lips. "I've always preferred a quiet life of contemplation and study. I believe it is best for the soul and the digestion. At least that's what Mama always says. But it is only fair, as you say. I'll go with you to your London, if you visit mine."

Connor smiled at Miss Charlotte—and to himself. He'd won round one.

* * *

Charlotte closed the door of her room gently and rested her forehead against the wood. The coolness of the smooth surface soothed her whirling senses. Connor's scent still filled her head, spicy and warm and all male. Dizziness had nearly overwhelmed her when he'd bowed over her hand in farewell, his fingers strong and large, his palm almost engulfing her hand. If his touch hadn't rendered her helpless, the light in his eyes would have.

Victory flashed there; he'd been mightily pleased with himself. Heaven knows why, she thought. Granted, she'd accepted his silly *Life in London* enticement, but it was little more than the hospitality Aunt Dorian had asked of her, and no less than the adventure that Cassie would have jumped at in a second. Now on second thought, in the quiet, orderly sanity of her room, Charlotte began to regret accepting his challenge.

"He wasn't bluffing, was he?"

Charlotte started at the sound of Cassandra's voice. When she turned, she saw her sister dressed in a fresh yellow gown and standing in the doorway that connected their bedchambers.

"You were right," Cassandra continued, her expression as sober and apprehensive as Charlotte ever remembered it. "Connor McKensie knows the difference between us."

"Yes, indeed, the Earl of Kinleith truly knows the difference." Charlotte threw her reticule and bonnet onto the bed as laughing images of Connor still flashed through her head. He'd worn no hat, allowing the sun and the wind to toy with his hair as they'd driven through the park. Strands glinted blue-black. His shoulder had brushed against hers twice as he'd managed the horses. Beneath his blue coat his arm had seemed fluid yet solid.

The idea of spending more time in his company over the next few weeks had disturbed her then. Now she was uncertain how she felt. On the one hand she liked him, though he was quite uncouth. On the other hand, he'd proven himself considerably more insightful than Edward, and now she wasn't certain she was prepared to deal with that.

"Who would have ever thought a boxer would be that astute?" Cassandra chewed on her lip as though she were truly puzzled. "I swear he knew the moment I walked into the drawing room. It could have been a bluff, but I saw his eyes grow instantly cold. He was angry."

"Was he? I thought he was offended perhaps, but he said nothing in anger to me."

"He didn't need to speak of it!" Cassandra exclaimed. "Couldn't you see it in his face? The man is not accustomed to being crossed. Don't you find that just a bit frightening? I do."

Charlotte blinked at Cassandra in surprise. "What troubles you, Cassie? You never fear anything."

"It's not exactly that I fear Kinleith," Cassandra said, frowning. "It's more like apprehension. This has never happened before, you know. Someone that we don't truly know can tell us apart without any difficulty."

Abruptly Cassandra turned to study herself in the dressing-table mirror. "Do you think something about one of us has changed?"

"Nothing that I've seen," Charlotte said, walking to her sister's side for a closer look in the looking glass. She saw the same two faces that she'd seen there earlier as Cassie prepared to greet Connor. Only now she saw one face—hers—the one Connor McKensie recognized immediately. A warm, mysterious glow grew inside her. "We look the same as always."

"I don't see any change either." Cassandra primped absently, plucking at a tendril on her nape, pulling it back into the desired curl, then she sighed. "Lord Kinleith must see something."

With a shrug, Cassandra turned to Charlotte. "Oh, but do come tell what happened. What did he say when you walked into the drawing room? How did he like the drive in the park? Were there many people there to see you?"

She reached for Charlotte's hand and Charlotte allowed Cassandra to draw her down on the bed where they sat hand in hand. "Did he say anything about Glen Gray?"

This was their ritual quizzing. It had always been so between them—the sharing of everything, with Cassandra pumping Charlotte for each gesture and word exchanged between Charlotte and their acquaintances. So Charlotte, with pleasure, launched into the details of her conversation with Connor—most of it, anyway. Cassandra listened eagerly, questioning Charlotte when she paused to take a breath or to consider her words.

Charlotte told her sister all except about the Glen Gray discussion; she dismissed it with a few words, implying that it was unimportant. For the first time in her life, she decided to keep some of her adventure to herself, like the feel of Connor's shoulder against hers and the glistening of his hair in the sunshine. Those were things of her own to savor, but she did tell Cassandra about *Life in London* and the challenge.

"You're going to do what?" Cassandra said with a gasp. "You're going to the disreputable parts of London in turn for every party he attends with you?"

"Something like that, I suppose." Second thoughts assailed Charlotte again.

"Do you think Papa would approve?" Cassandra asked, looking thoughtful. "I'm certain Aunt Dorian wouldn't. I don't think this is what she intended."

"Maybe not," Charlotte agreed, suspecting that Cassandra might be right about Papa and Aunt Dorian. She'd thought of that before, but was still uncertain about how to handle the problem.

"And what about Edward?" Cassandra asked. "Did you see him in the park today?"

"No, but I've explained to him that I'm merely being hospitable to Lord Kinleith at Aunt Dorian's request," Charlotte said, the memory of the sullen frown Edward had worn for the remainder of the evening at the *soirée* still clear in her mind. He'd not been happy with the arrangement, but he'd made no claim on her. "He will probably send me a note later today with some lines of poetry he wants me to admire. He sends something most every day. I'm sure he understands in his way."

"We shall see," Cassandra said, tapping her lips with a finger. "A gentleman tends to lack understanding about a new man in his lady's life."

"But does Edward consider me his lady?" Charlotte asked, remembering how possessive he'd suddenly seemed when Connor had been introduced.

"The fact that he sends notes to you daily indicates something, you know," Cassandra said, an impatient tone in her voice. "But he has never declared his feelings."

Unacknowledged disappointment and anger gnawed at Charlotte's insides. Time after time he'd had the opportunity, but had never opened his heart to her.

"You could lose Edward over this," Cassandra said. "Have you thought of that? Are you certain you want to go through with this preposterous adventure with Lord Kinleith? If Edward takes exception to it, he could back off. What if you devote yourself to Kinleith and he wins his big fight then returns to Scotland? You would be left without Edward or anyone. Your reputation could be ruined."

Charlotte studied her sister. The possibility of losing Edward was a risk she'd considered. But she'd not thought of the danger to her reputation. "You think Lord Kinleith would take advantage of me? Is that what you are saying?"

"I don't know." Cassandra leaned closer, peering into Charlotte's face. "How much do we really know about him beyond the fact that Aunt Dorian is sponsoring him into Society and that he wants Glen Gray?"

"For Aunt Dorian to sponsor him, he must be a gentleman."

"True, Aunt Dorian is seldom wrong," Cassandra admitted, apparently mollified by the thought.

Charlotte gazed into her sister's face, a familiar countenance, one she knew as well as her own—yet so much about them was different. And Connor McKensie had recognized the difference. "But you think he's not to be trusted?"

"I don't know." Cassandra shook her head. "There's *never* been more than a special few who could tell the difference between us. Mama. Tony. Aunt Dorian. Papa, sometimes. Never anyone we couldn't trust."

"Because he recognizes the difference between us doesn't mean that he can't be trusted," Charlotte protested.

"True, it doesn't necessarily reflect on his trustworthiness," Cassie agreed. "But it does mean that whatever adventure he has in store for you would be yours alone. I would be helpless to assist you."

A strange thrill curled in the pit of Charlotte's stomach. An image of Connor's heartwarming smile flashed through her mind's eye. Suddenly the opportunity of a lifetime seemed to loom before her.

"Charlotte, under the circumstances do you really believe you should go through with this escapade?"

"Why not?" Charlotte stared at Cassie and Cassie stared back in silence that hung between them.

"You tell me why not," Cassie urged.

The decision spoken aloud made Charlotte feel suddenly lighthearted. She shifted her position on the bed to face her sister. "Why shouldn't I risk it? Kinleith won't be in Town long. As you said, he will fight his big fight and then be gone. I've already explained to Edward that I am merely acting as a hostess for Aunt Dorian. I shall have to trust that he will understand."

Cassandra shook her head and touched Charlotte's hand. "Charlotte, the Brawlin' Scot is no fool. He's not about to submit to anyone's reform. He's already made that clear. And we don't truly know what he's after. Are you absolutely certain you want to take this risk?"

"Yes, I'm certain." Charlotte smiled, secretly pleased with her decision. This adventure with Connor McKensie, unlike any others in her twenty years on earth, would be hers alone.

SEVEN

"So just why do you think the St. John twins do it—trade places as if they be interchangeable souls?" Erik asked, bobbing in a circle around Connor. His feet moved rapidly on the canvas as his fists jabbed toward Connor's face without making a connection.

Connor threw a half-hearted punch at Erik, but the older man ducked and defended himself before dancing around Connor again.

"Yer not concentrating," Erik chided with a frown.

"I think they do it because they can," Connor said, knowing Erik was right about his concentration. But he still intended to use his last hour of time working in the ring at Gentleman Jack's. "Remember the Kennet twins?"

"Aye, nary a pair of boys more identical have ever been birthed," Erik said, standing back to appraise Connor's fighting stance. "Ye are dropping yer block on the left. Aye, the Kennet twins. Only their mother could tell them apart. Their mother and you, that is."

"They didn't mean anything by it," Connor said, as much to himself as Erik. He'd always been able to read people in a way that others found remarkable. His Irish mother had called it a kind of second sight. His father had denied its existence. But on numerous occasions Connor had unerringly pointed to the perpetrators of mischief. Soon after his father had begun to bring Connor into meetings and hearings. "The substitution o one for the other isn't meant to be an insult. 'Tis more a prank. 'Tis just something that they can do and it amuses them."

"Are ye saying that's what the Missies St. John be doing?" Erik bobbed around Connor again. "Amusing themselves? There's no more to it than that?"

"I'm not certain," Connor muttered, wondering why it seemed so important to understand Charlotte and Cassandra's deception when he had forgotten all about the Kennets' attempted pranks.

This time when Erik threw a punch, Connor blocked it and connected with the man's unprotected jaw. Erik staggered back against the ropes. Connor grinned. "What do you think of my concentration now?"

"Yer not angry about this thing with the St. John twins, are ye?" Erik mumbled with his hand pressed against his jaw.

"Not now," Connor said, feeling strangely better, not because he'd hit his friend, but because he was satisfied that the twins had merely been playing with him as they might anyone else. There'd been no grand design in their deception. To them it was a sport. A dangerous game, considering the damage his goal could do to their family reputation, but a game to them.

Erik charged Connor and swung a hard right. Connor ducked and returned with a quick jab to Erik's midsection. He missed by a hair, but the attack sent his sparring partner into retreat.

"Hi ho, there in the ring," hailed a well-dressed bystander.

In the boxing salon, men clothed in all manner of garments came and went continually. Most of the time Connor was too intent on his sparring to pay much heed to them.

At the sound of the hail echoing through the parlor, Connor turned to see Nigel Eldwick standing near the ring, rocking back and forth on his heels. The rich merchant's son peered up at the ring with a bemused smile.

"Hello, Eldwick," Connor said just before he swung another hard right at Erik. The blow connected with Erik's jaw again. Arms flailing, the curly-haired Scot staggered backward.

"You are looking good, Kinleith," Eldwick called. "Got another fight lined up yet?"

"Haven't heard from anyone willing to back one," Connor responded, vaguely aware of Erik scowling as he rubbed his jaw. "I think that's enough training for now, Erik."

Erik said nothing; he just hauled back and swung at Connor, who ducked. Undaunted, Erik followed up with an illegal cuff to the back of Connor's head that sent him stumbling toward the ropes.

"Good show, Drummond," Eldwick called, laughing so that everyone in the parlor turned to see what had happened.

Erik laughed in the face of Connor's glower, then hastily retreated to the far side of the ring and climbed over the ropes. "I'll leave ye to yer business."

"No backer, eh?" Eldwick hooked his thumbs into the pockets of his red-and-black-striped waistcoat. "You can always take some fights at Fives Court."

"That's not the kind of money I want." Connor was reluctant to be distracted from his goal—a big purse. He leaned on the ropes, pulled off his gloves he used only for sparring, and rubbed his knuckles which had healed nicely. He was ready for another barefisted prizefight, but he wanted it to be a step in the right direction, one toward a big match.

"Would you be interested if I told you I think I've got some investors who would be willing to back you in a bout against that young Welsh boy? He's a new fighter who has been impressing all the comers at the fairs."

"Perhaps." Connor frowned. Eldwick was a gentleman gambler; the man made no secret of it. He was as likely to be found at the races as he was at Fives Court and always with a tidy wager riding on some fancy of his. Connor had no illusions about what inspired Eldwick's deference and interest; it was the winnings he'd acquired from Connor's fights. "Doesn't sound like the kind of fight to bring in a lot of money."

"But he would attract the press," Eldwick pointed out. " think you might get a lot of attention matched against him."

"Is he experienced?" Connor asked, disappointed that Eldwick had nothing better to offer. "Has he had any training?"

"Some, I think." Eldwick looked around the salon to see who else was there.

Connor followed the dandy's gaze, aware that Eldwick was a man who liked to see and be seen in the right places and in the best company.

Portraits of famous boxers of the last century—Big Ben Brain, James Figg, Gentleman Jackson—looked down upon them from the walls high above the floor. In one corner a gentleman was testing the weights hanging in the rack. Across from him a fencing master was warming up with a partner. And in a third corner several bare-chested gentlemen were being coached by a retired fighter. One seemed to be a natural, but the two others had the coordination of a drunken organ grinder's monkey.

Eldwick finally turned back to Connor. "You could take a look at him yourself at the Battersea Field Fair next week. I think he's going to fight there."

"I want it to be a good match," Connor said. " 'Tis no challenge to meet with a youngster who is good in a brawl, but doesn't know how to defend himself."

"I know, but he is gaining a good following," Eldwick said. " 'Tis no fun for a crowd neither if the match is uneven. The point is, Lord Kinleith, are you interested? Even if it ain't as big a purse as you like, it could be enough to be worth your time."

"Aye, I'm interested," Connor admitted. He was proud, yet the condition of his own purse made it impossible to pass up even a modest opportunity. Connor climbed out of the ring and dropped down onto the main floor at Eldwick's side. He was well aware that this man was probably the closest connection he had to the big-money fight backers. "Find out more about the investors. If they're truly interested, I'd like to meet them."

"I told them you would," Eldwick said. "Now if you weren't so particular about who you do business with, I might be able to find some backers that would put forth a big purse for a fight."

"I prefer to know who I'm doing business with," Connor said, not out of any scrupulousness, just out of practicality. A purse full of promises was of no use to him.

"Still, you might take a look at the Welsh boy at the fair."

"I'll remember that," Connor said and waved to Grady, the towel boy, who had just come into the salon with an armful of clean linens. Actually, Grady was no boy, but a man of some thirty-odd years. He nodded to Connor and trotted across the room, offering a fresh white towel. Taking it, Connor began to wipe the sweat from his chest. Grady lingered, his arms still full of clean towels. Connor saw no reason to dismiss him.

"That's capital then," Eldwick said. "I'll see how the backers want to handle this. I should be able to set up something."

"Just give me the particulars and I'll be there," Connor said, wondering what Charlotte was going to think about attending a country fair.

"Good show." Eldwick's face lit up. He envisioned vast winnings, no doubt. "Did you see Eagan's newspaper write-up of the fight last week? Gave you a right good review, he did. I think this fight could turn out well for a lot of people. It could lead to big things. Well, I'd better be off."

Connor shook hands with Eldwick. The dandy strolled away, adjusting his top hat to a jaunty angle and speaking to several other bucks as he headed for the door.

Grady lingered and offered Connor another towel. Preoccupied, Connor took it and began to dry the perspiration dripping from his hair.

"Knows a lot of gentlemen that fancy the boxing matches, that one does," said Grady.

"Does he?" Connor stopped toweling his hair and eyed the aging towel boy. The deep lines in the man's face and his short, crooked, bulbous nose testified to a hard life lived in the back streets of London. Something shifty in the squint of Grady's light-gray eyes made Connor skeptical of his words but curious about what he knew. "Like who?"

"Oh, not the big ones, thems that can set up the big fights, like with the champ, Jem Ward," Grady said with a shrug. "But he might be able to get you a bout with the Deaf Un, Jimmy Burke, or another up and comer, the Trooper."

"A marathon bout?" Connor had never fought a fight the length that Burke was known to excel at, but he wasn't going to tell a towel boy that.

"There's good money in it." Grady relieved Connor of the first towel he'd handed him. "That's what yer after, ain't it?"

"Do you know who these men are?"

Grady rolled his eyes in a coy manner. "I might. Or I might know who might know 'em."

Connor resumed drying his hair. He had no intention of allowing Grady to bait him. Either the towel boy knew something or he didn't, and Connor was inclined to think he didn't.

Whether Eldwick's connections in the world of fight backers and betting bookies went beyond acquaintance with small operators or reached down into the darker depths of underworld power, Connor was uncertain. Eldwick was full of bluster and unwarranted self-confidence. That made him difficult to read. Grady, the towel boy, was playing his own game or one someone had put him up to. Connor could but wait and see how it played out.

EIGHT

The gaggle of ladies Davis found in the drawing room when he arrived home irritated him. He tried not to show his annoyance, but the feminine chatter was deafening and the sweet scent of myriad perfumes smothering. He'd just spent a long day sequestered with solicitors and clerks—this Glen Gray issue beleaguered him. After the headaches of the day, he'd been looking forward to a quiet evening in front of the fire alone with his wife.

He longed to settle into his favorite chair, light his pipe, and sit in a room where he had no need to explain himself to anyone and all his wants and needs would be anticipated.

But Susanna was nowhere to be seen in the crowd, though he suspected she was at the center of the commotion. In her own quiet, gracious way, his wife had become something of a darling of Society. He'd learned to share her most of the time, but tonight he had less patience with others' demands on her than usual.

Fastening a tight social smile on his lips, he began to make his way through the guests, greeting familiar faces as he went, taking care not to step on fashionable gowns or slippered feet. He would find his wife surrounded by admiring ladies who also deluded themselves into thinking that the study of the classic Greeks elevated their intellect.

When Davis neared the far end of the room, to his surprise the top of a dark, masculine head suddenly came into view.

Then he caught sight of Susanna standing alongside a tall, well-dressed, sun-tanned gentleman. With their heads bent close together, their attention was fixed on a folio opened on the table serving as a lectern. There had never been a gentleman in her Hellenic study group before—none younger than the age of sixty years, at least.

This man stood a bit taller than average and presented a fit figure, though he was shorter and slighter than Davis. His brown hair was sun-streaked with gold and his blue eyes lit a face darkened from hours spent out of doors in the sunny Mediterranean. He had the kind of features women liked—finely drawn and aristocratic.

Davis's minor irritation blossomed into aggravation. The thought of Susanna being attracted to another man, especially a man of quality, troubled him though he would never admit it. And he certainly had better sense than to embarrass his wife before her friends.

"Mrs. St. John," he began, forcing himself to sound as cordial as he could manage. "What fascinating fact about the Greeks have you discovered this day?"

Susanna's head came up immediately and she smiled that sweet smile that never failed to make him glad he'd married her.

"Oh Davis, I had no idea it had grown so late," Susanna exclaimed. "Sir Myron has spent the afternoon explaining to the ladies and myself all about the restoration work on the Parthenon."

"Fascinating," Davis said, his well-practiced eye instantly noting the fine cut but shabby condition of Sir Myron's coat. A most conservative knot in his cravat—ah yes, an academic, Davis concluded with some relief. He could probably buy and sell the man twenty times over if he wished. "I don't believe I've had the honor, sir."

"I am so sorry," Susanna said, obviously remembering her role as hostess. "Sir Myron, may I present my husband, Davis St. John. Sir Myron worked with Lord Elgin when he transported the marbles from Greece to England. He has been so kind as to speak to us this afternoon about the Parthenon restoration and about the discoveries his study of the marbles has brought to the fore."

Davis bowed, vexed that Susanna never took her gaze from the gentleman scholar the entire time she was making the introductions. "Sir Myron, you must have some interesting stories to tell about Greece and the ancient ruins," Davis said.

"It is such a pleasure to share them with a lady of such fine intelligence and sensibilities as your wife," said Myron, turning his handsome smile on Susanna.

She blushed at the compliment. "But we all have enjoyed hearing about your adventures in retrieving this great artwork as well as learning more about your scholarly endeavors."

Several ladies standing close by chimed in their agreement.

"It has been my pleasure," Myron said, taking Susanna's hand and bending over it so deeply that Davis thought the man was going to boldly kiss her fingers.

Not that Davis would have taken exception. He was a man of the world and no civilized husband became incensed over a mere compliment paid to his wife by another man. And no professor in a threadbare coat was going to make Davis forget himself now. He prided himself in not being a jealous husband. Thankfully, Susanna had never given him any reason to think that he should be.

"Such a shame that you have to go now," Davis said, taking Myron by the arm and leading the scholar toward the door.

Myron glanced over his shoulder at Susanna. "Yes, the lecture did go quite a bit longer than I'd expected. The ladies had many questions, but they really are quite well-informed. You are a fortunate man, St. John. Such splendidly educated ladies make charming companions."

"Yes, I am fortunate." Davis followed Myron into the front hall. "It is good of you to share your experience with Mrs. St John's study group, Sir Myron. Horton will see you out."

With the departure of their mentor, the ladies said their own farewells, finally leaving Davis and Susanna standing together at the drawing-room doorway.

"I'm sorry, darling," Susanna said, linking her arm through Davis's. "Sir Myron was so interesting, the time slipped away from us. And I thought you said you were going to spend some time at your club this evening."

"I was, my dear," Davis said, patting his wife's arm and more content now that everyone was gone. He led her down the hall toward the family parlor. "But I changed my mind. No harm done."

"You've had a particularly trying day?"

"Yes, Lord Linirk is making an issue of this Glen Gray property."

"Glen Gray?"

"You remember, that Scottish property I bought last year," Davis said. If he'd had any idea he was acquiring so much trouble when he bought the shipyard in Glasgow with sundry properties, he'd have passed up the deal. "Forbes and McKensie want it."

"Forbes and McKensie," Susanna repeated softly. "Not the Lord Kinleith, the prizefighter that Dorian was introducing around last week?"

"The same."

"Just what is the trouble?"

"Forbes is demanding that I sell him the property," Davis said, stepping aside to allow his wife to enter the parlor ahead of him.

"Can he meet the price?" Susanna asked.

"Money is not the problem with Forbes," Davis said, the stress of the day already fading now that he'd entered the cozy confines of the parlor. "But he's reputed to be a cold, heartless soul with enough power and influence to make things difficult for people if he chooses to do so."

Davis had recently managed to arrange several investments and sales of property to the benefit of the Crown. He was hopeful that his good services would be rewarded soon—with a long-sought-after title. He'd worked doggedly for years to reach the point where knighthood was within his grasp. Now this issue with Forbes turns up. Davis knew of at least one man that the Marquis of Linirk had ruined and that pitiful victim had been forced to remain on the continent living in genteel poverty. The last thing Davis needed now was for a disgruntled marquis to cast a shadow on his good services to the Crown.

"And McKensie, does he also want to purchase the land?"

"I believe so, but it's even more complicated than competition for the land. These two clans have been feuding over this particular glen for several centuries."

Susanna gestured to the footman to light the fire. "Isn't that against the law?"

"Yes, and I have no desire to contribute to the strife between two families squabbling over a rocky piece of ground that is ultimately going to end up divided by a railway."

"This McKensie is the same one that has been calling for Charlotte?" Susanna settled into her chintz chair and softly instructed Horton about dinner.

"McKensie with Charlotte was Dorian's idea, as you know," Davis said, stretching his hands out to the fire that the footman had just lit. Flames leapt up bright and warm in the hearth.

"Should we be concerned about ulterior motives?" Susanna asked, a shadow of concern passing across her face. "Charlotte seems a bit wary of his company."

"I don't know much about the McKensies," Davis admitted, crossing to his favorite chair. Surrounded by creature comforts, he could feel his tension already easing away. "The old laird was suspected of being a bit of a pirate though nothing was ever proven. And this young fellow is a known brawler, though Dorian assures me he is educated and can be trusted to behave as a gentleman, despite his rustic manners."

Davis had hardly sunk into his leather wing chair when he heard a commotion in the hall, louder and more spirited than anything that had greeted him upon his arrival. He cast a questioning look in Susanna's direction.

She shook her head, clearly as mystified as he was. "I have no idea what our daughters are up to now."

"It's all in here, everything you could possibly want to know about prizefighting," one of the twins was saying. From the sound of her voice she was scurrying toward the parlor. "It's right here, in Pierce Eagan's *Life in London and Sporting Guide.*"

"That's an old publication," the other twin protested.

Cassie appeared in the doorway, resplendent in a candy-pink gown with a white lace yoke. "If Charlotte is going to be spending time in a prizefighter's company, she should learn about pugilism, shouldn't she, Papa?"

"Personally, I'd rather she did not see that Brawlin' Scot fellow at all, earldom or no earldom," Davis said, annoyed with the noisy interruption but pleased nonetheless to see his daughters.

"But Aunt Dorian wants us to educate Lord Kinleith about London," Charlotte said, a full-lipped, Dorian-like pout threatening the pretty line of her mouth. "Polish his manners, not promote his fighting."

"But it's only polite that you take an interest in what he does too, my dear," Susanna said with her usual practical generosity.

"My objections to the man are his Scots-Irish ancestors and his manners, not his boxing," Davis said, speaking distinctly. "Charlotte, lest you become too disapproving of this boxing thing, let me remind you that not so many years ago the King invited a number of prizefighters to serve as ushers at his coronation."

"That's right," Cassie said as though she'd bean present herself.

Davis could not resist smiling at his hoyden daughter.

"And does your precious Edward know that Lord Byron was a pupil of champion fighter Gentleman John Jackson?" Cassie continued.

"Edward." Charlotte sighed forlornly and sank down onto the velvet-tufted ottoman in front of the fire.

Davis glanced at Cassie in time to see a guilty look pass across her face.

Susanna dropped her needlework in her lap. "You've not heard from Sir Edward today?"

Charlotte shook her head and continued to stare at the floor. "Nothing, for three days now."

"Only three days?" Davis said, impatient with his sensitive daughter's mood.

"Papa, Edward sends me a note every day and has since Christmas," Charlotte said, tears welling in her eyes and indignation lowering the tone of her voice. "And now, now . . ."

"He's just preoccupied with some great poem," Cassie said.

Davis wished he'd thought to say that for Charlotte's sake.

"Yes, I'm certain that's the case," Susanna said with a soft, reassuring smile. "He can hardly hold it against you for showing an acquaintance of your aunt's around Town—at her request."

"But I fear he does," Charlotte whispered.

"Nonsense," Davis said, determined to dispel the melancholy atmosphere threatening to settle over the room. To his way of thinking if Sir Edward, the poet, never called again, it would be no great loss—as long as Charlotte's heart wasn't broken. Another thought occurred to him. "When do you see Lord Kinleith again?"

"Tomorrow, why?"

"Has he said anything to you about Glen Gray?"

"No, not since the first day when we went for a drive in the park," Charlotte said. "We talk of the London sights and sometimes of Edinburgh since I do know something of that city."

"Really?" Davis was surprised that the Scottish laird had not begun to press Charlotte about her papa's business affairs. He certainly wouldn't mind knowing a bit more about McKensie. The young, unofficial laird of his clan—for the old clan hierarchy had been outlawed—was something of an unknown quantity. He'd only come into his title and position within the past year. Though McKensie was reputed to be something of a brawler and the only son and youngest child of the old laird, little else was known about him. Dorian seemed to have confidence in the young man, but where Dorian got her information about McKensie, Davis had no idea. Yet his sister's knowledge was never to be discounted. "So McKensie has asked you no questions about Glen Gray?"

"None," Charlotte said. "In fact, I think he quite liked driving in the park the day before yesterday. And yesterday he was rather taken with the Tower on his second visit. A great fortress, he said."

"Well, leave it to a Scot to have an eye for good battlements," Davis said. "There seems to be no reason not to fulfill your promise to Aunt Dorian. But if McKensie begins to talk of Glen Gray, you direct him to me. As far as Sir Edward Seymour is concerned, I suspect he will get over whatever is troubling him."

"That's what I told her," Cassie said. "He'll come around."

Satisfied that he'd solved his daughter's problems, Davis reached for his favorite pipe, which had already been laid out on the table beside his chair.

"Now girls, leave your father to his peace and quiet," Susanna said, always sensitive to his habits. "Dinner will be served soon."

Cassie and Charlotte departed the room, still arguing about the book Cassie carried.

Davis thoughtfully pressed the tobacco into the pipe bowl. The mantel clock ticked quietly and the smell of well-prepared food wafted up the back stairs into the room. Davis sank a little deeper into his chair and sighed deeply as contentment settled over him. He glanced at Susanna, who was working at her needlework once again.

"I'm glad your Greek study group has become a success, my dear," Davis said, feeling a bit guilty about not taking more interest in her activities. "You had quite a crowd here today."

"Yes, it has begun to fill a great deal of my time," Susanna agreed, clipping a thread with her elegant gold sewing scissors. "You are so occupied yourself, and the girls—as you can see—

are off on their own most of the time. I can hardly keep up with them."

"So the Greek study group is good for you then," Davis said, picking up the paper and opening it to the business section, cutting off the opportunity for further discussion. Later, in the dark, he and Susanna would have more time together. He drew on his pipe and released the smoke with a puff of contentment. In bed his wife would be warm and sweet, responsive to all his needs. She always was. Ah, yes, he mused, he was going to have his perfect, quiet evening at home after all.

NINE

Grady, the towel boy, ignored the jostling elbows and trampling feet of the Battersea Field Fair crowd and contorted his features into his most menacing expression. He leaned forward, glaring at the whey-faced little girl carrying a tray of meat pies hung from a strap around her neck. Without shrinking away, she stared back at him, wide-eyed and unblinking. But he refused to let her fearlessness daunt him. The chit couldn't be more than eight years old and he knew he could bully what he wanted from her.

With great deliberation he jingled the pennies in his pocket. "A whole sixpence? You've got a nerve asking that for one of them foul-smelling things, ain't yah? 'Tis highway robbery, sixpence for a meat pie."

"Please, sir, 'tis what Ma told me to ask for 'em." The stringy haired urchin paled, making the dark circles under her eyes appear darker, but she stood fast. No, she knew how to play the game well enough, Grady thought. He'd done it himself when he was a boy. Play the mark for a sucker. Look weak and underfed. Act mistreated. Whine. Genteel ladies might fall for it, but he was no fool.

"Please, sir," the girl piped, "Ma will box me ears if I come home with anythin' less than sixpence for every pie she gave me."

"Save yer breath on me, whelp," Grady snarled, and snatched

the fattest, freshest-looking pie off the tray. "Here's a thra' pence and tell yer ma to give yer ears an extra lick for me."

The girl barely glanced at the coin he tossed on the tray. She just gazed up into his face and studied him with those wide, pale eyes, as if she was fixing something in her mind.

"What do you think you're staring at, girlie?" Grady said, thinking he was going to smack her if she didn't stop glaring at him like that. He glanced around to see if anyone in the crowd was watching them. "Ain't you never seen a man who knows what he wants and takes it?"

That must have frightened her, because she turned from him then and disappeared into the noisy throng—swallowed up as if she'd never been there in the first place. He shrugged, his victory dampened by an odd chill that settled over him.

"By Jove, looks good."

Someone snatched Grady's pie from his hand. He swung around to collar the culprit, only to come face-to-face with Jerome Harby, who took an enormous bite out of the flaky crust.

"Just what do you think you're doing?" Grady's stomach rumbled with hunger. "That was my pie."

"Good choice," Harby said, his cheeks bulging with another bite of crust and meat. He wiped away a trickle of gravy from the raspberry birthmark on the point of his chin. "If you want one so badly, go find the girl and get another."

Grady glanced around in the direction in which the girl had disappeared and decided against pursuit. She wasn't going to allow him another pie easily after he'd already shorted her once. Street urchins had their own way of exacting revenge.

"Yeah, well, you owe me one, Mr. Harby," Grady said, frowning at his new acquaintance. He didn't want to let the man take undue advantage of him. On the other hand, he wanted desperately to do business with this well-dressed buck who looked as if he could offer more than one good opportunity to make a shilling.

"Is he here?" Harby mumbled, particles of food spraying from his mouth. "Have you seen the Scot yet?"

"He's here," Grady said, nodding in the direction of the spectators assembled around the fight ring already roped off on the green. "There's a lady with him."

"A lady?" Harby stopped chewing. "A lady? By Jove! He took Eldwick at his word and he brought a lady, too? Do you know who she is?"

"No doxie, from the looks of 'er." Grady had tired some time ago of following the Scot without letting himself be seen, but he'd managed to keep track of the giant in the crowd. Wasn't difficult. The striking couple—the tall Scot and the fashionable lady with a blue parasol—created something of a commotion wherever they went. "She's some gentle lady. And wearing white stockin's and shoes that's goin' to be ruined by the end of the day, if you ask me."

"Peeking at ankles again, are you, Grady?" Harby gulped down the last of the pie and brought his coat sleeve to his mouth to wipe away the grease. "Fancy that. He brought the St. John girl here to see the Welsh boy fight. Won't Lord Linirk find that interesting?"

Grady made note of Harby's pleasure. "That's good? The lady?"

"It's useful information," Harby said, looking over the sea of people. "Very useful. Where is he? Can you point him out?"

"Over there by the goods stall on the other side." Grady gestured in the direction of a booth offering wares. "He wanted to see the animals. But the lady said she wanted to see all the sewing things and the used-book stall."

"She hasn't insisted on seeing the waxworks?" Harby asked, picking at something between his teeth. "Have you seen them? The phantasmagoria of the murder of Maria Marten at the Red Barn is bloody good."

He chuckled, apparently amused with some cleverness Grady barely understood. Waxworks had never held much attraction for the towel boy. Why pay to stare at stiff, painted dummies when real, contorted, bleeding bodies could give a man's blood a rush?

"So you want me to keep following them?" Grady asked. He had no idea why the big Scot was of such interest to his new patron, but he was willing to do what he was told. Besides, he wanted to see the Welsh boy fight, too.

"Yes, I'll follow them for a while, too," Harby said. "McKensie doesn't know me from any other man in the crowd. But you keep your eye on him, too. But stay out of sight and report to me later."

"Awright, Mr. Harby," Grady said, turning away a bit disappointed. He hoped McKensie still wanted to see the fight because he intended to see it, by gum. He already had a pound wagered on the Welsh boy's opponent, the bloody mean Trooper.

"Can you believe that horse could actually count its age?" Charlotte said, the wonder of it too much to dismiss, even with a thousand other fair attractions demanding her attention. As they strolled away from the performing horse, she glanced up at Connor to see if he felt as much wonderment over the miraculous animal as she.

But he only grinned. "I believe an animal can do anything at a country fair."

Tucking her arm into the sizable crook of his elbow, Connor led the way through the crowd, the throng parting for the passing giant in a kilt. She ignored his laughing skepticism. She was having too much fun at the Battersea Field Fair to let anyone's cynicism diminish it.

From the moment Connor had handed her down from the carriage, the bright colors, musical sounds, and pungent odors of the fair had assailed her. It was like walking through a parade. So much that was new and wonderful—she could not take in enough at once. Colorful flagged pavilions, peep shows, waxworks, freak shows, puppet performances, rope dancers, and uniquely talented animals. It reminded her of her few trips to the market with Cook when she was a girl. But the fair was a million times more thrilling.

She was so glad she had some, though it was probably not something worthy of writing a poem about. Papa wouldn't be too pleased about her being here. He considered fairs far too common for his daughters to attend. Edward would absolutely turn livid if he knew she walked among the unread. With a toss of her head, she forbade herself to think of Edward, who had not written her for over a week.

This experience was hers to enjoy and even Connor wasn't going to take the pleasure of it from her. Fulfilling her half of the bargain she had made with Connor was proving to be more enjoyable than she'd ever expected.

"I still think it was miraculous that that animal could paw the correct number of years out on the ground when his trainer asked," Charlotte went on. She strolled along beside Connor, barely aware of her wide-eyed, openmouthed amazement. She didn't care how awestruck she appeared. It was all just too wonderful.

"The horse, really knew what to do," she insisted.

"Of course he knows, lass." Connor's amusement remained undiminished. "Haven't you ever seen a horse know exactly how many times he's to walk a trail?"

He stopped and Charlotte looked down to see that they had reached a large mud puddle left by the morning's shower. Connor grinned at her and untucked her hand from his arm. In one long stride, he stepped over the enormous mud hole. He reached back for her hand to help her over, but Charlotte hesitated. The puddle was long and wide. A booth stood at one end of the mud hole and a crowd being entertained by a dancing bear blocked the other side. There was no way she could hop across it without soaking one foot or the other.

Connor waved at her encouragingly. "Come on. You can do it. Just a little hop. Give me your hand and you'll sail over."

Charlotte rested her parasol on her shoulder and twirled it absently. She looked at the muddy water, then at the waterline on Connor's soft, leather-laced boots. His foot had only sunk in as deep as his instep. But her satin slippers would be covered and her white stockings soaked with black, oozing mud.

"I'll never make it." She glanced up at him and knew what he was thinking. "Yes, next time you tell me to change to walking boots before we leave the house, I shall heed your suggestion. But for now, what are we to do? Perhaps we can go another way?"

"No need." Connor stepped back across the puddle. Before she realized what he was doing, he slipped one arm around her waist, caught her beneath the knees with his other, and scooped her up. "Put your arm around my neck. Here we go."

To the laughter and cheers of the fairgoers around them, he carried her across the puddle—her petticoats and ankles on display to all who cared to look.

Mortified, a blush stained Charlotte's cheeks. "You are making a spectacle of us, my lord. Put me down."

On the far side of the puddle, instead of setting her down, Connor marched on.

"Where are you going?" Over his shoulder, she watched the puddle recede in the distance. "My lord, this is highly improper."

She wriggled against him in protest, but his grip was firm and his chest as solid as a rock. He grinned into her face. The devilish light in his eyes made her painfully aware that under the circumstances, with her breasts crushed against his chest and her knees in his clutches, physical assertion was not her best tactic. "Pray, do put me down now."

"Why?" he asked, walking on as if he could carry her in his arms all day. "This feels right, don't you think? Why don't you shift that parasol so the sun is out of my eyes, too."

For a moment, Charlotte couldn't believe that he was serious. She glanced uneasily around at the crowd, most of whom merely laughed as they passed. Then she realized, of course, that he wasn't serious. No one at the fair was. The spirit of fun had pervaded the crowd from the moment they'd stepped from the carriage. Smiles lit faces and laughter filled the air. No one heeded the rank smell of the farm animals or the muddy grounds. No one was serious about anything. And why should she be?

She glanced at him, reconsidering what she should do next. Playfully she moved the parasol to her other shoulder, shading them from the sun and the curiosity of the crowd. "Is that better, my lord?"

"Aye, lass, 'tis better." His naughty grin softened into a genuine smile.

She couldn't resist smiling in return. She breathed in the scent of him, a tantalizing combination of pine and man. She couldn't help but think he might be right. Being so close to him, being wrapped up in his arms, seemed right. She relaxed a little, enjoying the warmth of his body against her own.

"You know, there's a language of the parasol," Charlotte offered, thinking to use the pleasant moment to slip in a bit of a lesson.

"The parasol?" Connor said, a note of disbelief in the deep rumble of his chuckle. "I know there's a language of the fan, but I never bothered to learn it. Now you tell me there's a language of the parasol, too?"

"I'm serious," Charlotte said. "There are indeed basic signals given with the parasol that you should know as a gentleman."

"Such as?"

"If a lady carries her parasol over her right shoulder, you may speak to her."

"Right shoulder, I may speak to her," Connor repeated as though he was memorizing Charlotte's instructions.

"Over the left shoulder means you are too cruel," Charlotte continued. "I'm sure you never see that kind of signal."

"I don't need parasol language to know when a lady is rejecting me," Connor said. "I trust my instincts. But while we're on the subject, what does it mean when the parasol rests on the gentleman's shoulder?"

Charlotte huffed in frustration. Obviously he had no intention of availing himself of the knowledge she could impart. Disappointed, she glanced at her parasol handle resting on his broad shoulder and studied the curve of his ear. Her gaze followed the way his dark hair curled over his white cravat. She couldn't remember Edward's ear ever being so fascinating. "The parasol handle on the gentleman's shoulder means he really should put the lady down, my lord."

"Is that so? And what will you give me for carrying you across that puddle, saving your slippers from being muddied, and setting you down on dry land?"

"Payment is required?" Charlotte drew in a deep, indignant breath. How dare he require payment! Edward would never do such an outrageous, indecent thing.

She eyed Connor long enough to see his grin broaden and to note that he had amazingly thick, dark eyelashes. Whatever he was up to, it was no good. And she rather liked it. She fluttered her slippered feet, childishly delighted with the fun in this. "I fear I have no coins with me, my lord."

"I never said payment need be in coin," Connor said, sounding suspiciously reasonable. "I'm simply pointing out that a favor is usually exchanged for a favor, is it not? Even in high society, one courtesy is often given in return for another, true?"

"Well, yes, I suppose so," Charlotte said, beginning to wonder if she was going to suffer the embarrassment of being carried about in his arms the whole afternoon. He seemed absolutely tireless. Everyone who passed by laughed and saluted them. "What sort of bargain did you have in mind, my lord."

"How about a kiss?"

TEN

"A kiss!" Charlotte exclaimed.

Passersby turned their heads.

She bit her lip when she realized how loudly she had spoken and lowered her voice. "I mean, a kiss? It is not very seemly, even at a fair, is it?"

"Why not?" Connor stopped the next passing lady who was strolling along on the arm of a proper-looking gentleman. "Excuse me, ma'am and sir."

The couple stared at them, openmouthed.

"Connor, what are you doing?" The heat of a blush flooded into Charlotte's cheeks again as she comprehended what an astonishing sight they must make. A barelegged Scotsman carrying a lady and her parasol! A giggle threatened. Charlotte bit her lip.

"Do you think a kiss is too much to ask for carrying a lady across a mud puddle?" Connor asked the couple.

The woman gasped—almost enviously, Charlotte thought.

"I beg your pardon," the gentleman sputtered, drawing his lady companion away from them. "This way, my dear."

"Stop this." Horrified, Charlotte hissed into Connor's ear, then surrendered to a fit of giggles. She could hardly manage to order him to behave. "Put me down this instant. You'll have everyone here thinking you're daft and I'm a woman of loose morals."

Connor tossed his head back, laughing a deep, rich laugh that lightened Charlotte's heart. He marched on with no indication that he ever intended to put her down. Then he halted abruptly. "Are you hungry?"

Charlotte glanced at his face to see him intent on something before them.

She looked around to see a small girl with a tray of meat pies standing before them.

"Aye, I am," she said, only vaguely aware that she had adopted Connor's vocabulary. Connor shot a surprised smile at her before he lowered her feet to the ground.

"Erik?" The ever-present but invisible man sprang out of nowhere. Charlotte didn't completely understand their relationship. Erik treated Connor with an odd mixture of royal deference and comradely disrespect, but he unfailingly appeared the moment Connor wanted anything.

"The pies look tasty," Connor said, smiling at the girl.

"Sixpence, they are," the girl said, a warning in her voice and a belligerent tilt to her chin. Plainly if she got a penny less for the three remaining pies on her tray, there'd be a squabble. A few feet behind her loitered a small, ragged boy and two restless, sullen older youths. Their clothes hung on them, tattered, little more than rags. Their resentful eyes rested on Charlotte and Connor.

"Sixpence it is then," Connor said, gesturing to Erik to pay the child. "We'll take two and get one for yourself if you like, Erik."

A tentative smile broke across the girl's face and she eagerly handed the pies to Connor. She turned to the boys and shook her head at them. "No, not them."

As Connor handed Charlotte a pie, she stared at the girl, taking in the thinness of her ragged clothes, the wide, pale eyes with the dark circles beneath them. "Are you hungry?"

"Oh, no, yer ladyship," the girl said, hastily shaking her head.

Thoughtfully, Charlotte broke off a corner of the pie and put it in her mouth. When she caught the eye of the youngest boy, she saw naked hunger there. It tugged at her heart. From the way his lips moved as she picked at her food, she was certain the child was near-starving.

Without another thought, Charlotte held her pie out toward him. "This is wonderful, but I'm truly not hungry. Perhaps you will finish it for me."

Wariness in his eyes, the boy made no move to take the food. His gaze darted toward the girl with the tray.

The girl nodded to him. "Take it."

Taking a cue from the girl, Charlotte nodded, too. "Please have it."

Apparently reassured, the child stepped forward slowly and took the pie from Charlotte's hand. The moment he stepped away he turned his back on her and began to cram the food into his mouth.

Swiftly, Charlotte turned on Connor, who was about to take a bite of his pie. Without hesitation she snatched it from his hands. "Lord Kinleith isn't hungry either, are you, my lord?"

Connor gaped at her, openmouthed. "Ahh?"

Charlotte ignored his surprise. She broke the pie in half and held the halves out to the older boys. "Perhaps you young gentlemen would like to try part of his pie."

"Careful," Connor cautioned. Why he said that, Charlotte couldn't imagine. They were simply hungry children.

They turned sullen gazes in Connor's direction. She understood immediately. The Scotsman's size was intimidating.

"Don't mind Lord Kinleith—he won't hurt you," Charlotte said, and the boys seemed to believe her. One bolted forward and snatched the food from her hand as though he feared she would change her mind.

The other doffed his tattered cap and made a rough bow before he took the pie. "Thankee, yer ladyship."

Charlotte smiled, knowing that some mother would be proud to know that a remnant of the fine manners she'd taught her son remained with him.

"Yes, thank you, yer ladyship," the girl said with a smile.

Charlotte looked at the girl again, taking in the enormous

eyes, the pointed chin, and the hollow cheeks. The poor thing was starving, though she would not admit it. Charlotte turned on Erik, who met her gaze with his mouth full and his partially eaten pie in his hand. He froze.

Thankfully Connor, who seemed to have overcome his surprise and understood her purpose at last, turned on Erik, too. "You're not hungry, are you, my friend?"

"Nay." But the guilty look in Erik's eyes belied his true feelings. Charlotte hesitated, but Connor snatched the pie out of Erik's hands and gave it to Charlotte. She handed it to the girl.

"You heard him—he doesn't want it," Charlotte lied. "Here, it's only a few bites to keep you going this afternoon."

"You're too kind, yer ladyship," the girl said, bobbing an awkward curtsy as she secreted the food into her pocket. "Lord bless you."

Then the children were gone, melting into the crowd like deer into a forest.

"Wait," Charlotte called after them. "Oh, they didn't tell us their names."

Connor took her arm and steered her away from the direction the children had taken. "It's of no matter."

"But they looked so hungry," Charlotte protested. "If we knew who they are and where they live, maybe we could do something for them."

"It's not that simple, Charlotte," Connor said.

"But why not?" Charlotte asked, refusing to be led away. How could he dismiss those small, hollow-cheeked faces?

"Because they aren't ours to take care of," Connor said. "Because they may not be as innocent as they seem."

"What do you mean, not innocent?"

From the direction of the fight ring a trumpet call blared over the crowd's heads, calling for their attention. Charlotte and Connor turned in time to see the referee climb into the center and stand next to the trumpeter.

"Ladies and gentlemen," the referee began, each word drawn

out and distinct. The man began to announce the beginning of a round of fights. Charlotte's heart sank.

"I wanted to see this," Connor said, taking her hand and leading her in the direction of the roped-off ring.

"You promised no fights," Charlotte said, suddenly feeling her happiness crumbling away like a sugar lump in tea. Watching two men throw punches at each other had never appealed to her. The thought of attending such a violent spectacle at the fair tarnished the luster of the day.

"Charlotte, I promised that you wouldn't have to watch *me* fight." Connor leaned closer and spoke softly. "You watched an afternoon of fights the day we met."

"Yes, I know, but I was Cassie then," Charlotte said, refusing to meet his gaze. Surely he understood that was a very different situation. She could feel him studying her. "I'm not my sister."

"Of course not." He looked away, toward the fight ring. "I hadn't thought what difference that would make here today."

She could detect no anger in his voice, but she could tell he wanted to see the mill that was about to commence.

"Must we watch all the matches?" she asked, staring at the referee in the ring, already dreading the spectacle that would transpire.

He glanced at her, understanding in his soft smile. "No, I only want to watch a Welsh boy. He is said to be an ugly customer."

Charlotte stared at Connor, wondering what purpose there could be in watching an ugly boy fight.

He grinned at her. "I mean, he is supposed to be a good fighter."

"Oh, yes, well, I see," Charlotte said, reluctant to be a naysayer on an otherwise lovely outing. "Just one fight?"

Connor nodded. "I see Erik over there. I sent him to find us a good vantage point. Let's see what he found."

Charlotte soon found herself standing next to Connor in the midst of the crowd. Because Erik had saved them a place on a slight rise near the ring which was roped-off at ground level, she could see over the heads and shoulders around her. The noisy crowd proclaimed their approval or disapproval with each punch exchanged between the Welsh boy, a small but muscular dark-haired fighter, and a big, lanky pugilist called the Trooper.

Charlotte listened and watched, trying to gain an appreciation for what the men seemed to find of such importance. Erik stood behind them babbling an ongoing description of the match in Connor's ear.

"There be a marked difference in their manner of fighting," Erik said. "See how the boy hits right and left at the body while the Trooper aims at the nob alone."

Charlotte winced when the Trooper's blow connected with the boy's head and the boy reeled away, bleeding from the lip. Members of the crowd with wagers on the boy groaned. The throng in the Trooper's corner cheered.

The boy began to dance around the ring.

"He's going to rally," Connor said.

"Aye, here he comes," Erik said. "Look out. Ooh, that was a doubler to the Trooper's stomach."

"What are the odds?" Connor asked.

Charlotte noted that neither of the Scotsmen's gazes ever left the two men fighting in the ring.

"Seven to four," Erik said without pausing. "Trooper's favor."

The rounds proceeded quickly, but not quickly enough for Charlotte. By the ninth, the boy was retreating to every part of the ring, followed ruthlessly by the Trooper. Connor's ugly customer was clearly fatigued and near defeat.

"Why do they not declare the Trooper's victory and be done with it?" she asked, unrepentant about the impatience in her voice.

"Because neither man has gone down yet," Connor said, his gaze fastened on the two men in the ring.

"But the boy's eye is darkened and he is bleeding from the nose," Charlotte cried, trying to make herself heard over the shouting of the crowd. The Trooper's supporters could smell their winnings already and shouted their jubilation.

" 'Tis not enough," Connor said with a shake of his head.

Charlotte turned away, her stomach turning over with the rank smell of tobacco smoke and the sight of blood spattered across the dirty canvas. She put her hands over her ears. The smack of each fist striking the opponent's body seemed to echo over the cheers of the spectators. The whole experience was making her sick.

"Please, I'd like to go home." She tugged on Connor's sleeve to no avail.

Erik started. "What a mean upper left."

The crowd roared again—Connor and Erik, too. Charlotte risked a peek over her shoulder and the heads of the spectators to see the Welsh boy on his back, spread-eagle, out cold. The referee raised the Trooper's hand in the gesture of victory.

"Not much of a fight," Connor said, disappointment in his voice.

"Broke his jaw," Erik said matter-of-factly, as if the boy deserved no better.

Charlotte felt positively faint. "I want to go home."

Connor looked down at her as if he'd forgotten that she was there; then he glanced back at the ring. "He's not dead, Charlotte. It's just a broken jaw and a bloody nose. Look, the doctor is with him already. The Welsh boy will be all right. He'll live to fight another day."

Charlotte looked and indeed, a well-dressed man of medicine was already at work on the young fighter.

"The best medical men are always present," Connor added.

"I am glad to know that," Charlotte admitted, but the fun of the day had clouded over for her, just as the sky above had. The breeze blew damp against her cheeks and a chill settled over her. "But I'm really quite exhausted and would like to go home."

"Of course," Connor said without further argument. He spoke briefly to Erik, sending him after the curricle. Then he took her arm and led her away from the ring. "I can see this was a mistake. Let's get you away from the crowd and into the open air."

Charlotte allowed him to lead her away, relieved that she wouldn't have to watch another one of the fights. Relieved that she need not hear the smack of knuckles against bone or the labored breathing of the fighters as they reeled around the ring.

Connor navigated their way through the sea of people toward the open field where the carriages awaited. Charlotte did not yet see Erik, but she was certain he was there. She heard a woman cry out and a man shout some profanity. Then, without warning, a pack of ragged urchins erupted from the crowd. Small, stampeding bodies hurled their way through a forest of people—shoving unprepared fairgoers off balance, knocking baskets from arms, and tripping the unwary.

One boy's shoulder struck Charlotte's hip and spun her around so that her parasol was flung to the ground. Charlotte threw her arms wide in an attempt to regain her balance. The next boy struck her in the backside, nearly knocking her down, but he halted long enough to grab her arm before she fell face first into the mud. In a split second Charlotte looked down in time to recognize him as the boy who had doffed his cap to her earlier.

"Sorry, yer ladyship," he said, his thin chest rising and falling as he gasped for breath. He steadied her with one hand while his other little fist clutched a roll of pound notes that Charlotte knew couldn't possibly be his. Then he was gone before she could ask what had happened.

She glanced in Connor's direction in time to see him reach for her, grabbing her arm.

Shouts followed the boys, bellowed profanities that Charlotte could hardly interpret. Suddenly the crowd parted and a heaving, red-faced, wild-eyed man burst from among them, his arms outstretched, clutching for the boys' collars.

Instinctively, Charlotte stepped into his path. He slammed into her shoulder. The impact was so great he nearly pitched her to the ground. Only Connor's hand on her arm kept her from being pressed into the mud beneath the man's onslaught.

ELEVEN

"Grady?" Connor grabbed the fellow by the shoulder and hauled him around. The man's cap sat askew on his head and his shirttail flapped loose at his midriff. Off one shoulder hung his threadbare waistcoat pulled so that it hitched up on the other side where Charlotte could see that his pants pocket had been turned inside out.

"What's going on, man?" Connor asked, supporting the floundering man.

"Them boys, they picked me pocket, they did," Grady shouted, his lined face twisted in anger. His strange, crooked, bulbous nose shone shiny red and spittle sprayed from his mouth. "Set on me, they did, just like a gang of gypsies. Jostled me all around and fingers in me pockets. Hands everywhere. Took the coins out of me pocket, even robbed me of me fight winnings."

"You'll never catch them," Connor advised the man, and wisely, Charlotte thought. "Not in this crowd."

"But they took all I had. Getting even with me, they are."

"For what?" Connor asked, glancing at Charlotte, clearly as perplexed as she was. "You didn't give them cause, did you?"

"Ah, well, ah, it must have been 'cause I didn't want none of that skinny girl's pies." Grady's gaze shifted from Connor to Charlotte then back again. "Aye, that's what it was. I refused to buy her wares and look what she had them boys do to me."

"I see," Connor said, a faint frown turning at the corner of his handsome mouth. Charlotte knew instantly that the Scotsman wasn't quite satisfied with Grady's answer. "There's always a sneak or two at a fair, Grady. Go see Erik and tell him I said to advance you a few coins on your services to us at the boxing salon. But you don't go bullying your way through this crowd. You could start a riot, man. Give it up."

"Yes, well, thankee, yer lordship," Grady said, apparently mollified. He straightened his cap and turned to look around at the bystanders watching the exchange. "You said I could see Erik about an advance?"

"Yes, he's over there." Connor gestured toward the carriages. Grady seemed to gather what was left of his dignity and touched his cap in Charlotte's direction.

"So take that as a warning," Grady said to the crowd who had gathered round. "Watch the children. They be pickpockets."

Then he walked away, the crowd dispersing as he went.

Someone tugged on Charlotte's skirt. She turned and looked down to see the girl who had carried the pie tray earlier. With wary, pale eyes the urchin watched Grady take his leave.

As soon as he had disappeared beyond a pavilion, she bobbed an awkward curtsy to Charlotte. "Yer ladyship, that man, the one with the crooked nose who was accusing the boys—he has been following you and yer lordship all day. Just thought you should know."

With that she dashed off, too, disappearing in the same direction the boys had gone.

"What does that mean?" Charlotte turned to Connor. "Do you know him? You called him by name."

"No one of consequence," Connor said with a shrug. "Just a towel boy at the boxing salon where Erik and I spar. An advance will tide him over until he gets paid. Can't leave him penniless."

He took her hand and led her out of the flow of the crowd. "Are you all right? The girl was probably mistaken about Grady. Why would he be following us? I'm sure he is here to see the Welsh boy fight like we were."

"Yes, of course," Charlotte said, gazing back in the direction where the children had disappeared. Why would they lie to her about a towel boy? They gained nothing. Why would the youngsters take the trouble to alert her about Grady unless it were true?

"There's Erik with the curricle and none too soon." Connor glanced up at the gray sky and tugged on Charlotte's hand. "Let's go before it begins to rain."

Drops began to fall as they dashed toward the curricle, the cold, wet raindrops washing the question of Grady and the children right out of Charlotte's mind.

Connor credited Charlotte's silence during the ride home to exhaustion from the multitude of new sights and sounds that had bombarded her at the fair. He maneuvered the curricle through the traffic with his usual deftness while Erik rode on the back.

"So what did you think of the fair?" he asked, venturing a glance in her direction.

"Charming," she murmured as if startled out of some deep thought. "I've never been to one before. I loved the sights, but there were so many children there who look starved."

"I suppose," Connor said, surprised by her answer. He'd expected her to start babbling about the counting horse again. "Haven't you seen children selling wares in the marketplace before?"

"Yes, but I saw their mamas and papas nearby," Charlotte said. "These looked so alone. They had that wary look of wild things in their eyes. Do you know what I mean?"

"I hadn't thought of it that way," Connor said, struck by the accuracy of her observation. "But I suspect they are indeed more independent than some of the children you might have seen on market day."

"So you go to country fairs to see the fights," she stated,

staring straight ahead at the carriage traffic in the narrow, shiny-wet London street.

"And the livestock," Connor said, surprised at his own need to justify himself. "I'd like to see the Highlands used for more cattle grazing. And I think our stock needs to be improved."

"A worthy goal," Charlotte said, nodding without looking at him.

"Worthier than fighting?" Connor supplied for her, deciding to bring the topic out in the open.

She turned to him, her face pale and somber. "But how can you watch men hit each other, doing physical damage for the pleasure of others? Splitting lips and blacking eyes so someone like Grady gains on a wager"

"It's a sport, a competition, perhaps not as noble-appearing as jousting of old, but a competition in the art and science of hand-to-hand self-defense," Connor said, trying to explain something he feared she'd never understand. "There are even those who find a kind of grace in boxing and compare it to a ballet."

"I see no ballet in it," Charlotte snapped.

"I'll wager you don't ride to the hounds, either," Connor said as much to himself as to Charlotte.

"I don't," Charlotte said an odd tone in her voice. "But Cassie does."

His curiosity aroused, Connor asked in as bland a voice as he could manage, "Have you ever ridden to the hounds as Cassie?"

She glanced at him shyly, almost playfully. With a start, Connor glimpsed a mischievous Charlotte he hadn't seen before. "You won't tell anyone, will you?"

"Of course not," Connor vowed. At the moment he was willing to say anything to get her to tell him more about herself. He knew all he needed to know about Cassandra. But Charlotte—he wanted to learn more about the demure, mysterious Charlotte who masqueraded so successfully as her sister.

"I have ridden to the hounds as Cassie on several occasions,"

Charlotte said, looking at Connor at last, with a defiant set of her dainty jaw. "You see, she is a terrible horsewoman and I'm actually quite good. She did not want to embarrass herself with a poor performance in the field, so I rode instead."

She watched him as if she expected him to express amazement.

Connor filled in for her once more. "And no one noticed?"

"No, not even her fiancé, Dudley, knew the difference." She snapped her mouth shut and slid him a guilty glance as if she'd said more than she should have.

"And how did you avoid the taking of the brush?"

"It's not difficult to do," Charlotte said with a sniff. "There are often riders who do not make it to the kill. Aunt Dorian does it all the time."

"Now there's a sport I don't understand," Connor said, turning the curricle and its high-stepping pair of greys into the street of St. John's townhouse. "Why all the fuss over chasing a lone fox over hill and round dale when you could just set the terriers on it and be done with the varmint."

"But there is more to a foxhunt than that," Charlotte said. "There's the breakfast and the celebration afterward."

"Celebrating the killing of a fox?" Connor laughed. "And you Brits think the Scots are crazy."

"Well I suppose after killing a lion with your bare hands, chasing a fox must seem very tame," Charlotte said in a tight voice.

Harness fittings jingled as Connor pulled the greys to a halt in front of the St. John townhouse.

"I'll admit I drank near a full bottle of brandy the night I killed the beast, but it wasn't in celebration of his death, I promise ye," Connor said, never more honest in his life. "It was in thanks of having been spared my own. Now, we've got you home safe, at last."

The St. John groom dashed out of the kitchen door and up the steps to seize the horses as Connor climbed out of the curricle and strode around to help Charlotte disembark. The light rain had ceased so Connor decided he need not hurry up to the house and into the door.

He barely allowed Charlotte to set foot on the ground before he reached down and swooped her up into his arms. She cried out and clamped a hand on the crown of her bonnet to keep it from falling off.

"My lord," Charlotte cried. "What on earth are you doing?"

Connor turned and started up the steps to the front door. Carrying her was so easy, almost natural, the way she fit in his arms and against his body. She was soft and fragrant in his arms, her breasts pressed tantalizingly against him. He would have liked to take her somewhere private and hold her. "I believe when we were last in a similar position, our conversation was interrupted."

"What conversation?" Charlotte asked. "You were merely lifting me over the puddles. That was all."

"But I requested payment of my services and you refused to give me an answer."

"Nay, sirrah," Charlotte began, rearing back, stiff and unyielding in his arms, one hand pressed against his chest and her parasol dangling from the one around his neck. Her face posed only inches from his own. He ignored her resistance but took note of the faintest hint of a smile touching her lips. "I did not seek these services."

"I demand recompense nevertheless," Connor said.

"Connor, don't do this," Charlotte whispered. "The parlor maid is peeking through the lace curtains at us."

Connor grinned but made no move to release her. "Kiss me now, before I ring the bell, or you'll have to do it before your butler's dour visage."

"You are incorrigible," Charlotte hissed. "And this is entirely improper. No gentleman would do anything like this to a lady."

"I'm going to ring the bell and Horton will open the door and here we will be, standing on the step," Connor recited for her, paying no heed to her comments about propriety—gentlemen and ladies. "You in my arms, refusing my request for a chaste kiss of gratitude. What will happen then?"

"I have a clear picture of what we must look like, sirrah," Charlotte snapped.

He purposely leaned closer to add, "Did anyone mention that I'm sometimes called the Stubborn Brawlin' Scot?"

"No!"

"No, what?" Without making any move to set Charlotte down, Connor leaned toward the door and the bell handle. "Here goes."

"Very well," Charlotte muttered. "You said a chaste kiss of gratitude, though I've seen nothing said of that requirement for any service mentioned in the books of ladies' deportment."

"I wouldn't know about that," Connor said. "But I will accept a chaste kiss or any other type you would care to bestow, for that matter."

"You are dreadful," she whispered and he almost thought she meant it. Then a coy grin tugged at her lips. Connor forgot that they were standing on the doorstep for all the passersby and polite neighbors to see. Her arm was still raised as she clutched her bonnet to her head as if they were being buffeted by a gale. The soft blue patterned muslin of her gown stretched across her throat and pulled tantalizingly across the contours of her breasts. He could see her pulse beating in the hollow of her throat and he inhaled her earthy rose scent.

She suddenly stroked his nape and planted her lips against his. Dry-mouthed, Connor berated himself for not being prepared. But he made the most of the moment, meeting her lips with his, tasting the corner of her mouth and teasing her upper lip before she could pull away. Her mouth tasted warm and enticing. Her heart beat rapidly against his. He followed her mouth as she pulled away, turning her head so her bonnet brim came between them and hid her face. What had begun only as a jest to embarrass her, to make the color flood charmingly into her face, had suddenly become a longing, a stirring in his gut. He wanted to devour that prim, bow-shaped mouth.

The door swung open and Horton, shoulders square and drawn up to his full height, which was almost a foot shorter than Connor, glowered at Connor.

"Is there a problem, Miss Charlotte?" Horton inquired.

"No, none," Charlotte said, tapping Connor on the shoulder.

"No, no problem at all," Connor said, gently lowering Charlotte to her feet.

When Charlotte looked up at him, he saw the pink blush in her cheeks and dark confusion in her blue eyes. The thought that the kiss had disconcerted her, too, pleased him.

She looked away immediately and stepped toward the house. The frowning butler moved aside but remained at the door.

"When will I see you again?" Connor asked, reluctant to say good-bye without a commitment from her.

When Charlotte turned back to him, she seemed in full possession of herself. "Our next meeting is my choice, is it not?"

"It is," he confirmed.

"I was hoping you'd meet the literary group, but I am uncertain as to the date of the next meeting."

"Then I shall eagerly await your invitation," Connor promised, offering her a casual bow. He had absolutely no interest in her literary group, but he'd made an agreement with her and he wasn't backing out now. Not after glimpsing a delightful side of her he'd never guessed might exist. Not after tasting the passion those delightful lips promised.

TWELVE

Charlotte sat at her dressing table in a trance, hardly aware of the tug of the hairbrush her maid was wielding. In her lap her hands were cold and numb as if she'd just experienced a life-threatening ordeal. Dinner was over, but her head still swam with hot, sensual memories of Connor's lips touching hers, a featherlight touch, yet warm and full of smiles, full of approval. A kiss smelling of pine and musk.

Charlotte licked the tingle from her lips and wondered if Connor had been as affected by their intimate contact as she was. Probably not. He had such confidence in himself, such blustering, good-natured arrogance. He probably bestowed kisses like that all the time and the Scots ladies undoubtedly begged for more.

Charlotte huffed. Candle flames flickered and her reflection in the mirror wavered. Annoyed, she willed herself to forget all about Connor McKensie and his silly flirtation.

"I'm sorry, Miss Charlotte," Betsy said, distress in her voice and concern written across her face. "Did I pull too hard? I didn't mean to hurt you."

"Oh, no, Betsy, you didn't pull," Charlotte hastened to reassure her maid. "You're doing a fine job."

Betsy resumed brushing Charlotte's hair.

Unwilling to stare at the familiar face in the mirror any longer, Charlotte gazed unseeing at the silvery powder pots and crystal perfume bottles on her dressing table. All through dinner she had barely been able to take part in the family conversation. She murmured polite replies to Mama's questions about her afternoon with Connor and fibbed to Papa about a drive in the park. She was fairly certain that neither Mama nor Papa suspected that she'd gone to a fair and allowed a man to kiss her—in public. But fooling Cassie was another matter. Thankfully, Dudley had called, distracting her sister for a while at least.

She stared at herself in the mirror once more, the insistent warmth of Connor's kiss rising to her lips again. Fingertips to her mouth, she reminded herself that she was at home, safe at her dressing table, and not in the Scotsman's arms. There was nothing to be afraid of, not that she was afraid. But his touch, his attention, made her feel things that were strange and new. Things—doubts and uncertainties—that she shouldn't be feeling.

And he made her want to laugh, too. Charlotte shook her head at the image in the mirror. None of it made sense. None of it fit together.

But she did know that she should never have allowed him to take such liberties with her person. Of course, he'd only meant it in a lighthearted jest. She was certain of that. But she should never have allowed him to think that he could deal with her so frivolously. What kind of man toyed with a girl like that?

Her dreamy look faded into a frown. If Edward learned of this kiss stolen on the doorstep where any neighbor could see, what would he say? Charlotte's heart beat a little faster.

It was merely a jest she rehearsed silently, watching her own reflection in the mercurial depths of the looking glass. Yet instead of herself, she saw Edward's long, esthetic face in the mirror.

Jest, my dear? What woman allows a man, a near stranger, to kiss her in jest? She could see Edward's witheringly tolerant smile cast upon her as if he could expect nothing more from such a weak, mindless creature.

Charlotte's frown deepened. But the kiss had been only a frolic. The Scotsman had kissed her in fun. He found her a pleasant enough companion to tease, with whom to exchange a bit of light familiarity. Need that be considered a move to seduction? How ridiculous. A kiss stolen in the dark seclusion of the coach would be more suspect. But a kiss taken in daylight could have no significance. Need every bit of gaiety that passed between a man and a woman be considered of deep significance? Charlotte shook her head "no" at the reflection in the mirror.

"Is something amiss, Miss Charlotte?" Betsy asked, the hairbrush poised in midair. "I've only done forty-four strokes."

"No, really, I'm all right," Charlotte said, surprised at finding herself so faraway. Botheration, the Scotsman always seemed to leave her in a muddle. "Pray continue, Betsy."

The door latch clicked and Cassandra breezed into the room, a rose-colored dressing gown wrapped tightly around her.

"Here I am to do your hair, Charlotte." Hair brushing was a part of the twins' daily toilet that they frequently shared.

"Don't trouble yourself, Cassie," Charlotte said, eager to avoid Cassie's inquisition. "Betsy is almost finished."

"No, I'm not," Betsy said. "I've only done forty-seven strokes."

"Then let me finish," Cassie said, reaching for the hairbrush. "You may go, Betsy, thank you."

As Betsy bobbed a curtsy and hastened from the room, Charlotte silently chided herself for daring to hope that Cassie would not press her with more questions.

"Now, I expect the whole truth from you," Cassandra said, drawing the brush slowly through Charlotte's hair and locking gazes with her in the mirror. "Every detail of your outing with Lord Kinleith."

Charlotte briefly considered saying that she'd already revealed everything about her adventure with Connor at the dinner table. As she appraised her sister's reflection, she saw Cassie's eyes narrow ever so slightly and she knew that fibbing was useless.

"None of that shilly-shally stuff you recited for Papa and

Mama at the table tonight," Cassandra warned, shaking the brush at Charlotte's reflection. "We've shared everything, even our first kisses with Dudley and Edward. Why are you keeping things from me now?"

Charlotte bit her tongue. It was true they'd shared everything, yet this time she was reluctant to tell the details of her first intimacy with Connor. For the first time in her life, Charlotte had experienced something that seemed too precious to tell her sister—just yet.

"I want the truth, mind you." Cassandra began to brush Charlotte's hair. "You and Lord Kinleith didn't go for just another drive in the park. I know, for I have it on good account that you only passed through once and were gone. So just where did you go?"

"Promise you will not speak a word of it to Papa," Charlotte begged, still holding Cassie's gaze in the mirror.

"You know I won't," Cassandra said, tugging gently on Charlotte's hair. "If I did, which of my secrets would you tell?"

"Which one would you least like Papa to know?" Charlotte asked with a laugh.

"Where did you go after the park?" Cassandra said, wielding a practiced brushstroke on Charlotte's long, fiery tresses.

"We went to the Battersea Field Fair, and Cassie, it was so much fun." Before Charlotte could stop herself, everything spilled out—all about the freak shows, the rope dancers, and the waxworks.

When she finally glanced at her sister in the mirror again, Charlotte saw that Cassie had stopped brushing and a smile played across her lips.

"Did you see the seven-legged cow?" Cassie asked.

"No, but there was a fine-looking horse who could count out his age," Charlotte said. "You've gone to a fair with Dudley, haven't you?"

"Not the Battersea Field Fair," Cassie said, "but yes, he did take me to a fair. Remember, I told you. It was last fall, and the place was crowded with shepherds and wagoners all looking for employment."

"Yes, I remember now. Were there children selling wares at the fair?"

"There are always children selling things," Cassandra said, as if Charlotte had just asked the most ridiculous of questions. "Why?"

"I guess I never knew that," Charlotte said, staring at herself thoughtfully in the mirror. Cassie continued brushing. "At least I never thought about it."

"What are you getting at, Charlotte?" Cassandra asked, brushing with more force.

"Ouch," Charlotte protested. "Be careful. All those little faces and big eyes. Who are they? Where do they come from and where do they go? Who feeds them and dresses them and loves them?"

"They're everywhere," Cassandra said, stroking the brush through Charlotte's hair more vigorously now. "There are churches, missions, and orphanages to care for them. Papa gives to such institutions regularly and so does Aunt Dorian. That's as it should be, of course."

"Yes, it is," Charlotte said, relieved to know that Papa was doing something for the hungry mouths of London's streets. Even Connor had done his part. He'd instantly given up his pie without protest when Charlotte had snatched it from him. She realized suddenly that Connor hadn't appeared hungry at all. It had been his idea to buy the wares in the first place. He'd stopped because he wanted to help the girl. Who would have thought a fighter would take the food out of his mouth to feed a mere child? The thought made Charlotte like Connor even more, even though he had teased and toyed with her. Charlotte shifted impatiently on the stool. She wasn't sure she wanted to like the Brawlin' Scot.

"Sit still, Charlotte," Cassandra warned. "Did you see anyone we know?"

"No, well, yes, we did," Charlotte said, remembering that

Connor seemed to know the man, Grady. She explained the curious incident with the boxing salon towel boy, the stolen money, and the pickpocket.

"A prizefight," Cassie exclaimed. "How exciting. Who were the fighters?"

"The Welsh boy was called the Dirty Miner and he was fighting against an older man they called the Trooper," Charlotte explained. "The Trooper won."

"Was it a good fight?" Cassie asked.

"I don't know. I didn't watch."

"I hope Lord Kinleith is learning more about being a gentleman than you are learning about boxing," Cassie said. "La, Charlotte, when did you turn into a pacifist?"

"I don't think I'm a pacifist." Charlotte frowned at the idea of being cast as a creature as strange as a Quaker. Yet, she could not deny her feelings. "I understand that fighting is something a man does to defend himself or his family or his country as a soldier. And there is honor in that. But I can never understand fighting just for the fun of it. And Connor does like to fight, Cassandra. Have you seen him in the ring? He loves the adulation of the crowd."

"Perhaps, but it's not like he's a hothead or a sour bloke looking for any reason to knock someone about," Cassandra pointed out. "He fights in the ring by the proper rules."

Charlotte made a face at herself and Cassandra in the mirror. "I still do not like to hear the crack of knuckles against bone. But Lord Kinleith loves it. I do not think either you or I will ever change him."

"Probably not," Cassandra began, letting her hands drop to her sides, "perhaps it's for the best if you give up on this escapade, Charlotte."

The phrase "give up" struck a spark of misgiving inside Charlotte. "I'm not prepared to give up now."

She stared into the depths of the mirror. Who was the red-haired girl she saw there with wide blue eyes slanted so slightly and a bow-shaped mouth? Who was this young woman who suddenly discovered the street children—and the fact that not everyone had grown up with the same privileges that she'd been granted? Who was this daughter of a merchant who could not bring herself to watch one man strike another for the entertainment of the crowd?

Cassie reached into the pocket of her dressing gown. "I have something here that I think you've been looking for."

"And what might that be?" Charlotte yawned to display her indifference. Cassandra was always baiting her with something.

"Well, let's see." Cassandra put the brush down on the dressing table and pulled a letter from her pocket. "To Miss Charlotte St. John. The handwriting seems to be slightly reminiscent of—

"Edward." Charlotte whirled around and snatched the letter from her sister's hand. "What does he say?"

"How would I know?" Cassandra said. "Hurry, open it."

Charlotte ripped open the missive and scanned the lines of Edward's familiar script. A sigh of relief escaped her. The formal invitation invited her to Edward's monthly literary gathering. The words were not as casual and warm as he might have written her a fortnight ago, but at least he was not snubbing her. Charlotte released another long, low sigh.

"So, you are still in his good graces," Cassandra prompted.

"It would seem so," Charlotte said as she reread the last of the invitation. "Actually, it's even better than that. He has invited Lord Kinleith to attend also 'as guest of the Countess of Seacombe.' "

"How generous of him," Cassandra said without making the least effort to cover the sarcasm in her voice. "Better play it safe. Bid Lord Kinleith farewell and hasten back into Edward's arms. Metaphorically speaking, of course."

"Edward's arms?" Charlotte stared at herself in the mirror; Connor's kiss tingled on her lips once more. Had Edward ever held her with so much power and confidence? His embrace had never been like Connor's—never so warm and strong. Even if Connor had held her only in jest, nothing in Edward's touch had ever left her breathless, lighthearted, or content to be in that particular place at that particular moment.

"You're not thinking of asking the Scotsman to the literary group?" Cassandra asked, stroking the brush through Charlotte's fiery tresses. "Lord Kinleith will be no more thrilled with a literary afternoon than you were watching the prizefight at the fair."

"But he will accept the invitation," Charlotte said. "He has to. He made a bargain with me and I with him. This is perfect. Just perfect. When he is introduced to other possibilities, I'm certain his interest in fighting will wane."

"But I thought you said you didn't think he would change," Cassandra said.

"But I haven't really tried yet to make a change, have I?" Charlotte protested, feeling surprisingly more confident now that she knew that Edward was not going to snub her. Her idealistic poet was miffed, of course, but he would recover once he understood what she and Cassie were doing. "I've only just begun. With persistence and the higher example of others, Connor will reconsider this obsession with fighting."

Charlotte smiled serenely at the girls in the mirror. Her reflection smiled back at her, clear and unwavering. How could she ever have questioned who she was?

THIRTEEN

Connor surveyed Seymour's book-lined library, taking in the cold luncheon laid out on a sideboard, the cribbage board set up on a desk, and the chairs arranged in the garden beyond the opened French doors. A vase of fresh flowers decorated the mantel above the cold hearth. The day was too fine for a fire, but the room was inviting nonetheless. Hardly the sort of setting he'd expected of a literary group meeting.

"You thought it would be cold and stuffy, didn't you?" Charlotte said, smiling up at him, radiant in a green-sprigged muslin gown with puff sleeves, a green sash snug at her waist, and black silk pumps on her feet. Connor had never been one to take much note of fashion, but Charlotte in anything less than the most stylish design and feminine frippery would have looked wrong. To Connor she appeared very right and proper today.

Connor nodded reluctantly, annoyed that she'd read his thoughts so exactly. The place hardly appeared as formal as he expected and it certainly did not resemble the sparring ring he suspected it would become.

No man liked another sniffing around his lady. Seymour and Charlotte's relationship might not be considered a formal engagement, but Connor had recognized that possessive gleam in Seymour's eye when they'd been introduced. Officially promised or not, the poet considered Miss Charlotte St. John his own. However, if Seymour had not the courage—or integrity—to declare his intentions, then Connor considered the field clear.

"As you can see, Edward goes to great lengths to make his friends comfortable," Charlotte was saying over her shoulder as she led the way into the middle of the room. "He makes certain that the atmosphere is conducive to enlightening conversation and lively debate."

"How gracious of him," Connor muttered, his irritation with the situation deepening as he noted Charlotte's determination to present Seymour in the best light. He turned away from her, grinding his teeth over the worshipful shine in her eyes as she spoke of the poet. Yet, his own annoyance mystified him. Other than the fact that Connor needed Charlotte to remain on the marriage block for his own purpose—in the unlikely event he couldn't win the prizefight money to buy Glen Gray—it escaped him why he should care that she sought the attentions of a poet dandy. Except that he had taken an instant dislike to Seymour the moment they'd been introduced.

"Yes, Edward is considerate like that," Charlotte said. Before she could say more, Seymour appeared at the garden door in his shirtsleeves. His cravat had been loosened, his waistcoat unbuttoned, and his long poet's hair brushed away from his face.

"Here you are at last, Charlotte, my dear." He stepped into the room, reaching for her hand.

"Edward." Soft delight echoed in Charlotte's voice. Connor ground his teeth once again, but remained silent.

With a flourish, the poet bent low and kissed Charlotte's hand. A pretty blush stained her cheeks, revealing to Connor just how unusual Seymour's behavior was. If the man normally greeted Charlotte so, there'd be no pink flooding into her cheeks. She glanced uneasily in Connor's direction. "As you can see, Edward, I brought Lord Kinleith with me. He was pleased to be included in your invitation."

Seymour turned on Connor, offering a stiff bow no deeper than was polite, and his blue eyes once more turned cold. "How kind of you to come, my lord."

"Sir Edward." Connor responded with a curt nod of his head, hardly as courteous as Seymour's greeting.

"I hope you will enjoy our little intellectual *soirée*," Seymour went on. "I'd heard that you were going about London taking in the culture—theater, exhibitions, and such—so I thought to invite you here."

"Thoughtful of you," Connor grumbled as civilly as he could manage.

Seymour ignored Connor's reply and turned to Charlotte, placing her hand on his arm as he led her toward the garden. "Come outside, my dear, and listen to the discussion we were just having about this new dictionary published by an American fellow called Noah Webster. Can you believe it? He calls it *The American Dictionary of the English Language.*"

"Is not the King's English satisfactory?" Charlotte asked as though quite taken with the news of the American reference book.

"One does wonder," Seymour said with a sly smile that Connor suspected had more to do with the scooped neckline of Charlotte's dress than a dictionary.

In the coolness of the garden, young men as casually dressed as Seymour sat or stood in clusters, engaged in spirited conversation. The company included several ladies of varying ages and of much less inspiring appearance than Charlotte. Everyone seemed well-acquainted and relaxed in each other's presence. Despite the sometimes serious tones of the discussion, laughter rang out often. Connor soon found himself with a glass of port in his hand and Charlotte at his side, but he had little to offer to the discourse.

His concerns for years had been centered on lands, sheep, cattle, and fishing. More recently he'd turned his attention to the railroads, his financial instincts instantly understanding the benefit the new mode of transportation could offer the Highlands. But he enjoyed watching Charlotte debate rather ably the metaphors and images of a poem by a fellow named Shelley.

Color flooded into her cheeks once more, the lively hue of

interest and excitement. One of the ladies had expressed some confusion about the meaning of a stanza. At the moment Charlotte was in her element, weighing the craft of words and the art of symbols.

Connor watched in fascination—and disappointment, wondering at his own reaction. She had always professed to be studious and bookish. Why was he surprised to find that she had not changed after a few outings with him? Connor smiled ruefully at his own foolishness. Studious she was, and impossibly soft-hearted. By the end of an outing she was nearly always smiling and laughing and had managed to empty his pocket and her own with handouts to vendors, beggars, and urchins. Of course she had enjoyed the novelty of the Battersea Field Fair and their clandestine visit to Vauxhall, which was no longer the shining place that he'd remembered. But enjoying a carefree outing did not necessarily convert a shy scholar into a belle of the ball.

"How about a game of cribbage?"

The words spoken low and close to Connor's ear brought him around to find Seymour at his side. The poet's smile resembled an indulgent sneer. "You Scots do play cribbage, don't you? Or is throwing punches the only kind of competition you enjoy?"

"Aye, of course I play cribbage," Connor said, annoyed with Seymour's assumption that as a Scot he suffered from some sort of deficiency. "My only limitation is that I always like to win at whatever I do."

"Is it time for cribbage already?" Charlotte said, having overheard the invitation. "Edward is a dedicated cribbage player. He won't be satisfied until he defeats each new guest."

"So it's my turn, is it then?" Connor said, eyeing the poet's smirk. "Let's have at it."

"I'll be in to observe your game later," Charlotte said, clearly reluctant to leave the garden.

Inside the library the two men sat down across the desk from each other. Connor leaned back in his chair and stretched out his long legs. Seymour set the cribbage board, complete with pegs, between them, shuffled the cards, and put them out for Connor to cut. Then the poet took his turn.

"Low card, I deal," Seymour said, showing Connor the deuce he'd drawn against Connor's jack.

Connor waited in silence for Seymour to deal out the hand.

"As an athlete and a sportsman, you know there are all kinds of arenas of competition." Seymour picked up his cards and peered at them a little too seriously for this to be a friendly game of cribbage, Connor thought. Seymour went on, his gaze still on his cards. "Differences do not need to be settled with fists or a duel."

"Aye, that's so," Connor said, studying his own hand. He counted the values and the suits and concluded it wasn't a strong hand with which to win whatever it was he was going to have to win. As he stared at the queen of hearts and wondered what Seymour was up to, a flash of insight nearly blinded him. His instincts were working. He knew exactly what Seymour was doing. If he'd thought any less of Charlotte, he would have thrown down his cards and walked out of the poet's house.

"She is lovely, is she not?" Edward said.

"Who?" Connor said as if he had nary a clue to whom Seymour referred. No reason to make this easy for the scoundrel.

"You know who—Charlotte," Seymour said. "Your lead."

Connor decided on the best card and was about to lay it on the table when Seymour spoke up once more. "Wait. Don't play yet. I haven't finished."

Connor replaced the card in his hand. "Finished what?"

"First, perhaps we should determine what the wager is."

Connor's eyes narrowed as he regarded Seymour across the table. "Just what do you suggest?"

"Charlotte St. John's future."

"Is it yours to offer?" Connor asked, thinking it was a good thing Davis St. John wasn't privy to this discussion, or Charlotte's Aunt Dorian, either.

Unheralded, Charlotte swept into the room from the garden.

"I thought I should see how your game is going. So who's winning?"

The warmth of the summer afternoon had put color in her cheeks. The scent of roses clung to her. Wrapped all in green and white with her fiery hair piled high on her head, she was a picture of vibrant loveliness. Connor wondered if she'd perceived somehow that she was the topic of conversation.

"Neither of us is winning at the moment, my dear," Seymour said, rising from his chair. "We're just beginning."

"No, no." Charlotte gestured for them to remain seated. Sweetly apologetic, she smiled at Seymour and added uncertainly, "I didn't mean to interrupt."

"But such a delightful intrusion," Seymour said, reaching for her hand and squeezing it—for his benefit, Connor suspected. Charlotte's uncertain smile broadened.

"You need not trouble yourself over us." Connor studied his cards and spoke as evenly as he could, yet he was unable to keep the grimness from his voice. He hoped that Charlotte had not guessed the reason for their seclusion. "The game may take some time."

"There, you see, my dear?" Seymour quipped, smiling reassuringly up at Charlotte. "I expect the Scotsman here to be a worthy opponent."

"Yes, indeed," Charlotte agreed. "Then I shall review some poetry with Elizabeth. You will read some of yours for us later, won't you, Edward?"

Seymour brandished a knowing smile at Connor. "Yes, my dear. I'll read for everyone later."

As soon as Charlotte had left the room, Seymour turned to Connor. "So you see, it would seem the lady's future is mine, if I so choose."

Connor stared at the arrogant dandy, this time without grinding his teeth. His concentration had become too focused to be spent on useless efforts. "So you would play a game for her then?"

"That is what I'm offering." Seymour leaned across the table and fixed his icy blue gaze on Connor. "You may be a man of action, Kinleith, but I'm a civilized man. No need for pistols or sabers. Nor a referee in the ring. The loser of the game will leave the field and give the winner free rein to win the lady's affections and, eventually, her hand in marriage if he so chooses. Agreed?"

"And Charlotte, what about her feelings?" Connor asked.

"She need never know," Seymour said. "I wouldn't tell her. Would you?"

"Of course not," Connor replied without hesitation. He might or might not want Charlotte's hand in marriage, but he'd be damned before he'd allow this unfeeling rogue to cavalierly drag soft-hearted Charlotte to the altar. "So how many games do I need to win to make Charlotte mine, Seymour?"

"Two out of three," Seymour said without pausing. "Your play."

"Two out of three it will be, then," Connor said and led the first card.

FOURTEEN

The afternoon faded into a cool twilight, bringing the guests into the library from the garden. With a glass of sherry in hand, Charlotte stood near the sideboard where the cold food was now picked over. With growing concern, she watched the card game between Connor and Edward.

The intensity of the cribbage match had radiated into the room, and like a magnet had drawn all the young men to the table. The footmen moved unobtrusively among the guests to light the candles and clear up the used dishes. The group had grown quiet after Edward had rudely shushed one young man when he laughed out loud.

Connor had lost the first game. Edward had been all smiles and laughter. Connor's scowl had been so fierce it had kept Charlotte at bay. Then Edward had lost the second round and the foolish young man had laughed. Edward's temper had flared and he'd cast a murderous stare at the youth.

"Silence!" he had snapped. Quiet fell over the room. Now the outcome of this last game would determine the victor.

"Have you ever seen the like at one of Edward's gatherings?" Elizabeth whispered, selecting a piece of cheese from a plate on the sideboard. Hers was the only voice in the room.

"No, and I don't understand why men must take this sort of thing so seriously." Charlotte sipped her sherry. "It's only a card game."

Suddenly Connor threw down a card and announced his victory in a voice that echoed throughout the house. "The deuce of hearts. Look at that and weep, my poetic friend. Thirty-one. I win."

Murmurs of congratulations filled the room. But Edward's face paled and he glanced resentfully through the forest of spectators across the room at Charlotte. She read humiliation in his eyes. His glare brought a barb of apprehension to the back of her neck. Somehow she felt responsible for his defeat. Her first instinct to comfort him died as the coldness of his glower forbade her to offer him consolation.

Connor rose from the table, smiling like a cat—a huge, magnificent golden-eyed lion—that had just snagged a tasty morsel and was mightily pleased with himself. He was soon at Charlotte's side.

"When does this thing end?" he said, gesturing to the footman that he wanted another glass of port.

"You mean the literary group?"

"Yes, if that's what you call it," Connor said.

"Edward hasn't done his reading for us yet," Charlotte said, silently debating if she should go speak to Edward. Others had gathered around the poet to soothe him. Since Connor was her escort, perhaps she should stay away for now and send Edward a note later. "And we must all of us recite something. I told you about that. You did memorize the poem I gave you, did you not?"

Connor picked idly at the food on the sideboard. "No, I did not memorize the poem."

Charlotte blinked at him. "And what are you going to say when it is time for each of us to recite?"

"Never mind that. I know where we're going on our next outing."

"Where?" Charlotte asked, without the least bit of interest. She glanced back in Edward's direction, but he refused to meet her gaze again. What on earth, she wondered, had Connor done to make Edward behave so coldly to her?

"There's a place in Bloomsbury I think you'll find most fascinating."

"Bloomsbury," Charlotte repeated before she became aware of the significance of the locale. She dragged her gaze away from Edward and stared at Connor. He seemed to have forgotten all about the card game. "But Bloomsbury—I mean what could possibly be there?"

"I think a drive with a short visit to Bloomsbury should be a most illuminating venture after the interest you showed in the children at the fair," Connor added as if he'd settled on the decision.

"It has become warm in here," Charlotte said, waving her hand before her face as if it were a fan. She had no idea what Connor was talking about. And she could no longer stand the accusation she saw in Edward's eyes. All she wanted to do was escape him and the company who crowded around him to succor him in his defeat. "Would you be so kind as to accompany me into the garden, my lord?"

Connor sent her a quick, quizzical look. "Lead the way." With a mischievous smile, he followed her out into the twilight.

As soon as they were out of sight of the open doors and beyond earshot of the others, Charlotte turned on Connor. "What did you do to Edward?"

"What do you mean, what did I do to Edward?" Connor's dark brows shot up in apparent surprise. "He challenged me to a game of cribbage. You were there. I beat him at his own game. May I say, my lady, your poet is not a gentlemanly loser."

"And you *are* a gentlemanly victor?" Charlotte asked in terse, clipped syllables. "There you stand, near gloating. And Edward, humiliated before his guests."

Connor's good-natured surprise faded. "He challenged *me*, lady, not the other way round. I have spent all afternoon in this gentleman's house. I've done my best to be a good guest. And I fought hard for my victory at cribbage. As a matter of fact, I believe I deserve a kiss for my efforts."

A kiss? Charlotte could hardly believe her ears. The outrageous statement banished Edward's pouting from her thoughts. "You deserve what?"

"A kiss." The anger cleared from Connor's face and he was suddenly as open, appealing, and innocent as a choirboy. The man was maddening. "It seems to me that the feat of suffering through an entire afternoon of intellectual discussion is as worthy of a kiss as rescuing a damsel from a mud puddle."

"Suffering—as you call it—was part of our bargain," Charlotte reminded him.

"Then how about a kiss for the victor?"

"Connor—" Charlotte began in pure exasperation, but when she looked up at him and glimpsed the crafty gleam in his eye, she knew he was mocking her. She also knew nothing would solve their current impasse but a kiss. "Will you never grow up?"

" 'Tis only a wee kiss that I ask for," he said, obviously aware that she was weakening. He took her hand and led her into the garden shadows. "Just one small kiss, then we leave."

Charlotte blinked at him. "Very well, a small kiss."

She took a deep breath to fortify herself for the unaccustomed assault on her senses that contact with him always wreaked. Then she closed her eyes and held her face up to his. Thank heavens this kiss was in the dark privacy of the garden and not on the doorstep of her family's townhouse.

After a moment, when nothing happened, Charlotte opened her eyes and gazed curiously up into Connor's eyes. He leaned over her, so close that his breath tingled across her lips, but his eyes were hidden in the shadows.

"Are you sure you're prepared for this?" he asked. Charlotte could have sworn she heard the warmth of amusement in his deep voice. Exasperated with him though she was, the bass treble of the words settled over her, reassuring and familiar as a favorite blanket.

She closed her eyes again and nodded. "Yes, I'm ready. Go ahead."

Nothing happened for a moment longer; then Connor placed

his big hands on her shoulders. Immediately the warmth of his palms spread through her. His fingers gripped her gently as he drew her closer until she could feel the heat of his body radiating against her own. Fearful of a strange, new awareness of him, Charlotte quickly spread her hands across his chest, preventing her body from pressing too intimately against his.

He made a sound—a deep rumble of annoyance, Charlotte thought—but still he pressed her closer until she could smell his warmth as well as bask in it. With a finger he tipped her chin up a bit more and brushed his lips across hers.

The touch was tantalizingly light and gentle. It was more as if he was sampling her scent than tasting her. More teasing than kissing, which was exactly what he seemed to like to do to her. Tease. Tempt. Torture. A whimper escaped her when his lips did not find hers.

"Patience, kitten," he whispered against her mouth. Then his lips brushed across hers again. This time she stretched up on her toes to capture his mouth, allowing herself to taste him and savor the tender strength that their first contact on the townhouse doorstep had promised. He chuckled, the arrogant male rumble vibrating through his chest.

Then he kissed her in return, his lips demanding. Charlotte wantonly gave herself up to his demands. Warmth flooded through her. She leaned against him, thankful that her weak knees had no need to support her. Suddenly, he released her mouth. Charlotte would have collapsed if not for his hands on her shoulders.

Surprised and dazed, she opened her eyes to peer up at him once more. As before, she could read nothing in his eyes, which were still hidden in the darkness. Without a word, he firmly grasped her wrists and pulled her hands behind her back so that her body pressed against the full length of his.

Charlotte gasped. Thankful for the cover of shadows, she closed her eyes against the perverse feelings of pleasure that surged through her. She leaned against Connor, terrified that someone—that Edward—would walk out of the library and see them, yet she was too weak to break away from Connor's embrace. She relished the hard warmth of his muscled thighs pressed against hers and his flat belly solid against her midriff. And her breasts, swollen and sensitive in a way she'd never experienced, ached against his hard chest.

When he bent to kiss her again, she lifted her face to his without prompting. This time his mouth captured hers and his tongue sought entrance without delay. Charlotte mewled; she was confused, overwhelmed, and helpless, yet desperate to please for reasons she did not understand—and did not want to examine.

She opened to him, matching each of his forays, eagerly exploring him as he explored her. When at last they pulled apart, she gasped for breath. Connor trailed kisses along her cheek and down her throat, setting fire to her wherever his lips touched. In that moment Charlotte realized that he no longer held her wrists, but had spread his hands shamelessly across her bottom.

Appalled, she pulled away from him. "What are you doing?"

Still hidden in the shadows, Connor chuckled his self-satisfied chuckle once again. "I am accepting my kiss as victor of the cribbage game."

"You know what I mean," Charlotte snapped, stepping away from him and attempting to recover whatever decorum she might still have. To her horror she was breathless and her lips tender from the pressure of Connor's mouth. "That was more than a simple kiss."

"Aye, but I've no objection to it," Connor said. "Have you?"

"My lord, you are hardly a gentleman," Charlotte said, her exasperation returning.

"No, and you're probably not going to make one of me today," Connor agreed. "So can we be saying our farewells soon?"

"Leave?" Charlotte stepped farther from him and tucked a tendril of hair behind her ear, then smoothed the wrinkles from the front of her dress. What on earth were the others going to think when they saw the crushed state of her gown? "Edward has not done his reading for us yet and we each must recite our part."

"Must we stay for the whole bloody reading?"

"Of course." Charlotte took a deep breath of the evening air in an effort to soothe her jumbled emotions and the strange unrest that had come over her. She had been weak to allow Connor to distract her from her purpose. The literary group was hardly over. "We always conclude with the readings. Discussions first, then the readings. If you think you're going to be excused from any part of it, you're quite mistaken."

Connor regarded her for a long, thoughtful moment. Charlotte waited, not the least embarrassed about her demands. She would expect no less from him than he expected of her.

Finally he said, "Fair is fair. You stayed for the prizefight at the fair. I'll stay for the readings."

"Very well," Charlotte conceded. "Let's return to the library, shall we?"

Turning on her heel, she headed for the house and prayed that he would follow her without causing any more embarrassment.

"Wait," Connor called, almost treading on her heels in a few quick strides.

Charlotte turned just in time to see him reach for her bottom. She swatted his hand away. "Sirrah, what do you think you're doing?"

Connor straightened with a smirk, albeit a contrite one, lurking on his face. "I'm just trying to pull the telltale crimp from your sash."

Charlotte strained to look over her shoulder at her sash, but failed to spot the damage.

"You may certainly leave it all mussed like that if you wish," Connor said, a grin winning out. "But the way it's wrinkled might suggest something of our activities out here to those in the library."

"Well, straighten it then." Mortified and piqued, Charlotte frowned at him. "You really are a cad, you know."

Connor's grin broadened as he reached to tug on the offending green taffeta. "I know I am. And I enjoy every scandalous moment of it."

"Yoo-whoo out there? Sir Edward's reading is about to begin."

Charlotte looked back toward the garden doorway to see Elizabeth silhouetted against the library candlelight. "We're coming right in."

The brush of Connor's lips against the back of her neck sent Charlotte into a fit of shivers.

"Did Edward ever kiss you there?" He kissed her ear. "Or here?"

"My lord, any kisses that Edward and I may have shared are none of your concern." Charlotte closed her eyes against a renewed wave of tingling weakness. Her knees turned to jelly again. What on earth was the matter with her? She'd never felt like this before. "And any intimacy Edward and I have shared has nothing to do with this victory kiss nonsense you've perpetrated on me."

"Umm," was all he said, as he took her hand, stroking the palm with his thumb. When he stepped around in front of Charlotte, she could see his face. He was smiling faintly. "I'm beginning to wonder who's perpetrating what on whom. But I shall hold to my end of the bargain. Let's go hear Sir Edward's poetry.

FIFTEEN

The garden chairs had been moved into the library and arranged so that the poet could pose leaning against the fireplace mantel. The idea was to look wistful and artful, Connor supposed.

Most of the chairs were filled, especially those near the door to the hallway. Connor silently cursed their bad luck. He led Charlotte to the chairs that Elizabeth had so thoughtfully saved for them.

After that kiss in the garden and that damnable cribbage game, he was eager to part the poet's company. Yet as Charlotte had reminded him, he'd agreed to this. Still, his patience was tried.

His body ached with the remembrance of their kisses stolen in the garden. Charlotte had surprised him with her willing response to his demand for a victory reward. Beneath his lips, the passion she'd unknowingly promised during their first kiss had revealed itself again. It had been with the greatest reluctance that Connor had returned to the house with her. At the moment he yearned to be anywhere in the world with her other than in Seymour's library feigning interest in uninspired poetry.

The recital began with readings by several of the younger and newer members of the group, fresh-faced, aspiring poets. The works pretty much sounded the same to Connor. He knew he was no judge of such things, but Charlotte found the performance top drawer. At least she seemed to. She continuously caught at his sleeve and murmured something about a great image or a unique symbolism. Her soft voice was full of enthusiasm and her applause ardently delivered.

Connor suppressed a sigh of relief when Sir Edward took center floor. The poet and host of the occasion seemed to have recovered from his defeat, Connor thought. Seymour had shrugged into a frock coat, straightened his cravat, and brushed his hair. But his face remained pale and a shadow of his beard on his long, narrow jaw gave him a starved, spiritually urbane look. Connor glanced at Charlotte to see a frown pucker her smooth brow. No doubt she was taking pity on the arrogant bastard.

"Tonight I have chosen to recite some of my best work," Edward began, then paused.

A murmur of pleasure and anticipation ran through the crowd.

He smiled, clearly satisfied to be the center of attention, and unfolded the manuscript from which he was going to read. When the poet began, his voice was deep and varied, as practiced and smooth as a Drury Lane actor's. The poem contained fancy words about Greek gods and dedication to truth and beauty—all lofty notions that never paid a tenant's rent or a landlord's taxes.

Charlotte clutched Connor's arm. "Isn't it divine?"

Connor glanced at her in time to see the color rise in her cheeks. She released him and began twisting her handkerchief in her lap. Her gaze was fixed on the poet in a rapt, worshipful trance. Anger rose in Connor. If only she knew what the bloody idealist had tried to do. Gambling with her future. Connor longed to tell her the truth about the man. Seymour was a foppish hypocrite. But would she believe him? She needed to see Seymour's flaws for herself.

"Does he ever write anything a little more practical about everyday life?" Connor murmured in Charlotte's ear.

She shushed him, none too kindly. "I must hear this."

Connor sat back in his chair, folded his arms across his chest, and bit his tongue.

When the poet finished, cheers and applause resounded through the library. Connor saw no reason for such adulation. You'd have thought the man had distinguished himself in some fierce battle. But what did he know about poetry? Personally, he liked Bobby Burns's wise words about "the best laid plans of mice and men" as well as any.

At the front of the room Sir Edward bowed, accepting the adoration of the crowd as if he were the king's own poet laureate, which he was not. Charlotte sprang from her chair and rushed up to Seymour to deliver her praise confidentially. Connor forced himself to refrain from grabbing her by the wrist and dragging her from the library and the house.

But Connor remained in his chair, watching as Seymour drew away, out of Charlotte's reach as she tried to deliver words of praise. The poet turned aside, avoiding her beseeching gaze. Connor shifted restlessly in his chair. Seymour's coldness seemed to baffle Charlotte. The vulnerable confusion that clouded her face launched a wave of guilt within Connor. She leaned toward Seymour, seeming to plead with him. Finally Seymour nodded a slow, reluctant acknowledgment. Before Connor could get to his feet, Seymour turned to the audience.

"Thank you all for your kind words. Now Miss St. John wishes to recite for us."

Connor settled back into his chair as the rest of the audience did the same. A scattering of polite applause rattled through the room. Then the audience fell silent as Charlotte stood before them.

"I shall recite from the works of Shakespeare," she began. "In honor of our illustrious poet, Sir Edward Seymour. I'm sure that we all feel the great respect for his art that the great bard expresses here."

More applause, then the audience fell expectantly silent once more. Charlotte took a deep breath and began to speak, her voice strong and her phrasing lyrical.

Lord of my love, to whom in vassalage
Thy merit hath my duty strongly knit,
To thee I send this written message,
To witness duty, not to show my wit.
Duty so great, which wit so poor as mine
May make seem bare, in wanting words to show it;
But that I hope some good conceit of thine
In thy soul's thought, all naked, will bestow it:
Till whatsoever star that guides by moving,
Points on me graciously with fair aspect,
And puts apparel on my tatter'd loving,
To show me worthy of thy sweet respect:
Then may I dare to boast how I do love thee,
Till then, not show my head where thou mayst prove me.

The audience roared its approval. Seymour frowned. Connor sat unmoved, his anger flaring hotter by the minute, but his head told him a man didn't start a brawl in a baron's townhouse. He glanced at Seymour to see that the poet had the good grace to look embarrassed by such undeserved veneration, especially from Charlotte.

Suddenly Seymour turned to Connor, a smirk coming to the poet's lips. "There is but one of us remaining who has not recited tonight. Lord Kinleith, will you not share with us one of your favorite pieces of literature?"

Belatedly, Connor realized he should have seen this attack from Seymour coming. He glanced in Charlotte's direction to gauge her reaction. She ducked her head, looking away from him.

For the first time all day, she appeared embarrassed among the guests. She knew that he had not paid the least bit heed to the poem she'd given him to learn for the occasion. Rankled as he was by the thought that he was the source of her discomfort, Connor's lips thinned. At that moment he knew without a doubt that British women were as soft in the head as they were of heart. He rose slowly from his chair.

"Aye, I'll share some words that I've read and liked though the author knew nothing of Scots history. I've always found a lot of truth in Macbeth's words:

> *Tomorrow, and tomorrow, and tomorrow;*
> *Creeps in this petty pace from day to day,*
> *To the last syllable of recorded time;*
> *And all our yesterdays have lighted fools*
> *The way to dusty death. Out, out, brief candle!*
> *Life's but a walking shadow; a poor player,*
> *That struts and frets his hour upon the stage,*
> *And then is heard no more: it is a tale*
> *Told by an idiot, full of sound and fury,*
> *Signifying nothing.*

Connor let the word "nothing" hang in the air for a long moment before he added the rest of what he wanted to say.

"If you care to know, Macbeth killed Duncan on the battlefield, not in his guest bed as Shakespeare dramatized it. As king, Macbeth ruled for seventeen years, a prosperous reign for the Scots. 'Tis a great play, but we don't appreciate you English poets taking license with our history for profit on the stage."

Connor turned to Charlotte. "I think it's time for us to say good night, my lady."

"Yes, I think perhaps we should say our farewell to all," Charlotte said, edging toward the hallway door.

The stunned expression of disappointment on Seymour's face pleased Connor as he took Charlotte's hand. "I would have a word with you, sir."

Without saying anything, Seymour followed them to the door. Charlotte murmured her farewell to their host.

"Go ahead, Charlotte," Connor said. "Erik will help you into the curricle."

As Charlotte hurried down the steps toward the waiting vehicle, Connor turned on Seymour. "I won that game of cribbage today not to win Charlotte St. John's hand, but to win for her the right to choose between us. Neither you nor I has the privilege to determine where she bestows her heart. She has taken a mighty fancy to you though I can't imagine why. If she wishes you to court her, then you will. It matters not who won that blasted game because you'll compete with me whether you like it or not. Whether you have the courage or not."

Seymour opened his mouth as if he was about to deny Connor's words. Connor cut him off.

"If you don't continue to court her, we'll have another game and this time it will be one of my choosing. I will not be content with an old man's card game. Do you understand me?"

Seymour's eyes grew wide and his complexion turned chalky. He sputtered, his thin, blue lips wet with spittle. At the moment he looked more the wide-eyed country swain than an aristocratic poet. "I assumed two gentlemen of honor played that game in my library, sirrah."

"Well, you were wrong about that and I don't give a damn. I want to know if you understand me?" Connor demanded softly.

"You really are a barbarian." Seymour grabbed the door latch and tried to slam the door in Connor's face, but Connor's sizable foot stopped him.

"Do you understand?" Connor repeated without raising his voice.

"Yes, I understand perfectly."

"Good, that's all I wanted to know." Connor withdrew his foot and turned his back before the rush of air could hit his face. The door slammed closed with a bang that shook the house walls.

Lighthearted now, Connor jogged down the steps, the hem of his kilt swaying in the cool night air. His conscience was clear. He was satisfied with Seymour's answer and unaffected by the poet's insults. The identity of the real barbarian was clear enough to Connor.

And it wasn't the man wearing the kilt.

SIXTEEN

Davis dismissed his valet and ambled into his wife's bed-chamber where she was also preparing to retire for the night. Despite the fact that he was weary to the bone from a long day poring over contracts and negotiating a deal over supper at the club, he decided he'd better have a talk with Susanna.

Her maid glanced at him, bobbed a quick curtsy, then returned to loosening the laces of her mistress's dress. Davis pursed his lips, impatient with being confined to speaking of only the most prosaic things before the servants.

"We seem to be seeing the Scotsman around a great deal," he began, though Kinleith wasn't so much on his mind as was another visitor.

"You saw them come in?" Susanna said, looking at him by way of his reflection in her dressing-table mirror.

"Charlotte looked very sober," Davis said.

"Yes, quite," Susanna agreed, shrugging out of her dress with the aid of her maid. "She usually returns from an outing with Lord Kinleith blushing and full of giggles."

Without seeming too obvious, Davis admired his wife's creamy white shoulders, the sweet taper of her back, and the firm roundness of her silk-covered bottom. Even after the birth of the twins twenty years ago and after two pregnancies which had ended in disappointment and sorrow for them both, his wife's body still held an allure.

"You had a guest this evening." Davis spoke with studious

calm while he toyed with a ceramic dog on the mantel. The piece distracted him momentarily. He didn't remember the blue-and-white dog sitting there before. "When did you put this here?"

"What?" Susanna said, glancing up while removing her pearl necklace. "Oh, the Chinese dog—well I moved it when I added the blue hangings to the bed, sweetheart. Remember? I told you about that last week."

"Yes, I remember," Davis lied. Last week? He glanced at the bed and noted for the first time that it was hung with new blue draperies. Had it been that long since he'd been in his wife's room? Surely not, but he didn't remember any discussion about new hangings for the bed. There must have been one because Susanna talked of most everything with him. He examined the hangings more closely. "Very nice, my sweet. Very nice, indeed. Now, about your guest this evening."

"Sir Myron," Susanna said, moving behind the screen to remove her underclothes. "You may go now, Betsy. That will be all tonight."

"Yes, Sir Myron, that's his name," Davis said as if he had hardly remembered who the fellow was when he'd passed Myron on his very own doorstep this evening.

"You don't mind, do you?" Susanna said. "He came by to bring me some material I had requested for the ladies. It was such a ghastly warm spring evening and he had no plans. I invited him to dine. You were going to be out at your club."

"So it was just you and Sir Myron at the table tonight?"

"Oh no, Cassandra and Dudley were here, too," Susanna said with a laugh. "Davis, sweetheart, you don't think I entertain gentlemen when you're away, do you? Besides, he's only a professor," she added with a wave of her hand, dismissing Myron as if scholarly pursuits rendered a man a eunuch. Davis knew better, remembering about his own days at the university and about the Oxford dons.

"No, of course I don't doubt your hospitality," Davis said, smiling at his own foolishness. He trusted Susanna. He truly did. Still, he was unable to rid himself of an odd misgiving about the fellow. He'd even asked around about Sir Myron—nonchalantly, of course—and heard only respectable things about the man. A scholar, a penniless aristocrat who'd made something of a name for himself in antiquities. Exactly the sort of man who would capture a woman's fancy.

Davis glanced around at his wife just as she stepped from behind the dressing screen. His breath caught in his throat as he saw the flowing silk of her white nightrail and dressing gown stretch tantalizingly across her body. As he watched, she sat down at her dressing table and reached up to remove the combs from her titian hair.

A burnished cloud of curls descended to her delicate shoulders and down her back. Davis forced himself to remain by the mantel. He knew from personal experience that the skin of her shoulders was highly sensitive to kisses. Once bestowed, she would become as warm and pliable in his arms as the silk that covered her naked body. If he asked, she would wrap herself around him and he would lose himself in her. When they were finished, they'd lie together and he'd drift from their heaven into a sweet dreamless sleep.

Davis's exhaustion vanished.

"So have you learned any more about Lord Kinleith?" Susanna asked, drawing the brush through her hair.

"Who?" Davis began to blow out the candles on the mantel, one by one.

"Lord Kinleith," Susanna said, replacing her brush on the dressing table. "You're concerned about him seeing Charlotte? Isn't that what you said?"

"Yes," Davis said, moving on toward the other branch of candles on the mantel. "No, I haven't learned much more about him. But Forbes certainly is making his desires known. He's called upon all his supporters to exert pressure on me to sell the land."

"Ramsay Forbes, Lord Linirk," Susanna said softly as she began to braid her hair. "It is said that he is a ruthless man."

"I know and I'm beginning to see why," Davis said, turning to Susanna. He'd had to talk rather persuasively and at great length to dissuade his dinner guest from withdrawing his money from a railroad project Davis wanted to launch. Forbes had told the man it was a boondoggle. "What else is said about Forbes among the gossips?"

"I don't like to encourage gossip," Susanna said.

Davis had heard her change the topic of conversation more than once because she thought the talk had become too personal or speculative about someone.

"But tell me, is there more?" he asked, knowing that personal conviction did not prevent her from filing away every bit of hearsay she came across.

"Just that he does not go about in Society much and hardly anyone knows him well," Susanna said. "He is unwed and has already declared his nephew as his heir."

"And about Kinleith?"

A smile spread across Susanna's face. "You know, I like him, though he is something of a rascal. But I'm not certain his roguishness should be taken seriously. He's a bit like your sister Dorian. He rather seems to have a good time defying all the conventions."

"Well, you won't think the Brawlin' Scotsman so amusing if he breaks our daughter's heart—or worse, ruins her," Davis snapped, suddenly annoyed with Susanna for being so naive about the twins' future.

"I know, sweetheart," Susanna said, still smiling. "But mention of his name puts a spring in Charlotte's step and a saucy gleam in her eye. Sir Edward has never done that for her."

Davis moved across the room to blow out the candle by the side of the bed. "That is true. Though I'm not overly fond of the young man, Sir Edward is of good family and a baron with some property."

"Does a barony entitle him to be a bore?" Susanna asked. "For all his lofty literary aspirations, even you must admit Edward is something of a churl, is he not?"

Davis pressed his lips together in displeasure and strode around the bed to put out the candles on the other side. "You never let a title distort your views, do you, Mrs. St. John?"

She smiled at him knowingly as she tied a ribbon at the end of her braid. His dowsing of the candles was an old tradition, a well-established signal between them. "Never, Mr. St. John. Quality is more than mere rank or title."

"Don't say that too loud in the presence of certain people," Davis said. "That democratic notion might earn you passage to the colonies."

Susanna laughed, a light, pleasing, familiar sound. "And would you follow me, Mr. St. John?"

Davis blew out the next to the last candle on the dressing table. "Just as soon as I could get all my business affairs transferred to Boston."

Susanna opened her arms to him and he bent over her. "It would take you that long to come for me?"

His lips moved across hers, tasting her familiar taste and inhaling her customary perfume. The scent still excited him. A moan escaped him as his hands slipped down along her throat, beneath her dressing gown, and inside the neckline of her nightrail. Her skin was smooth beneath his fingers. He knew what she wanted to hear, but he couldn't resist baiting her. "Would you be waiting for me?"

In the lamplight that penetrated the room from the street below he could see her face tipped up to his, her eyes closed, and her eyelashes a dark fringe against her fair cheek. He kissed her again as he slid the silk dressing gown and nightrail from her shoulders. The warmth of her skin soaked into his palms. He held her mouth with his as he knelt before her. Sinking to the floor beside the stool, he released the kiss and drew her gown down her arms until her breasts were gloriously bare.

She tangled her fingers in his hair and whispered his name. It sounded so good on her lips. "Would you join me sooner if I conferred upon you the title of king of my heart?"

Davis pulled away, feasting on the sight of the pink peaks of her breasts, hard and taut for him already. The sight nearly drowned out the reserve in her words. Women always babbled nonsense when more satisfying occupations required attention. He'd say what she wanted to hear and be done with words.

Filling his hands with her generous beauty, he sought her mouth once more and whispered against her lips. "Mrs. St. John, if you could bestow a title upon me, I'd join you anywhere in the world instantly."

SEVENTEEN

Connor's performance at the literary group had astonished Charlotte. He was no stage actor, no Edmund Kean, but his deep intonation and clear cadence of Shakespeare's words had rendered every guest in Edward's library speechless.

She'd said little of her surprise to him, but his recitation had made her realize there were many sides to this man. She'd glimpsed only one or two.

At home she had described the literary scene to Cassie—without any details of the kiss—who also had been surprised by Connor's recitation. But the story came bubbling out once again three days later at tea with her mother, Cassandra and Aunt Dorian.

"Well, of course, you knew Sir Edward would try to embarrass Lord Kinleith," Aunt Dorian said, handing a full dish of tea to Charlotte.

"I didn't want to think it of Edward," Charlotte admitted without looking up from her cup, "but I did suspect he might resent having to compete with a prizefighter for attention."

"So what did Lord Kinleith do when Sir Edward asked him to recite?" Mama asked as she accepted tea from Aunt Dorian.

"The whole of the 'Tomorrow and tomorrow' speech from *Macbeth*," Charlotte said. Macbeth's words spoken in that authentic Scottish burr had sent chills down her spine. "The thing of it is, as far as I know, Connor rehearsed nothing before the literary group."

"I thought you selected a poem for him to read," Cassie said, daintily stirring her tea. A furrow creased her brow, notifying Charlotte that Cassie was hurt that the entire story had not been told to her before.

"I did copy a poem for Connor and he tossed it aside when I gave it to him. I was honestly afraid he would decline Edward's invitation to recite."

"And if he had, Edward would imply Lord Kinleith was illiterate," Aunt Dorian said, waving the silver sugar tongs in the air. "When Sir Edward couldn't put Lord Kinleith to a disadvantage with his renowned cribbage game, he tried to do it with literature."

"That appears to be the gist of the thing," Mama agreed.

Charlotte sat helplessly staring at her tea and wondering what she could say to make Edward look better. After all, she was his fiancée, or so she hoped to be, and she should support him with her loyalty.

"Well, no one should be surprised," Aunt Dorian said, pouring a cup of tea for herself. "Kinleith is hardly the illiterate Highland bumpkin that he allows people to think him. He may not have done the continental Grand Tour, but he's an earl, after all, and from a very old family. I've heard he's an alumnus of St. Andrews—studied the sciences, I believe."

St. Andrews? A fine old university, even if it was Scottish. Bumpkin, indeed. Charlotte continued to stare unseeing into her teacup until Cassie's elbow in her ribs almost made her spill the hot brew.

"If only Aunt Dorian had told us that sooner, you wouldn't be in this fix," Cassie whispered.

"I'm not in a fix," Charlotte muttered in return. "Edward sent me a very nice note just this morning."

In truth, the phrasing had something of a stiff, dutiful turn to it, but her poet had written her much as he'd always done. In the scribbled message he'd reassured Charlotte that he was too generous to hold Connor's behavior against her. "I'm in no fix at all."

"But do you truly care how Edward feels?" Cassandra asked with a shake of her head.

"Of course I care!" Charlotte said, shocked that Cassie would think that she didn't.

Cassie shrugged. "Anyway, it's about time for the grand poet to realize he has some competition for your affections. I think he's been rather cavalier in his treatment of you, Charlotte."

"Cassandra, did I hear you call Edward 'cavalier'?" Mama chided with a frown. "That's not fair."

"I don't know," Aunt Dorian said, taking a sandwich from the tray the footman offered her. "I think 'cavalier' sums up Sir Edward's behavior very politely. I'm afraid our aspiring Byronesque poet has successfully acquired the selfish conceit of his idol. If only his poetry displayed a similar ability."

The conversation died for a moment and once more Charlotte thought she should defend Edward and his poetry. No words of praise came to mind. With a sense of guilt, she sipped from her teacup. The note from Edward that very morning had thanked her for attending his gathering and for her engaging delivery of Shakespeare's sonnet. He'd not written a word about her momentary desertion of him while she'd slipped into the garden for a tryst with Connor. Edward had been a generous host. She had repaid him by standing in the dark with the Scotsman, surrendering to his demand for victory kisses. And she'd given them—long, hot, passionate kisses—and caresses.

Charlotte frowned into her teacup. A fine way for a guest to behave. In time perhaps Edward would prove them all—Aunt Dorian and Cassie—wrong, she hoped.

"Charlotte, dear," her mother was saying to her, "your aunt is speaking to you."

"What?" Charlotte shook Connor's kisses from her mind and turned immediately toward Aunt Dorian. "I'm sorry."

Dorian smiled a bemused smile. "That's quite all right, dear. I say, a lady with two gentlemen vying for her heart is rather entitled to a bit of woolgathering."

Cassie elbowed Charlotte in the ribs and Charlotte blushed.

"I was just wondering if you know where your next outing with Lord Kinleith is going to take you?" Dorian asked. "I overheard him talking with Anthony last night and he was saying something about the Foundling Shelter."

Mama's teacup clattered against her saucer. "The Foundling Shelter? Why would he possibly be taking you to the Foundling Shelter? I don't think your father would like that."

"The Foundling Shelter is for illegitimate children and orphans, is it not?" Cassandra's brows arched with speculation. "Surely Lord Kinleith is not—does not—"

"Of course he does not," Mama said, reproach in her voice. "You're not even to think such a thing, young lady, let alone utter the idea aloud. 'Tis improper."

"No, it's really very respectable and quite safe," Dorian said, unperturbed by her niece's implication or her sister-in-law's scolding. "Nicholas is a staunch supporter of Captain Corkham's Foundling Shelter, as it was originally called years ago. They only accept infants and children from women of good character. I believe Kinleith adopted the Foundling Shelter as one of his charities. Although I understand he's hardly in a financial position to indulge even the worthiest of causes."

"But why the Foundling Shelter, of all places?" Cassie persisted. The promise of some secret scandal gleaming in her eyes. "He must know someone there. He must."

"It's more likely that there's a boxing match there," Charlotte quipped, not at all pleased with Cassie's insinuations. She would not allow herself to believe for one moment that Connor's interest in the Foundling Shelter was more than something akin to Uncle Nicholas' interest.

Mama smiled and Aunt Dorian laughed at Charlotte's comment about a boxing match. Then the conversation drifted on to important matters: balls, *soirées,* teas, and betrothal breakfasts.

Nevertheless, Charlotte was curious about an outing to such an unusual place. The Foundling Shelter was another famous London institution of which she and Cassie had read, but had never seen. Papa would think a visit inappropriate; Mama was right about that. Too lowly. Too common for his daughters. Why should the St. Johns rub elbows with the poor homeless and unwashed? Indeed, why would Connor take her there? Why would she want to go?

The answer to that came without difficulty. Because Connor had stood by his side of their bargain and acquitted himself handsomely at Edward's literary *soirée,* Charlotte reminded herself. She would do no less than meet his challenge.

Connor was aware of Charlotte's misgivings about this visit as he handed her down from the curricle. Uncertainty paled her face and her eyes never left the front columns of the Foundling Shelter that loomed above them.

Once her feet were on the pavement, her gaze flickered toward him. She tugged apprehensively at the narrow sleeves of her gown. "Am I appropriately dressed for a visit to an orphanage?"

Connor considered her trim, dark blue dress and her flattering beribboned bonnet. The sober color deepened the indigo of her eyes and softened the fiery shade of her hair. She made a pretty, if subdued, little package, he thought, but he was unable to keep from laughing at her question. "You would ask fashion advice of a Scotsman in a kilt?"

Her lips pursed in annoyance. "I don't make calls at orphanages often."

"Nor do I," Connor said, bent on goading her a bit. "Am I to take it you haven't even toured Bethlehem Madhouse? One lady at your aunt's *soirée* told me it is a most amusing sight, those poor mad souls."

"I wouldn't know," Charlotte snapped, fidgeting with her reticule and parasol. "I do not take delight in another's misfortune. Will this take long?"

"Once my mission is complete, we will stay as briefly or as

long as you wish, Charlotte," he said, nodding to Erik to see to the horses and the curricle.

Taking her arm, he started up the stone steps to the Foundling Shelter. He knew he was stretching their *Life in London* bargain a bit, but after his experience with Edward and his narrow literary group, Connor was convinced Charlotte needed to be introduced to more of the real world than she seemed to understand. And it would be good for her to meet a true Scots lass with honor and courage.

Inside the doors at the top of the steps, the smell of lamp oil and unbathed bodies greeted them. Discreetly, Charlotte took out a scented handkerchief and pressed it to her nose. From the depths of the building the ringing of bells and the trill of children's voices reached them.

Connor led her toward the desk across from the entrance past a group of women, young and not-so-young, dressed in an array of dingy gowns and faded bonnets. Charlotte stared at a few who were clearly in the later stages of breeding. The silent faces stared in return, their eyes round and stoic and their lips pressed in a hard, thin line. Charlotte paused, shrinking back against him, but he offered her no shelter. He knew that she could not possibly have met many young breeding women in her soft, protected world. Yet, what surprised him was that she didn't seem as shocked as she was curious. Tugging on her arm, he ushered her to the desk.

"I believe we're expected," Connor said without preamble to the horse-faced woman wearing a white apron. "This is Miss St. John and I'm Connor—Lord Kinleith" He'd not become accustomed to thinking of himself as a lord. "We're calling on Miss Clyde."

"Yes, my lord." The horse-faced woman's countenance brightened. She curtsied and introduced herself. "Miss Clyde is expecting you. Follow me, please."

"Who is Miss Clyde?" Charlotte asked, looking up at him warily as he touched the small of her back to urge her to follow the woman.

"I shall introduce you to her." Connor had no idea what Charlotte expected, but he was enjoying keeping her off balance.

Without delay the aproned lady led them around the corner, down a narrow hall—the worn wood floors creaking beneath their feet—and into a spacious but sparsely furnished office.

The moment they entered the room, Janet rose from behind her desk, a snowy-white cap covering her smooth blond hair and an apron tied at her waist. Her familiar smile and open arms warmed Connor's heart.

She bustled toward them, her eyes flashing with pleasure and her usual energy nearly crackling in the sway of her skirt. "Connor, how good to see you."

Connor took her up in his arms, laughing as she was, and gave her a hearty embrace. "Janet, 'tis good of you to receive us when I know you are so busy."

"Now, put me down, Baby Cousin," Janet protested. "You've been in London for weeks now, and you're just calling on me."

"Aye, I've been tardy at that," Connor said, setting Janet on her feet.

"And where are your manners, Connor McKensie?" Janet asked, turning her attention to Charlotte, who stood pale and stiff in the doorway. "Please present your lady companion to me."

"Forgive me, ladies," Connor said, still laughing with the pleasure of seeing Janet. "Miss Janet Clyde, may I present Miss Charlotte St. John. Janet is a cousin of mine."

"Connor is my baby cousin," Janet said, squeezing his arm and looking up at him with a proud smile. "I used to wipe his nose for him, and look at him now."

EIGHTEEN

"Your cousin?" Charlotte said, a peculiar sense of relief nearly overwhelming her. So that was why they'd come to the Foundling Shelter. They'd come to call on Connor's cousin—not some love child. A smile touched Charlotte's lips. Eagerly she stepped forward and extended her hand to the charming little woman in the snowy-white cap. "Miss Clyde, 'tis my pleasure."

"Janet chose to come to London to live and work among the poor about two years ago," Connor explained, grinning down at the tiny woman. "She is the strongest and most courageous lady in a white apron that I've ever known."

The warm approval in Connor's voice wiped the smile from Charlotte's lips. She bristled. Just what did the Scotsman think of her? Charlotte studied the spirited lady closer. So this was the kind of woman Connor admired. A little dynamo of energy dressed in a housekeeper's apron and mobcap.

"The McKensie clan thought you were daft, lass," Connor said, suddenly seeming to remember something. "I've brought this for you."

He reached into his coat pocket and pulled out a letter. "Your mother made me promise to deliver it to you myself."

Janet accepted the missive with another laugh. "Mama doesn't trust the post, you know. Never has. And thank you for bringing this to me. But I assumed from your message that you were coming to visit for some reason other than just to deliver my mama's letter."

"You know me too well," Connor said. "The truth is your father asked for a report on this place. I promised I would see for myself what good work you were doing. He needs his mind put to rest. Seemed the least I could do for my only uncle."

Janet glanced questioningly in Charlotte's direction.

"Miss St. John was kind enough to agree to accompany me," Connor explained.

Charlotte smiled and nodded, thankful that he made no more explanation of their bargain. But now that she was here, all kinds of questions came to mind. After meeting Janet, she wasn't about to let Connor think she was too timid to tour the orphanage. No, not she. If he thought a few bad smells and the sight of women in out-of-fashion clothes and heavy with child would daunt her, he was greatly mistaken.

"Actually, I've been concerned about the children I see in the streets," Charlotte volunteered. With satisfaction she saw Connor's brows arch in mild surprise. "When Connor said he was coming to the Foundling Shelter, I was curious about the work done here."

"I'm so glad to hear that," Janet said, leaving Connor's side to link her arm through Charlotte's in a comradely fashion. "We do wonderful things here for children, and there's no place in the world where I'd rather be. Let me show you."

She led Charlotte down the hall as she launched into the story of how Captain Corkham had established the hospital in the last century to deal with the problem of homeless children he saw on the street. Janet's expressions were animated and her conversation charming. She loved her work and Charlotte could feel herself being caught up in the Scotswoman's enthusiasm.

Janet talked of the sad problem of orphans and abandoned children with a frankness and honesty that Charlotte had to admire. "Please, do call me Charlotte. And tell me more about what the children do here."

"Charlotte then, let's go this way." Janet led her out of the office and down the hall.

Connor straggled along behind them. In his kilt he towered

over the children scampering up the hall and women scurrying past. Charlotte was so fascinated by what Janet was telling her that she hardly had time to notice that he looked more than a little out of place and ill at ease.

Charlotte allowed Janet to show her first through the dormitory rooms, the laundry, the sewing room, the kitchen, and the dining hall. Much of the furniture was simple and worn, but the chambers were clean and functional. Chattering children littered each room. Charlotte noted that every pair of hands was engaged in doing the chores necessary to keep the institution running.

"You see we believe that poverty itself is not a sign of individual moral failure," Janet explained. "It is a cycle that can be defeated by learning self-help. We give the children safe harbor and teach them skills that will make them employable when they grow older."

The children they passed in the halls looked well cared for and well-enough fed. Smiles lit their faces and polite greetings tumbled from their little mouths. Occasionally a running or skipping child had to be reminded to slow down.

"And their education?" Charlotte asked as she studied the faces of the children who passed them in the hall. She saw no fear in their eyes, no resentment or reserve, no starvation. "Do you give them any kind of education?"

"Indeed, education and religion," Janet said. "We teach them to read, write, and cipher. Attendance to church services is required. And when the boys turn fifteen, we apprentice them out if they appear to be talented in a particular craft or we secure employment for them. They may go to a printer or a furniture maker or a cooper or the like. The girls frequently go into service."

Suddenly, Charlotte turned to see Connor strolling along, silent and bemused. She'd been so interested in what Janet was telling her that she'd almost forgotten that he was there.

" 'Tis impressive, is it not, my lord?" she asked. "And they appear so happy, the children. What wonderful work this must be."

"Janet likes it," Connor said with a nod, his expression as unreadable as his words. " 'Tis her work and her life."

Another group of children passed them in the hallway.

"But Janet, do all the children come from the streets?" Charlotte asked, forgetting about Connor once more.

"Many are born here," Janet said. "Their mothers apply for admission and give proof of their previous good character. Many of the children are sent to us by churches or landlords who find children deserted."

"How sad," Charlotte said, thinking of how she'd read stories of such things, but she'd never really thought of the tales any more real than a play acted on the theater stage. It truly happened—a child abandoned by an uncaring parent or given away by a mother unable to provide for it. Someone had to take care of these children. The idea excited Charlotte. One of those someones was a bright, busy, valiant woman like Janet Clyde.

"But you must see and hear our pride and joy," Janet said, her eyes shining with excitement as she drew Charlotte down yet another hallway. "It is time for choir practice. This way to the chapel."

Charlotte and Connor were soon settled in the back pew of the small chapel while Janet hurried to the organ. The simple sanctuary was appointed with stained glass and a fine brass chandelier. The children gathered in the choir box, their faces scrubbed shiny clean, their cheeks rosy, and their eyes bright with eagerness to sing. Soon their sweet voices were raised in song.

"And the children look so well-fed," Charlotte whispered as she and Connor sat in the shelter's chapel. She couldn't stop smiling. "No haunted, hungry look like those children we saw at the fair."

"Not a starved child among the lot," Connor agreed, his gaze fixed on the choir.

"Tell me, how did Janet get started in this work?" Charlotte asked.

"I believe she started by helping the cotters on her father's lands," Connor said, speaking softly as his gaze fixed on the choir.

"She never married?" Charlotte asked, her mind cluttered with the excitement of many new discoveries. "Surely there is some man who would be delighted to wed such a selfless woman."

"This work was her choice, to give to many instead of a few," Connor said. "Much to the disappointment of her family."

"I'm so glad you brought me here," Charlotte said.

"I'm glad you found the visit enlightening," Connor said without looking at her.

"Well, I admit I had my doubts at first," Charlotte said. "But I actually believe I learned something today. Just as I'm sure you've learned from the outings with me."

Connor laughed as though her assumption was preposterous. "Really? And what have I learned?"

Vexed, Charlotte squared her shoulders and lifted her chin. How could he ask such a question? The answer was so obvious. "That the world of literature, ideas, and philosophy can be just as interesting and stimulating as fights and prizes."

"I see—that's what I learned," Connor said without explaining exactly whether he agreed or not. "What have you learned?"

"I learned that there are people who care about the street children, too," Charlotte said, staring ahead at the singing children. "And these caring people work very hard to help the children."

"People such as Janet," Connor said as if he wanted to confirm what she was saying.

"Yes, but I also learned something even more important," Charlotte said, forming the idea as the words came to her lips. "I also learned that there are worthier things in life than—"

"Than what?

"I learned that there are other things for a woman to do with her life," Charlotte finished, as surprised with the sudden clarity of the idea as Connor seemed to be by her words.

"Other things?" He stared at her, clearly perplexed. "I brought you here to show you there are places that help children."

"But, look at Janet," Charlotte said. "She's a perfectly lovely girl from a good family. But she has chosen another direction for her life. Something other than marrying and living as a man's wife."

Connor blinked at her, then snapped his mouth shut and returned his attention to the choir. When he spoke he seemed to choose his words very carefully. "Seems to me that she is wasting her life on those children."

"Well, I suppose some people might think of it that way," Charlotte said a little surprised by his reaction. "But her true courage of which you speak so highly comes not in facing those children and the challenges of caring and providing for them every day but in making the decision to turn her back on her family and Society's expectations. I'm truly glad that you introduced us. Janet is an inspiration."

NINETEEN

Inspiration to defy the conventions of marriage and family was not exactly what Connor had intended for Charlotte to reap from her introduction to Janet. He wanted to initiate her to a part of London he was sure she'd never seen. He'd also wanted to show her what a strong Scotswoman was like. He'd expected Charlotte to be horrified by the unpleasant odors and the chaos. He'd expected her to plead with him to take her home within a quarter of an hour of arriving. He'd almost laid a wager with Erik.

Instead she'd wandered the halls with Janet, engrossed in every word his cousin had to say. It was not surprising after the Battersea Field Fair that the orphaned children of the shelter had captured her fancy. But defiance of Society and family had not been the lesson he'd hoped she would learn.

Without betraying his astonishment at Charlotte's revelation, Connor endeavored to navigate the carriage through the streets from the Foundling Shelter back to the St. Johns' Mayfair townhouse.

Heaven help him if Davis St. John or Lady Dorian knew he'd been instrumental in putting rebellious notions in Charlotte's head. Not that he was afraid of Charlotte's father, but Connor felt pretty certain that life as a spinster working with street urchins was not the future that Charlotte's papa or aunt had planned for her.

Connor glanced at Charlotte again, taking in her preoccupied half-smile and the thoughtful, faraway luster in her blue eyes. There was nothing missish, spoiled or withdrawn about this Charlotte. And she wasn't playing her sister's role, either.

When they reached the townhouse, Connor escorted Charlotte up the steps, still marveling at her unexpected reaction to the orphanage. At the door, she turned toward Connor, snapped her parasol closed, looked up at him, and waited.

Connor took her hand and bowed over it. "Thank you for your company, Miss St. John, on my call to the Foundling Shelter."

"But the pleasure was mine, my lord," Charlotte said without making a move toward the door.

Connor reached around her to ring the bell. Still Charlotte did not move. Connor hesitated, wondering what she expected of him. He would see her into Horton's safe company before he left. Was there some obscure gentleman's manners that he'd forgotten?

"Have I forgotten something?" Connor asked, confused by the absence of her usual eagerness to part company with him.

The smile disappeared from Charlotte's face and was replaced by perplexity.

"You have nothing to ask of me?" she asked. She fluttered her eyelashes at him, then looked away.

Connor almost shrugged in his confusion. "No. Am I supposed to?"

Charlotte continued to stare down the street and a blush rose in her cheeks. "No kiss?" she whispered so softly, Connor almost didn't understand her at first.

"Kiss?" Surprise robbed Connor of his laugh.

"Shhh!" Charlotte looked up and down the street guiltily.

"You are asking for a kiss?"

"No, of course, not," Charlotte said, disappointment glimmering in her kittenish eyes. "It's just that every time we— It's just a silly notion. No, I am not asking for a kiss."

Delighted, Connor let his laugh roar up and down the quiet respectable street. "Say no more, kitten."

Just as Horton pulled open the door, Connor seized Charlotte by the shoulders and planted a big, smacking kiss on her lips. Brief though the contact was, she kissed him back and turned all soft and warm against him. A tiny moan escaped her.

New feelings stirred in Connor, pleasant feelings beyond desire.

"My lord," Horton said with a gasp.

Connor released Charlotte and she staggered a step or two. Horton steadied her.

"It's all right, Horton," Charlotte said. "We were just saying farewell." With that she disappeared into the house and Horton shut the door behind her.

Connor climbed into the curricle, took up the reins, and clucked to the horses. The stiff-backed young woman with cold hands that he'd met at Lady Derrington's *soirée* had disappeared. He fancied this new Charlotte. Yes, he fancied this Charlotte a great deal. As disappointed as he was at the outcome of this outing to the Foundling Shelter, he wasn't at all disappointed with that farewell.

"Kinleith took her where?" Harby demanded, leaning over the counter of the Covent Garden gin shop, his glass raised halfway to his mouth. His sour breath blasted Grady in the face, but the towel boy hardly noticed it. The smell wasn't much worse than the stink of the juniper berries and stale tobacco smoke that saturated the room.

"The Foundling Shelter," Grady repeated, more interested in having a glass of gin himself than how Lord Kinleith chose to entertain his lady. "I could hardly believe the sight meself."

"Certainly not the place a gentleman takes a lady he wants to impress," said Harby, wagging his head in drunken disapproval. Then he threw back his head, the raspberry birthmark on the point of his chin clearly visible, and drained the contents of the glass.

Grady watched and licked his lips as Harby finished.

"Did they stay long?" Harby asked.

"As a matter of fact, they did stay a surprisingly long time," Grady said, envying the baby across the room sucking 'blue ruin' from its mother's own glass. Lucky tyke. "They stayed there near an hour, they did."

"Shopkeeper, refill." Harby stared at his glass as the shop-keeper filled it from a stoneware pitcher. "What would occupy a buck and his lady in an orphanage for over an hour?"

Grady shook his head, his gaze never leaving the newly re-filled glass of liquor.

Harby leaned on his elbow and lurched closer into Grady's face. "Did the lady look upset when they left?"

"No, not a'tall," Grady said, recalling the scene with sudden clarity. "No, the ginger-pated lady was smiling, but his lordship didn't look so happy."

"Isn't that interesting." Harby stared off into space for a very long time. Grady watched, beginning to think the man had passed out with his eyes open. Grady started when Harby spoke up suddenly. "I wonder what Linirk will think of that bit of news? Kinleith courting the lady with calls to an orphanage."

Grady contemplated Harby's glass longingly and tapped his finger on the wooden countertop. Surely it weren't too much to expect Harby to buy him a glass of drink.

Harby turned on Grady so suddenly the towel boy jumped. "Has Kinleith said any more about getting a fight set up?"

"Fight?" Grady parroted. The mention of boxing edged the temptation of gin from his mind. "Yes, as a matter of fact, he and his man were talking something about getting a prizefight set up with some buck who has been calling at the salon off and on."

"Why didn't you tell me that sooner?" Harby stood up straight, the drunken slackness disappearing from his face when Grady didn't answer promptly. Harby grabbed Grady by the lapel of his secondhand coat. "Who's the fight with? When' Where?"

Surprised by the violence, Grady tried to peel Harby's finger from his coat. "Details ain't been settled yet. But it's going to be something special."

Recovering his decorum, Harby released Grady and stepped away, looking around the room. "Find out who Kinleith is fighting—and quickly. Lord Linirk will want to know all that. Do you know how much the purse is?"

"No, but the rumor is it's to be a big one," Grady said, unconcerned about any loyalty to Kinleith. All he knew and cared about was that Linirk was a Scot nobleman who had some difference with Kinleith. Not that he disliked Kinleith, but if a clan feud put money in Grady's pocket, he wasn't going to trouble himself over principles.

"Good," Harby said, sounding relieved and appearing amazingly sober. "Good, get to it then and I'll let Linirk know that Kinleith is about to fight again."

"I'll get right to it," Grady said without making a move to leave the half-full glass of gin Harby had just abandoned.

"Right, then. You won't fail me, will you?" Harby said, striking his walking cane decisively on the straw-littered floor. "Lord Linirk can be a very unpleasant man to deal with when he's displeased."

"You'll get your information, Mr. Harby," Grady said, caring little about how nasty Linirk was. And he knew Harby wasn't real quality even if the man could talk like it when he wanted to. Grady wasn't fool enough to leave a half-glass of gin sitting on a counter.

The minute Harby was out of the door, Grady reached for the buck's gin glass. From the other side of the counter, the shopkeeper did the same. Their hands collided. Knuckles knocked. Fingers tangled. The glass tottered precariously. Before either of them could grasp it, the glass clunked over. Clear liquor sloshed across the counter. The glass rolled toward Grady, gin spreading in every direction.

Frantically, Grady tried to scoop it up into his hands, only to succeed in catching a few drops. He licked the spilled gin from the heel of his hand and ignored the three drops that dripped over the counter edge onto the toe of his worn boot.

"Now look what you done," the shopkeeper complained.

"Naw, don't you take me to task," Grady growled. "The gent paid for it and you was going to try to sell it again. I know yer game."

The shopkeeper shrugged and turned away. Grady licked the last drop of gin from his hand and cursed to himself.

He sure hoped he had better luck finding out what Harby wanted to know before all of London knew it anyway. Only then would he get paid. When he got paid, he could afford to buy his own gin.

Connor liked Tony Derrington's gentlemen's club. He felt at home there, or at least as at home as he did in any of the London clubs he'd been invited to visit. But being comfortable didn't make the decision he had to make any easier.

Sir Benton rose and held out his hand to his host first. "Well, I thank you, Derrington, for a fine meal. And Kinleith enjoyed meeting you."

Tony, Eldwick, and Connor also stood.

"My pleasure." Tony shook the baron's hand. He was clearly taking delight in his role as host of the meeting.

Connor took Benton's hand when it was offered, finding the elderly man's grip soft and fleshy. "I'll give your proposal careful thought."

"You do that. I'll expect to hear something from you or Eldwick by the end of the day tomorrow."

"Right you are," Eldwick said, pumping the elderly baron's hand more vigorously than necessary. He grinned at Connor. "I'll bring Kinleith around to seeing this our way, sir."

"Good, good," the baron said. "Good night, then."

As soon as Sir Benton was out of hearing, Tony signaled to the footman to bring the cigars and brandy.

Connor settled back in the well-upholstered leather chair and took a long, deep draw on the freshly lit cigar. The tobacco was fresh and rich and perfectly wrapped. He savored the flavor as he watched the club footman pour two fingers of amber brandy into the three glasses on the table.

"Well, what do you think of Benton's offer?" Eldwick spoke with his cigar hanging out of the corner of his mouth like a trader haggling at a horse fair.

Across from Connor, Tony blew a soft ribbon of smoke into the air and watched it curl up around his head. "Benton has direct connections with the Pugilistic Society and he knows how to put a fight together. Where to hold it. How to get the word out without upsetting the authorities. He knows the business. That's for certain."

"I think there's something here that we can work with," Connor said, unwilling to commit himself to all of the prizefight details that Benton had put on the table. This was still not the fight he'd hoped for.

"After that fight at the Battersea Field Fair a few weeks ago, plenty of folks will traipse out to the countryside to see the Brawlin' Scot and the Trooper square off," said Eldwick.

"A fight between a pair of prime milling coves will attract a lot of people," agreed Tony.

"He's an ugly one, that Trooper," said Eldwick, eyeing Connor across the table. "Do you hesitate because of the opponent?"

"I'm no Welsh boy fresh from the coal mines," Connor said, frowning at Eldwick. Connor knew he was being baited but that didn't prevent his ire from rising. "As a matter of fact, I do hesitate because my opponent is the Trooper. Not because I fear him, but because he's not the champion. I want to fight for the title. A championship bout will bring in the crowd with the money."

Eldwick sat forward in his chair and took the cigar out of his mouth. "Sorry, ol' chap. Didn't mean to offend you. The Trooper killed one of his opponents a couple of years ago."

"I'm not afraid of him," Connor said, discovering that the

cigar had suddenly lost its flavor. For some reason, death made Ramsay Forbes come to mind. Now wouldn't his demise in the ring please the marquis. "The Trooper won't kill me, though I reckon a few folks would like to think they're paying for the chance to see just that."

"You're in then?" Eldwick asked, inching forward in his chair with little attempt to hide the eager gleam in his eye.

"I'll let you and Benton know when I've made my decision," Connor said, refusing to be stampeded into a verdict.

"Right, then." Eldwick drained his brandy snifter. Leather creaked as he rose from his chair. "Thank you for the dinner, Tony. If you don't mind, I think I'll go see what's going on in the card room. Look forward to hearing your answer, Lord Kinleith."

As soon as Eldwick was gone, Tony took another sip of his brandy and regarded Connor over the top of the snifter. "You didn't like something about the fight arrangements?"

"As I said, it's not the match that I desire," Connor said. "I want to fight for the championship."

"And Benton is the man who can make that possible," Tony said. "All he has to do is say the word in the right ears and it will happen."

"But that's not the offer he put on the table tonight," Connor said.

"No, it wasn't," Tony agreed. "The more fights he can set up while you're trying for the championship, the more money he and his friends make. And so could you."

"I suppose that's true," Connor said thoughtfully.

"Have you told Charlotte about this fight?"

"I see no reason to confide the details of my fighting career to your cousin." Connor had learned his lesson when he'd taken Charlotte to the fight at the Battersea Field Fair. "I would prefer that you keep what you know in confidence."

Surprise erased the complacency off Tony's face. "But she knows that you have fought recently, doesn't she?"

Connor stared into his brandy. "Why share the details of what I do if it is likely to upset her?"

"She doesn't know that you've won two bouts at Fives Court?"

"Those were private wagers," Connor said. He'd fought those two bouts for the money. He had bills to pay. He'd won them both and the victories had brought Eldwick and Benton knocking on his door. "I was just keeping in practice. So you will not speak to her of it."

"But don't you see, perhaps if she saw you in action, she'd get accustomed to the idea," Tony offered. "Some of the most fervent boxing fans I've seen are women."

"But your cousin Charlotte is not among them," Connor pointed out, finishing the last of his brandy. He remembered the paleness of her complexion and the blueness around her pinched mouth by the time the Battersea Field Fair fight was over. Connor had no intention of exposing Charlotte to another experience like that if he could help it.

But Tony was right about this fight with the Trooper. Benton had definitely indicated that a victory against that mean fighter might lead to the match Connor wanted—against English champion Jem Ward, known as the Black Diamond.

A victory over Ward would guarantee Connor more than enough money and influence to tempt Davis St. John into selling Glen Gray back to the McKensie clan.

Then Connor could go home, back to the Highlands and start building the life he truly wanted.

"You're going to do it, aren't you?" Tony asked, eyeing Connor from over his brandy snifter again. "You'd make a lot of people happy if you did."

"I'll do it," Connor said, knowing he was close to getting exactly what he'd come to London for. His decision might please a lot of boxing fans, but he knew of one young lady whom he suspected would be most opposed to it.

TWENTY

"I do so wish the king were here at the opera tonight," Charlotte said to fill the awkward silence that had fallen over her, Connor, Cassie, Dudley, and Mama at the conclusion of the first act.

She snapped open her fan and stirred the air energetically to hide her disappointment. Her frustration was actually threefold. Edward was nowhere to be seen, either, and she had hoped for the opportunity to tell him how much the notes he'd been sending meant to her. But when she glanced at Connor sitting next to her, handsome in his black velvet coat, she decided perhaps it was best that Edward did not see her on Connor's arm. Her other upset centered on Papa's absence from Mama's evening at the opera.

"Yes, 'tis thoughtless of the king not to appear for Mama's birthday," Cassie observed dryly. Next to her sat Dudley, impeccably dressed in a deep purple damask coat with a handsome purple striped cravat perfectly coordinated with Cassandra's opera gown and elegant plumed headdress.

Dudley laughed obligingly at his fiancée's droll humor.

Charlotte frowned at her sister. "You know what I mean, Cassie. 'Tis more exciting when King George IV marches in with all his lords and ladies in attendance. All the jewels and satins. Like having another drama to watch while the singers perform."

"I'm quite satisfied with the performance that's been put on for me this evening," Connor said. He'd been staring off distractedly into the audience below them.

"Did you see someone you recognized, my lord?" Mama asked politely, looking ever so cool and unconcerned about the fact that Papa had made no appearance on her birthday. He'd sent a message that he'd been regrettably detained at the office, but Charlotte thought that a poor excuse. He should be here with them. Business could wait until the morrow.

"Well, you never know who you might see at the opera," Cassie said. "Everyone who is anyone comes to the performances at the King's Theater in Haymarket."

"I thought I glimpsed a familiar face," Connor said, looking out over the audience once more. "But 'tis of no significance."

"I see that the king's absence hasn't kept anyone else of interest away," Cassie continued without looking up from her program. "The Duchess of Litchmond is here and the Duchess of Cargyle, and I do believe that is Lady Melberlade over there. Have you ever seen such a scrumptious gown?"

Charlotte stared at her sister, amazed that Cassie had spotted all those people without ever seeming to take her eyes from the printed page before her.

"Your father is missing a very fine performance," Mama said, idly flipping through her program. Charlotte noted that Mama's smile was only a shadow of her usual one. "I hope you are enjoying the performance, Lord Kinleith."

"I'm enjoying the performance tremendously, Mrs. St. John," Connor replied, with a genuine warmth. Charlotte smiled a silent 'thank you' at him for lying. She had convinced Connor that he must witness a magical performance of the opera to complete his tour of Town. But the restlessness of his posture told her he was bored beyond words, yet too polite to say so in front of Mama. "It was so hospitable of you to include me in your party and on the occasion of your birthday. 'Tis a pleasure to hear the music, but I must admit my Italian is a bit rusty."

Mama tipped her head in sympathetic fashion. "I confess, so

is mine, my lord. I am always so relieved that they print a summary of the story in the program."

"There is Aunt Dorian and Uncle Nicholas with Tony," Cassie said, waving demurely across the theater at their relatives in the opera box opposite them.

"You must go say hello," Mama urged, including Connor in her suggestion. "Cassie and I spoke with them earlier. Dorian will want to know what you two have been doing in your journeys through Town."

"Yes, what a good idea," Charlotte said, pleased with the prospect of escaping the awkward conversation in the box. Charlotte started out into the crowd. Connor followed.

And a good deal of Society was there to be seen in the corridor—and to see them, she thought with satisfaction. If only she could have talked Connor out of wearing that kilt.

She slid him a covert glance and decided she didn't mind his dress after all. He did look fine in his trim-fitting, cutaway coat and snowy-white shirt. The fresh gash above his brow hardly marred his looks at all. A sparring injury, he'd told Charlotte earlier when her gaze lingered on it too long. She'd tried not to be anxious about the reminder that he was a prizefighter. Evidence of his calling was bound to present itself from time to time.

She'd even become accustomed to his kilt. The way he moved in it enchanted her these days. She had to admit no trousered man could match the way a kilted man walked. She'd seen the manner in Erik and other Scotsmen, but the way Connor wore a kilt expressed something unique and undeniable. An energy of stride, a swagger of hip, a supreme confidence of step. Nothing soft or timid dwelled in a man with a tartan flapping at his knees.

By merit of his aristocratic title, London society accorded Connor a certain level of social respect. But when Lord Kinleith strode into a room, his narrow hips swathed in a kilt and his broad shoulders filling the doorway, the ladies' heads came up and they stared, curious and attentive. The men turned to watch, wary but courteous.

His earldom had little to do with their reactions. The truth was, his entrance and presence was so forceful, even with his smile, that no one was willing to dismiss Connor McKensie on account of his picturesque dress.

Now that she'd come to appreciate his style, Charlotte rather liked being seen with him. She suspected that envy devoured most of the ladies who stared rudely.

"So is the opera as dreadful as you expected?" Charlotte asked as they made their way through the crowded corridor around to the Derrington box.

Connor looked blank. "Dreadful?"

"The music and wailing voices?" Charlotte asked, leading the way through the stylishly dressed throng, each of whom was clearly bent on showing off gowns, coats, waistcoats, and jewels—a bevy of peacocks on parade. "You made your aversion to an evening at the opera rather clear."

"I did not intend to be rude in doing so," Connor said, sidling beyond the reach of a plumed headdress. "But I see now that there are reasons to attend the opera other than for the singing. Everyone of influence is here. I've noted the presence of some interesting personages myself."

"But isn't the music lovely—and the costumes?" Charlotte said. "I love the dazzle. The color and the finery. But the music is wonderful."

"If I can hear the song over the chattering of the dandies and the rattling of snuffboxes," Connor said. "Townfolk make a rather rudesome audience—almost as noisy as village rabble."

"But the actors don't mind," Charlotte said, relieved to finally arrive at the Derrington box.

"But the actors have no choice," Connor reminded her.

Charlotte reached for the box curtain, but an arm in black velvet caught it and yanked it open before Charlotte's touch could do so. "Uncle Nicholas."

Tall and stately as ever, Charlotte's sea-captain uncle smiled at her. "Dorian, we have guests."

The Derrington family filled the box—Aunt Dorian, Uncle Nicholas, and Tony. In the corner sat Uncle Nicholas's elderly Uncle George with a servant in constant attendance. Greetings were exchanged and the gentlemen stood while the ladies were seated. Dorian demanded to know if Papa had appeared yet. When Charlotte admitted he had not arrived yet, Dorian muttered something Charlotte didn't understand.

"But enough about your papa," Dorian said. "Have you shown Lord Kinleith everything there is to see of London?"

"We have not missed much," Connor said with a laugh.

"And the tour of the Foundling Shelter was interesting?" Dorian asked, tapping Charlotte on the knee.

"Well, yes, Connor's cousin Janet told me all about it," Charlotte said, memories of her visit flooding back. "Did you know that the shelter has the most charming little choir? I told Mama that we should invite them to sing for a *soirée*."

"Yes, I've heard them before," Dorian said, turning to Connor. "That might be a fine fund-raising project. Let me congratulate you, McKensie. What an original way to entertain a lady—a trip to an orphanage."

"I only wanted to call on my cousin," Connor said, his gaze falling on Charlotte, his smile unreadable. "Miss St. John was kind enough to make the outing something special."

"I quite enjoyed it, Aunt Dorian," Charlotte said, quick to defend Connor's choice, which made more sense to her now than it did the day she first stood on the steps of the Foundling Shelter.

"That orchid color looks absolutely ravishing on you, Charlotte," Dorian said, mysteriously changing the direction of the conversation in a blink of an eye. "Good choice. And congratulations to you, sir, on your recent victories."

Charlotte thought she caught the subtle gleam of mischief in Aunt Dorian's eye. Suspicious, she turned to Connor. The smile slipped from his face. Charlotte did not miss the uneasy glance he cast first in Tony's direction, then in hers. "Thank you, Lady Derrington."

In an effort to cover her annoyance with the realization that Connor had not told her the whole truth about his fighting, Charlotte snapped open her fan and fluttered it in front of her. "Just what victories do you speak of, Aunt Dorian?"

"Did Connor not tell you of his bouts at Fives Court? *The Times* reported about it in some detail. Tony said the Brawlin' Scot fought a thundering good bout. I believe those were your very words, Tony. Pleased the crowd beyond words."

Charlotte glared at Connor, who clasped his hands behind his back and suddenly found the theater ceiling immensely interesting.

Tony caught his mother's enthusiasm. "Some bucks dropped huge wagers, and the fight promoters were flush. I tell you, it was a good show. One good right punch, actually—"

"I don't think we need to discuss the details," Uncle Nicholas interrupted after a glance in Charlotte's direction. "But I must say, McKensie, your victories are exciting. You bring both color and gentility to the ring after a few years without it. Gentleman Jackson has been missed."

"Thank you, Lord Seacombe," Connor said, still avoiding Charlotte's gaze.

The theater bell tinkled over the noise of the crowd.

"Well, then, we must get back to Mama and Cassie," Charlotte said, rising abruptly, thankful the timing required no comment from her about Connor's fighting.

The theater hallway was rapidly emptying. Certain of some privacy, Charlotte rounded on Connor, her move so unexpected that he almost walked into her. "Why did you not tell me you fought again?"

"You have expressed a dislike of it, so I decided not to trouble you with it."

"You received that cut over your eye in the fight, did you not?" Charlotte demanded.

"I did. But I could just as easily have gotten it from Erik."

"So you lied to me about an injury."

"Only in favor of sparing your sensibilities," Connor said, wagging his head in exasperation. "It seemed the thing to do, Charlotte. What else would you have me say?"

"I would have you be honest with me," Charlotte snapped. "You were honest enough with me to show me the Foundling Shelter and introduce me to your cousin. Can you not be honest with me about this?"

"Even though the truth upsets you? What interest is my fighting of yours, after all?"

Charlotte hesitated, hurt that he would dismiss her concern, yet without an answer to that question herself. She grasped for the only reason that came to mind. "Are we not friends?"

Connor frowned and threw his hands up in a helpless gesture.

Charlotte's anger blossomed afresh. "Surely you would accord our relationship the respect you have for an acquaintance at the very least. Why would I not be concerned for your welfare?"

Connor glanced around them and put a warning finger to his lips. "I don't think this is the place for this discussion."

For the first time in her life Charlotte cared little for what other people thought. "Why is this not the place? Do you think me such a weakling that I have not the stomach to hear news that displeases me?"

Angered beyond words, she slapped his solid chest with her fan. In that moment she almost understood what it felt like to want to strike someone or kick his shins or at the very least bellow into his face like a common fishwife.

If she could have found a chair to climb up on at that particular moment, she would have bellowed right in Connor McKensie's face. Blast that they stood in a public place where every move they made would be reported to the gossips. With every ounce of her dwindling dignity she finished in a whisper. "Yes, I want to know the truth about your fighting. I insist on knowing the truth, even if it will upset me."

Connor studied her for a long moment, skepticism written in

every plane of his face. "Then there is something more that you should know about, besides the fights at Fives Court."

Charlotte sucked in a breath, sorry that she'd just begged for the truth. "Tell me."

"I'm scheduled to fight the Trooper at the end of the month."

Breath escaped her as if she'd been dealt a blow. "Oh, no Connor, not him."

"It's a great opportunity, kitten." Connor took her arm gently and began to lead her toward the box. "It will be a feather in my cap when I defeat him."

Excitement danced in Connor's eyes. Charlotte stared at the expectant gleam. She could hardly believe the enthusiasm lilting in his voice as he talked of the bout. The Trooper! She remembered how dreadfully the Trooper had beat up on the Welsh boy at the Battersea Field Fair. She could only stare up at Connor in horror.

"Be happy for me, Charlotte."

"I want to be, Connor, but I'm not."

They had arrived at the box curtain. Charlotte stopped him, wanting to say something more, but uncertain of exactly what or how to say it.

"Your father is here," Connor said, giving a nod in the direction of the stairs, a gentle warning that they must not continue their private disagreement.

Charlotte swallowed the lump of dread in her throat and turned toward her father.

Papa came striding up to them, his coattails flapping and a lock of his fair hair dipping over his brow. "Charlotte. Lord Kinleith. So sorry to come trailing in like this." Papa dropped a light kiss on Charlotte's cheek and offered his hand to Connor. "How much have I missed? Is your mama too angry with me?"

"Well, she is rather disappointed," Charlotte began.

"I know," Papa said, stepping toward the box and reaching for the curtain. "I never dreamed this particular business arrangement to help fund the king's building plans could become so troublesome. I'm so sorry, love."

Papa swept back the curtain and every face in the box turned toward them: Cassie, Dudley, Mama—and Sir Myron.

For an awkward moment no one said a word. Sir Myron rose slowly from Papa's chair next to Mama. Papa did not move to take it.

On stage the soprano launched into her aria. In the box, no one said a word.

The Greek scholar had been calling at the St. John house with some frequency for several weeks now, mostly when Papa was away from home. Charlotte and Cassie had observed the fact, though neither had been brave enough to speculate about any reason for Myron's visits beyond those innocent ones Mama gave them.

Papa stood, stiff and frowning.

Myron bowed formally.

"Davis." At last Mama rose also, her fan fluttering over her heart—in surprise or relief, Charlotte couldn't be certain. "You're here at last, my dear. Sir Myron—"

"I see you have not wanted for company," Papa said, his voice cold and his face hard as stone. Charlotte glanced from Papa to Sir Myron in confusion. Her annoyance with Connor and his fight vanished. Was it possible? Was Papa jealous?

"I saw your lovely wife and daughters here so I stopped by merely to bid all a good evening and wish Mrs. St. John many returns of the day. It is her birthday," Sir Myron said without apology or retreat, his voice even and his manner quite civilized. "I have no intention of intruding."

"And you're not intruding, Sir Myron," Mama said. "I'm always pleased to see you."

Charlotte and Cassie stared at Mama, then exchanged glances. Surely Papa had no reason to be jealous.

"Thank you, Sus—Mrs. St. John." Sir Myron bowed again. "So nice to see all of you again. Enjoy the performance."

Papa, Charlotte, and Connor stepped aside as Sir Myron took his leave from the theater box.

Papa slipped into the chair that Sir Myron had just vacated

and made a hasty excuse about a business arrangement that threatened to fall apart because of some outside influence. His immediate attention had been required. Mama accepted Papa's apologies without a fuss and turned her attention to the opera.

The rest of the performance passed without incident.

After the opera the Derringtons and the St. Johns enjoyed a midnight supper together at a tavern suggested by Uncle Nicholas. Amid the critique of the singers' performances and the composer's music, there was hardly any time for more private conversation between Charlotte and Connor.

The moon had set by the time the St. Johns' landau dropped the family at the doorstep. Mama and Papa made their farewells brief. Cassie and Dudley exchanged a chaste kiss inside the door and Dudley was off in his own carriage.

But questions assailed Charlotte. She and Connor were friends, weren't they? Why had he frowned when she'd asked him that? She had a right to tell him how she felt, did she not?

"Where is Erik?" Charlotte asked, looking up and down the street and very aware of Horton, the butler, stifling a yawn as he stood just inside in the doorway.

"In bed, probably," Connor said.

"But how will you get home?" Charlotte asked.

"I'll walk," Connor said. He had become distracted since their conversation in the theater lobby. "Walking is good for my wind."

"I see," Charlotte said, not truly understanding but guessing that he referred to something important for his fighting. "You're not concerned about footpads then?"

"Why should I be?" Whatever had been on Connor's mind seemed to slip away. He grinned and reached for her. "All I want to steal is a kiss."

"I didn't mean you would be stealing." Charlotte held him at a distance. "Please, Connor, do not mock me. I have something to ask of you."

"Ask."

"Connor, don't fight this fight."

TWENTY-ONE

Connor let his hands drop away from her delicate shoulders. He had hoped to avoid this conflict. After spying that hauntingly familiar face in the opera crowd this evening he was more determined than ever to move ahead with his plans for the fight. Nothing was to be gained by a confrontation with Charlotte.

There was no way he could explain how the sight of black-clad Ramsay Forbes stalking through the crowd like the very devil himself had renewed his determination.

He stepped away and shook his head. "Charlotte, prizefighting is what I do. This bout is what I have planned for from the first day I came to London. I've never told you anything else."

"So you won't listen to me? What I ask of you is of no consequence?"

Connor studied her face, so innocent and troubled. How he would have liked to grant her wish just to see her smile. For the life of him he could not understand why the fact that he liked to box distressed her and her distress touched him.

But he could not let her deter him from his purpose. He'd wondered all evening what the man he'd seen in the audience had to do with the sudden ease of arranging this fight with the Trooper. The range of Ramsay Forbes's influence was legendary. How long had Forbes been in London, he wondered.

Connor shook his head. He didn't want to disappoint Charlotte, but what he'd come to London for was more important than a society miss's distaste for pugilism.

"Charlotte, I like to fight and I'm good at it," Connor said, wondering why in the name of the almighty she couldn't have been one of those blood-thirsty Society bawds who clamored at the ropes, cheering the fighters on—the bloodier the fisti- cuffs, the louder their voices.

Connor eyed Charlotte in her orchid opera gown, pearls glow- ing softly against her smooth throat. He tried to picture her encouraging him to throw another punch. He almost snorted. Not bloody likely. For the first time he had to wonder if Char- lotte had urged him on, would she have come to mean so much to him?

Connor shook his head; he was letting frivolous issues com- plicate things. "This fight is what I came to London to do, Charlotte. I will not give up my goal when I've come so near to reaching it."

"I know you want to win the purse to purchase Glen Gray, but the Trooper is brutal. I heard *you* say so. At least think of yourself, Connor. You could be hurt."

Connor laughed. He'd suffered his aches and pains after a fight. The swollen eye. The sore ribs. The stitch in his back. But he had no fear of the pain. "Not me. I'm indestructible, Charlotte. Don't you know that? I've never lost a bout."

Charlotte shook her head and stared at his feet.

"Come to the fight." With a finger, Connor lifted Charlotte's chin so she was forced to meet his gaze. Her somber expression troubled him. "I went to the opera. Now it's your turn. Come to the fight. Tony will bring you just as he did the day we first met. After you've seen a fight or two you'll see for yourself that it's not so terrible as you think. Did you suffer so that first time?"

"I did not care for it one bit," Charlotte said, a full-lipped pout on her lips and her brow furrowed. "And I didn't even know the men in the ring then. But knowing you—"

She turned from him again and he allowed her to move away. He knew what she was going to say and his heart sank.

"I know you always win and I'm glad of it. But I won't watch you fight. Please don't ask. Thank you for coming to the opera. Good night."

With that, Charlotte stepped into the townhouse. Horton shut the door so soundly that the thud echoed up and down the deserted Mayfair street.

Connor shrugged to himself. She hadn't even asked for a kiss. Ignoring the aching disappointment in his gut, he took each step down to the street one at a time, his pace slow and thoughtful until he reached the walk.

If Charlotte were a Scottish miss, there would have been none of this silly faintheartedness over a good mill in the ring.

On the other hand, he reminded himself, if Charlotte was a Scottish miss, he wouldn't have a second chance at gaining Glen Gray should he lose the fight.

He wasn't going to lose. He'd never been defeated before and he wasn't taking up the blasted habit now. But if he lost, there would be Charlotte.

Fortified with that thought, Connor's step quickened as he started off toward his east side rooms. As he walked he thought of Ramsay Forbes again. The unexpected glimpse of his enemy seated across the theater had shaken Connor.

Just before the curtain went up on the third act, something had drawn Connor's gaze toward the boxes opposite the St. Johns. There sat Forbes, dressed in solid black as always except for his tartan sash. The marquis had stared back at him with those hard, green eyes. They had not seen each other in person for almost eight years. But there was no missing Ramsay's long, haunted face—the narrow, hard countenance of a man determined to have what he would have.

They held each other's gaze for a long moment, until the baritone had begun his solo. No expression had crossed Ramsay's face. Connor had masked his own reaction. An opera house was not the time or the place for displaying the cold, violent emotions Connor felt for his nemesis. Each carried a burden of hatred three hundred years old. A burden no parliament or king could banish with law or decree.

Connor had said nothing of the sighting to Charlotte or her family. He suspected that Davis St. John had been too preoccupied with his wife's birthday to realize that the Marquis of Linirk had been in that audience.

Forbes's appearance had been totally unexpected but if Connor gauged the marquis's expression right, Ramsay had wanted to be seen. It was his way of throwing down the gauntlet.

How long had Forbes been in London, Connor wondered once more as he walked beneath a streetlamp. How far was Forbes willing to go to defeat Connor in his bid for Glen Gray? Not far enough, Connor decided, because he was willing to go farther.

Davis dismissed his valet for the night. Then he stepped back and took stock of himself in his mirror. After a short appraisal he tied the sash to his dressing gown a bit snugger to show off the trim youthfulness of his figure. Not bad for the father of twin twenty-year-old daughters, he thought.

Stepping closer to see better in the candlelight, he studied one jaw and then the other. Drawing his fingertips over his cheek, he decided he did not need to shave again. Maybe his face was a bit rough, but it was smooth enough to leave Susanna's face unchafed in the morning. Besides, she'd confessed in an intimate moment she enjoyed a little scratch from his beard. A grin of anticipation broke across Davis's face. Maybe Susanna's birthday had gotten off on the wrong note, but at least the occasion was going to end right.

His day had been a succession of disasters, beginning with the notification of withdrawal of one of the partners on the king's building project. Then the note of displeasure that had come from the king's advisor—the very man Davis was counting on to put his petition for a title before the king. That qualified for a late emergency meeting at the club, which ended in his subsequent tardy arrival at the theater.

Davis frowned at himself in the mirror. But the true final

disaster of the day had come in finding Sir Myron sitting next to *his* wife in *his* opera box on her birthday. Davis had had to summon every bit of strength he possessed to avoid losing his temper. The scene in the opera box had been perfectly innocent, but Davis could not prevent the spark of jealousy from nearly burning through all his civilized restraints. All he needed to do was strike a gentleman in public to totally ruin his reputation and chance at knighthood.

But the scene was over. Davis picked up the gift box that he'd had the jeweler send over earlier in the day. There was still a chance that he could recover something of the final hours of Susanna's birthday and make something worthwhile and pleasurable out of the day. Pearls and diamonds should please her. Patting the box in his dressing-gown pocket, Davis knocked on the door to his wife's room and opened it.

To his surprise, Susanna was already lying on the bed with only a single candle burning on the bedside table. A cloth compress covered her brow and her eyes. At the dressing table Betsy was pouring water into a wash bowl.

Davis closed the door. "You may go, Betsy."

Susanna held up her hand to forestall her husband's order. "No—stay, Betsy. The cool cloths seem to help."

Davis stood speechless for a moment, uncertain of what to do. Susanna never contradicted him. "Is something wrong, love?"

Betsy looked from Davis to Susanna, whose eyes were closed. The lady's maid bobbed a curtsy. "Begging your pardon, sir. I must fetch some fresh water, ma'am. I'll be right back."

"I have a headache," Susanna said as soon as the door closed behind the maid.

"I see." Davis stepped closer to the bed, concerned and confused. Susanna never had headaches. Susanna was never unwell. "I'm sorry to hear it, my love."

When he reached the side of the bed, he sat down on the edge of the mattress and touched her hand. Her fingers were cool and limp in his hand. When he looked into her face, he noted the paleness of her lips. "Is it very bad?"

"Quite unrelenting," Susanna murmured without moving, as if any kind of movement was too painful to attempt. Her thick titian hair fanned across the white linen of the pillow and gleamed in the candlelight.

Davis cradled her hand in his palm but the absence of life in her touch left him feeling lost. Whenever Susanna was unwell, helplessness overwhelmed him as it had when she had lost their last child. The powerlessness terrified him.

For days she'd lain in the bed, trying to regain her strength. The twins had danced in and out of her room and at first he'd thought their presence exhausted Susanna. Then Dorian had observed that her eyes followed the girls' every move when they were permitted into her sickroom. He'd allowed the twins to visit for longer and longer periods of time—against the doctor's orders. Only then had she seemed to regain her strength.

But dancing children was not what she needed now.

"I brought you your birthday gift," Davis said, the only offering he could think to make. He reached into his pocket.

"Thank you, sweetheart, but this is probably not the best time for me to receive a gift." Susanna raised her hand to press the cloth against her brow.

"No, I suppose not," Davis admitted and tucked the box back into his pocket. There had to be something he could do for her. "You know, my love, I am terribly sorry about being late this evening. It couldn't be helped. So much seems to be going awry right now."

Davis paused, realizing that his tardy arrival at the opera was not the best topic to bring up at the moment. "Perhaps I could read to you. Would that help? Where is that novel you were telling me about?"

"No, dearest, thank you. No reading tonight. I'd like to rest."

"I know what you need." Davis jumped from the bed and hurried around to the other side. "I'll just lie here with you and keep you company. You found that comforting before when—you know—"

"I've quite forgiven your late entrance," Susanna snapped before he could crawl onto the expanse of bed and take her into his arms. "Davis, do not fuss so. If you truly wish to do something for me, in the future you could be more civil to the people who were thoughtful enough to offer their best wishes. Sir Myron, for instance."

Brought up short by the mention of Myron's name, Davis drew back and leaned on his elbow. "I did not realize that I was uncivilized," he lied. He had not lost his temper, but he had not behaved well. "Now that you mention it, the man seems to be ever-present when I find you."

"That is not so, Davis," Susanna said without removing the cloth from her eyes, but her voice grew stronger. "Unless you mean to imply that a few minutes of conversation at the opera before my daughters and their escorts is some kind of tryst. It is hardly Sir Myron's fault that you are seldom in the company of your family and when you do choose to bless us with your presence, poor Myron has the misfortune of putting in an appearance."

Poor Myron? Annoyed now, Davis climbed off the bed. "The frequency of that man's appearances is hardly some coincidental misfortune as you portray it—or as he would have you believe."

"How would you know that?" Susanna said, pulling the cloth from her forehead and sitting up in the bed.

"Because no single man wastes his time sniffing around a married woman unless he finds some pleasure in it."

"What?" Susanna bolted off the bed as if sharing the counterpane with Davis was intolerable. The wet cloth dangled from her hand. "Just what do you mean by that?"

Davis knew he was treading foolishly into uncharted territory but his jealousy urged him on. "I mean you are encouraging him."

"What?" Susanna countered, more as a squeak than a word.

"You don't mean to be so beguiling," Davis said, leaning over and bracing his fists on the counterpane, pleased to see her as angry as he was. Insane as it seemed, he wanted her to be as hurt and insecure as he suddenly felt. "But you flutter your lashes at him and admire his—his antiquities—and the man is snagged by your charms."

Susanna's eyes widened and her mouth formed an 'O'. "I can't believe you are saying these things to me."

Davis straightened. "While I'll try to be civil to your Sir Myron, I would appreciate it if you would behave decorously enough to avoid any gossip that would threaten my petition for a title. My elevation in society is bound to benefit you and the girls, too, you know."

Understanding flashed in Susanna's wide brown eyes. Her mouth pressed shut in a thin, pale line. Before Davis realized what she was doing, she reared back and pitched the wet towel over his head. It snagged at the back of his neck and fell into his face. "I should have known that was what this is all about, your lordship. Your ambition. Sir Unworthy-unless-I-have-a-title."

Davis gasped from the icy coldness of the cloth and the barb of Susanna's words. He snatched the towel from his head and glared back at his wife, his anger a bit dampened by the towel and daunted by her ire. He'd never seen Susanna so angry or heard her speak such sharp words. But she had said them and she glared at him, making it clear she had no intention of taking a single syllable back.

"I do not wish to see Sir Myron in the house again," Davis said, aware of his rights as the man of the house. "Have I made myself clear?"

"Without a doubt," Susanna snapped. "You will not see him in this house again. I swear."

"Good." Davis turned to take his leave. There would be no welcome for him in his wife's bed tonight. When the bracelet box slapped against his thigh, he stopped, pulled it out, and opened it. Diamonds glittered and pearls glowed in the light of the single candle in the room. "Here is your birthday gift."

Susanna cast it a disapproving glance and lifted an indifferent shoulder. "Save it to give me when you get your title."

"Good idea," Davis said, snapping the box shut and thrusting it back into his pocket.

In the darkness of his room he cast off his robe and crawled into his cold, lonely bed, certain that Susanna would forget her anger when he was knighted. She would be remorseful about mocking his aspirations. His hard work and ambition had given her a life of luxury—the time to dabble in Greek antiquities and scholarly discussions. And once he was knighted Sir Davis and she became Lady Susanna, Davis was willing to wager that Sir Myron would not look so good to her then.

TWENTY-TWO

Charlotte did not see Connor for the next fortnight—no social calls, no notes, nor was he at Aunt Dorian's musicale on Friday last. When Charlotte caught herself peering out the upstairs window for the tenth time to see who had rung the doorbell, she had to ask herself who she hoped to see. Not Connor, but Edward's footman, she told herself.

The poet's daily correspondence filled with poems had resumed. Though she was flattered by the attention, the poems no longer seemed as romantic as they once had. In fact, they seemed rather lame.

The fault was hers, she decided, not Edward's. She was in an unexplainably blue mood and her literary judgement was not to be trusted.

But by the end of the fortnight she realized she would like very much to look out that upstairs window and see a giant Scotsman in a kilt standing there.

But he was never on the doorstep. She scolded herself for caring. He did not call nor did he send a note nor ask after her as far as she could tell. Tony said Connor was training for the fight with the Trooper, which did not enlighten her much more. She had thought she and Connor were better friends than that; at least she had hoped as much. His apparent lack of interest took the light out of her days, but she tried to hide the fact. She vowed to herself she would never admit her longing for Connor's good-natured company to anyone. Not even to Cassie.

The spring day had dawned fine and clear. Cassie had suggested that they go to the linen-drapers to look at summer fabrics. Mama was preoccupied with some Greek lecture and Papa was off to his office as usual.

At first Charlotte resisted, thinking to spend another day in her study working on the translation of Homer that she'd started weeks ago. But when she looked down at the papers and books on her desk, they held no appeal. Suddenly Cassie's suggested trip out of the house sounded good. So off the girls went, planning orders for several new gowns and bonnets to wear to the summer teas and garden parties on their social calendar.

"There's hardly anyone here," Charlotte observed when they entered Harding, Howell & Company in Pall Mall. "We shall be able to look and shop at our leisure."

"So we shall," Cassie agreed, perching herself on a tall stool near the counter and promptly pointing to the bolts of fabric she wished to see. A courteous shop clerk quickly complied. Soon the counter was piled high with linens, muslins, chambrics, and silks, all in hues the girls preferred. They fingered this one and that, holding lengths up to their faces and asking for advice from the other.

Cassie's sharp wit and discerning eye for fashion soon made Charlotte forget all about Connor and Edward. She could feel her depression slipping away. Nothing like a shopping trip on a fine day to lighten a girl's heart—until Cassie changed the subject.

"You seem rather subdued these days Charlotte," Cassie said. "Is anything amiss?"

"Subdued?" Charlotte studied the muslin she was holding, though she had no interest in this particular shade of pink. She tried not to frown. "I believe this is your color, Cassie. Whatever do you mean, 'subdued'?"

Cassie was quick to read much into a frown—or even the hint of it. "You've spent more than your normal number of hours moping around your study."

"I've not been moping," Charlotte said, purposely occupying

herself with another bolt of silk. "I've been reading. You know how I love to read and I've been working on that translation."

"I'm so glad to hear that," Cassandra said with a light note that Charlotte recognized as skepticism. "You know how I hate it when my sister mopes. I won't allow it."

Cassie's imperial statement brought a smile to Charlotte's lips. Even though Cassie didn't rule the world, she could at least make you think she did. "I assure you, no moping from me."

"Splendid," Cassie said. "So tell me, how can you read when you stare out the window with that pensive smile?"

Charlotte opened her mouth to protest.

Cassandra held up a hand to avert it. "This wouldn't have anything to do with the fact that Lord Kinleith hasn't called or corresponded with you since the opera, now would it?"

"It has absolutely nothing to do with Connor," Charlotte said.

"You can't pretend with me, you know." Cassandra slid the bolt of cloth she'd been examining onto the counter. "I knew it. Did you two have a set-to that night?"

"No, of course not," Charlotte said, feeling guilty and confused about arguing with Connor, then lying to her sister about it. But she had her pride. She was not going to admit to anyone that she'd asked him not to fight and he had so little regard for her opinion that he'd almost laughed in reply.

"I'm glad to hear you two did not argue." A wide, knowing grin spread across Cassie's face when she finally succeeded in making Charlotte meet her gaze over a bolt of silk. "You and he parted on good terms then? And you're going to go see him fight?"

"You know about the fight?" Charlotte asked.

"Dudley has been following all the excitement in *The Times*." Cassie unwrapped a length of pink muslin and stroked it thoughtfully. "They say if Connor wins this match against the Trooper, he may be offered a bout with the champion, Jem Vard."

Charlotte paused, pretending to be fascinated by the weave of the linen in her hand. She wanted to be glad that Connor was getting what he wanted. Since they'd disagreed about the fight at the theater she had told herself over and over that she was pleased for him. But deep in her heart there was no pleasure. She feared he was destroying himself for a piece of land and there was nothing she could do about it.

"Tony is going," Cassie said, a sly smile on her lips. "He's terribly excited about the mill and I think Aunt Dorian is also going though she is too thoughtful to say so to you. She is McKensie's supporter, you know."

"I know," Charlotte said, feeling left out. "But I am not a supporter. Not of his boxing, at least."

Suddenly very interested in the same piece of linen Charlotte had been examining, Cassandra talked on as if she had not heard Charlotte. "I'm certain Aunt Dorian would be pleased to have you accompany her to the fight. You should get out and do some new and different things. Get some fresh air. An afternoon in Edward's garden hardly qualifies as fresh air. I don't believe this fabric is my color after all. Too pink."

"I'm perfectly content to spend an afternoon in Edward's garden and in his company. We read poetry and discuss ideas. There's no blood and we don't go nosing around for the sad, tragic stories that the streets have to tell."

"All that literary stuff sounds boring to me."

"Our relationship, Edward's and mine, is civilized, courteous, intellectual," Charlotte continued, saying at last what she'd been telling herself for the last two weeks. No ups and downs. Cassie couldn't possibly understand how important the steadfastness of their relationship was.

"No passion between you?"

"Passion?" Charlotte echoed, lost. What on earth was Cassie prattling about? Cassie was usually too practical to bring up useless, invisible emotions. "Passion? I believe what the poets say about passion. It is fleeting. It fades just as youth does. Truth and beauty are the stuff of life. When youth fades, we Edward and I, will always have our mutual interests in literature music, and art."

Cassie's silent study of her made Charlotte feel a bit uneasy. "Charlotte, when did you become an old woman?"

Charlotte gasped. "I am not an old woman. Do you and Dudley share passion? For that matter, can you define passion for me?"

"Actually, I believe I can," Cassie said with certainty in her voice. "It's the gleam in Uncle Nicholas's eye when he glances at Aunt Dorian every time she wears wine-colored silk. And you know when you see that gleam that when they finally retire to their bedchamber, when the door closes on them, things are going to happen." Cassie turned around on the stool to face Charlotte. "You can tell sparks are going to fly."

"Sparks?" Charlotte repeated.

"You know, heat between them," Cassie said, obviously frustrated with Charlotte for not understanding.

"Heat from what?"

"Desire for each other," Cassie said, frowning in exasperation. "They want to touch each other, hold each other, sleep together, naked."

Charlotte knew better than to gasp. Cassie always enjoyed shocking her. But, *sleep together naked?* "I can't imagine anything like that between Aunt Dorian and Uncle Nicholas at all."

Charlotte glanced up to see the shop clerk drifting dangerously close, close enough to eavesdrop. "Do you have any ribbon to match this muslin? Pink, I think, or green. Bring me all the shades of green."

The clerk frowned, but hurried away to do her bidding.

Cassie continued. "Well, I can imagine it. And between Mama and Papa, too. Papa gets that gleam in his eye too, but not recently."

"I'm not listening to this," Charlotte said, tossing a cloth bolt onto the counter. Then another thought occurred. "Have you ever seen that gleam in Edward's eye or Dudley's?"

Cassie frowned. "No, as a matter of fact I haven't. I've seen some gleams, but not quite the same as Uncle Nicholas's or Papa's. Charlotte, there is one other thing I wanted to ask you.

Have you noticed that Mama and Papa have been very cool toward each other?"

"Yes, but I'd hoped I was wrong," Charlotte admitted. Any strain, even the smallest day-to-day friction between Mama and Papa, upset her.

Cassie leaned closer. "Do you have any idea what it is about?"

"Well, Mama was disappointed that Papa was so late to the opera," Charlotte said, barely noticing that she'd just contradicted her denial.

"Oh, Papa has been late to one event after another as long as I can remember, and Mama never seemed to take exception," Cassie said. "Unless it was—"

Charlotte ceased stroking the bolt of cloth on the counter. "It was what?"

"Sir Myron?" Cassie turned around on the stool again, her eyes wide in the disbelief that also fluttered in Charlotte's heart. "Papa seems to have taken a dislike to the man."

"But Mama seems to find Sir Myron very entertaining," Charlotte said. "And it is only because of his work with the Greek antiquities."

"Maybe Papa is jealous."

Charlotte's mouth dropped open. "But Mama would never—"

"You and I know that, but does Papa?"

Charlotte stared at her sister in disbelief. What Cassie was proposing seemed impossible. Papa couldn't possibly believe that Mama would do more than share a charming conversation with a man. And Mama, surely she never worried about competing with another woman for Papa's affections. Mama and Papa—true and faithful to one another. No other conjunction of souls was possible in Charlotte's universe. Mama and Papa were two and one, joined just as the moon circled the earth. Together they shone as constant and bright in Charlotte's sky as the North Star.

"Is this serious?" Charlotte asked, ready to beg Cassie to tell her it wasn't. Her knees felt weak. She caught the shop clerk's attention. "May I have a stool, please?"

"I hope not," Cassie said.

When one was brought and Charlotte was seated, she touched Cassie's arm. "Tell me, is there anything we can do?"

"You know as much as I do," Cassie said with a shrug that Charlotte knew was feigned indifference. "I'm hoping they will get over it."

As they sat staring unseeing at the bolts of fabric before them, their hearts downcast over Mama and Papa, Charlotte realized that the shop clerk had reappeared and was staring at the floor behind them.

Slowly, Charlotte followed his gaze downward and behind her to the sight of a pair of large feet in black leather laced boots, bare legs, and the swaying hem of a kilt. Her heart stopped beating and her gaze darted up in the hope of finding Connor smiling at her. Instead she found herself staring into Erik's dour countenance.

He bowed. "Miss St. John. I hope ye don't mind. Yer man, Horton, told me that I might find ye here."

Charlotte glanced questioningly at Cassie, who shrugged once more and turned to the clerk.

"Would you be so kind as to fetch me the French pattern book?" Cassie said.

Disappointment crossed the clerk's face, but he disappeared toward the back of the shop.

"Yes, Erik, what is it?" Charlotte asked, looking beyond him, still hoping foolishly to catch a glimpse of Connor somewhere.

"His lordship isna with me," Erik said in response to her searching gaze. "But he sent me to ask a favor of ye."

Charlotte turned away, disappointed. "And what might he wish to ask of me?"

Erik shifted awkwardly from one foot to another. "Well, he always carries something for luck into a fight."

"The Scots are so superstitious," Cassie said.

Erik frowned at Cassie. "A man has to do whatever he can to bring good fortune to his ventures."

"Be it prayers or a token?" Cassandra finished.

"Aye, whatever it takes," Erik confirmed without embarrassment. He turned to Charlotte, pointedly ignoring Cassie. "So he—we have a favor to ask of ye, lass."

To cover her curiosity, Charlotte fingered a length of willow green muslin. "Ask."

Erik spoke softly, forcing Cassie to lean over on her stool so far that Charlotte feared her sister would topple to the floor before he finished. "Connor would like a token from ye, for good luck. He said it has to be from ye. No matter if ye donna come to the fight, but he wants to—"

Erik paused, then huffed in seeming frustration. "Truth be, lass, it donna make much sense to me neither, but it be important to Connor, so I'm here asking for something for him to carry with him into the fray."

"If you don't approve of this fight, how can you give him something for good luck?" Cassandra asked.

Charlotte glared at her sister.

Cassandra sat up straight and rearranged her skirts on the stool.

"I think it's touching that Connor should ask for something from me," Charlotte said, genuinely moved. "A token. It's like a knight wearing his lady's colors into the joust."

"Aye, that's it," Erik said in eager agreement, though the bewilderment on his face revealed he hadn't a clue as to what Charlotte meant.

"I do not approve of the fight, but it's not as if I wish the man ill," Charlotte said, reaching for her reticule, which she'd laid aside when she began looking at fabric. As she searched its depths, she wished that she had something more appropriate to give the man who had asked for a good-luck token. She would have liked to give him a lock of her hair neatly tied up with a ribbon and pressed between layers of tissue—or perhaps one of her favorite blue silk scarves. "All I have with me is this handkerchief. It is very dear to me because Mama monogrammed my initials on it in blue. Blue is my color and pink is Cassandra's. See the letters and the flowers right there?"

Erik snatched the handkerchief out of her hand. "Aye, 'tis exactly what Connor needs." He hastily stuffed it into his sporran and backed away as though he was in a great hurry. "Thank ye, lass. Thank ye."

Charlotte and Cassandra sat staring after him as he disappeared out the door and turned down the street.

"What a strange man," Cassandra said.

"Connor relies on him a great deal." Charlotte returned to the fabric. She found, as she fingered the willow green muslin once more, that her heart was strangely lighter than it had been even after they'd come into the store. Lighter than it had been for nearly two weeks.

Connor had not forgotten about her. A little sigh of relief escaped Charlotte. He had not taken mortal offense at their argument in the theater. She hadn't realized until this moment that it meant so much to her to know that he had not lost his regard for her because of her dislike of his fighting.

As he said, boxing was what he did. What he liked to do and he was good at it. Each match had rules and referees. In that sense prizefighting was civilized—just as jousting had been. Had a knight's lady ever refused him the favor of her colors before he went into battle? Of course not, but how many knights' ladies had hidden their eyes from the sight, all the time hoping and praying that their knights understood that they just couldn't witness the combat.

Beside Charlotte, Cassie was flipping unconcerned through a pattern book. "Does this change your mind about going to the fight?"

"No, not one bit," Charlotte said, more certain than ever that she could not watch Connor fight, but satisfied that he would know that she cared. "That morning dress is quite nice."

Charlotte could feel her sister's eyes on her, studying and appraising. She prayed silently that Cassandra would ask no more from her.

Finally Cassandra agreed. "Yes, I like that gown, too. The capelike collar is most unique. Let's order one for each of us."

Charlotte grinned, grateful to Cassie for not pressing her to say more about her feelings than she understood herself. "Yes, let's do order one for each."

TWENTY-THREE

The tinkle and clink of fine gravel striking Charlotte's window brought her out of her restless sleep. There was no mistaking the sound. Someone was in the side garden throwing stones at the window. Whoever was trying to rouse Cassie was aiming at the wrong window.

The landing clock chimed midnight. Annoyed with having her sleep disturbed by her sister's friends, Charlotte flung back the counterpane, padded to the window, parted the draperies, and threw open the sash.

The moon bathed the lawn and garden below, casting it in silvery light and shadow. The figure standing on the grass seemed familiar, but too tall to be Dudley. Shadow cloaked the man's face though it was turned toward her window.

"Charlotte. There you are. It's Tony."

"Tony? You have the wrong window. Cassandra's room is on the corner of the house."

"No, I don't have the wrong window," he called in return. "I've come seeking you. It's Connor."

"What about Connor?" Charlotte demanded, leaning out of the window farther. Connor's match with the Trooper had been fought that afternoon. Cassie and Dudley had gone, leaving early in the day with Aunt Dorian, Uncle Nicholas, and Tony. They had returned jubilant over Connor's victory. He'd trounced the Trooper, but it had been a close fight, according to their accounts.

"The Trooper lived up to every ounce of his reputation," Dudley had asserted.

But their real excitement had been over the riot that broke out afterward. A disagreement had erupted between a bookie and some bloke who had placed a wager with him. The conflict had come to blows which had turned into a brawl which had rapidly escalated to a riot.

Upon hearing the news of the victory, Charlotte had nearly collapsed into a chair. Because of the suspense of the outcome, she'd spent a torturous afternoon of appearing unconcerned about the fight. But it had never left her thoughts. She'd nearly been reduced to sitting at the door awaiting Cassie and Dudley's return.

"Connor won, didn't he?" Charlotte called down to Tony, a niggle of panic threatening her composure. If the bout had ended well, what was Tony doing in their garden at midnight, babbling about Connor? "He's well, isn't he?"

"He won, Charlotte, but it was a brutal fight," Tony called back softly. "He's hurting and he's asking for you."

Charlotte's belly did a little spin and dropped. "Hurt? How badly? Has a physician been called? Where is Erik?"

"The physician has come and gone." Tony shook his head. "Erik is in jail. He got caught in the riot and was arrested by the local magistrate."

"Oh, my." Charlotte pictured Connor alone, without Erik to wait on him. Still she hesitated. It wasn't that she was afraid to go with Tony or that she'd never left the house without her parents knowing about it. She'd done so several times at Cassie's urging. But how hurt could the victor of a fight be? Why would Connor ask for her? Except that there was no one else. And they were friends—she and he had agreed to that.

"Charlotte, the doctor said Connor needs a lot of rest and he has no one there to help him. One eye is swollen shut and he can hardly see."

Charlotte's belly spun once more and sank a little deeper. In her mind's eye she could see Connor, battered and alone, slouch ing in a chair. The image made her heart ache, but it also seemed unreal. Connor helpless?

"What about his cousin Janet?"

"She brought him a basket of food earlier and he was glad to see her, but she couldn't stay," Tony explained. "She can't leave her post at the Foundling Shelter that long. Please say you'll come now, Charlotte. He's asking for you."

"Asking for me?" she repeated softly. Connor asked for her. He was hurt. He was helpless. How could she deny him?

"I've got my carriage here," Tony said, gesturing toward the street. "I'll have you there in a flash. But you must come. Please say you will."

"I'm coming," Charlotte said, her heart aching for Connor, the wounded hero. "Wait there, I'll be right down."

In the next few moments she pulled on a plain gray button-down-the-front walking dress and half boots, tucked her hair into a simple bonnet, grabbed a good, serviceable shawl, and seized her reticule. Without knocking, she burst into Cassie's room.

"Where's the ladder?" she demanded, shaking her twin awake.

Cassie came to the surface slowly, mumbling, "Ladder? What ladder?"

"This is me, Cassie," Charlotte snapped, dropping to her knees and reaching under her sister's bed. "Where did you hide it? Is it still under here? Oh, I've got it."

Charlotte pulled out the rope ladder, navy issue equipment acquired through Tony, who patronized the chandler's shop near the docks. In no time she had Cassie's corner window open and the ladder dropped down the side of the townhouse.

Cassie reared up on her elbows. "Charlotte, what in heaven's name are you doing? You can't go out there without me. And are you going to wear that gown?"

Charlotte stopped, shocked by her sister's selfish assumption. "This is hardly the moment to be worried about fashion. I most certainly can and will go where I like without you."

With that, Charlotte hiked up her skirt and swung her leg over the windowsill as she had done a few times before.

"Where are you going?" Cassie asked, scrambling out of bed at last. "At least tell me what's going on so I can cover with Mama and Papa for you."

"I'm going to see Connor," Charlotte said, clinging to the windowsill and gazing down at the yew shrubs so very far below. She shoved second thoughts and rising panic from her mind. "Tony said he needs me."

As Charlotte watched, confusion, then envy, crossed Cassie's sleep-flushed face before her twin looked away.

"What is it?" Charlotte asked, puzzled by Cassie's hesitancy—she who had been the ringleader of so many adventures.

"Nothing, nothing at all, Charlotte." When Cassandra met Charlotte's gaze again, a soft smile had formed on her lips. She grabbed the rope ladder to steady it for Charlotte. "Godspeed, sister."

"I won," Connor mumbled to himself in the dark, his head throbbing too painfully and his mind too muddled with sleep for him to truly grasp the significance of the feat. He'd been trying to explain it to Charlotte in his dream. The significance. The value. He knew in a fuzzy way that his defeat of the Trooper had been an important—and lucrative—event. The cheers of the crowd still echoed in his head as he tried to roll over on his narrow bed. Aches and pains thwarted every move. The victory left him overjoyed, but Almighty above, he hurt all over—from his toes to his scalp.

He lay on his back now, staring into the darkness. The familiar shadows cast on the ceiling by the streetlamp below told him he was back in his own lodgings. How had he gotten home he wondered. Tony. Yes, Tony. He relaxed against his pillow and relived what had happened starting with the long, arduous journey up the stairs with Tony's help.

"Just lift your foot one more time, Connor, and we'll have you back in your own lodgings," Tony had urged.

Horrified that he was nearly being dragged up the stairs, Connor had tried to pull his arm away from around the young man's shoulders.

Tony grabbed Connor's wrist. "Don't upset the applecart now, man. You'll send both of us tumbling back down these steps and into the street for everyone to see. We can't have the man who pounded the Trooper into the canvas rolling in the gutter, now can we? Hold on, we're about there."

"I won," Connor said, his pride as bruised as his body. "I'm the victor and I don't need help to get home."

"You won in twenty-three exhausting rounds, Connor," Tony said. "And the man was an animal. A helping hand from a friend is no sign of weakness."

At the top of the stairs Connor hesitated, aware that he'd left something undone. "I can't rest yet, Tony. There's something I need to do."

Then he'd remembered the mob scene. The referee had just declared Connor the winner and raised his arms in victory. The crowd roared in jubilation. A whistle shrilled over the thundering voices. The roar lapsed into screams. Magistrates and uniformed local police swarmed down on the spectators.

Tony and Erik scrambled through the ropes; one grabbed Connor by the arm and the other shoved him out of the ring. By then the riot was in full tilt. Spectators, fighters, and fight officials were fleeing in all directions.

Somehow in the chaos a blue-coated officer collared Erik. Connor started after his relative and retainer, but helplessly in the grasp of the blue-coated officer, Erik warned him off. "No! You go, Connor. I can take care of meself."

Confused and befuddled from the long bout, Connor allowed Tony to drag him away. "I remember now. It's Erik. I've got to do something for Erik."

"Let Father take care of Erik," Tony said, gently urging Connor through the door he'd just thrown open. "He said he would.

No one will resist the wishes of the Earl of Seacombe. No offense, Connor, but Nicholas Derrington's influence will go farther than yours right now."

"Right," Connor admitted, slowly stepping into his familiar, low-ceilinged lodgings. He knew without looking in a mirror that he'd make a sorry picture standing in front of a magistrate right now. "I need a tankard of ale."

"You need a physician," Tony countered "Mother has already sent for him. He should be here any moment."

Connor turned on Tony. "I don't need a sawbones with leeches. All I need is a tall, cool yard of ale."

"I'll send for it," Tony said, standing in the middle of the room scanning the litter of clothes, dishes, and newspapers scattered across the table, floor, and chairs. "Your housekeeper hasn't been in today."

Connor laughed—even that hurt—and collapsed into a chair. "What housekeeper?"

The cool wood had felt good against the back of his legs, and he'd closed his eyes, enjoying the solid support of the chair, but he could feel Tony studying him. "It looks worse than it is, lad."

"What?"

"The bruises and the cuts," Connor said, giving himself up to the weariness. He knew what to expect at the end of a fight and it held no terror for him. "I always look worse than I am. Don't take a swollen eye and purple knuckles as cause for concern. A couple days rest and some good roasted beef will put all back into order."

Tony shook his dark head; Connor saw a despairing twist to his mouth, an expression so like his cousin Charlotte's.

The reminder of Charlotte sent a mystifying pang through Connor. He frowned, but even that hurt. Lady Dorian, Lord Nicholas, Tony, Cassie, and Dudley had been at the fight. Connor had seen their open carriage parked prominently among the spectators. Curiously, he thought he'd even glimpsed Sir Edward Seymour among the throng on the other side of the ring. For an agonizing moment—balanced between triumph and rivalry—he'd thought Charlotte might have come in the company of her poet.

But no Charlotte. Her absence left him unaccountably disappointed. What good was a victory without someone to share it with? He'd hoped against hope that she might change her mind at the last moment and decide to attend. Aloud, he chortled at his own foolishness. The abrupt laugh sent a lancing pain through his side.

"What?" Tony started toward him.

Connor stayed him with a hand. "It's nothing a good night's sleep won't heal, lad."

Someone knocked on the door.

"I'll get it," Tony had said, reaching the latch. "It's probably the physician."

And so it had been. The doctor had examined Connor closely, but agreed not to bleed his patient. "He's right, Lord Anthony," the physician had said to Tony. "It looks much worse than it is. He needs good food and rest. He'll live to fight again another day."

"Are you certain?" Tony persisted, hovering over the doctor and Connor. "That eye and the way he groans when he moves."

The doctor shook his head. "Rest is all he needs and a few good meals."

"Hear that?" Connor asked, pleased that the doctor had agreed with him. "Where's my ale?"

Tony had appeared somewhat relieved. As soon as the physician had left, he'd bolted down the stairs and returned from the tavern below with a yard of ale. Connor had downed it, grateful for the cool taste. Just what he needed to slake his thirst.

Over the ale he and Tony agreed that Tony should check on Erik. When Tony had gone, Connor drew Charlotte's handkerchief—a bit bloodied now—from his belt. He wrapped it around his aching knuckles and gingerly stretched himself out on the bed to get the rest the doctor and his body demanded.

Sometime in the early evening, when the lamplighters had been hard at work, Janet had awakened him. She stayed long enough to make him eat a near-feast that she'd managed to pack into a basket. She'd fussed over him, but to Connor's relief, she had not hovered like Tony had done. Janet had tended Connor after more than one fight—not all of them in the ring—and she knew what to expect. She'd entertained him with stories about the children, then dashed off when her time away from the home had come to an end.

His body aching in new places, but his stomach full, Connor had thrown himself down on the bed and slept again, until now. He wondered if Tony had learned anything about Erik or if he'd returned at all.

Finally, he lay in the dark alone, his mind clearing, his memory returning, and the gratification of his victory taking shape in his head. He'd finally taken the important step he needed to earn a bout with the champion. He closed his eyes and took a deep breath. The satisfaction was almost worth every last ache and pain that troubled him now.

His only regret was Charlotte. But too much was at stake to let a missish female keep him from his goal. He wanted to deny that he missed her and her proper ways, but he couldn't. Not to himself, at least. The only solace he had was that she'd readily given up her handkerchief. Erik had described how she'd offered it without pause. Connor smiled into the darkness. He didn't like to think of himself as just another superstitious Scot, but he was certain that lace-edged scrap of linen wrapped around his knuckles had helped him win.

From the street below, the voice of the night watchman called out, "One o'clock in the morning," and "All's well." The watchman's voice had barely faded down the street when Connor heard the clatter of horses' hooves on the cobbles. The equipage stopped below his window. Without troubling himself to move, he wondered who was out at this time of the night.

Maybe Erik had been released at last, Connor thought. His head cleared more. That was good enough news to make him summon the energy to climb out of bed, but as soon as he tried to rise to his feet, dizziness struck him. The shadows whirled around him. Connor sank down onto the bed and put his hands on his head to still the swirling light and shadows.

Someone pounded on the door.

"Connor? Are you asleep?" Tony called, then he knocked again and opened the door a crack. "Connor, Charlotte has come calling. She's concerned about you. May I bring her in?"

TWENTY-FOUR

Connor's dizziness vanished. He raised his head. Charlotte here? Now? At one in the morning? Beyond the door, he could hear Tony talking. "No, Charlotte, I swear I heard him call your name in his sleep, I tell you. He wants to see you."

Charlotte? Suddenly Connor found himself amazingly clear-minded. Charlotte was here. She'd come to see him. The delight was enough to make him laugh. He knew she couldn't stay away. Then another thought occurred to him. He'd heard Tony. Had he called out her name in his sleep? He remembered dreaming of her.

The strange, fragmented dream had begun with a sexy kiss, then transformed into a chase. Charlotte was being stalked by a dream-world lion that was sometimes huge and black and at other times small and weasel-like. The weasel image mystified him, but he knew exactly who the lion was—Forbes. In the dream, no matter how fast Connor ran, he could not catch up with Charlotte. She was always just out of his reach. Connor shook his head. He was not one to put a lot of stock in dreams, but this one had brought Charlotte to his door and he was not going to argue its merit.

He could hear her whispering to Tony. His heart did a strange flipflop, a ridiculous, boyish sensation that he hadn't felt since he'd had a fancy for the miller's daughter—the one who'd taught him the fundamentals of lovemaking.

"Connor, may we come in?" Tony called again.

"No, wait." Connor looked down, aware that he was wearing the same clothes he'd fought in right down to the shirt he'd used like a towel when the other linen had been soaked. It stunk of sweat. When he'd returned, he'd been too weary to bathe or wash without Erik's help.

"Tony, take her home," Connor called, reminding himself that he'd never intended these rooms to be appropriate for receiving guests—especially lady guests. Certainly one in the morning was too late—or too early to receive a proper lady. "I fought yesterday. I'm in no condition to receive guests. Whatever were you thinking to bring her here, man?"

Connor heard the murmur of another conference on the other side of the door. Then Tony spoke up once more. "You know this isn't a social call, Connor. We've come as friends."

"Enough," Charlotte snapped. "We're coming in."

The door swung open, banging against the chair sitting against the wall. Charlotte marched into the room, back stiff and chin high. She halted in the middle of floor. Connor tried to rise, but the aches slowed him. All he could do was watch her searching the shadows for him.

Spying him at last, Charlotte flung aside her shawl and dashed to the bed. Connor managed to gain his feet. She put her hands on his shoulders and attempted to push him down onto the edge of the bed again. But he resisted her, pushing her away at arm's length.

"Go home, Charlotte."

She ignored him. "Light some candles, Tony."

She stood her ground, tearing at her bonnet ribbons. Even in the darkness, Connor could see the determination flashing in her eyes. When the ribbons were loosened, she flung the hat aside and her braid dropped down her back. Though Connor could only see her profile in the darkness, she looked blessedly good to him.

Candlelight flooded the room. Burnished lights leaped in her red hair and the earnest blue of her eyes studied him. Connor was so glad to see her he could hardly resist sweeping her up in his embrace. He forced his arms to remain at his sides and frowned. "Charlotte, you should not be here."

She stared back at him, apparently unmoved by his cool reception. "There's no other place I'd rather be."

"Charlotte—"

"Bring a candle closer, Tony," she ordered, cutting off Connor's protest. "Let's have a look at you, Lord Kinleith. Let's see just how bad the damage is."

"It's not as serious as it looks," Connor found himself repeating.

Tony brought a candle closer as Connor stared at Charlotte, pleasure and embarrassment warring inside him. Given her views on fighting, he'd have preferred she not see him like this, bruised and unsteady. In a day or two, he wouldn't mind. The swelling would be gone, the bruises faded, and he'd have his feet under him. But not now. Not with his head still throbbing.

Charlotte stood in front of him, her fists braced on her hips, her neck slightly arched in order to look up at him. There was a defiance in her stance that was new to Connor, but not altogether foreign to her character.

How was it that he'd never noticed that her throat was so long and slender—so exposed? The pleasure of seeing her made him long to touch her fragile neck. Starting at the base of her throat where the frantic pulse was beating, he allowed his gaze to meander downward along the row of buttons to the shadow beneath the muslin that hinted at a deep cleft between her breasts. She was breathing rapidly. Muslin and buttons strained dangerously to contain her bosom. Even in his condition, Connor found it damnably difficult to keep his gaze off that private spot.

Under his scrutiny the starch seemed to evaporate from Charlotte's stance. Her hand fluttered uneasily at the top button, which held his attention once more.

"You look dreadful," she said, her voice soft and pleasantly familiar to his ear. She looked away when he searched her face again.

You look delicious. The words longed to form on the tip of his tongue, but he would not say them. She should not be here, but her refusal to leave did not diminish his growing estimation of her. Whatever had made him think she had no courage? What other proper British miss would present herself in a prize-fighter's lodgings in the middle of the night simply because her cousin had convinced her the man had uttered her name? Soft-hearted Charlotte. All he could bring himself to say was, "You shouldn't have come."

"What should I have done? Sit down." Charlotte put her hands on his shoulders and urged him to sit on the edge of the bed. "I'm already here, so let's not argue about it, shall we? It strikes me as quite contradictory that you would rather I watched you beaten in the ring, then disappear while you lick your wounds without help."

He had no reply to that.

She studied his face, her eyes searching for damage, he assumed.

When her face crumpled up, Connor feared she was going to cry. "Connor, your eye."

"Charlotte, believe me, lass, it's not as bad as it looks," he hastened to explain once again. "The physician said so. Tell her, Tony. Lord, get her out of here. Whatever possessed you to bring her here anyway?"

"You were calling her name," Tony insisted, as if that exonerated him from all crimes. "I heard you mumbling in your sleep."

Connor peered over Charlotte's head at her cousin.

"I swear you did, Connor," Tony said. "And with Erik in jail and Janet gone, I thought—"

"Erik won't be released until tomorrow or the day after," Charlotte said. "Tony says Uncle Nicholas is seeing to it. So now we must tend to you. I'd say that eye requires a slab of beefsteak. Tony, find the butcher."

"It's one in the morning," Tony protested.

"I'm sure you can manage," Charlotte said, leaning closer to

Connor. "And you—" Charlotte's voice broke again. "Connor, what are we going to do with you?"

"Well, I'll leave you two to sort it out," Tony said and backed out of the room. "I'll find meat somewhere. Beefsteak?"

"Yes. Raw beefsteak." Charlotte still stood before Connor; her bedtime braid had come to rest on her shoulder and lay shining against her bosom, rising and falling with her breath. The movement, soothing and stimulating all at once, held Connor mesmerized.

Without warning, Charlotte lifted her hand.

Connor almost jumped when she ran her fingers through his tangled hair. The touch was so unexpected and tender that he closed his eyes, allowing himself to experience the sensation throughout his body.

"Did I hurt you?" Charlotte whispered, bending closer, her scent reaching him at last.

Connor opened his eyes and met Charlotte's soft, blue-eyed gaze. He saw such caring and tenderness there he almost forgot to breathe. His aches and pains slipped away. The urge to touch her was overwhelming. He felt almost good enough to dance around the room with Charlotte in his arms. He forced himself to take a deep breath and let his head instead of his loins prevail.

Just what would Charlotte do if she learned he would be as good as new after a night's rest and a good meal? She would probably spring for the door like a hare before the hound, he reasoned. If he knew her as well as he thought, Miss Charlotte preferred to believe that he'd suffered from his ordeal in the ring and his recovery required her attentions.

Pride be damned, Connor decided.

He allowed himself to slump a bit on the edge of the bed. He closed his eyes and forced a moan from his lips. "Yes, that does hurt some."

"Your head?" Charlotte asked, touching his stubbled cheek with the back of her hand. "Or your ribs or what?"

"Everything," Connor lied, his mind racing to think of his next complaint. Where did he want to be touched? The truth was, the pain had become somewhat embarrassingly localized. The aches from the fight were fading in the presence of a more persistent pain. Connor wanted Charlotte—not with the same desire that had made him flirt with her, bedeviling her until she surrendered to his demands for kisses. That had been a mere game.

Only a moment ago he'd wanted to lock her outside, but now he'd do damned near anything to keep her within these four walls. He truly wanted her—to hold, possess, protect, and please her in any fashion required. This was a new sort of desire to Connor, but it did not frighten him. "Perhaps, if you could stay for a bit—"

"Of course, I'll be glad to help," Charlotte said, her breath brushing warm against his cheek. "Whatever I can do to make you more comfortable, just ask."

"I will," Connor said. "I promise I will."

TWENTY-FIVE

"Then, do you feel too bad to clean up?" Charlotte asked, speaking as lightly as she could to hide her shock at the sight of Connor's swollen eye, cut lip, and purpled jaw. She didn't want him to know how dreadful he looked to her, but the sight of his dark good looks all battered and bruised was enough to make her weep. Pressing her lips together, she met his gaze levelly, swallowed the lump in her throat, and held back the tears. She was here to help him and tears were useless.

"Yes, washing up is a good idea." Connor rested heavily on the bed as though he was unable to get to his feet. "I was too weak before."

"Of course." Charlotte looked around the room, taking in the disorder. Exasperation pursed her lips. Obviously the housekeeper had not been in for some time. And how did one go about arranging for a bath?

"There's fresh water in the pitcher on the wash table," Connor said, as if he'd heard her thoughts. "I think there might be more in the kettle over the fire. I feel better now. I'll just wash up and put on clean clothes."

When he tried to rise again, he groaned. Clamping a hand to his side, he dropped back down on the edge of the bed.

Charlotte grabbed his free arm to support him. "Now don't try to be the brave soul after that brutal fight. Take it easy. Tony said the physician wanted you to rest and eat a good meal. Do you have any food here?"

"Janet brought some bread, cheese, and fruit," Connor said, gesturing toward the basket on the table. "But I've eaten once already and I'd rather clean up."

"You rest here and I'll see to the water and your clothes," Charlotte said. When she was satisfied that Connor was safe on the bed, she investigated the basin on the table in the corner of the room.

"Yes, the water is fresh, just as you said," Charlotte replied, picking the linen from the floor. "But these towels are used."

"But only once," Connor said. "They're good for another round, at least. Now what are you looking for?"

Charlotte glanced about the room once more. "Where is your dressing room?"

She turned to Connor as he sputtered into a coughing fit which had begun suspiciously like laughter. But she could see he was in far too much discomfort for merriment.

"I'm afraid the accommodations do not afford a dressing room," Connor finally managed to choke out.

"Then where are your clean clothes?"

"In the wardrobe," Connor said, still coughing.

Indeed, in the wardrobe Charlotte found what she was looking for, clean shirts and more heaped in a jumble on the shelves. "There's a dressing gown here."

"I am that civilized," Connor quipped with a surprisingly healthy dose of sarcasm in his voice.

Charlotte chose to ignore it. "Are you sure you don't want me to order you a bath? Surely these lodgings provide that."

"A wash in the basin is fine," Connor said without moving.

"Ah, well, will you need help washing?" Charlotte looked around the room again, wondering how they were going to accomplish this task with as little embarrassment to either of them as possible.

"I can manage to wash and shave myself, thank you," Connor said, the coughing fit having subsided. He watched her from the bed as though to gauge her reaction to his next statement.

"But I will need some help getting over there, clear across the room."

"Yes, of course, I'll be glad to do what I can." Charlotte arranged the dressing gown next to the towels, soap, and razor on the washstand. Then she hurried across the room to Connor's side. "Here, put your arm around my neck and lean on me."

Connor stared up at her for a long moment. He seemed to be studying her throat again. "Connor? Are you going to be able to do this?"

"Lord, I hope so," he whispered. He got up slowly, leaning so close to her that his lips almost brushed against her bare throat as he rose. The contact sent a thrill through Charlotte. She sucked in a quick breath and chided herself for her silliness. This was no time to act like a giddy miss. Determined, she braced herself to bear as much of his weight as she could.

Connor's arm slipped around her neck and clutched her shoulder almost painfully as he steadied himself. Charlotte staggered a bit under his massive body but managed to steady herself. Then she slipped her arm around his waist. He smelled very much like a man who needed to bathe, but to her surprise the scent was not unpleasant; it was Connor, musky and piney. It made her lightheaded.

"Am I too heavy?" Connor's warm breath tickled her ear.

"No, as long as you feel well enough to walk, I think we're all right," Charlotte said, looking up into his face so near her own that she could see the shadow of his day-old beard. "If you don't feel up to it, we can wait until Tony returns."

"No, we can do this, you and I," Connor said, gazing down into her eyes with a confidence that made her feel strong and brave. With a firm hand he drew her arm close around his waist. The hard cords of his back moved against the bare inside of her elbow and her breast pressed intimately against his ribs beneath his shirt. A strange warmth grew inside Charlotte—from the inside out—and she knew it had nothing to do with Connor's body heat.

"That's better." Connor released her shoulder and his arm

dangled dangerously close to her bosom. "Now if we walk slowly, I think we'll be fine."

So they started off across the room, Connor leaning heavily on her shoulder, his cheek pressed against her hair.

"Have I grown too heavy yet?" he asked, his chin pressed against the top of her head.

"No, of course, not," Charlotte insisted. But his weight against her lightened suddenly, yet his proximity to her did not change. "We've almost reached the wash table. See, here we are."

"That didn't take long," he muttered, sounding oddly disappointed. Charlotte slipped out from under his arm. He leaned heavily against the table with both arms braced on the edge and his head down.

"Steady enough?" she asked, noting that Connor's right hand was bound. She touched it lightly so as not to cause him any pain. "What's this?"

"This?" Connor lifted his right hand and slowly unwrapped a bloodied lady's handkerchief from around his knuckles. He held it up for her inspection. "Sorry, about the condition."

Astonished and touched, Charlotte stared at the lace-trimmed good-luck token she'd given Erik in the draper's shop. "You carried my handkerchief into the ring?"

"Wrapped around my hand just as you saw," Connor said, a grin spreading across his battered face at last. "You know, I think it brought me luck."

His pleasure coaxed a reluctant smile to Charlotte's lips as she looked up at him. "I'm glad you won, Connor, truly I am."

"Then give the victor a kiss."

She laughed, immensely relieved to know he was well enough to devil her. She stretched up to brush a kiss along his cheek, but he caught her shoulders—surprising strength in his grip—and pressed his lips firmly against hers.

His grasp tightened on her shoulders. Charlotte tilted her face up to his, too eager to know his kiss again to resist. He smelled of sweat and blood, and she didn't care. He was in her arms again. She wondered ever so briefly if their separation had been as bleak for him as it had been for her. The sun had shone in the sky every day, but her life had been dark without his prodding and teasing.

When he took her mouth again, she opened to him like a flower, inviting him to deepen the kiss and steal away her breath and good sense. The tang of ale was an unexpected flavor on his tongue; she was delighted to offer herself to him once more. She moved her lips against his and stroked the powerful contours of his back. His grip on her grew painful, but it was he who groaned.

Suddenly she feared he was asserting himself more than he should. She pushed away. "You shouldn't be squandering your strength like this."

He uttered a sound suspiciously like a chuckled curse, but she knew he was too injured for that kind of levity.

His lips brushed along her ear to her jaw. The melting that had begun inside her with his first touch continued.

"Sorry, kitten," he whispered against her ear. Charlotte's senses lurched. What did he have to be sorry about? She licked her lips, longing for more of him.

"I forget what a sorry sight I must be," Connor murmured, his lips moving tantalizingly against her ear.

Charlotte shivered.

"Let's reserve the victor's kiss for when I'm cleaned up."

Breathless, Charlotte steadied herself against the table, waiting for her knees to stop shaking. "Yes, later."

He turned toward the basin. "You've laid everything out already."

"You can manage on your own from here, can't you?" Charlotte asked, still trembling, still overwhelmed by the solid maleness of him that drew her close. She hoped she'd laid out the proper things. She'd glimpsed Papa at his shaving mirror from time to time, but she knew little else about a man's toilet. "Soap razor, towels, dressing gown."

"Perfect," Connor said, drawing away from her and eagerly scanning the things she had laid out.

Charlotte hesitated, uncertain how to phrase her next questions. "Ah, do you need my help with anything more? Perhaps with your shirt?"

"No." Connor's response was short and sharp. "I can manage fine. Why don't you sit by the window and watch the sun rise or something." He gestured toward the other side of the room.

"Sunrise? I'll sit by the window, but I think it's a bit early for the sun to come up," Charlotte said, noting the chair Connor indicated, its back turned toward the washbasin. "Let me prepare the water for you. Then I'll just catch a breath of fresh air while you wash. But if you need help—we need not stand on useless proprieties."

"Of course, but I can manage this for myself," Connor said, his lips thin either in pain or determination, she wasn't certain which.

"Good. Here's the hot water." Charlotte took the kettle from over the banked fire and warmed the water in the basin. When she left Connor, he was reaching for the tail of his shirt.

She turned her back on him to appraise the chaos that she'd ignored when she'd first entered. She picked her way across the room toward the chair at the window. The clutter was appalling. Clothing, papers, tankards, and plates littered every surface. Obviously someone was not doing her job. "I shall have a word with the housekeeper immediately upon the morrow."

"No need to trouble yourself," Connor said over his shoulder. "We don't have a housekeeper. The landlady, Mrs. Needham, provides breakfast and laundry. Nothing more."

"Connor, how do you live like this?" Charlotte asked, finding the setting completely unacceptable. "Don't you know that a disorderly room is bad for one's peace of mind?"

"Never troubled mine or Erik's," Connor said. Water splashed in the basin. "Erik takes care of some things."

"He needs to do more." Charlotte reached for a stray sock dangling over the edge of the table and shook her head. How was she to remedy the situation if she couldn't give orders to the housekeeper?

Charlotte contemplated the chaos once more. How different could setting a room to rights be from putting her study to order? Upon specific instructions, the maids never touched her books and papers. Charlotte had her own system. Keep your wits about you and deal with one thing at a time, she told herself as she stared at the bachelors' anarchy. That's how she organized her study when the disorder had gone too far. Inspired by her plan, she reached for the discarded shirt slung across the back of a chair. "What do you do about laundry?"

"Erik leaves the laundry by the door," Connor said. "Mrs. Needham comes for it in the morning."

Mrs. Needham would have a goodly armload to carry away when Charlotte was finished. She tossed the garments toward the door where they landed with a rustle.

In the silence the additional sound of rustling fabric caught her ear. She paused, another dirty shirt in her hand, paralyzed with the realization that Connor was undressing not ten feet from her. He'd be wearing next to nothing and standing in the same room with her. Quickly she grabbed more garments and moved noisily around the room so neither of them could forget her presence—or his *déshabillé*.

Soon the pile at the door had grown to knee-high. She could hear the splash as Connor dipped into the washbasin. Nervously she began to gather the news sheets, shaking the paper as she went.

"The newspapers should have fine stories about the fight out tomorrow," she chattered awkwardly, endeavoring to fill the silence and her mind with images other than Connor's bare chest. She'd glimpsed it once at the first fight nearly two months ago and she did not need to see it again to make her cheeks burn with embarrassment. "Tony will buy a copy of each newspaper and read every last one. I suppose you and Erik do the same."

"Erik buys them. I never read about my own fights," Connor said. She could hear him lathering the soap on himself. He mind's eye teased her with an image of Connor smearing soap bubbles through the gleaming dark hairs of his bare chest.

Charlotte's mouth went dry. She began bustling around the room more loudly, rattling the newspapers and scraping chairs around the floor toward the table. Then she stopped.

"You don't read the newspaper stories? Why not?" His admission seemed odd to her. The Brawlin' Scot she knew loved attention.

"I don't know," Connor said. She could tell by his voice that his back was still to her and he was speaking over his shoulder—a broad, well-muscled shoulder. "I guess because when I read the journalists' comments I always wonder if we were really at the same event. Of course, the writer saw it from his perspective outside the ring, but it looked different to me on the canvas."

"Of course." Charlotte reached for another news sheet hung over the back of one of the chairs. "But do you not want the public attention?"

Connor paused so long, Charlotte almost wondered if he'd heard her.

"Only because it will lead to the fight I want, the championship match," he said with a shrug of indifference.

"I see." She tossed the papers into a stack and found a tray with as much clatter as she could manage and began to gather the used cups and plates. But she knew as she cleared the table of everything except for Janet's basket, she was only mouthing polite words. "No, actually, I don't see. You want this big fight to win the money to buy a piece of property called Glen Gray. So which is important? The property or the fight?"

"Aye, both," Connor said. "I win one to gain the other."

"But why is Glen Gray so important?"

Charlotte heard Connor rinse his razor in the water. "Glen Gray belonged to the McKensies before the Battle of Culloden. It was confiscated by the English after the Scottish defeat. We want it back."

"But I thought it belonged to the Clan Forbes," Charlotte

said, recalling something her father had said about the Marquis of Linirk trying to purchase Glen Gray. She allowed herself to sink down on a chair at the table. "So who owned it before we—the English confiscated it?"

"The McKensies." Then Connor was silent for a long moment. Charlotte heard him draw the razor along his jaw again, then the splash of soap lather dropped into the water. "But once the property belonged to Clan Forbes, very long ago."

"And—?" Charlotte looked up from the table. With a shock she caught sight of a naked man reflected in the mirror between the windows. His back was to her and he had no idea she was watching him. Guiltily she tried to look away from Connor's reflection. But she was too hungry for the sight of him and too curious about the mysteries of the male body, of which she knew so little. His beauty drew her gaze back to the mirror.

She devoured every detail of him standing with his back to her without a stitch of clothing on, his feet braced, his back straight, and his shoulders square. Charlotte couldn't look away and her breath came in quick, shallow gasps.

She studied anew the beauty that had captured her the first day she had seen him. The dark curls against his strong neck gleamed in the candlelight. The muscles of his broad, well shaped shoulders rippled with power as he shaved. The gentle 'S' curve down the middle of his back flexed as he bent to scoop water to rinse the remaining soap from his face. The movement drew Charlotte's eyes down to his narrow waist and below, to the tight behind and the long, muscular thighs.

Charlotte dragged her gaze to the floor and took a deep breath. The rest of his leg—the shape of his calf—she was familiar with. But her unruly gaze strayed once again. She wanted to see for herself once more the three long, white, parallel scars across his back, the only mar in his beauty. The lion he'd told her of, she thought, and wondered what it would be like to touch those scars, to feel their texture beneath her fingers or her lips. With that thought, the air in the room became uncomfortably hot. Charlotte began fanning herself with her hand, bolting from the chair in order to deliver herself from the spell of Connor's reflection in the mirror.

"It's warm in here, don't you think?" she said, wondering how long Tony was going to take anyway. "I believe I shall open this other window, too. Now, what was it you were saying about Glen Gray?"

"So you would have the entire story of Glen Gray?" Connor asked, his voice muffled by the towel he was using.

Charlotte allowed herself to peek into the mirror again. She noted with some perplexity that his stance was remarkably solid and steady for a man exhausted from a prizefight. This time she did not pull her gaze away from the image in the glass. Surely it was not too sinful for a girl to gaze upon such beauty, especially if the man seemed so unconcerned about the possibility. "Yes, I would have it all—the whole story of Glen Gray, I mean."

TWENTY-SIX

"I'll tell you as much of the history of Glen Gray as I know," Connor said, his back to Charlotte.

Finally she turned away from the mirror, listening to the silken rustle of the dressing gown as he pulled it on.

"I believe the story began sometime in the late 1500s when a Forbes lass was promised to a McKensie." Connor padded barefoot toward the table. When he sat down across from her, he was wrapped in gold silk, his dark hair wet and tousled and his chest hair gleaming black at the 'V' of the throat. The scent of soap and his natural piney fragrance drifted to Charlotte.

Even with a black eye, he was a handsome man. The image of his strong, naked backside drifted through her mind once more. Her heart fluttered. Charlotte studied the tabletop in the hopes that he would not see the blush his nearness brought to her cheeks.

He talked on, clearly oblivious to her reactions. "It was a love match, they said. But both families were pleased with the arrangement, I believe. The Forbeses were satisfied to have an alliance with a Highland clan with grazing land and the McKensies glad enough to connect with the influential Lowland family."

"What happened? Did one of the couple cry off?" Charlotte asked, forcing herself to pick up the thread of the story.

"No, they were wed and it was a happy occasion with relatives and retainers traveling from far and wide to be part of th celebration," Connor said, peering at Janet's basket. "You know, I am hungry even after that feast Janet put before me. What's left in here?"

Charlotte rose and pulled off the cloth napkins to better explore the basket's contents. "It looks as if we have half a bottle of wine, some cheese, bread, and fruit."

"Pour the wine." Connor took the cheese and bread and began to slice off hunks of each.

Charlotte found one clean cup in the basket and held it up.

"We'll share it," Connor said, clearly unconcerned about the lack of refinements for their meal. "Here, have some cheese and bread. You must be hungry, too."

Charlotte accepted the food and sat down again as Connor poured their wine. "And so it was a big, happy wedding. Glen Gray became a McKensie property. A dowry gift?"

"Aye, and all was blissful for about six months," Connor continued, going to work on the apple Charlotte had fished from the basket. "The couple lived in a well-fortified house on the west coast. But not fortified well enough. One night pirates raided the house and the bride was taken captive and never seen alive again."

The cheese in Charlotte's mouth lost its flavor. "Heavens, how dreadful."

"According to the story, her husband was distraught beyond words," Connor said, handing her a slice of apple. "He offered a reward for her return. He sailed the seas for years, searching for her. Stories came to him of a ghost ship with a Scottish lass crying for help from the deck, but he never found her."

Charlotte swallowed the glob of cheese, the ghost ship taking shape in her head so that she could almost hear the poor girl's cries through an evil fog. "How horrible."

Connor frowned and handed her the cup of wine. " 'Tis but an old tale, Charlotte. Don't let it upset you."

Charlotte washed down the cheese with a draught of wine. "And Glen Gray. What happened to it?"

"Aye, well the Forbes Clan was most unhappy that their female relative had not been better protected. There was even some hint that perhaps the young husband had actually done her in. But no one on the McKensie side gives credit to that idea. Remember this all happened before the couple had even been married a full year and there were no children. Since there were no true heirs, the Forbes Clan demanded return of the dowry property, Glen Gray."

"And what did the McKensies do?"

"We refused, of course," Connor said, slicing off more cheese and bread with a thump. "As I understand it, the groom was so distraught, so grieved, and so determined to find her that for years he refused to declare her dead. If she was not dead, why should he even consider returning the dowry?"

"So that was the beginning of the famous feud?" Charlotte finished.

"Aye, that's it," Connor agreed. "But that is not all there is to the story."

Hoping for a happier ending, Charlotte perked up. "They found the bride?"

"Oh, no, she was long gone, poor girl," Connor said, settling back in his chair as if indifferent about one poor girl's life. Apparently he had a much longer story to tell. "The feud soon turned nasty and there were a number of bloody raids back and forth between the clans for the next century. Sheep stolen. Homes burned and lives lost. By the early seventeen hundreds a well-meaning churchman suggested that a single pitched battle be fought between the two clans to settle ownership of the property and bring peace to all. The victor—McKensie or Forbes—would win Glen Gray."

"A sort of duel," Charlotte said, fascinated by the barbaric simplicity of the solution.

"Aye, a duel of armies," Connor said. "The churchman was clever and sincere, I think, and he got the laird of each clan to agree to the battle and a time and place."

Charlotte perched on the edge of her chair. "Who won?"

" 'Tis not that simple," Connor said, chopping up the last o the apple with a resounding thud of the knife against the wooden table. "You see, the Forbeses actually won the battle on the field, but everyone knows they cheated."

"Cheated?" Charlotte was beginning to understand why the British found dealing with the Scots so exasperating. "But a churchman arranged this. How could they cheat?"

"At the last of the battle, they brought in more men," Connor said. " 'Twas stipulated how many men could be on the field, but just as the McKensies were about to be victorious, a second force of Forbeses swarmed down onto the field. They brought in more than their allotted number. The battle only succeeded in deepening the feud. The McKensies were nigh butchered. The churchman was so shocked and disappointed that the McKensies were allowed to hold the title to the land until the defeat of Scottish forces at Culloden in 1746."

"At which time the property was confiscated," Charlotte filled in for him, not very proud of being British at the moment.

"The McKensies who fought with the Jacobite cause were allowed to retain only the lands entailed by the earldom. The remaining clan properties, including Glen Gray, were usurped by the Crown."

"And in due time Glen Gray came into Papa's possession," Charlotte murmured, suddenly reminded of the true reason for Connor's interest in her. She wondered if her heart was to be one more victim of a three-century long Scottish feud. Raising her head, she studied Connor once more. "So you want the return of Glen Gray just to keep it out of Forbes hands?"

"No, 'tis more to it than that," Connor said, reaching across the table for her hand. Charlotte allowed him to take it. "Glen Gray is a considerably large property and it was of vital economic value to the clan. Many McKensies and their retainers have suffered from the loss over the years. We need that property, Charlotte. I don't fight for Glen Gray because I'm a damned good fighter, though I won't deny that I've always loved a good brawl. I fight for the glen because it means bread in the mouths of McKensie children. Janet does what she can for the starving children. She came to London because all the children of the world are hers. But the clan children are mine, my responsibility."

He squeezed Charlotte's hand as if to press home his point.

She squeezed in return, understanding so much more than she had before. "I'm so glad you told me the story behind the feud."

"I don't expect that to change your feelings about boxing," Connor said with a shrug.

"I'm afraid it doesn't," Charlotte admitted, feeling as if she had to remind him that she could offer him little help. "And you know I have no influence over Papa and his business affairs."

"Charlotte," Connor said with a soft smile. He leaned forward, bringing her fingers to his lips. "That was never why we embarked on this friendship in the first place."

His lips brushed warm and firm against her knuckles. She watched, charmed and touched. The gesture was so spontaneous and genuine, so unlike the practiced motions of a society gentleman, that tears momentarily welled in her eyes.

"I know," she whispered, finding her natural voice untrustworthy. How she wanted to believe him.

The jingle of a carriage in the street reached them through the open windows.

Connor's head came up and he straightened in his chair. "That must be Tony."

"Yes, indeed, Tony," Charlotte repeated, trying to free herself from the enchantment that Connor had just cast over her. "You stay right here. I'll let him in."

Tony returned with a slab of beefsteak, sausages, and a ham. He set out his loot on the table before them with the light of victory gleaming in his eyes.

"Once I made the butcher open his shop, I had to make it worth his while," the young man explained as Charlotte stared in astonishment at the amount of meat on the table.

She laughed in her amazement. "You did well, Tony, and I'm sure Sir Butcher returned to bed satisfied with the exchange."

"Well, he should have, I gave him . . ." Tony glanced at Connor.

"Present the charges to Erik," Connor said, admiring the ham.

"I'll hear no more of commerce," Charlotte said, unwrapping a small slab of red meat. "We have a patient to heal, Tony. Lean back, Connor."

Charlotte advanced on him with the beefsteak.

"Wait—what are you going to do with that?"

"I'm going to put this on your eye to take down the swelling," Charlotte said, aiming for the right side of his face. "Now sit right there. Don't try to get up. This is going to feel good. You'll see."

"I'm at your mercy, kitten." Connor settled back into his chair and grinned up at her. "You'll be gentle, won't you?"

Charlotte blushed, aware that he was playing some man-woman game that she didn't quite understand—but oh, how she longed to. His teasing did not keep her from applying the cool slab of meat against his black eye.

As Tony looked on, Connor groaned—a long, drawn-out sound of shock, then relief. "Aye, lass, 'tis cool. You told the truth of it."

"I can't believe you never put steak on a black eye," Charlotte said. "After all your fighting."

"At home, I just threw myself into the nearest icy stream," Connor said, his eyes closed. "And where did you, learned-miss-of-the-study, acquire this particular bit of healing wisdom?"

Charlotte exchanged a glance with Tony, who shrugged.

"I believe it was something that Cassie learned from the boxing matches," Charlotte admitted. She reached for Connor's hand to place it on the meat. "Now, you hold the meat in place."

Connor caught her fingers with his before she could move away. "No, my arms are too weary. You'll have to hold it to my eye for however long this takes."

Charlotte looked helplessly toward Tony. Her cousin shook his head. He was no help at all.

"If you don't need anything more, I've got to get home," Tony said, starting toward the door. "Mother will have my hide when she finds I've been out and about like this. Are you ready to go, Charlotte?"

Consternation seized Charlotte. "But I can't leave yet. I want to see some improvement in Connor's eye."

"Of course," said Tony, reluctance crossing his youthful face. "But how will you get home?"

"I'll see that she gets home safely," Connor said, the authority of an older man in his voice. "I'll send her home in a cab. There's usually one at the corner."

"Yes, of course," Charlotte agreed, though she'd never taken a cab, let alone any sort of carriage ride alone in Town.

"I'll be back tomorrow as soon as I've seen what I can do for Erik," Tony said. Then he was gone, the clatter of his carriage swiftly fading down the street.

Connor patted his knee. "Sit down and rest yourself, kitten. You're safe here with me."

"Well, of course I am," Charlotte said, sounding more casual to her own ears than she truly felt. Suddenly she realized what a delicate position she truly was in: an unmarried miss visiting a gentleman in his bachelor lodgings in the dead of the night. Edward and her literary friends—though they loved to dabble in scandalous things—would think the situation highly improper. But Cassie or Aunt Dorian would only be concerned that she was keeping safe company. Could Connor be considered safe?

Charlotte eyed the injured man with beefsteak over his eye. He was safe company for the time being, anyway. She perched on his knee.

"This doesn't feel so good anymore," Connor mumbled from beneath the slab of meat.

"That's because the meat has taken the fever from your injury," Charlotte explained, moving to the table and cutting off another piece of meat. "Now you discard the old and put on a fresh one."

Gently she removed the first piece. As she bent over him, Connor opened his eyes. The swelling had gone down some. His gaze met hers. She was fascinated by the topaz gold of his eyes and the dark sable thickness of his lashes—Apollo's golden eyes.

With a start she realized he was staring at her mouth.

"Is it time for the victor's kiss?" he asked in a deep, husky voice.

TWENTY-SEVEN

Charlotte stared down at Connor. The neck of his dressing gown had fallen open and a broad, expanse of his chest lay before her. She longed to touch him, a longing she knew was far too improper to even allow herself to contemplate. "No, it is not time for the victor's kiss."

Instead of giving in to the temptation to kiss him, she slapped the fresh piece of steak over his eye. Connor winced and groaned—out of shock this time, she was certain.

"Why not?" Connor asked, the large piece of meat she had pressed to his face muffling his voice.

"I'd like to see you looking more like a winner before I kiss you," Charlotte fibbed, turning away so he could not see her face with his one uncovered eye.

She dared not tell him how beautiful he was to her, even with his blackened eye, his hair wet and uncombed from his bathing and his body bruised from fighting—even with a piece of beefsteak on his face. He was beautiful to her and she loved him. The realization flooded through her like an emotional rip tide.

Heaven help her, she loathed fighting, but she would kiss him if he won or if he lost. No matter. She loved him. The immensity of the emotion threatened to drown all her good sense.

No matter how much she abhorred fighting, she loved Connor. Whether he fought for money or the pure love of the spectators' cheers, she loved him. That was why she could never watch him fight. Each blow to his jaw would make her head throb and each body jab would make her belly ache. She had neither the stamina nor the courage to watch round after round.

Her lack of courage was why he would never love her. She had no fortitude. No backbone. She could never be a Janet or a detached spectator like Aunt Dorian. She could not be the kind of woman who could watch Connor beat a man and be beaten in return.

As much as she longed to be more than she was for him, Charlotte knew it was not within her being to be what he wanted and needed her to be.

Charlotte frowned.

"Well, I don't much like the looks of that sad face," Connor said, the half of his face that was not covered frowning back at her. "What's the trouble, kitten?"

Charlotte shook her head.

Distracted and dismayed by the sudden comprehension of the impossible chasm yawning between them, Charlotte's heart ached. She could not look at him.

"Tony called you from your bed, didn't he?" Connor murmured, reaching for her braid.

Charlotte nodded. "I was fast asleep."

As she watched, powerless to object, Connor's agile fingers pulled the knot from her hair ribbon, tossed it aside, and began to unbraid her hair. He touched only her hair, but Charlotte could feel each brush of his fingers.

When most of the braid was unraveled, Connor said, "Shake your hair loose."

Charlotte did as he asked. He smiled, his single eye clearly taking pleasure in the sight of her. Charlotte suddenly knew that she was drifting into uncharted waters. The idea surprised her, but it did not shock her. She had no fear of him. For reasons she could not possibly put into words, she trusted him—even longed for him—to touch her in the sweetest and gentlest ways.

"Let's see how your eye is doing now," Charlotte said, endeavoring to break the spell she could feel descending over her—and Connor, too. Carefully she peeled away the meat and was relieved to see that the swelling had subsided considerably.

"Can I wash my face now?" Connor asked, his eyes still closed as she examined the results of her remedy.

"Yes, it must feel sticky." Charlotte picked up a damp towel from the table and began to clean Connor's face. He did not move nor did he open his eyes. She took her time, lovingly wiping the evidence of the meat from each plane and contour around his eye, his brow, and nose. She found an old scar just below his lower lip and satisfied herself that the cut in his brow from his previous fight was healing nicely.

She could have gone on forever, exploring his face, but she could feel a strange force gather inside of him. She drew the towel away. "Is that better?"

"Aye." Connor's voice was low and rough.

Before she could rise and move away from him, he opened his eyes and captured her gaze. "Much better. Don't stop, if you don't want to. Touch me here."

Connor pressed her hand against his bare chest. His springy chest hair tickled her palm. Beneath her hand his heart beat rapidly.

A tender devilishness gleamed in his eye. Before she realized what he was doing, he bent to kiss her throat. Charlotte checked any movement, afraid he might stop trailing feathery kisses along her neck. She closed her eyes and clung to him, giving herself over to the delightful magic he stirred in her. She raked her fingers along his hard chest, widening the opening of his dressing gown. She whimpered with pleasure.

When he lifted his head and she opened her eyes, she found him breathing heavily and his heart thundering beneath her palm.

"Listen to me, kitten," he murmured. Fiery gold flashed in his eyes. "You've got me huffing like I've just gone ten rounds."

"I did that?"

"And you don't even know what you're doing," he said.

They held each other's gaze. Then slowly, his right hand

trailed over the slender arch of her neck, tracing the modest neckline of her walking gown. Her heart raced. His fingers drifted lower, working each button holding the muslin taut across her breasts.

At last his hand settled on her breast, fitting snugly over the full, generous mound cupped in his palm. She was embarrassed to see herself nubby and protruding against his hand.

He did not move. When she met his gaze again, she found the heat of his eyes searching her face. She fought to take a breath. He was waiting for a sign from her, a signal to go ahead.

"Does this frighten you, kitten?" he asked, his voice still rough—yet soft.

"Yes," she admitted, then realized that was the wrong answer. She grasped his wrist before he could take his hand away. "I mean, no. I mean, I've never been touched like that, but it feels—delightful."

With hooded eyes he looked away from her. "Not even by Edward?"

"Heavens, no. Not Edward." Charlotte shook her head, astounded that Connor could even think such a thing of Edward—or her.

He laughed and brushed a kiss against her ear. "Kitten, I love your honesty."

But shame over Edward lingered guiltily in her heart. How could she feel all these things for a brawlin' Scot when she should be feeling them for her poet?

For a long moment Connor's hand remained cupped over her breast and the heat returned to his eyes.

Charlotte melted under his gaze. "Victor's kiss?"

Connor's breath caught sharply.

Charlotte bent over his lips, kissing him with a passion that she had never suspected she was capable of. Her arms wrapped around his neck, pressing herself against his chest. She made a sound like a moan deep in her throat and parted her lips for him before he had done much more than touch them with his tongue.

Charlotte knew enough now to kiss him as he kissed her, caressing, exploring. She imitated every foray and repeated those she found especially pleasurable.

Her fingers combed through his damp Apollo curls. Her heart thundered against her ribs. She surrendered to the pleasure of such intimate giving and receiving. She would gladly share with Connor anything he wanted of her. Anything that was hers to give. Because she loved his carefree heart, and his generous spirit.

"You know there is a lot more to kissing than this," he murmured, lifting his mouth from hers after the long, spellbinding kiss. He began to tug on her buttons again. "But we need to be more comfortable."

Charlotte stopped his hands with hers. "Connor, no."

His hands went still; he was obviously puzzled.

"I mean, let *me* do the buttons," she whispered against his temple.

"While you do that, I'll just make us more comfortable over here."

Connor slipped his fight-weary arms under Charlotte's knees. With remarkable ease he rose from the chair and walked across the room with her in his arms.

"Connor?" Charlotte gasped in surprise, wrapping her arms around his neck and clinging to him for dear life. The room whirled around her. Then he was gently setting her down on his curtained bed in the corner. He sat down beside her.

"How are those buttons coming?" he asked, reaching for her bodice once more.

Charlotte blushed. "I almost have them. There."

Connor slipped the bodice off, planting a kiss on her bare shoulder as he freed her hands of the sleeves. Then he reached for the tape of her skirt. Soon he had her skirt, petticoats, and drawers peeled down over her hips and knees.

Suddenly awkward in nothing but her shift, Charlotte sat on the corner of the bed, shivering despite the warmth of the summer evening. She did not know if she should remove the flimsy garment for him. Was it true that people made love naked? But Connor's touch on her skin always seemed to be just what she wanted.

When Connor turned back to her after tossing her clothes aside, Charlotte reached for the ribbons of her shift.

"No, mine," Connor said, reaching for the gold satin that guarded the last barrier between him and her bare skin. He took his time untying the front of her shift, his fingers brushing ever so briefly, so lightly against her swollen breasts. Charlotte drew a shaky breath, barely able to wait for his next touch. Even as the thin silk fell away and his eyes feasted on her, he did not touch her again. Charlotte's nipples pearled once more and ached for his caress.

Under the guidance of his hands, she lay back naked on the bed. She trembled with need as his eyes moved over her.

"Look how lovely you are, kitten," Connor said, still wearing his gold dressing gown. Charlotte longed to see him naked again. She reached for his sash, but he stopped her. "Not yet. I haven't even touched you yet. Haven't even given you your advanced lesson in kissing."

"Then let's begin." Charlotte reached up to draw his face to hers.

"No, that's not the kissing we're doing now," Connor said. "This kind of kissing goes like this." His hand stroked over her throat. His fingers found her nipple and rubbed his palm across the bud, then he bent to place a light kiss on it.

Charlotte cried out, her legs moving restlessly as a strange new ache grew inside of her.

He soothed her with his voice before kissing circles over her breast, leaving her quivering and whimpering beneath his lips. Then his hand slid down her body, stroking, the strokes always followed by his lips. Each rib. Her navel. Tiny maddening, whispering kisses low across her belly just above the private place between her limbs. The aching coalesced into a shameless throb between Charlotte's legs. She moaned.

At last his strokes caressed the thatch of hair covering her mound. Charlotte shut her eyes as his fingers toyed with the tiny curls.

"As red as the hair on your head," he chuckled softly, the arrogant note of a conqueror in his voice. To Charlotte's mortification he leaned over her and kissed her red curls. "Shh, it's all right, kitten. Lie back and open for me."

Connor placed his mouth on Charlotte's again, but this time his fingers never gave up their quest, sliding between her legs as if searching for the ache that lay hidden and demanding inside her. Overcome, Charlotte parted her legs for him. His stroking fingers drew exquisite sensations from her, each intimate foray moving deeper into her than anyone had ever been. He continued to cover her mouth with tiny kisses and teasing nips.

His fingers worked magic, robbing her of all but enough strength to move in response to his intimate exploration. The ecstasy grew when his lips traveled down her throat and found her breasts again. Tasting her nipples, kissing the sensitive undersides of her breasts, his fingers delving ever deeper into her, tempting her with a joy she had yet to discover. What more could there be? Charlotte sighed.

Then he took her nipple into his mouth and began to suckle her like a babe. The suction, the roughness of his tongue, sent extraordinary waves of pleasure flooding through her.

"Connor," she whimpered, threading her fingers through his hair. "Connor, no more. It's unbearable."

Connor left her breast, raising himself up on his elbow to search her face. The heat still burned in his eyes, but Charlotte was too weakened and overwhelmed to try to understand it. She closed her eyes against the wave of pleasure that threatened to contract within her.

When she opened her eyes, Connor was still watching her. He slipped an arm under her head and took her hand, placing it on his sash, but he held her gaze all the while. Without uttering a word, he was asking her if she wished to go on.

Charlotte understood vaguely what happened next. She and Cassie had pieced it together between the things their mother had told them and with answers to the questions they'd put to Aunt Dorian. Charlotte knew that she could remain herself if she called a halt to the wonderful things they were sharing now.

Connor would honor her wishes, though he could clearly take from her whatever he wanted. Even if she wasn't helplessly spread across his bed in the throes of passion, she could never fight him off if he chose to force himself on her. But she knew Connor would not do that. He might not like being denied, but he would take only what she wished to give.

But she'd seen what truly separated them. She knew the chasm would only yawn wider. As Connor's fame as a boxer grew, there would be more horrifying fights. She was beginning to understand how prizefights and championships worked. One victory led to another fight. Victory. Fight. Victory. Fight. She saw an endless stair step of bouts and victories until defeat ended it or success satisfied Connor. And with his success would come his return to Scotland. Their future was uncertain at best, and in reality, most likely impossible.

"Are you going to think it to death, kitten?" Connor whispered, a note of teasing in his voice. But the hand that held hers to his dressing gown sash trembled. "Don't translate and conjugate now. This is not an ancient poem to press in the pages of book. This is an invisible and absolute force between us—since that first day. Surely 'tis meant to be."

Connor's burning gold eyes awaited her answer.

TWENTY-EIGHT

Charlotte understood Connor's words. This was not the moment for intellectualizing. With all her heart, Charlotte wished to give him this moment, here and now, whatever else might befall them in the future. Prizefights or feuds, this was their moment together. It was a time for loving.

Without hesitation, without allowing herself a second thought, Charlotte untied the sash of Connor's dressing gown and choked back a gasp. None of her discussion with Cassie had prepared her for the sight.

Connor seemed to understand. "I'm only so big because I want you so badly, kitten. You're ready for me and I'll make it as easy as I can. You'll grow to like this," he promised, dropping another teasing kiss on her nipple. The bud tingled and ached for more.

The sweet helplessness swept through Charlotte again and she fell back against his arm, closed her eyes, and offered herself up to him.

Without pause, he covered her, pressing her deep into the mattress. Charlotte stretched, opening herself to him as her heart and her instincts told her to do. The ache inside demanded quenching. It demanded she take him into her, that she hold him in her body. She would.

He found his way inside, thrusting ever so gently but persistently, deeper and deeper, her body stretching and straining to accept him. Charlotte's breath came in short, ragged gasps. She wrapped her arms around Connor, her hands spreading across the magnificent cords of his back. He pressed his mouth against her ear, murmuring her name, whispering his own pleasure warm and wet against her ear. The understanding made her open herself more, and he moved deeper. The undeniable pain could not burn away the pleasure of drawing him inside her.

Then he began to move.

Charlotte murmured Connor's name. More new and wondrous sensations began to grow inside her until they spilled over into an explosion of tiny thrills singing along every fiber of her being. Charlotte cried out.

Connor shuddered in her arms and his cry echoed hers. A moment later he rolled off her. Whispering soothingly to her, he gathered her up in his arms and they both fell into an exhausted slumber.

The pounding on the door roused Connor from a deep sleep. He opened his eyes to sunlight flooding the room and the morning cries of the street vendors drifting in through the window. He sat up on the edge of the bed, his head clear and his defenses alert. The visitor wasn't Mrs. Needham. She always called through the door and if neither he nor Erik responded, she left.

This visitor was rather more insistent. The pounding began again.

"Who's there?" Connor called, pulling his dressing gown around him and cinching a firm knot at his waist.

"Lord Kinleith 'tis Miss Charlotte St. John come to congratulate you on your victory of yesterday," announced the cultured voice of the St. John footman.

Connor frowned. What in thunderation? He turned to find Charlotte still sleeping in his bed, her red-gold hair spread across his pillow and her nakedness covered with only a corner of the rough counterpane and his tartan. The sight of her brought a tender smile to his lips. He reached for the bedclothes and tugged on them, exposing a full, round breast flush with sleep.

"Connor, 'tis me, Charlotte," came a female voice this time, a voice very nearly like Charlotte's. Connor recognized Cassie's timbre, just a fraction firmer than Charlotte's. "I apologize if I've called too early, but do let me in. I needn't stay long."

Then Connor understood. "I'll be right there."

He leaned over Charlotte. "Kitten, wake up. I think your sister is here to rescue you."

With a soft smile of happiness, Charlotte stretched without opening her eyes, her limbs long and graceful as a nymph's. To know that he'd brought that smile of happiness to her lips made Connor feel almost as good as a victory in the ring did. Her limbs tangled carelessly in the bedclothes and her satiny skin nearly glowed in the shadows of the curtained bed.

Tempted to strive for that happiness again, Connor was about ready to crawl back into bed and start loving her once more.

But reality set in for Charlotte; she bolted upright, grabbing for the sheet to cover herself. "What? Who?"

"Cassie is here," Connor said, resigning himself to the fact that their interlude was over. Instead of tugging the sheet away from her, he snagged her discarded petticoat and bodice from the floor.

"Cassie." Wild-eyed, Charlotte looked around at the bed and curtains. "Connor, what have we done?"

"The most natural thing in the world," Connor said with a grin. He bent toward Charlotte and placed a quick kiss on her nose in the hopes of bringing that beautiful smile back to her lips. "You seemed to think well enough of it last night. You're not going to fret about it now, are you?"

Charlotte groaned. "I must have been mad last night. Whatever was I thinking?"

"I don't know, kitten, but it wasn't of Edward." Connor handed her her skirt. "You purred for me last night and it was my name you cried out."

A blush reddened Charlotte's cheeks and brought satisfaction flooding back to Connor.

Charlotte shook her head as she fumbled with the ribbons of

her shift. " 'Tis hopeless, Connor McKensie. I'll never make you into a gentleman."

"No, but I like what I'm making of you," Connor said, unable to resist displaying a bit of male triumph.

"I don't know what you're talking about," Charlotte said, tunneling her way into her petticoat.

The pounding on the door resumed.

"Do you want me to send her away?" Connor asked, more concerned for Charlotte's feelings than her sister's. He wanted more time with Charlotte, enough time to reassure her and himself of something—but he wasn't quite sure what. "I can take you home when you're ready."

"And how would that look?" Charlotte cried, more troubled over their night together than Connor liked to see. "The whole world would know that I spent the night in your rooms."

"I don't mind what the world thinks," Connor said, frowning as he spoke a truth he might have to reconsider. Until last night, marriage to Charlotte had always been the second option toward acquiring Glen Gray, should boxing fail. But in a weak moment he'd compromised her—part of his plan he'd never expected to implement—but, she'd been so tempting and ripe in his arms.

Now what the world, or, more accurately, what Society, thought made the compromise useful to him—or hurtful to Charlotte. He found the thought of hurting her distasteful. And her obvious dismay in the light of day displeased him. He longed to believe that she'd enjoyed every last touch and taste as much as he had.

"But I do care what everyone thinks," Charlotte said, shaking her hair free of the petticoat. "For Papa and Mama's sake and Aunt Dorian."

Connor understood about appearances before family. He rose from the bed and pulled the curtains to give her privacy. "Then finish dressing and I'll admit your sister."

When he opened the door, Cassie, wearing a voluminous pelisse in Charlotte's favorite blue, nearly fell into the room. She tripped over the mound of men's clothes that Charlotte had deposited near the door the night before. But she quickly regained her balance and rounded on Connor with a sweet smile.

"Wait for me there, Betsy," she called to the maid who lingered in the hallway.

The minute Connor closed the door, her smile vanished. She advanced on Connor with a stony fury that threatened to stir up a whirlwind. Connor braced himself.

"Where is she?" Cassie demanded. "What have you done with her? If you've hurt her, I'll bring every power in England and Christendom down on you. Don't think I can't do it. No title or clan will save you."

"Whoa," Connor said, holding up his hands to ward off her rage. Then he gestured toward the bed. "Charlotte is right here."

Cassie glared at him suspiciously at first. "Charlotte? Are you there? Are you all right?"

"I'm fine, Cassie," Charlotte replied from behind the curtain. "You haven't told—"

"No one knows you were here last night," Cassie finished. "I'm sleeping late this morning and you are calling on poor battered, but victorious, Lord Kinleith."

Cassandra started toward the bed, but Connor cut her off.

"I've some fresh clothes for her," Cassandra explained, producing a bundle from beneath her pelisse.

Silently, Connor took it and handed it through the curtain to Charlotte, fully intending to remain between the sisters until Charlotte was content to show herself.

"This is a maid's gown," Charlotte complained from behind the curtain.

"And who will notice one more maid in Charlotte St. John's entourage?" Cassandra asked.

"Yes, of course, I see," Charlotte said in a small voice.

Connor could hear the rustle of clothes as Charlotte apparently went about dressing.

Cassandra drew closer. Connor folded his arms across his chest and remained planted before the bed.

"I can't believe you did this to her."

"I did not hurt your sister," Connor said, the memory of Charlotte's willingness still fresh and precious in his mind. Cassandra had no right to the details.

"But if this gets out, you have ruined her reputation," Cassie said. "Do you know what she has done for you? Things she would never dream of doing—for anyone but me. Things like climbing out of a second floor window and riding off into the night with her cousin. Because she thought you might be hurt. And you would humiliate her and her family."

"That was never my intention," Connor vowed, marveling at the thought of Charlotte risking her neck and defying her father for him.

"Then just what is your intention?" Cassandra demanded in a hot, angry whisper. "To break that soft, sweet heart of hers?"

Connor frowned. "Of course not."

"I will not quibble with you about maidenhood or honor or compromise," Cassandra murmured in a low, angry voice, her gaze darting around the room. "Those are words for you and Papa to talk of. And I have little notion of what Charlotte means to you, but know that I will not stand aside and see Charlotte brokenhearted over a conniving thug of a prizefighter."

Connor drew in a long, deep breath. Cassandra's words struck too near the truth of what he'd been up to. "Nor have I any wish to see Charlotte hurt."

"Then we are in agreement on the issue of Charlotte's heart, at least?" Cassandra asked, catching his gaze and holding it.

Connor studied her, his respect for British womanhood, and in particular for the St. John twins, growing. "We are in agreement."

"I need help with the buttons," Charlotte said, groping her way out from behind the bed-curtains. She shook out her skirts and turned her back to Connor and Cassandra before lifting her hair up on her head, revealing a gaping bodice and her shift-covered back to them.

"Here, I'll—" Cassandra began starting toward her sister.

Once again Connor blocked Cassandra from reaching Charlotte. "I'll do the buttons."

He quickly set about fastening the back of Charlotte's bodice. She was still his, as long as she was in his room, and he would not relinquish a single privilege of possession as long as she remained with him.

Cassandra paused, then stepped back, still angry but seemingly resigned.

Connor worked at the buttons, a foreign task to him, but his fingers quickly closed the gap in Charlotte's bodice.

"Tuck your hair well up into the bonnet I brought," Cassandra instructed, "and no one will know who you are."

"There can't be many people about yet," Charlotte said, hope in her voice. "It's far too early."

"I recognized Pierce Deacon, *The Times* boxing writer, loitering on the street corner," Cassandra said, tapping her foot impatiently. "Since the fight yesterday, Connor has become a very visible man."

"I believe your sister is right to get you out of here as early as possible," Connor said, putting the last button through its proper opening. He pulled Charlotte's hands from atop her head, allowing her tresses to brush his face as they fell about her shoulders. He closed his eyes and inhaled her scent, hardly believing that only twenty-four hours ago he had yet to defeat the Trooper—or make love to Charlotte St. John.

"Put on the bonnet," Cassandra urged.

Charlotte turned to retrieve the bonnet from the bed.

Feeling suddenly empty with the prospect of Charlotte leaving him, Connor shoved his fists into the pockets of his dressing gown and turned away. He wandered across the room to the window, leaving Cassandra to go to her sister's side at last. They chattered softly about the bonnet and Charlotte's hair. He did not listen to their words, but the sound of their sisterly prattle was somehow soothing and he knew he would miss it when they were gone.

A commotion in the street below caught his attention. He

peered out the window just in time to see the Earl of Seacombe's phaeton, followed by another carriage, pull up beside the St. John equipage at the front of his lodgings.

"I think Tony is back," he said to the twins. "Does he know you've come, Cassandra?"

"He'll keep his wits about him," Cassandra said. "Tony is an ally."

"Good," Connor said as he watched Tony, Erik, and Nicholas Derrington disembark and start toward the stairs. Three men climbed out of the other carriage. "Because I haven't any idea who these other people are."

"We're almost ready." Cassandra turned to Connor. "Here is the story. Charlotte came calling this morning to congratulate you on your victory in the boxing ring yesterday. She was accompanied by two maids and a footman. She didn't stay long."

Connor watched Lord Seacombe, Tony, and the three men gather at the doorway below. They talked among themselves, giving Connor time to identify Sir Benton, the fight backer who had hinted at connections with the Pugilistic Society. Instantly Connor knew what this visit was all about. The last thing he wanted was for Charlotte to witness any of it.

"Go now," Connor ordered, striding across the room to hold the door open for the twins.

The girls stared at him in blank surprise. Before they could move, Tony burst into the room, followed by Erik. Tony took a look at Cassandra and Charlotte and without expressing a ghost of concern, doffed his hat. "Good morning, Cousin Charlotte. What a pleasure to see you today."

Cassie bobbed a demure, Charlotte-like curtsy. "And good day to you, too, Cousin Anthony. I was just congratulating Lord Kinleith on his victory of yesterday."

"Indeed, it was a good mill," Tony said. "So good, in fact, the officials had to break it up."

Connor welcomed Erik back with a slap on the shoulder. "Just had to sample the hospitality in an English jail, didn't you?"

Erik grinned. " 'Twas no great imposition. I've spent worse nights on the floor of a Scots tavern."

Connor laughed, relieved to see Erik still had his sense of humor.

Nicholas Derrington and Sir Benton came into the room. Derrington, who seemed mildly surprised to see his niece, made the presentations of all the gentlemen, including two of the most influential members of the Pugilist Society. Connor could feel the air around the men was electric with excitement.

He glanced uneasily at Charlotte, who had kept her head down so the bonnet hid her face. During the presentation she had edged her way toward the open door.

"We'll not mince words with you Lord Kinleith," the society member said, too exhilarated with his mission to take note of who was present. "We of the society, without exception, were impressed by your performance against the Trooper yesterday. We've been dispatched to invite you to fight for the championship against Jem Ward."

Connor offered them a noncommittal smile, careful not to appear too eager or too indifferent. But he could not keep himself from fixing his gaze on Charlotte, who remained near the door standing slightly behind Cassie as a dutiful maid should.

He saw her shoulders go stiff. He continued to stare at her, hoping to force her to look at him. When she did at last raise her gaze to meet his, the disappointment and fear he read in her blue eyes stunned him.

He wanted to curse. Could she not understand? These men were offering the fulfillment of his dreams, the chance to save the McKensie clan from poverty. He would not lose it—not even for Charlotte.

"Sit down, gentlemen," Connor said, gesturing to the chairs but without taking his eyes from Charlotte. He could only pray that she would understand.

"Aye, sit," Erik said, drawing up a chair for each man. "Let's talk about what you're offering with this boxing match."

"Gentlemen, I shall take my leave. Good-bye," Cassie said.

forgotten amidst the excitement. She took her sister's hand and started for the door.

Charlotte ducked her head, the bonnet obscuring her face, and she brushed something suspiciously like a tear from her cheek, Connor thought. Then she, too, disappeared out the door, leaving him alone with the Pugilistic Society and the opportunity of a lifetime.

TWENTY-NINE

"I heard the most fascinating tale at the club this afternoon over luncheon," Papa said without looking at Charlotte as the footman began to clear away the dinner dishes.

Under the table, Cassie nudged Charlotte's foot, their sign to each other that something was up. Charlotte had been so dispirited after leaving Connor that she'd barely noticed that the dinner-table conversation had been cool and formal throughout the meal. Papa had spoken short, crisp sentences, like a man with something important on his mind. Nothing extraordinary about that. Charlotte ignored the signal.

But then he'd said, "Bring the port in here, will you, Horton?" Charlotte surfaced from her melancholy and met Cassandra's glance across the table. They were in for a lecture.

Mama gestured to the footman to bring her tea. Overhead the crystal chandelier glittered in the candlelight, casting rainbows on the polished wood of the dining-room table.

Charlotte leaned back in her chair so the footman could take away her dinner plate still full of food. She'd shoved the lamb chop around, but had eaten almost nothing. Food had no flavor since leaving Connor that morning, and she didn't think she would ever eat again. Enough had been said in his lodgings before she'd left for her to understand that he was lost to her forever. He'd fight his prizefight and return to the Highlands as the English boxing champion and the clan hero. He'd marry some strong, practical Highland woman and have dozens of children with her. Food had no flavor. Life had no color. Nothingness filled Charlotte. Her future had blossomed, then vanished in one glorious night. Impatiently, she wondered what Papa could have to say that was of any importance?

She glanced uneasily across at Cassandra, who'd begun to toy with her napkin in her lap.

In silence, Horton, his white gloves gleaming in the candlelight, poured the rich, red liquor into a glass for Papa. With a clink the butler dropped the ground glass stopper back on the decanter and stepped back into the shadows of the room.

"Do you have any idea what I might have heard at the club?" Papa asked, peering from one daughter to the other as soon as the footmen had departed. "Charlotte? Cassandra? Do listen to this, because I think there are some lessons for you to take away."

Cassie glanced across the table at Charlotte with a small, knowing smile. Cassie often found Papa's lectures far more amusing than Charlotte did.

"I'm sorry, Papa, but I don't know what you're referring to," Charlotte said. Clearly Papa knew something, but probably not all of it. Fortunately for them, he seldom did.

"It was brought to my attention this afternoon that Connor, Lord Kinleith, has been invited to challenge Jem Ward for the championship," Papa said, sipping his port.

"Dudley has been anticipating this for days," Cassandra said with a that-is-old-news tone of voice.

"Speculation is not news, Cassandra," Papa informed her. "The point is that the story going around at the club is that when the gentlemen of the Pugilistic Society arrived to issue the invitation at nine o'clock this morning, Miss Charlotte St. John was in attendance to Lord Kinleith."

Charlotte took a deep breath as she folded her napkin slowly and laid it on the table before her. She knew exactly what she must say. "That's true, Papa. I called on Lord Kinleith to congratulate him on his victory. Betsy rode along with me and

Albert, the footman who usually accompanies us when we shop."

"Yes, Albert is quite good company on calls and shopping excursions," said dear Mama, who most always tried to avert Papa's ill humor. "I've always told the girls to take him along, Davis. However, Albert's attendance is not the issue. I believe your father is concerned about the hour of your call. So very early is a bit unseemly, Charlotte."

"Well, perhaps," Charlotte admitted, creasing her napkin once more. "I had some other errands—a fitting for the gowns we had ordered from Hardings'. Cassie hadn't risen yet so I made the call at Lord Kinleith's my first stop."

"You know that kind of thing starts all sorts of rumors," Papa said, studying the liquor in his glass. "Some bloke even asked when we would be announcing your betrothal to McKensie."

That shook the emptiness out of Charlotte.

Cassie's head came up and she fixed an inquiring look on Charlotte's face. "That was quick work, sister."

Charlotte shook her head, warning Cassie not to get any ideas.

"I don't believe you want that sort of thing to get around to Sir Edward, do you?" Papa asked, then drained his glass.

Her mind groping wildly through a fog of confusion, Charlotte stared across the table at Cassie. Betrothal? Connor? Edward? What did she want Edward to think? Did she even care what Edward thought? Cassie stared back, her small, knowing smile offering no answers.

"No, of course, it wouldn't do to get erroneous rumors going around about a betrothal that has not happened," Mama said, watching her daughters. "Charlotte doesn't want that, do you, dear?"

Charlotte turned to her mother, who gave her a reassuring smile. "No, I don't want false rumors spreading. It never occurred to me that calling on Lord Kinleith to congratulate him on his victory would be misconstrued so. It seemed only a courtesy at the time."

"Well, give your actions more serious thought in the future," Papa said, pouring himself another glass of port.

"Yes, I will, Papa," Charlotte said, hoping he was about to dismiss them from the table. She and Cassandra might be able to put the morning's escapade behind them with no more than this scolding. But Papa made no move to leave the table or to excuse them. He shifted in his chair so that he faced Cassie more fully.

"I also heard another interesting tale from Dudley's father," Papa began as he swirled the port around in his glass. The candlelight flashed ruby red through the liquid.

"Lord Moncreff was at the club today?" Cassie asked, her voice light and casual, but the quick glance she cast in Charlotte's direction betrayed her unease. "Dudley told me his father had been in the country all through May."

"Yes, well, Moncreff had a fascinating tale to tell about some young pups playing at highway robbery," Papa said, continuing to swirl the port, never taking his eyes from his glass.

"Highway robbery?" Cassie repeated with a false note of amusement in her voice. "What does old Moncreff know about highway robbery?"

"It seems a rather troublesome old widow in his neighborhood was accosted by two highwaymen in May," Papa said, then took a sip of his port. "About the time you went to Kinleith's boxing match."

Charlotte creased her napkin again. Highway robbery? Was that what Cassandra and Dudley had been up to the day of the boxing match? She dared not look across the table at her sister for fear of giving anything away.

"You must be speaking of old Lady Mannerly," Cassandra said. "She's a rather grumpy, frumpy old dear who tattles on everyone around the village."

"Yes, well, it seems that Lady Mannerly's carriage was stopped by two masked horsemen, one of whom she thought resembled Dudley," Papa said. "Would you know anything about that?"

"Dudley?" Cassandra exclaimed. "Masked highwayman? Papa, what a laughable notion. The old dear is quite deaf, you know. Rich as Midas and just as tight with her pennies. But how shocking for her to be robbed. Pray tell, no real harm came to her?"

"No, no real harm was done," Papa said with little conviction in his voice. "Interesting that you should guess that."

Cassandra sat back in her chair. "Whatever do you mean? It's just that I can't believe that any highwayman from the Moncreff neighborhood would be so villainous as to harm an old lady."

"Curiously, the valuables taken from her were later found in the poor box of the village church," Papa said. "The vicar was enormously pleased. Moncreff said the churchman kept the coins, but I believe he was persuaded to return the heirloom jewelry."

"See, no real harm was done," Cassandra said, dismissing the issue with laughter and a wave of her hand.

"But shock sent the poor lady to her bed," Papa said, clearly not finished with his story and not about to permit Cassie's interruptions to deter him from the telling. "Lady Mannerly complained to Moncreff about not keeping his son suitably occupied to prevent him from gallivanting across the countryside accosting old ladies and throwing their heirloom jewelry to the poor."

Cassandra was silent, suddenly as intent on her napkin as Charlotte had been on her own earlier. Charlotte ducked her head and bit her lip. For the first time all day, laughter threatened to escape her.

"Lady Mannerly swore she'd press charges with the magistrate next time," Papa continued. "Actually, it's quite difficult for me to see Dudley dreaming up and executing a prank like this on his own. The boy doesn't seem to have that much imagination or gumption to me. Do you think he fell under the influence of disreputable friends?"

Charlotte saw Cassie wince.

"I couldn't say," Cassie said, smoothing her napkin once more.

"So," Papa concluded, "I was very glad to know that you were at the boxing match with Tony that day and could not possibly have been a party to Dudley's prank."

The urge to laugh vanished. Charlotte stared across the table at her sister. The threat of the magistrate intervening banished the humor in the pranks. Cassie's escapades had always been outrageous, but surely this one had gone too far.

"Yes, I see what you mean," Cassandra said, glancing across at Charlotte at last.

"I was wondering why old Moncreff decided to confess all this?" asked Mama, who had been silent throughout Papa's tale.

"He just wanted us to know, Susanna, in the event the story got back to us," Papa said. "Something of an apology, I think. I've no great concern over a prank. Actually, I was a party to one or two myself at university, but I don't want the nonsense to get out of hand. Are you listening to me, Cassandra?"

"Yes, I'm listening, Papa." Cassie stared contritely at her hands in her lap. "I'm sure Dudley meant no harm."

"Perhaps not, but he must learn to think about those things before he goes off frightening old ladies," Papa said. "And you, Charlotte, I never thought I'd be warning you, but no more early morning calls on gentlemen, lest you find yourself betrothed where you care not to be."

"Yes, Papa," Charlotte pledged, her vow heartfelt. How foolish she had been to go to Connor's lodgings! But he had needed her, and now what was done was done. She could not change it—would not change it. Her heart fluttered at the fleeting memory of Connor's touch, of the thrilling intimacy they'd shared. The sweetness of sleeping in each other's arms and sharing dreams. The only thing she wanted to change was the call from the Pugilistic Society.

When Connor invited those men in, Charlotte had known that nothing had changed for him. He had made love to her in the dark hours of the night, but had returned to the pursuit of his goal in the light of morn. But everything had changed for her. She had given Connor her heart and her body. With the rising of the sun, her life revealed itself in a new light. She could not turn back now.

The Homer translation that lay on her study desk and the new morning gown that hung in her dressing room seemed to have belonged to another Charlotte, one who had not discovered the direction of her life. Not that she didn't still want those things, but in a different manner, a manner secondary to loving Connor and being with him.

But there was no future for her with him.

All she could do was put her life in order and move on. She would do so as quietly as possible and pray that Papa and Mama never learned the truth. Yes, and there would be Edward to deal with, but she could manage him now. Somehow she had gained the strength for that.

Was it possible she'd gained so much from Connor in one night? Was it possible that Papa and Mama and Cassie could not see the change in her face?

"Then if you girls will excuse us, I wish to have a word with your mother," Papa said, filling his port glass once more.

Escape offered, Charlotte and Cassandra stood up from the table at the exact same moment. Charlotte read relief on Cassandra's face, which she knew mirrored her own. Papa might know and guess at some of the truth, but he didn't know it all and neither of them was going to tell him.

THIRTY

Davis watched his daughters leave the dining room, their faces properly sober from their chastisement. As soon as they were out of earshot, he looked across the table at Susanna.

"I think they accepted that well," he said, hoping to hear Susanna agree with him. "I trust they will not get themselves into any more questionable situations."

"They are bright and spirited girls," Susanna said. "Even our Charlotte, who seldom reveals herself as readily as Cassandra, has a mind of her own."

"They are both more like their aunt Dorian than I care to think sometimes," Davis admitted, longing for the evaporation of the distance that had yawned between him and Susanna since the night of her birthday.

She had been the obedient wife as always, but she had put him from her in that invisible, indefinable way that women have. A coolness in her smile, in her touch, in her manner as she went about her wifely tasks. A remoteness that a man could not rage at nor argue with, for she would deny it existed, even as it hung there stony as a castle bulwark.

He'd even gone to her room as frequently as usual and slept beside her, comforted by her nearness, by even the meager concession of sharing her bed, but nothing more. For the wall stood between them.

He knew he could force a touch. He could demand his husbandly rights and only last night he had almost talked himself into doing so, until he thought of the consequences.

Susanna might, indeed, submit to him, for she was a dutiful wife and a passionate soul. Lord, how well he knew her passion. She never refused him anything, but she could withhold herself. And he hated that. The sense of her being in his arms—all his, seemingly—yet the essence of her lying somewhere just beyond his grasp. That made him grind his teeth.

No, he would not force her into anything. Yet, he knew that if this difference between them was not resolved soon, the invisible wall would only grow stonier, colder, and all the more insurmountable.

Davis sighed in his perplexity and sipped his port. "I'm thinking perhaps we should forbid Charlotte from seeing Lord Kinleith. We have no idea where things are going with him. Heaven knows what his intentions are. That's why I had to scold her for her behavior."

"Yes, I agree." Susanna's smooth brow furrowed. "I do fear for Charlotte. Lord McKensie is so genial, and she seems to enjoy his company. His down-to-earth ways are good for her, I think. Yet, everything about him is so unlike that she professes to desire from life."

Davis was relieved to hear the doubt in Susanna's tone. "It might be best to forbid McKensie to call on her again and squelch these rumors of betrothal as soon as possible."

"Perhaps," Susanna said. "But it seems a bit extreme to me. And such a rejection adds credence to the stories the gossips love spreading."

"Not at all," Davis insisted. He was becoming eager to break connections with the two Scots lords who threatened his happy family life and his attempt for a title. Today he'd learned why his petition for knighthood was stalled.

He'd had a response to his enquiry as to the reason for the delay, only yesterday—vague and formless excuses. But this morning a letter from Marquis of Linirk made it clear that his most recent rejection of the Forbes bid for Glen Gray might bring an end to all his aspirations.

But the marquis had not withdrawn all hope. In fact, Forbes had offered assistance if Davis would eliminate McKensie from the picture. The offer had thrilled Davis and angered him. He did not like the idea of allowing Forbes to influence him with power and money.

"But Charlotte seems to like Kinleith." Susanna scowled at him. "And Kinleith has title to an earldom, Davis, a rank of considerably more significance that Sir Edward's."

"And just what do you mean by that?" Davis snapped, forcing himself to listen to his wife's objections.

"I'm simply pointing out the inconsistencies in your thinking." Susanna's voice was soft and cool with inscrutable female logic. "If you are truly ambitious for the prestige of a title in your family, you would wed Charlotte off to Lord Kinleith if she is so inclined."

"Kinleith? Never!" Davis exclaimed, half rising from his chair and wondering if Susanna knew of the letter he'd received from Forbes that morning. "No marriage to Kinleith. I will not have my daughter's happiness sacrificed for a man's ends, earldom or no."

With wide, startled eyes, Susanna regarded Davis for a long moment. Under her scrutiny, Davis turned away. She couldn't possibly know of Forbes's letter. Nor could she possibly know how tempting the marquis's offer was.

"I will not use my daughters' future for gain," Davis said. "I only dictate to them for their own happiness."

"I am glad to hear you say that," Susanna said, the uncertainty in her voice contradicting her words. "Does this have something to do with your title? I wish you would give up this notion of knighthood, Davis. We move in the most exalted social circles. Your daughters and I have been presented at court. We want for nothing. There is no member of the *haute ton* who has more land, houses, furnishings, servants, horses, or carriages than we do and many of them have less. Why must you have this title?"

"But don't you see?" Davis said, exasperated enough by her lack of understanding to pound his palm on the table. "How do you think I felt when you and the girls were presented at court under Nicholas and Dorian's sponsorship?"

Susanna said nothing, but stared at him with her lips parted as if she did not comprehend a word of what he was trying to explain. It was all so clear to him; why could she not see it?

"Susanna, you and the girls should have been presented as *my* wife and daughters," Davis said, softly pounding the table again. "Not as Dorian's relatives. Not like poor relations at a party. You should have been there as Lady Susanna, wife of Sir Davis St. John."

Susanna shook her head slowly as if she didn't understand.

Davis went on, determined to make her see the omission as clearly as he did. "And when we are announced at balls or receptions it should be as Sir Davis and Lady Susanna. We have earned that."

"But I care not whether I'm announced as Mrs. or Lady," Susanna said, slowly shaking her head as if she were disappointed in him. "Titles are chances of birth, Davis. Titles are but face cards dealt out. Face cards to respect, but nothing more. Sometimes they are not even very powerful when played upon the game table of real life. Can you not see that?"

"Perhaps, but I will not settle for it," Davis said, angered that she was so blind. "You think well enough of Sir Myron's title."

Susanna's face closed.

Anger flashed through Davis like fireworks across a night sky. "Why can you not understand?"

"I do understand," Susanna said, rising from her chair, her hands spread on the table as she spoke, the candlelight sparkling in the diamonds of the wedding band Davis had given her for their tenth anniversary. "This is not about me and how I feel about titles, or about you or Myron. This is about how you feel about yourself. I will not argue with you about it again as long as you promise me that you will not use our daughters' future to further your longing for a title."

Davis stared back at his wife, too filled with guilt to say a word. When he'd learned the unfortunate history of Glen Gray, he had resisted the idea of selling it. In fairness to the feuding clans, he thought to keep the property. He had no real need for the money.

Now Ramsay Forbes was baiting him with offers of support of his petition for knighthood. But if he sold the glen to Forbes in exchange for that support, he'd risk the displeasure of his sister, Dorian, who had become a Connor McKensie supporter and his daughter who had not the good sense to call on the prizefighter at the proper time of day. He might even risk being the cause of the resumption of a Highland feud.

But most important of all, if he accepted help from Forbes, he would risk the love of his wife. Davis contemplated Susanna who stood at the foot of the table looking lovely in a soft green gown. They'd been man and wife for twenty-one years. She was his life and his passion. He'd be lost without her.

"Davis, you do promise that you will not risk our daughters' future happiness for the sake of your ambition?" Susanna was talking at him again. "Davis? I can forgive you your jealousies but I could never forgive—"

"No, of course, I would never risk our daughters' futures," Davis said, uncertain whether he believed himself or not.

THIRTY-ONE

Charlotte had been working in her study, sorting books since breakfast. She looked up to find Cassie in the doorway, holding the silver correspondence salver laden with a letter.

"I think you should take a look at this immediately," Cassie said, thrusting the silver tray toward her sister.

Charlotte had been toiling steadily and studiously, concentrating on reorganizing her study and not thinking of Connor. Errant questions pestered her. When would he fight? Where? Was he eating enough? Was he getting enough rest? Good heavens, would he be hurt so badly again? She was buried so deep in her thoughts that Cassie's appearance startled her.

Without haste, Charlotte dropped two more books into the box on her desk and turned toward her sister. "So now you are hand-delivering Edward's notes to me in the place of Horton?"

"It's not from Edward," Cassandra said cryptically and waved the salver at Charlotte again. "If it were, I would not have troubled myself. Connor's man, Erik, delivered it and he waits downstairs for a reply. He said Connor is occupied at the boxing salon."

"From Connor?" Charlotte searched Cassie's face for a clue about what the letter contained. In two days since Cassie had rescued Charlotte from Connor's lodgings, Charlotte had shared as much as she dared about her night with the Scot. To Charlotte's relief, Cassie had been curious, but had not pressed for details.

"I have not read it, if that's what you think," Cassie said, snatching up the missive in her free hand and waving it at Charlotte. "See, the seal is unbroken. The Earl of Kinleith's crest is whole and undamaged right there on the paper."

Charlotte took the letter and studied her name scrawled across the front in a bold, simple hand. How like Connor. He would add no flourish to anything, certainly not his handwriting.

"Well, open it," Cassandra said, bouncing on her toes like an impatient child.

"I don't know if that would be wise," Charlotte said. What on earth could Connor have to say to her now? They had shared so much when he needed her, but as much as it pained her to admit it, he didn't need her now. He was well on his way to accomplishing what he'd come to London to do. And there was no place in that goal for a woman who did not approve of fighting. As much as she loved him, she knew she could never be woman enough to watch him fight. "Does Papa know this arrived? I mean, after what he said at the table—"

"Papa is at his office across town and Mama is out," Cassie said. "No one knows anything about this letter except Horton and me, and we've always been able to trust Horton. Besides, you didn't take Papa seriously, did you? He has to scold us from time to time to satisfy his need to be a good father."

Only half listening to her sister, Charlotte slowly turned the letter over and inspected the seal. Indeed, it was intact. Charlotte brushed her fingers across the paper where Connor had lettered her name, wishing she could feel his presence from those markings. She longed to divine the contents of the message without opening it.

"Well?" Cassie prodded. "What are you waiting for?"

Charlotte shook her head. She didn't dare do it. She didn't dare allow this desire to know more of Connor go any farther. "Give it back to Erik."

"Unopened?" Cassie leaned toward Charlotte as if poised to snatch the missive from her hand. "Are you mad?"

"Yes, send it back unopened." Charlotte handed the letter to Cassie and turned away. In the dark hours of the night, Charlotte had made up her mind. She was thankful to Connor for awakening her sensibilities to the injustices of the world. She must remain true to that awakening. No self-delusions permitted. Connor's life might not have been changed by their night together, but hers was forever altered. In the bleakest hours, when even the streets of London were quiet, she had decided just how she would shape a new life for herself—without Connor.

"But don't you think you should see what he has to say for himself after you two—" Cassie said. "Well, you know."

"I think it best we not see each other again," Charlotte said, avoiding Cassie's gaze.

"The temptation is too great?" Cassie asked, hovering over Charlotte's shoulder. "Oh, Charlotte, you did give him your heart, didn't you? And he turned away from it, choosing his prizefighting instead."

"I guess that's one way to put it," Charlotte said, pretending disinterest as she stared at the titles on her bookshelves. But she could only think of Connor's lips at her throat. His hands on her back. His gentle words in her ear and his bold touch in the most secret of places. He'd made her feel so beautiful and special. He'd made her feel strong and gloriously feminine.

"Strange." Cassie perched on the desk edge. "Honestly, Charlotte, I never thought the Scotsman a fool. A bit of a blundering rustic, yes. But never a fool."

"Perhaps it was not Connor who was the fool," Charlotte said, edging her way around her sister. "But he never made me any promises, nor I him. We were friends and we entertained each other with the sights of the city. One night, when he needed me, I rather foolishly gave him more than was wise."

"Are you sorry?" Cassie asked.

The question surprised Charlotte. She could feel her sister's scrutiny following her as she dropped more books into the box. Cassie made a great show of taking no particular pride in her intellect, but she had a knack for asking the shrewdest questions at the most propitious moment. Charlotte sighed.

"Well?" Cassie prompted, touching Charlotte's arm.

Was she sorry? Charlotte hesitated before answering.

"Now, no nonsense about disappointing Papa or Mama," Cassie said. "I want to know how you feel—for your own sake."

"I feel . . . liberated," Charlotte said at last finding a word to describe the lightness and gloom that had settled by turns inside of her.

Astonishment crossed Cassie's face. "Free? Truly? Why?"

"Because I have discovered so much about myself that I didn't know before I met Connor," Charlotte said. She would not confess her love for Connor to her sister. That belonged to her alone. But she could tell Cassie all the other things she felt.

"Such as?"

"I still love my books," Charlotte said. "But now I know that the world contained in these volumes is also out there on the streets of London. How am I to write about it if I'm cloistered in here scribbling another translation of Homer, who has been translated hundreds, maybe thousands, of times already?"

"Yes, I see," Cassie said. "But what about your heart? What about Connor? I mean, when I saw you two together, I saw a light in your eyes that never burns there when you're with Edward. That glow makes you so beautiful it makes me jealous."

"You? Jealous of me?" Charlotte said with painful surprise. "Because of Connor?"

"Because of something that is between you and that great lout, yes," Cassie waved the letter in the air once more in a gesture of aggravation. "That thing between you seemed to be something special—almost as special as what you and I share. But, if you think returning this letter is the right thing to do, then I will take care of it."

Charlotte turned away from Cassie to hide the pain she knew must show on her face. "It is the right thing."

"What if he says he needs you?"

The thought tugged at Charlotte's heart, but she squelched it. "But he doesn't. He has Erik and now, with the championship fight, he will have anything or anyone he needs at his beck and call."

"If you do this, you may never see Connor again," Cassandra

observed. "He can only interpret the return of his letter unopened as a sign that you do not wish to see him again."

Charlotte's throat tightened so that she dared not speak. Never to see Connor again, never to hear him laugh or lean so close that his breath tickled her ear and sent shivers down her spine. Never feel his lips against hers. No self-delusions. She nodded.

"Very well." Cassie turned away, tapping the letter against the silver tray. "I shall return this to Erik and send him on his way."

"Yes, and tell Erik and Horton that I will not be at home to the earl should he call."

Cassie paused as if she wanted to say something more, then decided against it. "Very well, as you say."

Once her sister's footsteps had faded away, Charlotte's shoulders slumped. Her newfound courage abandoned her. The energy that had sustained her through the morning as she'd sorted through her books, translations, and life's work seeped away. Weak and a little bewildered, she allowed herself to sink down onto her desk chair. The new Charlotte, despite her best efforts to deny it, wanted nothing more than to see a certain Scotsman.

" 'Tis unopened, Erik." The words were out of Connor's mouth before he had time to realize what the fact truly meant. "She sent back my letter unopened?"

He and Erik stood in a corner of the boxing salon where Connor was sparring most of his daylight hours in preparation for the championship fight. Two full days had passed since he and Charlotte had parted and Connor was eager to hear from her.

He stared in disbelief at the sealed letter. He had anticipated a number of reactions from her—coyness, embarrassment, regret perhaps. But never this. Never rejection.

"Aye, unopened," Erik echoed with a shrug. "She sent it back that way."

"You're certain it was delivered to her?" Connor demanded.

"Aye, I believe so," Erik said. "At least I waited long enough for it to be delivered and for her to write a reply. So I was as astounded as ye are when her sister brought it back unopened and said the lady wouldna accept it."

Bewildered, Connor sat down on a bench against the wall and stared at the sealed letter once more. A bead of his own perspiration fell on it, blurring the letters of her name. "Not accepting my letter? And it was Cassandra that you talked to?"

"Least I think it were," Erik said with a shrug. "The one that likes to wear pink."

"That's Cassandra," Connor muttered as he rose and began to pace the length of the room. "Cassie may be a wee sly, but I don't think she would not hide a letter from me to Charlotte. No, this was Charlotte's decision."

"And there be a message sent along with it," Erik said, shifting uneasily from one foot to the other.

Heartened, Connor halted, turning to Erik. "What is it?"

"Miss St. John, whichever one she was, said to tell you that Charlotte would not be at home to the Earl of Kinleith should he come a-calling again."

Connor swore, using several oaths that he'd not uttered in years. The message left no doubt about the meaning of the unopened letter. Charlotte was denying him, denying everything that had happened between them that night in his lodgings, in his bed. She did not want to hear from him again.

He'd had no illusion about the disapproval on her face when the Pugilistic Society had come to call. He'd been ready to curse the bad timing of it all. That morning of all mornings. Had the gentlemen been any other callers, Connor would have sent them packing. He'd prayed then that she understood. She knew what these fights were all about. He'd never led her to think he desired anything less than the championship.

"Very well, then, if she doesn't want to see me, that's fine," he muttered to himself. Deep inside his gut, he remained unconvinced. Even as he sank down on the bench again he knew he had to see her. He wasn't sure why or what he wanted to say, but he had to see her oval face framed in fiery tresses once more.

He rose and paced the length of the room again, long, angry strides that made the other fighters cast him uneasy glances.

How clearly he could see her face, pale and sober in the shadow of the maid's bonnet she had donned that morning. She'd heard Sir Benton of the Pugilistic Society extend the invitation to fight for the championship. She'd known he would accept.

It had all transpired so fast and he had not had the opportunity to tell her how much it meant to him that she'd come to help him when he needed her—and that she'd stayed. Gentle, soft-hearted Charlotte. Risking her safety and her reputation.

Connor cursed louder this time, then muttered to himself, "Maybe you have a right to be so unhappy with me, kitten."

"What do ye want to do about the letter?" Erik asked, standing restlessly by the bench.

Connor stared down at the unopened missive burning against the palm of his hand. Charlotte was entitled to reject him, whether he liked it or not. He'd bargained with Seymour for her freedom. She could turn her back on him if she pleased.

"Forget it," Connor said, angrily tossing the letter into a rubbish can in the corner.

Unbidden his favorite image of her came to him—Charlotte wrapped in the tartan he'd pulled over them during the night. Her flaming hair curled across her creamy-white shoulders and her breasts rising and falling with her slumber. He couldn't keep a smile of relish from spreading across his face.

Fight it as he might, he could not bear the thought of Charlotte retreating to the confines of her study or the clutches of a self-important poet. Not after he'd watched her open up like a precious flower to all the things he'd shown her.

With a painful twist of his heart, Connor realized he cared too much about Charlotte to let her go.

THIRTY-TWO

"I asked you to call on me today, Edward, because there is something I must tell you," Charlotte said over her shoulder, spitting out the words breathlessly as she led the way into her book-lined study. "I thought it too important and personal to put it in a letter."

Edward had responded to her invitation with inordinate speed. Now that he was here in person following her through the house, what had seemed like such a necessary plan the day before took on a less appealing luster.

"Is something amiss?" Edward asked, his hands tucked into his trouser pockets as he sauntered into the study behind her. His wool coat was ill-fitting and his boots wanted polishing. But he was freshly shaved. "I'm not going to have to share your company with that boxing cove, am I?"

Surprised by the reference to Connor, Charlotte halted before turning around. "No, of course not. I believe it's time for me to return your books. Please, Edward, sit down."

"Books?" Edward exclaimed. "You asked me to call on you so you could return my books today? I'm in no great rush to have them back."

"Yes, well, I know that," Charlotte said, stepping behind her desk and putting a barrier between herself and Edward. She always felt safe and at home behind her desk—not that she feared Edward. But she was uncertain about his reaction to what she intended to tell him. "It is also time for me to tell you how I feel."

Edward flipped the skirt of his frock coat out and seated himself on the one straight back chair in Charlotte's study. A slow, puzzled smile spread across the poet's thin face. When he realized that Charlotte was watching him, he ducked his head and ran his hand through his wild hair to hide his expression.

"Dear Charlotte, you must feel free to share your feelings with me at any time," he said, leaning forward, obviously eager to hear her confession. Charlotte couldn't imagine what he thought she was going to tell him, but she suspected it was not what she was about to say.

Charlotte balanced herself on the edge of her desk chair. Concerned that Edward misunderstood her intentions, she clasped her hands in her lap. Second thoughts assailed her. She could just return his books and the lock of hair from Lord Byron and say no more. Their relationship could go on as it was—monthly invitations to Edward's literary discussions and occasional outings to balls and social affairs. Feelings spared. A relationship undisturbed and placid as a mountain lake. He would send her poems and lend her books and she would translate Homer, preening over the praise the literary group showered on her. How tempting. But what would she have accomplished? Who would be better off for her existence?

Charlotte shook her head. No, to leave things as they were would be dishonest. To leave her life unchanged would not be true to the new person she was becoming.

She looked at Edward, who assumed an air of earnestness as he regarded her across the desk. The prospect of hurting him held no relish for her.

Charlotte took a deep breath and dived into her rehearsed speech. "Edward, we've been friends for a long time," Charlotte began, aware that her hands were cold.

"And will be for a long time to come, I hope," Edward said, peering at the titles of the books on Charlotte's desk. "Pauperism? I had no idea you had an interest in the poor. So gloomy and unclean."

Edward's indifference to her speech annoyed Charlotte. She was turning her life in a new direction, and he'd rather have a look at the books she was adding to her library. Get on with it, she scolded herself.

"Yes, well, about our friendship. I know that you are a very sensitive man," Charlotte went on, clasping and reclasping her icy fingers. "If you were not, you would not be such a great poet. But I also know that you are a man of great moral strength and character."

That seemed to capture Edward's attention. He sat up and met Charlotte's gaze at last. "Well, I'm no boxer, but what's this all about, Charlotte?"

She took another deep breath and launched into what she wanted to say. "Edward, I've decided that it's time to make some changes in my life."

Edward frowned. "What sort of changes?"

Charlotte hurried on. "Edward, I've always been so flattered that you considered me a part of your literary group. It has been a joy and an enlightening experience to be a part of London's intellectual circle."

"And it is always a pleasure to have you there, my dear," Edward said, casting her a patronizing smile.

"Thank you, but I feel it's time for me to devote myself to more practical and worldly matters."

Edward's light blue eyes became round and his mouth dropped open. "Surely you're not saying—"

"Yes, that's right, Edward," Charlotte said, nodding as her fickle courage came back to her. "I don't think it would be appropriate for me to continue to attend your literary group."

"You mean that you do not—but you and I—" Color rose in Edward's narrow face, rushing to the roots of his artistically untamed hair. "You know how highly I esteem you. And all the poems I've written for you. You have been my muse."

"And I have been so flattered to serve as your muse," Charlotte said, prepared for this argument and noting the word "esteem." Not love, *esteem*. "It has been an honor to be immortalized by you, Edward. But you are a true poet—you will write poetry whether I serve as your muse or another fills that role. It has always been so with the great writers through the ages."

"Yes, you are correct about that," Edward agreed thoughtfully. But some second thought made him jump to his feet. He pounded on the corner of the desk. "McKensie is at the root of this, isn't he?"

"Connor has nothing to do with this."

"He has won you over to his barbaric ways, has he not?" Edward insisted.

Charlotte stared at him, wondering how she'd missed seeing this shallowness in him. How fortunate she was. She'd waited for so long for his declaration of love and now she was relieved that he'd never offered it.

"I heard about your early morning call at his lodgings," Edward ranted. "Now that he's going to fight for the championship and his name is bantered everywhere about Town, you'd rather be connected with him than me."

Charlotte stared at Edward in confusion. His voice had the petty ring of jealousy in it. She resented the implication that she was motivated by Connor's notoriety. Anger brought a flush to her cheeks.

"I was right." Edward thrust an accusing finger into her face. "I knew I should have warned you the day you brought him to my salon. But I feared the truth would hurt your tender sensibilities."

"You should have warned me about what?" Charlotte asked, rising from her chair at last.

"McKensie bargained with me for your favors."

Charlotte sucked in a deep breath. "He what?"

"He used the right to your favors as a wager in our cribbage game." Edward smirked at Charlotte. In his agitation he strode across the carpet then back. "I would not have you know that for the world. I vowed to myself to remain silent on the subject.

But now—why else do you think I was so upset to lose that cribbage game to him? He has no respect for anything, the barbarian."

Charlotte stared at Edward in shock and dismay. She remembered clearly Connor's smug pleasure with his victory. His demand for a kiss in the garden as if he had a right to such an intimacy. She had yielded, guileless fool that she was, as if she had no other choice.

"I had no idea," Charlotte said, dumbfounded by the revelation but unwilling to betray her shock to Edward. "I thank you for telling me what actually happened."

"My poor darling Charlotte," Edward said, his voice full of malice. "McKensie has influenced you so that you do not even understand his control over your thoughts. You must reconsider your decision."

Charlotte rose, standing as tall as she ever remembered standing in her life. "There is nothing to reconsider, Edward. And I can assure you, if it sets your mind to rest, that this withdrawal from the literary group was my own decision and not influenced in the least by Lord Kinleith."

The wind gone from his sails, Edward drifted to a halt before Charlotte's desk. " 'Tis Cassandra's influence then? She has never liked me and forever mocks my work."

An unbidden smile threatened to spread across Charlotte's expression. Petty though his words were, Edward was exactly right about Cassandra.

"That's not so," she said, refusing to attack her sister on his behalf. "It's just that Cassandra does not have much appreciation for literary works that are not performed on the stage. This is my decision and I can but hope that you will respect it."

"Reconsider, Charlotte. You will be much missed. And I must warn you—without my help, the poetry of your translations will suffer."

"I'm afraid I must risk that possibility," Charlotte said, astonished to discover that Edward was not only shallow but narcissistic as well. "I shall miss seeing everyone there. Elizabeth, and the university students. But I must do this, Edward. I must see where else my destiny might lie."

Edward drew back, his mouth twisting in distaste. "Take care that it is not with the Scotsman, for that sort of man is not above seduction. He would think nothing of using you, Charlotte, and leaving you ruined and outcast."

A blush flamed in Charlotte's cheeks once more. She'd feared as much about Connor's intentions herself—and now with Edward's new revelations, what was she to think? "I shall take care, Edward. Thank you for your warning."

A warning that had come several days too late, Charlotte admitted to herself as she saw Edward out the door with Albert, the footman, carrying his books and the lock of Lord Byron's hair.

Had Connor been plotting her seduction all along, she had to ask herself. She had been so much happier believing that what had transpired between them had ignited spontaneously. But if what Edward said was true, Connor had been plotting to have her all along. And she had walked right into his trap.

Charlotte stepped back to allow Horton to close the door on Edward's retreating back. What Edward had told her changed none of her decisions. She brushed her hands together to clean off the book dust. Edward was gone. And Connor?

Edward's revelation about Connor only made her more certain that she'd done the right thing in returning his letter unopened.

Charlotte glanced around at the hall table to see what lay on the silver salver. "Any more letters in the post, Horton?"

"No, miss, nothing," Horton said. "Were you expecting something?"

"No, nothing," Charlotte said, satisfied that Connor had understood her well enough. He was not going to be so tiresome as to try to write her again. She had no desire whatsoever to see him—especially after this latest bit of news. She turned back to her study, ignoring the growing grief in her heart.

* * *

Two days later a warm summer rain drummed on the roof of the St. John phaeton as Charlotte climbed out onto the street and looked up at the fine colonnades of the Foundling Shelter.

"Albert, bring those two boxes of books for Miss Clyde," Charlotte directed before she walked up the steps and between the stately columns.

Janet was expecting her. Charlotte smiled to herself; her plan was going smoothly. She'd written to Connor's cousin to make an appointment to donate the books and to talk more about the shelter. Janet had replied immediately.

As she waited for Albert to unload the books, she glanced across the street just in time to see a plainly dressed man turn away and lean against the lamppost.

She would not have thought much of the man except it was drizzling and the street was otherwise deserted. She had the sense that she'd seen him before. She peered closer. That strange bulbous nose. Where had it been? Who was he?

Then she remembered the Battersea Field Fair. If she was not mistaken, the man leaning against the lamppost with his back to her was Grady, the towel boy, the man who had nearly run her down in pursuit of the children. What was Grady doing here?

Albert jogged up the steps, gingerly balancing both book boxes in his arms as the rain began to fall faster.

"This way, Albert," Charlotte said, forgetting the man across the street in her haste to get the footman and the books out of the rain. "Follow me."

The lobby of the shelter was occupied by only a couple of women. As before, the woman at the front desk promptly led Charlotte and Albert to Janet's office.

As Charlotte followed the woman down the hall, everything about the shelter was as she remembered: the dark, lofty hall, the creaky floors, the scent of children's bodies and oil lamps. She smiled. It all seemed so strangely familiar, as if she'd been here a hundred times and she belonged to this place. She was glad she'd come again. She hoped to walk down this hallway more often in the future.

"Charlotte." Janet stepped out of her office and smiled, the expression lighting up her round, fair face. As before, her silken hair was tucked neatly under a snowy-white cap and her apron was spotless and starched. "I'm so glad you've come, Charlotte. And these are the books for the library? Two boxes!"

"I hope you and the children can put them to use," Charlotte said, directing Albert to place the boxes on the table by the doorway, then dismissing him.

"Yes, indeed," Janet said with a laugh. "We can use them. So kind of you to think of us. We encourage the children to practice their reading often. Come in—hang your wet things on the coat-tree and have a cup of tea with me, won't you? I just set the kettle on the fire."

Soon Charlotte found herself sitting by the cheerful hearth in Janet's office asking after the children she'd met before and sipping tea as if she and Janet had been friends for a long time.

"So you are interested in being a volunteer here in the shelter." Janet sipped thoughtfully from her cup after Charlotte had asked her the question that had been on her mind since her first visit to the shelter.

"Surely there is something I could do," Charlotte said. She'd spent her entire life under Papa's roof and she feared that perhaps she didn't have the skills needed to help at the shelter. "I could work in the library. Or perhaps I could teach reading or penmanship? I have a very good hand."

"We have excellent teachers," Janet said with a tolerant smile.

"Yes, I'm certain you do," Charlotte said, disappointed there was no place for her. "But there must be something I could do to help."

"Your aunt, Lady Dorian, is an effective fund-raiser for us," Janet offered.

Charlotte shook her head. "I know, but I want to do more than collect money. I'd like to work with the children like you do."

"Have you discussed this with your parents?"

"Papa and Mama will agree to anything that Aunt Dorian approves of," Charlotte said. "I can win her over."

"I'm sure you can." Janet set her dish of tea down on the corner of her desk, folded her hands in her lap, and fixed Charlotte with a level gaze. "You do understand that the jobs volunteers do here are not very glamorous."

"I didn't expect the work to be glamorous," Charlotte admitted, balancing her cup and saucer on her knees. "I want it to be useful."

"And the children are not always delights," Janet warned. "Not all of them appreciate what is offered here. Sometimes they behave most distressingly. They use bad words and call each other—and us—well, by dreadful names. The likes of which I suspect you've never heard, Charlotte."

"I'm certain I would have a lot to learn," Charlotte said. "I haven't done much work with children, but I think I could learn to get over the shock."

Janet eyed Charlotte a moment longer. "I must admit I'm impressed with your sincerity. And I've seen how the children take to you."

Inwardly, Charlotte prayed that success was at hand. "Janet, I'd be so pleased if you could find a place for me."

"Let me review my staff," Janet said, tapping on the ledger on her desk. "I think I might be able to place you."

"Thank you," Charlotte began as Janet checked the watch pinned to her apron.

"In the meantime, I see it's time for me to accompany the choir to practice," Janet said. "You must come listen to them."

Delighted with the prospect of soon being part of the volunteer staff at the Foundling Shelter, Charlotte allowed Janet to take her by the arm and lead her down the hall to the chapel.

"I believe they are shaping up nicely on this new hymn that the music professor has them rehearsing." Janet opened the door to the chapel, darkened by the rain clouds outside. She ushered

Charlotte to a seat a few rows down the aisle. "Sit right there, wait, and listen."

Janet strode off toward the choir box to aid the professor. With a sigh of satisfaction Charlotte settled into the pew, taking in the gold, blue, and red light falling from the stained-glass window to wash across the chapel pews despite the gloominess of the day. Ancient wood paneling cast soft, dark shadows into the corners and across the door. Overhead the unlit brass chandelier gleamed in the colored rays. Only two candles burned against the darkness of the chapel, one for the music professor and one for Janet at the organ.

Elated by her success, Charlotte smiled to herself as she waited for her private performance to begin. She was soon going to have her hands full with her work at the shelter and the new research she intended to do on London's pauper housing. There was so much to learn, so many new, exciting things.

As the choir's voices rang out through the chapel, a movement near the door caught Charlotte's eye. With a start she turned to see Connor materialize from the shadows, the length and breadth of him wrapped in a black cloak, dark and magnificent as Apollo descended in mortal form from Mount Olympus. His dark hair gleamed in the dusky light and a frown darkened his beautiful face.

Silently, he slipped into the pew beside Charlotte, blocking any possibility of escape.

THIRTY-THREE

Charlotte's heart hammered in her breast and she gripped the back of the pew in front of her, wanting to take flight, but intensely aware that Connor had purposely made that impossible.

"What are you doing here?" she demanded, sliding to the far end of the pew. "How did you know—Janet told you?"

"I asked her to," Connor said with maddening casualness, as though they were making small talk on a street corner. "And I am well, thank you, Miss St. John. I hope I find you well? I see roses in your cheeks and a brave smile on your lips—before you spied me, that is."

"I am very well, thank you," Charlotte muttered. He had no need to know that she hadn't been able to eat a proper meal or sleep through an entire night since she'd left him. "Don't patronize me, Connor. Surely we know each other too well for that. What do you want?"

"I want to speak with you, kitten," Connor said, looking toward the choir. "You left the other morning before we could talk."

The sound of the pet name made Charlotte's belly flutter. She drank in the sight of his face. The black eye had faded and the gash on his brow was healed. She knew exactly why she had returned his letter and refused to see him. The sight of him made every courageous and strong emotion that she'd discovered inside of herself melt into weakness. She didn't want to be the weak Charlotte again. She looked away from him and tried to concentrate on the music. "There seemed to be little to say."

"On the contrary, the problem was not a lack of words, it was the interruptions. First by your sister, then by my gentlemen callers. Then suddenly you were gone and wouldn't even accept my request to see you."

"And what would be the point of seeing you?" Charlotte asked, barely able to find her voice. "Everything has changed between us, Connor. You have your invitation to a prizefight. You have achieved what you set out to achieve. I have no part in it."

"Everything has changed, kitten." Connor studied her. "Surely you don't think I take a lady to my bed and send her off in the morning without even a fare-thee-well."

"Shh! Connor, not here." Charlotte's face burned with embarrassment and she was thankful for the noise of the music and darkness of the chapel.

Connor stretched his arm out toward her, along the back of the pew. His cloak fell away, revealing a powerful hand and a sinewy wrist. The gold seal ring of the Earl of Kinleith gleamed in the gloom. But he did not touch her. "Truly, Charlotte, I'm not certain what we have to say to each other, but there is more between us than we had a chance to speak of before Cassie dragged you away."

Charlotte pressed her lips together, refusing to remember that morning. "Edward had the most interesting tale to tell me."

Connor withdrew his arm and turned to face the choir as she had done. "What does Edward have to do with this?"

"He told me you had wagered my favors in your game of cribbage." When Connor made no reply, Charlotte went on. "Cassie and I suspected that your interest in me had to do with pleasing Aunt Dorian, who is very influential, and with Papa's ownership of Glen Gray. We were hardly so sheltered that we could not see your motive for what it was. But wagering favors that were never yours to offer—how disgusting."

Still Connor stared ahead and said nothing.

"Have you no response to that?" Charlotte demanded.

At last he turned to her and spoke with a deceptive softness in his voice that raised the hairs on Charlotte's neck. "Seymour lies. What would you have me do? How do I prove my word against his? Challenge him to a duel? Isn't that what a gentleman would do?"

Charlotte gasped. "You know I would never expect that. Never. But I want to know the truth."

"The blackguard lies. The truth is that his lies make me so angry I would like to split the wood of this pew with my fist and shout profanities to the rafters, the likes of which should never be heard in a house of God. But all I can say to you here and now is that Edward lies."

Charlotte's breath came in shallow gasps. She wanted to hear the truth in Connor's words, but it only whispered to her. Edward had been her friend so long—how could she trust a brawlin' Scotsman?

Connor watched Charlotte turn back toward the choir as she weighed his words. He'd seen the blush of excitement in her cheeks when he'd first approached. The visit to the shelter was responsible for the color, he decided. But he'd also seen the shadow of unhappiness around her eyes. The sight of it made his heart ache.

At least now he knew why she was unhappy. Edward. Under his breath, he cursed Seymour. Then he berated himself for not realizing that the bastard poet would turn the tables, twist his own deceit into Connor's sin.

For himself, the lie mattered little. Connor had faced liars before and the truth always came out. But he resented what Edward's lies did to Charlotte, confusing her, forcing her to question herself—and those for whom she cared.

"But why would Edward lie?" Charlotte asked, looking at Connor once more, seeking an answer to a dishonesty that her truthful soul would never understand. "Edward is a gentleman,

Connor. Why would he abuse your reputation or mine in such a foul way?"

"I can only tell you what I believe," Connor began, fully prepared for her to disbelieve him. "Edward is a little man who longs for devotion. He seeks adoration. He desires admiration. For him love is only a theme for a poem. Pity him, Charlotte."

"I don't know who to believe," Charlotte said, shaking her head.

Connor took a deep breath. He could gladly throttle one aspiring poet at the moment. Charlotte would have to choose for herself who was telling the truth. He leaned closer to her again. "Believe in yourself, Charlotte. Not in your sister. Not in Davis St. John's daughter. Or in the Charlotte who was Edward's devotee. Listen to *your* heart, kitten. It is true and honorable and you will hear the truth."

"I am listening to my heart," she said, continuing to stare at her hands in her lap. "I pray you are right. And that it won't betray me."

"It won't. I know you well enough after this past month of our *Life in London*. Whatever you choose to do—turn away from me if you must," Connor said with more generosity than he felt, "but believe in yourself."

Charlotte turned her gaze on him, her blue eyes probing and searching his. He prayed that she understood his meaning. She was no fool, his Charlotte.

But she turned away before he could be certain that he'd reached her. Her gaze remained fixed on the children in the choir. He sat close enough now that he could smell the rosy fragrance of her perfume. It stirred memories of their passionate night together.

"I have returned Edward's books and told him I will not be coming to his literary group again," she said.

Relief washed over Connor and he swallowed the momentary urge to shout in victory. "Then you don't believe him?"

Charlotte shook her head. "I'm not certain, but even if I did I could never go back to being the Charlotte I was that day first met you. The Charlotte who was content with a literary group. And I thank you for challenging me to that silly *Life in London* game. I have learned so much. I should have thanked you sooner."

"No thanks is required," Connor said, watching her thoughtfully. If Edward was out of the ring, he had a fighting chance.

Charlotte distractedly chewed on her lower lip. He sensed that she wanted to tell him something more.

"About that night we were together," she began at last, "I realized that we will never come to terms about your fighting."

"I was afraid of that." Connor moved closer to her on the pew. Charlotte scooted away maintaining the distance between them.

"I think if you understood the sport better, Charlotte, you might feel differently."

"I have changed, Connor," Charlotte said. "But not that much. I don't think it would do any good for me to know more about boxing. The change I'm talking about brought me to the decision to devote myself to the Shelter."

An unpleasant thought struck Connor. "You're not going to devote yourself to the cause as completely as Janet, are you?"

"I admire Janet very much," Charlotte said, a rebellious tilt to her head.

The prospect did not please Connor. He shifted uncomfortably and turned to watch the orphans' choir. If Charlotte made Janet's unselfish choice, she would be as lost to him as surely as if she'd promised herself to Edward. Panic flickered. He glanced at her, at her young, earnest face intent on the singing children. He knew with a rush of emotion that almost knocked him out of the pew that he loved Charlotte.

He released a long slow breath and grasped the pew in front of him to brace himself against the surge of feelings. Gallantry be damned, he loved her and he wanted her for himself. Dare he declare that now? She'd just told him she saw no future for them. "You have a huge heart, Charlotte. You deserve a husband and your own children. Why lock yourself up with these orphans?"

"They need me," Charlotte said. "But I haven't made Janet's choice, yet."

"I'm glad to hear that," Connor said, relieved she was not determined to turn herself into the little nun his cousin had become. And he liked to think that their intimate night together might have something to do with that. He released the back of the pew and sat back.

"But whatever has changed in me, a particular part remains constant," Charlotte continued. "I cannot approve of your boxing."

"I would not ask you to give up what you believe," his said, treading softly with his words. "But I would ask you to keep an open mind and come to the fight. See for yourself that it is civilized, in its way."

Charlotte tapped her toe impatiently as if she did not like what she heard, but he could see that she was listening.

"Hear me out," Connor said, hope growing in his heart. "I never want you to witness anything that upsets you, Charlotte. But at that first fight, you watched me defeat a man. And you didn't appear to suffer greatly."

"I had no idea who you or he were," Charlotte said, facing straight ahead. "And I did it for—"

"Cassandra, I know," Connor finished for her. "You are not Cassandra. You were Charlotte that day, underneath your masquerade. If you could do it for Cassandra, could you do it for me?"

"Don't play games with my head and heart," Charlotte implored, her lips dangerously close to trembling. "Please, don't do that to me."

Connor took a deep breath. He would press her no more. "Then, would you think about it? Think about coming to the fight."

Charlotte pressed her lips together and nodded." I will think about it."

Connor sat a bit longer, listening to the tuneful voices of the children singing "Be Thou My Vision" which had often given him comfort. He should have known that he would not be able to change her mind. When the song ended, he bade Charlotte farewell and without waiting for her reply, he slipped out of the pew and the chapel.

He strode down the hallway, angry and annoyed and confused with his failure to win her over. He knew now that he loved Charlotte and he had reason to suspect that she might care about him—in some small way. That was good to know. But he also knew "some small way" would never be enough for him.

Halfway down the hall he heard his name being called. Abruptly, he turned to see Charlotte following him as she drew something out of the pocket of her gown, a modest dark blue frock that made her look dainty and demure.

"Here, take this," she said, offering him a clean, white, lacy handkerchief.

Surprised and a little bewildered, Connor hesitated.

"To carry into the fight," Charlotte explained, her gaze on the handkerchief. She held it forth as if she were afraid to look up into his face. "I noted that the other was rather beyond repair."

Filled with a sudden desire to draw Charlotte into his arms, Connor did not move. After their conversation touching her would be a mistake.

"Yes, the other is the worse for wear," Connor agreed. "But it served me well."

"And so shall this one, I hope," Charlotte said, a false note of cheer in her voice. "I can't watch you fight, Connor, but that doesn't mean that I don't wish you to win. It would make me very happy for you to win your prizefight, purchase Glen Gray, and return to Scotland victorious and rich. I have never wished you anything but the best."

When Connor took it from her hand, she smiled at him, a tender, tremulous smile.

Connor tucked the linen square inside his sash and took heart, his old devilish confidence welling up inside him. "But a token is of little use without a kiss for luck."

Charlotte paused. Her lashes fluttered against her cheeks when she turned away from him. "Don't, Connor."

" 'Tis true, you know," Connor insisted, unable to resist grinning at her. "Have you ever heard anyone say different? Just a small kiss."

"Just a small kiss," Charlotte echoed, still not looking up at him. Her tongue flicked tentatively across her lips.

Connor's entire body warmed.

"Just lips," she added, casting a furtive glance back toward the chapel. "This is not the proper place for—"

"Aye, if you insist," Connor said slowly, a bit disappointed but his strategy already shifting to fit the opportunity. "Just lips. But no peck on the cheek would ever qualify for a kiss for luck."

At last Charlotte eyed him, her blue eyes flashing with suspicion. "Is there some book of kissing deportment that I have yet to discover in the lending library?"

"Not yet," Connor said, attempting to remain as sober-faced as possible. "I'm still writing it."

"That's what I suspected," Charlotte said, a smile lurking on her lips.

"But that makes the rules no less valid," Connor said, eager to keep the exchange going and to make that tempting smile broaden. "I'm merely attempting to record what men and women have known about kissing for centuries. I would certainly welcome a partner in this work."

"You're hopeless," Charlotte said amusement in her voice. "But I'll give you your kiss."

With a quick movement, she stretched up and planted her mouth on his.

Speed had always been one of Connor's assets. He seized her arms before she could draw away. He moved his lips across hers with all the love and tenderness that had surprised him in the chapel. He sampled her lower lip and savored her upper with a series of little kisses. He poured into them all the emotions and stirrings that he had no talent for putting into words.

Charlotte moaned. With all his strength, Connor resisted the sweetness of her mouth. He had promised lips only. But when Charlotte's mouth quickened beneath his and her body pressed against the length of him and her lips parted, he took what was offered. Hot, wet, satiny, and so eager to return what he gave. There was no hearty Scottish stock anywhere who would ever stir more passion in him than Charlotte St. John did.

At last he had to come up for air. "Kitten?"

Charlotte seemed to recover herself and pushed at his chest until he released her. She was gasping for breath almost as rapidly as he. "I think that's quite enough for a good luck kiss."

"I'll win in three rounds," Connor said, laughter bubbling up inside him. "If you are there, it won't even take that long."

The smile slipped from Charlotte's lips. "No, I can't, Connor. I can't. Don't you understand? I can't bear to watch the blows, the purpling bruises, the bleeding brows."

Panic filled her eyes, and she shook her head as she turned away and ran back toward the chapel—the back of her hand pressed to her mouth.

Connor stared at the lacy handkerchief she'd pressed into his hand. So fragile, so delicate, like their love. He fancied boxing. She deplored it. He took what the world offered. She contemplated each new offering. Was there to be no compromise for them?

THIRTY-FOUR

Davis's evening had begun with an attempt to extract information about the championship bout from Sir Benton. Over dinner at the club with Sir Benton and several other gentlemen of the Pugilistic Society details were revealed.

Just as Davis had suspected, Forbes's name was mentioned. The Scottish marquis was supporting the champion, Jem Ward, dubious though the champ's reputation was. The support came in every form, from securing Ward the best boxing coach and sparring partners, to financing his training. Lord Forbes, the Marquis of Linirk, was doing everything in his power to defeat McKensie.

The knowledge didn't sit well with Davis. Not because he had a soft spot for underdogs, but because he knew with the instinct of an astute businessman what Forbes would do to him if he didn't oblige the marquis. Once McKensie was out of the picture, Forbes would set his sights on Davis.

Davis had not yet composed his reply to the marquis, because he had not yet decided how he wanted to answer. All he had to do was agree to sell Glen Gray, naming his price, and he'd have his knighthood. Why was the decision so difficult to make?

The hour had grown late at the club, and all the gentlemen had departed, one by one. Then Benton had begun to talk of having nowhere to spend the night—though he had a house on the edge of Town. Davis had been trapped.

"Thank you again, old chap, for bringing me home with you,"

Sir Benton said, settling himself into Davis's favorite chair by the library fire.

"With all the beds at the club spoken for, offering you a room is the least I can do, my lord." Davis flipped open the cigar box and extended it to a foxed peer of the realm. "Care for a smoke?"

"Yes, don't mind if I do." Benton reached into the box, missing a cigar on his first attempt, but snagging one on his second try. "Are these the fine Carolina smokes that you were passing around at the club?"

"Oh, yes, indeed." Davis smiled. He liked being known for offering good tobacco. "The very same."

They proceeded through the ritual of snipping off the ends and lighting the tobacco from the candle flame on the mantel.

"You said your wife was home," Benton mumbled, after they had each released the first savored draws on their cigars.

"Yes, I believe so." Davis wondered where Susanna was.

"A treasure," Benton said, leaning his head back and sending a great plume of smoke into the air. "A doting wife. A treasure. How I envy men like you."

"Me?" Davis looked around the library, wondering if someone had entered whom he had not seen. What was there to envy? Coming home to a gaggle of women babbling about old Greek stones that any sensible civilization would have usurped for new structures. Fending off a throng of young bucks who thought they had a right to your daughters and their dowries. And that infuriating way a woman could let her husband crawl into her bed, all the while closing him out of her heart. All because he aspired to a title. What was to envy?

"Coming home every evening and find the servants in order and a meal prepared." With bleary eyes Benton watched the cloud of smoke rise toward the plaster ornamented ceiling.

"Are you hungry, my lord?" Davis asked, eager to move on to a more relevant and less personal topic. He rang the bell just as Susanna swept into the library.

"There you are, Davis." She paused inside the door, a gracious smile on her lips though the hour was late. Despite the

plainness of her brown gown with a cameo pinned at the throat
and the errant flame-hued curls framing her face, Davis thought
she looked marvelous. "I was worried when I didn't hear from
you. But here you are and with a friend."

Davis stepped toward her, grateful for the interruption in the
strange, drunken conversation.

"Susanna, Sir Benton has accepted my invitation to spend
the night," he said. "The club rooms were all spoken for."

"And I can't bear to go home, my dear," Benton said, his
words slurred. At the club Davis had watched his lordship empty
two bottles of port and start on a third. "I simply can't bear to
face that great echoing place of mine."

"How unfortunate, my lord," Susanna said, exchanging an
understanding glance with Davis. "I've already ordered a room
readied. It won't take but a few minutes. In the meantime, Sir
Benton, perhaps you would like something to eat."

"Yes, I just rang for Horton," Davis said.

"A cold supper would be tasty," Benton said, comfortably
puffing on his cigar. "Make no fuss."

When Horton appeared at the door, Susanna went to him.
"Davis, would you be so kind as to help order for you gentlemen?"

"Excuse me, my lord," Davis said, knowing a wife's cue when
he heard it.

"What are we going to do with him?" Susanna implored.
"Thank heavens the girls are abed. We can't have them see him.
He's rather in his—"

"Cups. I agree," Davis said. "Order a cold supper and—"

"And cider, I believe?" Susanna said, thoughtfully tapping
her chin with a finger. "I believe his lordship has had enough
port."

"Quite," Davis agreed. As soon as Horton headed for the
kitchen, Davis took Susanna's hand. "When he's eaten, he'll
probably be ready to retire. Serve him breakfast in his chamber
tomorrow. The girls need never see him in this state."

"Yes, you're right." Susanna turned toward the library. "I'll do what I can to help. He seems so lost. But we'll have him tucked into bed soon."

"Thank you, Susanna," Davis said, touching her arm before she walked back into the room with Sir Benton.

"Ah, there you are, Mrs. St. John," Benton began, eyeing Susanna with a drunken man's leer. He patted the arm of the chair beside his. "You do look lovely as ever tonight. Please, come sit down by me, my dear."

With a patient smile, Susanna sat down in the chair next to Sir Benton. Davis posted himself behind his lordship.

"I apologize for keeping your husband out so late," Benton said. "You see, we became involved in a deep discussion about the championship fight four days from now. You know the one."

"But all of London knows about it," Susanna said, a shadow of disapproval crossing her face. " 'Tis as much a part of the news sheets as the Duke of Wellington's antics as Prime Minister."

A look of surprise crossed Benton's face and he peered at Susanna. "Wellington? Prime Minister?"

"Since January, my lord," Davis muttered into his lordship's ear. Benton's lapse was not surprising, Davis mused. Boxing was the lord's life, not politics. If he wasn't at Fives Court or at one of the boxing salons, he was at the club talking fights to anyone he could corner.

"Oh, yes, of course, I knew that about Wellington," Benton blustered and brushed the matter aside with a wave of his cigar.

Susanna suppressed a smile of amusement. Davis choked off his own laughter. They smiled at each other over his lordship's head. The exchange warmed Davis inside, filling him with a precious familiar pleasure he'd almost forgotten. It was good to really share something with Susanna again.

"Ah, as I was saying, about the fight," Benton continued. "It is becoming the match of the year. I believe in McKensie myself. A win is in the bag for him I think, unless he should fail to show for the fight. Forfeiture that. But place your wagers accordingly St. John. The Scotsman will win. Bright man, your husband, Mrs. St. John."

"Yes, I know, my lord," Susanna said, smiling softly at Davis again. The expression warmed Davis's heart.

Benton studied her with a satisfied gleam in his eye before he spoke over his shoulder to Davis. "I tell you, she's a treasure, St. John."

"I know it, my lord," Davis said, grateful to see that Horton had arrived with a food-laden tray.

Davis drew up a chair. For the next half hour or so all three supped on bread, cheese, biscuits, fruit, and cider.

The conversation turned to light and amusing topics. Davis had the distinct impression that Benton was purposely trying to entertain Susanna. Not out of any lecherous designs, but simply because the man truly enjoyed the company of a cordial and genteel woman. Davis sat back, nibbling on a grape and basking in a glow of pride.

"Let me say again how good it is of you to have me in your home tonight, Susanna, dear," Benton said, finishing his last mug of cider. "I may call you Susanna?"

"Of course, Sir Benton," Susanna said, taking his lordship's cider mug and gesturing to Albert to refill it.

"And you must call me Benny," he said, retrieving his refilled mug. He leaned toward Susanna confidentially and said with a chuckle, "My full name is Benton Rowland Benton the Third. But my friends call me Benny."

Davis wondered if his lordship would remember in the morning that he'd given Susanna permission to call him by his nickname.

Abruptly Benton became very still, stiff as a statue. Cider sloshed in his mug. Davis sat forward in his chair, wondering if his lordship was about to pass out, or worse, get sick.

Leather creaked as Susanna reached for the forgotten mug.

His lordship shook his head and looked about him as if seeing the room for the first time. "Time for me to retire."

"Excellent idea." Davis jumped to his feet to help Benton rise from the chair.

Susanna hastily set the mugs and food aside and rose to take his lordship's other arm. Slowly they made their way out of the library and toward the stairs, Benton's right arm wrapped around Davis's shoulders and Susanna steadying the man on the left.

"I had a lovely wife once," Benton muttered in Davis's ear as they attempted to scale the steps one at a time.

"Lady Benton is at your country house, I believe," Susanna said. Davis had heard the same thing and wondered why Benton insisted on carrying on as if he were a bachelor.

"Yes, she prefers the country house," Benton said, with a bitter laugh. "Has lived there for years, you know, leaving me to come home alone every day to that great, hulking estate on the edge of Town."

"I suppose 'tis lonely," Davis said, trying to be agreeable.

"Lonely?" Benton shook his head. "You don't know what it's like. The boys are both grown and gone. Every day I walk into that house and my footsteps echo through the halls. I hate the sound. Even bought a wagonload of carpets to hush the maddening echoes. But it doesn't help."

Benton finally made it to the landing and leaned heavily on Davis, speaking directly into his ear. "You can't eat dinner with a rolled carpet at the other end of the table either."

Susanna smiled at Sir Benton's attempt at humor.

"True," Davis agreed again, without anything more to add.

"Just one more short flight of steps, your lordship and we'll be at the door of your room," Susanna encouraged.

"A loving wife is a true treasure," Benton said once again. "Actually, 'loving' is not necessary. 'Friendly' will do. Friendly and loyal."

Susanna laughed. "Perhaps you need a good dog, my lord."

Davis sucked in a breath, fearing his lordship would take offense.

But Benton gave a short laugh. "Dashed good sense of humor is also an excellent trait in a good wife."

"Susanna has a sense of humor all right," Davis said, casting her a reproachful glance. He hoped there would be no more dog comments.

"You know why my wife likes the country house, don't you?" Benton continued, making the next few steps without difficulty. "She's in love with the gamekeeper."

Susanna stopped in her steps. "I'm sorry to hear that, my lord. That must be very difficult for you."

"Yes, it is," Benton said.

Davis scowled at Benton, regretting that the lord had chosen this particular moment to reveal his personal circumstances. Benton's unfaithful wife was news to him. He'd only heard that Lady Benton never came to London and he had assumed, as many others had, that the lady did not care for Town life.

"She has a right to him, I suppose," Benton continued. "I neglected her. We men never appreciate our wives. When we're young we want to bed them and get our heirs and our pleasure. We overlook the other delights they bring to our lives."

"Here we are, my lord," Davis said, leading the gentleman into the room Susanna had had prepared for their guest. Davis released his lordship slowly to see if Benton could stand on his own.

"Sorriest thing I've ever done, neglecting my wife." Benton swayed slightly. "Probably the easiest, too. I should have sat by the fire with her a few more evenings and flattered her and made a great fuss over the anniversaries and the birthdays. Women like that sort of thing, you know, St. John."

Benton waved a finger in Davis's face. "And this is important too. When women tell you what they want, listen."

Benton wagged his head from side to side. "Don't be a fool and think you know better than they about what they want."

That statement struck a chord with Davis and he glanced at Susanna who was staring back at him. The debacle over her birthday had not happened all that long ago.

"Yes, special occasions mean ever so much more to them than jewels alone," Benton continued. "No, not even houses mean much to some of them. At least, to the women worth going home to. Don't do it, St. John. Don't make my mistake."

Susanna helped Benton into a chair.

Davis stared at the older man, understanding the wisdom in his words at last. Benton was right about jewels. Susanna's birthday gift lay tucked safely in the house strongbox. She had not been in the least tempted by the diamond-and-pearl bracelet. She'd not even asked to see it again, let alone wear it.

"That's good advice," Davis said. "Take off your coat, your lordship, and let's get you settled."

Susanna helped their guest out of his coat.

"So after my wife made her position known I found me a ladybird," Benton said allowing Susanna to begin to work on his crushed cravat. "My ladybird threw me over for a younger man, you know. Dashed embarrassing, it was. A mistress is never the answer. When it's all said and done, they are merchants looking for the richest customer."

Davis decided that was enough said about wives with lovers and gentlemen with mistresses with his wife present. He brushed Susanna's hands away from his lordship's cravat.

"Why don't you retire, my dear," Davis said in a stern voice. "I shall see to whatever his lordship needs."

Susanna stared at him, her expression unreadable.

"Please, Susanna," Davis said. "Thank you for your help."

"Of course." She turned to Benton. "Good night, my lord."

Benton bade a garbled but respectable good night to Susanna. Davis managed to get the elder man undressed and rolled into bed without much more advice or confession. By the time he was out of Benton's chamber, his lordship was snoring.

To Davis's surprise when he opened the door of his own room, he found Susanna sitting on his bed and wearing a thin white nightrail. Her titian hair hung in loose curls about her shoulders and she looked almost girlish, except for the sober set of her mouth. She seldom came to his room these days, mostly because he could never wait for her and went to her bed first.

"Sorry you had to hear all that," Davis said, going to the mirror to untie his cravat.

"I have a question, Davis." She concentrated on the invisible circles she drew on the counterpane with her finger.

Davis began to tug at his own cravat. "I had no idea he and his wife were estranged."

"Here, let me do that," Susanna said, rising from the bed to come to his aid. "My question is not about Sir Benton."

She paused and took a deep breath. "I wanted to know if you have or have ever had a mistress."

Davis let out a slow, exasperated sigh. He could wring his lordship's aristocratic neck. But he had questions of his own "Let me ask you—have you taken Myron as your lover?"

"Of course not. How can you even think to ask," Susanna said, giving a surprisingly energetic tug on his cravat.

Unprepared, Davis gagged.

"Sorry," Susanna muttered as she continued to loosen the knot, her head tipped so he could not see her face. A face he'd gazed across the table at for over twenty years.

"I have never taken a mistress," Davis said truthfully as he tried to gaze into her face, but all he could see as he looked down was the tantalizing lace of her nightrail against her rosy, smooth breast. And lower, the dusky hint of her nipple beneath the fabric. His body reacted in a familiar, urgent way.

Needing to draw her closer, he grasped her upper arms. "Think on it, sweetheart. I can hardly manage the three females who live under my roof now. Why on earth would I add another woman to the fold?"

Susanna shook her head, her expression still hidden. Her floral scent filled his head. He ached for her.

"Then are you sorry you married me?" she asked. "Me, a widow, without a title or a dowry? You could have done better."

"Never," Davis cried, stunned by the question. "How can you ask that? I married the woman I love."

"And I love you, Davis." Still, Susanna refused to look into his eyes. "I would be crushed if anything separated us as it has Sir Benton and his wife. 'Tis so sad. He is so alone. Tragic, really."

"Sad, yes," Davis agreed, thinking how empty his house would seem if Susanna were not there to greet him, even when she was vexed with him. How empty his soul would be if he thought that she turned to another for love and companionship. "But as his lordship admits, he was a bit of a fool. He let little things come between him and his wife."

Susanna continued. "Davis, I wish we could put this title thing behind us once and for all."

Without warning, she took Davis's hand and pressed his knuckles against her cheek. She looked up at him, her amber eyes lustrous with unshed tears. Her lips trembled. "Please, Davis, we—the girls and I beg of you—give it up. A title is not worth all the trouble you take, the hours away, the compelling need to impress others. All we want is your love and company."

Davis studied her beloved face and was lost. She asked for so little. All he had to give was himself and she was welcome to every last part of him. Davis pressed his lips against Susanna's, tasting and teasing. She kissed him back, wrapping her arms around his neck and pressing her breasts against his chest. He lifted her up into his arms and carried her to his bed. Then he wiped away her tears and made love to her all night with more passion than he dreamed he had left in him after twenty-some years of marriage.

As dawn glimmered in the east and Davis drifted off into exhausted slumber with Susanna cradled against him, he decided at last what he must write in his reply to the Marquis of Linirk.

THIRTY-FIVE

Grady leaned one elbow against the gin shop counter and with a toss of his head took a long, satisfying swig of gin. This time he'd arrived early for his appointment with Harby. He was determined to enjoy his drink before the buck arrived and started in with his infernal questions. Where'd the Scotsman go? How many times? Did he take Erik with him? Has he seen the St. John miss again?

Watching McKensie had been of little interest during the last week—except for the day he'd met the St. John girl. The Scotsman mostly had spent his days sparring at the boxing salon, eating a good meal in the evening, and staying in his lodgings. Jem Ward had better be preparing himself for this one, Grady thought.

The gin shop was crowded with midday drinkers. Grady had just managed to get out of the boxing salon in time to walk over to the gin shop some blocks away. Harby had sent a message by way of a street vendor's child that he absolutely required a meeting with Grady today at midday. There must be no delay.

The messenger boy had had the gall to make a face at Grady when he only tipped him a pence. Cheeky urchin.

The chance for a noontime shot or two of gin was just fine with Grady and here he was, about half finished with his first and thinking how good the next one was going to taste.

Harby burst into the shop, shouting Grady's name. Grady

waved to the buck then thrust his gin glass at the man behind the counter. "Fill it up, shopkeep."

Harby elbowed his way to the counter and ordered his own glass of gin. When the drink arrived, he drained the contents in one toss and pounded the glass on the counter for more.

"We have our orders at last," Harby said, speaking so softly, Grady could hardly hear him over the noise of the other patrons.

"Orders?" Grady repeated. "Ain't you going to ask what I've seen over the last week?"

"Well, of course," Harby said. "Lord Forbes knows exactly what he wants and when he wants it. His messenger arrived this morning breathless and excited. Something had gone wrong during the past few days. He received a reply in a letter from some rich bloke that made him very unhappy. He wants us to take care of McKensie. And he's willing to pay plenty for the job. We need to find two strong men and a good chemist. Then we need—"

Pleased to know at last that payment for all his work was close at hand, Grady leaned closer and listened to Harby's grand plans.

"My Lord McKensie." A well-dressed man stepped out onto Bond Street in front of Connor, blocking his way.

The unseasonably warm day was drawing to a close. The summer sun had just set, but the street was still full of light. The lamplighter had yet to appear on his appointed rounds. Many people were still about, taking in the evening air.

The young man in blue coat and buff breeches doffed his brown top hat and continued to block Connor's path. "I don't expect that you remember me, my lord."

"We've no use for another one of ye newspaper fellows," Erik growled none too politely. Illustrations of Connor in the news sheets and *The Times* had made him recognizable. Suddenly he was known by nearly everyone in London. Erik had been warding off gentlemen and ladies of all ranks for the last week. He made to step in front of Connor to fend off the man.

"No," Connor said, holding out a hand to stay Erik. The small raspberry birthmark on the chin was familiar. "I remember you. Harby, isn't it? You're a friend of Eldwick and Tony Derrington, I believe."

A smile of delight spread across the young man's face. "You're right, my lord. I'm flattered that you should remember me."

"What can I do for you, sir?" Connor said, glad to speak with someone he truly did know and had met before all the newspaper nonsense had begun.

"Well, my lord," Harby began, "truth is, I'd like to issue an invitation."

"I'm not accepting social invitations these days, Mr. Harby," Connor said, regretting the fact. He missed being out with people and most especially with Charlotte. But that was not a matter of refusing an invitation, for she had sent none and he'd expected none. "Training for the fight, you know."

"Yes, of course," Harby said, obviously a bit flustered. "We—I—we understand, my lord. It's just that a few of us who visit Gentleman Jack's and have watched you from the beginning, well, we'd be ever so pleased if you'd come down to the Hound and Hare to have a glass or two of ale with us. Surely ale wouldn't have no effect on your training."

The man's bashful delivery and the fact that he was a fellow boxing fan moved Connor. He glanced at Erik, who was shaking his head. Erik had become something of a naysayer in these last few days. Nothing suited him—not the number of hours Connor spent sparring nor the mornings he spent walking. While Connor agreed with Erik that this fight was an important move in the feud against the Forbeses, he was beginning to think his friend and retainer had become obsessed with the bout. Connor was weary of it. He'd spent nearly all his waking hours in the sparring ring. If Erik wasn't filling his head with fight strategy, speculations about Charlotte flooded his mind—what was she doing or feeling? The thought of sharing a bit of talk over a mug of ale with a few friendly boxing fans held a lot of appeal.

Connor shook off Erik's hand on his arm. "I've been known

to down a mug or two of ale now and again. Don't believe I've heard of this place, the Hound and Hare."

" 'Tis just down the street and 'round the corner." Harby gestured vaguely toward the corner. At his signal, a cab pulled up to the curb. "You see, I took the liberty of hiring us a conveyance."

"Connor, the fight is only the day after tomorrow," Erik declared, his brows drawn together in anger. "This is not the time for ye to get yerself jug-bitten and waste away a night regaling some young bucks with your boxing stories."

"We just want to wish you well, my lord," Harby said, dancing nervously from one foot to the other. "Your man can come with us if you wish. The more the merrier. Or he can go on along to your lodgings if you like. We won't keep you long. No, by Jove, we've all got wagers on you. We'll have you home in an hour or two."

"I'm dry after a day on the canvas," Connor said, clapping a hand on the young man's shoulder. "Your invitation sounds too good to refuse. Let's go, then."

"Really?" Harby exclaimed, almost seeming relieved. "Yes, well, let's go, then."

Harby opened the cab door and waved his hat to indicate that Connor should climb in.

"Carry on, Erik," Connor said, unmoved by Erik's arguments. "I'll be along directly."

Erik's angry frown deepened into a scowl and his fists doubled at his sides, but he said no more. Looking forward to a break in his long, exhausting routine, Connor turned away, and climbed into the cab.

Reaching the Hound and Hare took longer than Connor had anticipated. Harby prattled on so, hardly taking a breath between questions and Connor's answers that it was almost impossible for him to be certain just where the cab had taken them.

The tavern was on the seedy side of respectable, but it wasn't a bad place. The aroma of stale beer, cheap tobacco, and burned pie crust reached Connor. Dirty hay crunched underfoot, but the condition of the place did not trouble him. He certainly had refreshed himself in less reputable places in England and Scotland and come to no great harm.

Harby's friends turned out to be two big men in frock coats with shaggy haircuts. They looked as though they would be more at home on a London dock than in any boxing salon. And Grady, the towel boy, was also sitting at the table in the back room. All greeted Connor with raised mugs and loud songs for a hero.

The barmaid shoved a full mug into Connor's hands and Harby found the two of them a place on the bench. Connor sat down, glad that he'd come. This was going to be much more enjoyable than sitting in his rooms listening to Erik potter about while he wondered what Charlotte was doing and if she was thinking of him.

Harby grinned at him. "You said you were dry, and so you've proved. We can remedy that."

Halfway through his third mug and the telling of his second boxing story, the strangest feeling hit Connor. The room up-ended, like the deck of a ship on a stormy sea. The three men sitting across from him seemed to lose their smiles. Earlier they could hardly stop laughing, but now they watched him with sober, guarded expressions.

The room took another turn. Connor braced his arms against the table and forced himself to take a deep breath. The room settled back where it belonged. No one else at the table seemed to think anything was wrong. The candle flame never flickered or wavered. He'd had too much ale, he decided, though no brew had ever made him feel quite this strange.

"Gentlemen, I thank you for your hospitality, but I'd better go home," Connor said uneasily, shoving his mug away. He couldn't quite put his finger on it, but something was amiss here. The sooner he got out of the Hound and Hare and away from the drink, the smoke, and these men, the better.

THIRTY-SIX

"But you must finish your story," Harby insisted, reaching for the pitcher that the barmaid had finally left on the table after complaining about the frequency of their demands.

Connor shook his head, refusing the offer in hopes of clearing his head. He looked into his mug, wondering just how powerful this concoction was. Some locally brewed ales could be potent, but this was way beyond anything of his ken. "I think I've had enough."

"One more," Harby urged, filling the mug to the brim again. "Then we'll have you home straightaway."

"So how did that fight turn out, my lord?" asked Grady. He tapped Connor's arm, demanding attention. "You won it, of course. But we want to hear about the match with the Trooper."

Connor glanced about the room once more, waiting to see if it was about to betray his senses again, but it did not. Hesitantly, he launched into the story about the Trooper, but he kept finding himself at a loss for the wit and words for the telling of it.

Finally, he caught himself simply staring at the table before him, fascinated by the grain of the wood and the nicks in the surface. As he stared he realized that someone drew his cup aside and dropped something into it. He continued to stare at the intriguing, undulating wood grain, captivated by the flow of lines and colors, all the while the back of his mind struggling to put together the pieces of the puzzle. The invitation, the separation from Erik, the confusing cab ride, the boxing afficionados who looked like dock workers.

Harby sat the cup before Connor once more. Connor studied it this time, mesmerized by the concentric circles on the surface of the liquid flowing out toward the brim from the impact of being set down.

Soft, fuzzy alarm ran through Connor. Did the fool Harby think he didn't see what he'd done? Did he appear so beyond normal consciousness that no one at the table feared discovery or retribution?

This devilry could only be the work of one man, Ramsay Forbes. Nothing would stop the marquis from having what he wanted, which was for Connor to lose this match. Nothing, not even murder.

"Here, have some more ale," Harby urged, shoving the mug into Connor's hand, which lay at rest on the table. "We want to hear all of your stories. We don't want you to get dry."

Connor drew a deep breath, marshaled his strength, then lurched up from the bench. With all his might, he thrust his hands against the edge of table. It toppled away. Mugs scattered everywhere. Pitchers flew through the air, sloshing dark ale across the floor. Taken by surprise, the three gents on the far side of the table tumbled backward.

Harby lost no time throwing himself against Connor, but Connor was ready. He tossed the young buck aside. Kicking the bench away, he turned to escape the room, but his feet were leaden. Like limbs in a bad dream, they refused to move. His legs and feet remained planted on the floor as if he had no will over them.

Grady latched onto Connor's arm, but Connor was maddened now by his inability to move. With sheer will, he dragged at his feet until he was able to get to the door into the taproom. The door refused to open. Connor rattled the latch and pulled with all his strength, but the door remained fast. He could no reason. Was it locked from the inside or outside? Frustratio welled up inside him. Strong hands grabbed at his arms dragged at him. He had to escape. Shrugging off his attackers, he doubled up his hand, hauled back, and splintered the door with his fist. Whatever held it, gave way. Connor kicked the remainder of the door open. He was out.

The front room of the tavern was empty. No one was there to come to his aid. No one was there to hinder him, either. He charged toward the front door, still fending off hands and blows.

The front room tilted. Connor staggered, but kept moving. Instinct told him that if he'd been drugged he needed to keep moving. One foot in front of the other. One, then the other. He heard shouts and feet scuffling behind him. He forced himself to ignore them. He kept moving, slogging along like a man knee-deep in water. Keep moving. Move. Move.

Just as the latch of the front door of the tavern seemed to be within Connor's reach, someone grabbed him from behind. He was spun around. Fist doubled, Connor plowed into the man's gullet with all his might. Air whooshed from his attacker. An agonized groan fell from the man's mouth as he dropped away, making way for another. Connor swung at him, too, but the wily fellow ducked. From behind, someone dropped something heavy and dark over Connor. He flailed at the dense fabric. It smelled of the sea. A bag or a sail. Connor braced himself, but he couldn't prevent someone from looping a rope around his ankles.

Suddenly his feet were pulled out from under him and he hit the floor with a painful thud.

Still, Connor fought. Ramsay Forbes was not going to win this match. Connor was not going to be defeated. He rolled around the floor, using the leverage of the men holding his ankles to throw himself against someone's legs. The man yelped and scrambled away.

"Get something," he heard Harby say. "We can't handle him like this."

Several sets of footsteps moved around Connor's head. He knew they must be acquiring a weapon. He tried to battle his way out of the cover to reach the men's ankles but a rope was already being wrapped around him. Despite all his efforts, he was being trussed up like a lamb for the slaughter—or the river.

"Here, use this," he heard Harby say.

Light exploded in Connor's head.

Then nothing.

Charlotte sat down in the chair by the cold hearth in Janet's office and stared at her hands. Her left index finger throbbed from the most recent needle prick and her right hand cramped from cutting fabric with old shears.

"Battle wounds?" Janet asked, striding into the room with the rustle of starched skirts.

"I'm not sure I'm the one you should have selected to teach the little girls needlework," Charlotte began, holding up her hands for Janet's inspection. "I only learned the rudiments of stitching myself, but I'm having a good time with the little ones."

"And they seem to be learning from you," Janet said, bending over the basket on her desk. "The rudiments are exactly what we want them to learn at their young age. Charlotte, if you continue to bring a lunch basket like this every time you visit, I shall have to put you on a daily schedule."

"Cook put in her cherry tarts," Charlotte said, glad to contribute whatever she could. "You must try one."

"And so I shall. And I see ham and fresh bread, too." Janet looked up from the basket and over her shoulder as they both heard the hallway boards creaking as someone approached her office.

The horse-faced woman from the front desk appeared at the door. "Miss Clyde, you have a caller."

Erik stood at her side. His dark hair that was usually tied back hung wild about his shoulders and his shirttail was carelessly tucked into the waist of his kilt. Tony appeared at his side, equally disheveled.

"Tony?" Apprehensive, Charlotte rose from her chair, dreading—yet hoping that Connor was with them. She placed a hand over her fluttering heart to calm herself. How could she be so foolish about a man she'd not seen in over a week, she wondered. "What are you doing here?"

"Have you seen Connor?" Tony blurted out, hardly glancing in Janet's direction as she came around the desk.

"I don't believe we're acquainted, sir," Janet said.

"I'm sorry," Charlotte said and quickly performed the presentations. "Now what's this about Connor?"

"He's gone, Miss Clyde," Erik said, his gaze lighting briefly on Charlotte but not acknowledging her. "If Connor is not here, I donna know where he is. He's just disappeared."

"Disappeared?" Janet asked, peering into Erik's face. "What do you mean?"

Charlotte could only stare dumbfounded at Janet and Erik, her shocked mind echoing Janet's questions.

"Tell them what you told me," Tony urged.

"Sit, Erik, and tell us." Janet offered the troubled Scotsman a chair. He started with the last time he'd seen Connor, the night before on Bond Street outside of Gentleman Jack's boxing salon. He'd gone off to drink with some gentlemen. Connor had never returned from his drinking party.

"Miss Janet, ye know he's no angel when it comes to a few drinks with friends," Erik said.

"But he takes his training serious," Tony added.

Janet nodded. "Go on. What did you do?"

Before it was hardly light, Erik had located the Hound and Hare locked up tight. When he'd pounded on the door and hollered loud enough and long enough, the tavern keeper had finally come to the upstairs window, seeking the cause of the rumpus. He'd vowed he knew nothing of any Mr. Harby or of a drinking party with a boxer for a guest of honor. If such a man had been in his barroom, he would have remembered.

"I went to the tavern later," Tony said, "and the man met me at the door and told me the same thing."

So Erik had gone to Gentleman Jack's to question everyone

he could. All he'd learned was that someone named Harby had visited a few times as a guest of Nigel Eldwick, but no one knew anything more about the chap.

"Surely you don't think Connor has come to harm," Janet said. "He can take care of himself. There must be some explanation."

"Aye, I have a bad feeling about it," Erik said with a righteous nod of his head. "The name of that harm is Forbes. He'd do most anything to keep Connor from winning this fight."

"But would he harm Connor?" Janet said, frowning. "Forbes is ruthless, but surely not to the point of injuring someone."

"Aye, I think the dark marquis would do whatever he thought necessary to get what he wants," Erik said with another righteous nod. "The bad feelings over Glen Gray are old and run deep."

A shiver of fear tingled down Charlotte's spine, but she could not make herself believe that Connor was in trouble. Fearless, trusting, self-assured Connor, Earl of Kinleith.

"Was there anything else amiss?" Janet prodded. "Think. Who else might we talk to for clues?"

"The only thing odd at the boxing salon was that Grady, one of the towel boys, hadn't come in to work," Erik said.

Charlotte's head came up. "Grady—I remember him. He ran into me the day of the fair. Remember?"

Erik nodded. "Aye, he's the one. Ain't it strange that he'd not turn up at work the very day that Connor goes missing?"

"I saw him over a week ago or so, just outside the door here, leaning against the lamppost as if he wanted to go unnoticed," Charlotte added, gesturing toward the front of the building. "That day at the fair, the children told me he'd been following us. I thought it strange last week when I saw him again, then Connor was here and I forgot about it."

Janet had turned to her. "Yes, that was the very day that Connor was here waiting for you. He must have been following Connor."

"Could be." Distaste twisted Erik's ruddy face. "Spying fo

Forbes, I'll wager. This is not like Connor, lass. This fight means everything to him and it's not like him to go off missing at a time when it could mean forfeiting everything he's worked for over the last year. It must be foul play."

"I agree," Janet said.

"It's not like him," Charlotte agreed, her mind suddenly focused on what must be done. "Tony, have you talked to Eldwick? Erik, you said Harby dropped Eldwick's name."

"No, I haven't spoken to Nigel yet," Tony said. "That's the next step, of course."

"And take Cassie with you," Charlotte said. "Nigel likes to flirt with her. We can send her a message and you can pick her up on your way to see Eldwick."

"Of course," Janet said. "Write what you wish and I'll send out some of our messenger boys immediately."

"Good," Charlotte said, reaching for paper and pen. "I think we must find out everything we can about those two—Eldwick and Harby. And Grady? How can we learn more about the towel boy without letting anyone suspect that Connor is missing?"

"I'll ask around the boxing salon again," Erik said. "Leave it to me."

"Good," Charlotte said, beginning to compose her messages. "There's no time to lose. Connor has to be in the ring tomorrow at midday or he forfeits the championship."

By midafternoon, Cassie had joined their forces and they had managed to speak with a number of people who might know something about Connor's whereabouts. Charlotte discovered that Connor had not used the curricle and horses that he sometimes borrowed for some days. And the others had learned more than Charlotte had dreamed they might discover in so brief a time.

"Eldwick doesn't know Harby well, he said," Tony reported when they—Tony, Cassandra, Erik, Janet, and Charlotte—reassembled in Janet's office.

"The two struck up an acquaintance at the boxing salon,"

Tony continued. "Eldwick said he never asked much about Harby's circumstances. They talked mostly of boxing."

"But Nigel did say that he thought Harby put on airs and often wagered more than he probably should," Cassie added, her eyes sparkling with excitement. She was in her element and Charlotte could think of no more trustworthy and resourceful ally in a crisis than her sister. "And he also said that he thought Harby had aspirations above his station."

"That could be said of nearly half of London," Janet said, a look of apology on her face. "Present company excepted, of course. Even if it is so, it doesn't mean that the man did any harm to Connor."

"No, of course it doesn't," Charlotte agreed. "Erik, did you learn anything more about Grady?"

Erik shook his head. "Nay, except that his favorite drinking establishment, after the gin shop, is the Hound and Hare. At the gin shop the keeper told me he'd seen Grady in there frequently with a gent who liked to put on airs and has a raspberry birthmark right on the point of his chin."

"A connection to Harby," Cassie exclaimed, softly pounding the top of the desk with the palm of her hand. "We have a connection."

"So it is likely that Connor did go with Harby to the Hound and Hare," Tony said, a furrow in his brow as he spoke. "Grady might have met them there."

"Harby didna say anythin' about Grady when he stopped us on the street last night," Erik said. "But he did say there be some other boxing enthusiasts waiting for him and Connor."

"We need more information about the Hound and Hare," Charlotte insisted.

"I agree," Janet chimed in. "They may have been paid to keep quiet, or the tavern keeper might not have known what was going on."

Erik nodded. "Aye, but I canna go back. I made too much of a fuss. They know me."

"Me, too," Tony said.

"I could go," Cassie offered.

Janet paused. "Forgive me, Cassandra, but why would a tavern keeper or a barmaid confess to a young Society lady if they won't talk to two men?"

"But she wouldn't go as a young lady of Society," Charlotte said, instantly understanding her sister.

"I'll go as a young woman from the country looking for work," Cassandra said airily.

"What do you know of a country girl looking for work?" Janet asked, a frown of disapproval marring her usually cheerful countenance.

"As much as we know about being a highwayman," Charlotte offered.

Cassie shot Charlotte a guilty look. "We know what a new maid looks like when she comes to train in the kitchen. That eager-to-please line of the mouth—"

"And the uncertain darting of the eyes," Charlotte finished. "See, we know something. You can teach us the rest, Janet."

"Us?" Cassandra repeated, eyeing Charlotte skeptically.

"Why not?" Tony said, suddenly catching Charlotte's enthusiasm. "I think the novelty of being twins might make people more willing to talk to you."

Janet began to nod slowly, an incredulous but amused smile spreading across her face. "Yes, I see what you mean. Twins from the farm. 'Twould be a novelty that has possibilities."

"I beg your pardon," Cassie snapped. "I am *not* a novelty."

Charlotte looked to her sister, ignoring the irate expression Cassandra threw her. "If novelty is what is needed, then we'll do it, Cassie. Because Connor is going to fight his fight."

THIRTY-SEVEN

"Confound, it, these drawers are scratchy," Cassie complained, tugging at the tapes at her waist. "And these boots must weigh a stone. No wonder those poor country girls always look like they're dragging their feet."

"Shush, you sound spoiled and petulant," Charlotte snapped, annoyed with Cassie's whining when Connor might be in danger or even hurt. She didn't dare allow herself to speculate or she would lose her control. This was not the time for paltry complaints. "What do you think these people would say if they could hear you?"

They were standing on the street corner near the Hound and Hare amid a crowd of thin, haggard wives, sober-faced children, and surly men going about their daily business. Tony had dropped them a few blocks away to avoid the attention the sight of a shiny curricle in this part of Town would draw. Above all, they wanted to blend in with the ordinary people.

"I *am* spoiled and petulant and I shall never take silk for granted again," Cassandra muttered, eyeing a ragpicker who strolled by, a greasy-faced, grizzle-haired creature clothed in multicolored shreds and tatters.

Janet had dressed them for their role. Cassie wore a rough scoop-neck brown gown with her red hair tucked up in a deep brimmed bonnet without trim. For Charlotte, Janet had found a plain gray frock, a bit snug through the bust. A straw bonne covered her hair. Their homespun apparel was authentic down to their undergarments.

"Don't stare, Cassandra," Charlotte warned. "We're runaway girls wearing layers of our best clothes and we've never seen the sights of London before."

"If that's the case, I can stare," Cassie said, continuing to defy her sister's advice. "I've never seen the sights before."

"Janet said to avoid looking strangers in the eye," Charlotte reminded her sister, turning her back on the ragpicker.

"But was that a man or a woman?" Cassandra asked, continuing to stare.

"It matters not to us," Charlotte said, her patience rapidly eroding. She was anxious to get on with their plan, to find Connor safe and ready to fight. Fear for him overshadowed her curiosity about a world she would otherwise wish to examine. "There's the tavern right there, just as Erik told us."

The faded green and gold sign of the Hound and Hare hung crooked from one corner while the other swung in the damp breeze of the overcast day. As they watched, a thin, scruffy man with graying hair emerged and tossed a bucket of filthy brown liquid into the street. Several women scurried aside to keep the slop from splashing their skirts.

"What was Connor thinking to go into such a place as that?" Charlotte whispered in distaste and fear.

Cassie followed Charlotte's gaze toward the tavern. "I suspect Connor has been in more than one place such as that."

Charlotte secretly feared Cassandra was right. "Now, let me do the talking this time."

"You?" Cassandra turned to her sister. "I always handle these things."

"I do my share," Charlotte corrected her. "This time I'm doing the talking. Remember what Janet told us?"

"Blast, did you memorize every word that woman uttered?" Cassie exclaimed. "I still don't think you can be forward enough."

"I will be now," Charlotte said, starting off down the street with determination in her steps and her head held high. She brushed shoulders with a fruit vendor without even wrinkling her nose at the stench of rotten produce. She was the new Charlotte St. John, the girl who trusted her instincts and faced the world Connor had shown her. Now he needed her help, and she would do anything for him. Over her shoulder she called, "Just watch me."

Cassie shrank from the fruit vendor, hitched up her overlong skirt, and hurried after her sister.

Dismal daylight fell through the doorway to light the inside of the tavern. Charlotte paused on the threshold, hesitating long enough to allow her eyes to become accustomed to the gloom. The reek of stale beer, rancid meat, and old tobacco smoke assaulted her senses. Periodically, a thundering rumble filled the building and shook the floor. Once her eyes had adjusted, she could see that a door was open at the back of the building and a wagoner was rolling barrels of ale into the back room and down a ramp into the cellar—the source of the noise.

She stepped into a large taproom. Grit crunched under the soles of her worn, borrowed boots, but she marched on. The sound of her footsteps turned the heads of the two men at the serving counter. The thin man, the one with the bucket, was sweeping with his back to her.

He glanced around to catch sight of her. "We ain't buying nothing here. Just turn yourself round, girl, and head out the door."

Charlotte swallowed the lump of cowardice that threatened to choke her and kept walking deeper into the tavern, searching for any evidence that Connor might have been there.

The place was in chaos with tables and chairs sitting upright, but mismatched as if they'd just been set up without any order in mind. Two men leaned against the counter, imbibing from their tankards at regular intervals.

"Please sir, my sister and I aren't selling anything," Charlotte ventured, speaking to the gray-haired man's back. "We come to Town looking for work. Can you help us?"

The man made a sound much like a growl and stopped sweeping long enough to turn to her.

Charlotte continued to scan the dingy establishment for signs of Connor—anything.

Cassie was tripping along behind her now. "Blast, what happened here?"

Charlotte saw it, too. The door to the back room stood splintered and swinging from one hinge. Charlotte's breath caught in her throat. What was it Connor had said to her in the chapel? He was so angry he'd like to splinter the pew.

"The door?" the man said, his voice as thin and raspy as his person. "Some of those boxing fans were in here drinking too much and having differences of opinion about who is going to win the championship."

"So much damage," Cassie sympathized. "Looks like you could use some help to me."

"I'll be the judge of that," the man said, resuming his sweeping. "Be on your way. I told you I weren't buying nothing. Got me daughter to barmaid for me. And I got paid well enough for the door and the trouble."

Charlotte elbowed Cassie into silence. "So who did the men think was going to win?"

The owner looked up at her and halted. "Why, you two are just alike."

"Yes, sir," Charlotte said, grateful at last to have engaged his full attention.

"Well, by gum," the man exclaimed as he leaned on his broom and continued to look at the girls. He pointed at them for the men at the counter. "Look at that, two peas in a pod."

The men displayed little interest.

"So, who did the men last night think was going to win?" Charlotte asked once more.

"They were all Jem Ward men," the owner said finally. "Had their row and carried one of their own out. I heard one of them say they was headed for Molly Driscoll's. Say, now there's somebody who's hiring. She'd have an eye for twins. You do like men, don't you? Know how to please 'em?"

"Of course we like men," Cassie said, as if the man was an imbecile. "And we know how to please them."

Charlotte instinctively knew there was more to this remark than either she or Cassie completely understood. "Where would we find this Molly Driscoll, then? I mean, if she's hiring and all."

"Just down the street," the tavern keeper said, gesturing on down the way. "The big fancy house on the corner. Go in the back entrance and tell them that Clive from the Hound and Hare sent ye."

"Thank you," Charlotte said, uncertain as to whether she'd just discovered something important or not. "Thank you, we'll do that."

She turned abruptly, grabbed Cassie's arm, and hurried toward the door, trying not to look as excited as she felt.

"I know what you're thinking," Cassie said as soon as they reached the corner where Tony was waiting for them. "A splintered door is hardly proof that Connor was there."

Charlotte shook her head. She didn't want to hear any negative thoughts. "He was there. I'm certain of it. They tried to keep him in that room and he did not want to stay."

"Cassie is right, Charlotte," Tony said. Like the girls, he too wore borrowed clothing from Janet's wardrobe to blend in with the people on the street. But removal of his fine outer clothing had little effect. His tall, dark-haired good looks and shiny Hessian boots still caught the eye of every female in the vicinity.

Charlotte did not like the attention they were receiving from passersby. She drew her companions back around a corner and into a side street. "I realize the shattered door wasn't proof, but think of what the man said. 'They were Jem Ward men and they carried one of their own out.' "

"You think that was Connor?" Cassie asked.

"No, I don't think they could do that," Tony objected. "No Connor."

"Unless they overcame him somehow," Charlotte said, her mind racing along, putting together the image of Connor alone being pulled down like a stag attacked by wolves. "Then they'd carry him out and hide him somewhere until after the fight. If what Erik says is right about Forbes, that's probably the plan."

"So, say you're right and that's the plan," Tony said. "Where did they take him?"

Cassie looked at Charlotte. "What sort of place is Molly Driscoll's?"

Tony paused. A blush spread across his handsome face. "Well, I think it's—probably, a brothel. Why would they have to carry a man like Connor off to a place like that?"

"Because he couldn't walk himself," Charlotte said, pressing her lips together in disgust with her cousin's unspoken speculation. "He didn't go willingly. That's why the door in the tavern was smashed."

"And they're hiding him at Molly's until after the fight," Cassie added. "Maybe Forbes intends to embarrass Connor with the fact that he was hiding in a brothel. And it's not the sort of place most people would search."

"Exactly," Charlotte said, Cassie's words merely an extension of her own thoughts. "We have to go to Molly Driscoll's."

Tony's blush faded rapidly. He shook his head. "Here, now, I don't think that would be appropriate."

"Appropriateness has nothing to do with it," Charlotte said, feeling bolder than ever now that they'd uncovered a trail.

Cassie nodded and turned her gaze on Tony.

"We're going in there to find Connor," Charlotte began.

"And we're getting him out," Cassandra finished.

Charlotte smiled at their cousin, who paled under her scrutiny. "And you're going to help us, Tony."

Awareness came slowly, painfully, to Connor. Errant images circled through his head—cruel hands and tight ropes. He couldn't remember where he was or why. Aches radiated through his body, shimmering up from the cold stone into his bones, rendering his joints stiff. But he forced himself to stretch his arms. A moan escaped him as the aches knifed into pain.

His tongue was dry and his mouth tasted like cotton wadding. Only a pale light penetrated the cloth sail tied around him. It smelled of mould and bilge water.

Memory flooded back. The championship fight. In the clarity of it, Connor almost bolted upright, but his bindings held fast. Lying helpless on the stones, he snorted with impatience. What time was it? Where was he? From the sound of carriages above somewhere, it was afternoon or early evening—he hoped. Or could it be later than that? Had the fight time passed?

No, he wouldn't believe that. Whatever time it was, he was still in London. They had not carried him away to the country or dumped him on a ship. Where was Erik? How much did he know or guess? Connor renewed his struggle against his bindings, this time with more strength.

"So yer coming round, are ye?" a deep voice said from across the room.

Connor ceased his struggles. He did not recognize the voice, but he had to be in a cellar. Why else would the sound of the carriages come from above him?

"What day is it?" he demanded in a voice so scratchy and hoarse he didn't even recognize it as his own.

"A day too late," came a second voice. "And that is all you need to know. Harby said to tell him it's too late."

Gingerly, Connor tested his range of motion. His hands were bound behind him and his legs were tied together and to something else. A post of some kind?

"Don't get restless, now," the first voice warned. "Ye ain't goin' nowhere for a long while yet."

"Not for a long while?" Connor murmured, the clue he needed to know that it wasn't too late. Because if it was, they would set him free. "Tell Harby I want to talk to him."

Silence followed his request. He could imagine his guards

probably two of the men who had sat across from him at the Hound and Hare, exchanging glances.

"Mr. Harby is occupied above right now," the second voice said at last.

"We'll give him your message when he shows his face down here," the other said, derision in his tone. "Otherwise you mind your manners or we'll give ye another clout with this axe handle."

Connor thought better of causing more trouble at the moment. But his nimble fingers went to work on the bindings at his wrists, which were concealed from his guards' sight by the sail they'd bound around him.

THIRTY-EIGHT

Aghast Charlotte stood back-to-back with Cassie and looked around Molly Driscoll's office. The paintings of nude women at picnics and cavorting in harems left her speechless. If she and Cassie looked as astonished as a couple of green girls from the country, so much the better. Their naive wonder could only support the story they told the man at the door, who looked more like a well-muscled stable groom than a butler.

"Did you ever guess—?" Cassie began in a whisper, her voice full of awe.

"Never." Charlotte swallowed a gulp of air and stared at the statue of David, which took on a whole new meaning in a place like Molly Driscoll's. "You're sure it was Harby you saw in the hall?"

"Absolutely," Cassie said, staring at a painting of a nude goddess in a swing. "If Erik is right about Harby being part of Connor's disappearance, then—"

"Then where is Connor?" Charlotte asked without taking her eyes from a painting of two women touching each other. "The place is a maze. Where do we—"

The sound of a voice in the hall interrupted Charlotte. The door to the office swung open and Molly swept into the room. "So you two girls are looking for work at Molly Driscoll's?"

The lady herself was as much an original as Charlotte had expected. The white-wigged madame gowned in black satin reminded her of an actress who'd just stepped off the stage, he makeup bright and garish, her glamorous gown tarnished once the stage lights no longer gave it dazzle.

"Yes, ma'am," Charlotte said, still surprised that it had been so easy for her and Cassie to walk right into the brothel. They'd simply told their story to the man at the back door and he'd admitted them as if he did so every day. The difficult part of their scheme still lay ahead of them. "Clive of the Hound and Hare said to tell you he'd told us you were hiring."

"Twins, and identical, too," Molly said, settling herself into the leather chair behind the desk and looking them up and down. "Let me have a better look at you. Take off your bonnets and shawls."

Charlotte took off her bonnet, shaking out her hair and wondering if Tony had managed to get in downstairs as they had planned.

"Well, you two are pretty enough with that bright red hair. Some gents will like that, too," Molly said, sizing up each of them with a practiced eye.

Charlotte wondered briefly why twins should be of such interest.

Molly motioned at their feet. "Pull up your skirts and show me your legs."

Cassandra glanced at Charlotte. She gave an imperceptible shrug and reached for her skirt. Boldly, they each thrust their legs forward.

"Higher," Molly demanded, eyeing first Charlotte's ankles then Cassie's.

Charlotte obeyed, inching her skirt up to her knee. But the borrowed boots and heavy stockings that Janet had loaned them hardly looked seductive.

"Hmm, legs aren't bad," Molly observed and folded her hands across the top of the desk. "You know what we do here?"

"Entertain gentlemen with games of chance and the company of ladies," Cassie said before Charlotte could open her mouth. "And what I want to know is will we get silk underthings like the girls we saw downstairs?"

The blush Charlotte had held at bay from the moment they'd stepped through the door colored her face. They'd been led down the hall past a couple of pretty girls wearing nothing more than their drawers and stays trimmed in lace and ribbons.

Cassie had studied the girls, hardly able to navigate her way down the hall. Mortified, Charlotte had stared straight ahead and deplored the idea that Connor might be here in this velvet-lined house, this rabbit warren of rooms full of girls and vice. Just how much was he suffering, anyway? If he wasn't truly here under duress, his suffering would really begin after she found him.

When they'd been led up the back stairs and around the corner, they'd almost run directly into Harby himself. Charlotte had immediately ducked her head, but Harby had been too distracted to notice her or Cassie. The scantily clad girl he was with had blatantly grabbed him by the crotch, pulled him into the room, and slammed the door.

"Yes, I never mislead my girls about what they're here for," Molly said with a sharp, mirthless laugh. "We could make a lot of money with the two of you. Certain gentlemen would find two identical partners very entertaining and would pay well for it. And if you're virgins, well, the initial price could be very good. But frankly, you look too old for virginity, especially being from the country."

Charlotte cast Cassie a guilty glance.

Cassie's eyes widened in understanding, but she gave no other outward sign. "You're right, ma'am, we're too old."

Molly pursed her lips. "More's the pity. But we'll make the most of this—you'll see. You'll be glad you came to Molly Driscoll's, where we—"

The crash of shattering glass from the room below caused Molly to pause.

Charlotte held her breath. Tony was here at last, she hoped. She'd learned as much about Molly and her business as she cared to know.

When nothing followed the crash, Charlotte resumed breathing, quick and shallow. She and Cassie dared not look at each other.

Molly continued. "Never mind that. Just some gent in high spirits. As I was saying, this a place where we give our gentle-men—"

A scream rent the air, then a chorus of screams rose.

Molly rose and marched from around her desk. "Excuse me, girls, I have to see to whatever this is."

The moment Molly went out the door, Cassie and Charlotte were right behind her.

At the top of the stairs, Charlotte turned to her sister. "You work your way up and I'll go down."

Cassie nodded. "And if we find him, go out the back door where Erik will be with the curricle."

"Let's go," Charlotte said, starting down the stairs.

Anarchy reigned on the first floor. Girls and men were running in every direction. A brawl was raging in the front drawing room. Without stopping long enough to see if Tony was there as he should have been, Charlotte charged through the confusion toward the side hall. She threw open one door after another, only to find half-dressed strangers struggling into their pants while frightened girls clung to them. Several of the rooms were already empty. She didn't see the man Cassie called Harby anywhere.

Around another corner, Charlotte descended a barren wooden stairway leading to the ground floor. She hurried along the passage, peering into odd, cell-like rooms furnished with wooden benches, chains fastened to the wall, and lots of leather straps. Each smelled of musk, urine, and sweat. In one cell, a coiled whip lay on the floor. The sight turned Charlotte's stomach. She backed out of the room; the thought of Connor being here sickened her. Fighting back queasiness, she scurried on, moving purposefully from one door to the next. Thankfully, each time she peered through a doorway, she found the chamber empty.

At the end of the passage she turned, frustrated and frightened. Where to next? She started back toward the steps when she saw the door under the stairway. The cellar. It had to lead to the cellar. Where else would you hide a prisoner?

She reached for the latch and it clicked open easily in her grip. She opened the door carefully, just wide enough to see light coming from the bottom of another set of stairs. The sound of voices reached her, men speaking in low tones of excitement and concern.

"I tell you the noise ain't nothing to fret about," one said. "This is a bawdy house. Ye can expect some noise now and then. We'd better stay here with the Scotsman."

"Yer probably right," the other said. "Harby would let us know if there was trouble."

Charlotte hesitated, struggling to control her breathing and to make sense out of what she'd heard. Harby? The Scotsman? They could only be referring to Connor.

Throwing open the door with a great flurry, she began to march down the steps, rustling her skirts and clomping her boots. There was no advantage in her surprising the men.

"Well, what do we have here?" greeted one of the guards, sitting on a stool beside an upturned barrel of ale. "What's the cause of the ruckus above stairs?"

A candle burned on the barrel top and playing cards lay scattered across the makeshift table. He was a huge man, nearly as big as Connor, with brown hair, his jowls soft, and his shoulders hunched. Across from him sat a black-haired man with his back to Charlotte. He was big, too, with long arms. But he was more wide than tall, carrying his strength low to the ground.

"So Molly decided to send us some company," the black-haired man said to his companion, turning to look Charlotte up and down. "Aye, Miss Ginger-pate, what's going on upstairs?"

Charlotte smiled reassuringly at the men while quickly searching the shadows. On the floor lying in the corner she spied the figure of a huge man wrapped in what looked like canvas. Her heart tripped. It had to be Connor lying there, still and lifeless. She'd found him.

* * *

Connor lay very still, listening to the noise from above. The shattering of glass had caught his attention first. He'd stopped working on the ropes around his wrists when he'd heard the first thundering crash. Then had come the pounding of feet trampling across the floor and up the steps. Carriages in the streets. Screams and more screams. Frantic shouting. Angry voices.

Then the sound of a lone set of feet pattering back and forth across the floor above.

His guards had become concerned then. Their talk had turned from the card game to choosing which one of them went above to see what was going on. Then he'd heard the rustle of a woman's skirts and the guard's greeting. Miss Ginger-pate? A redhead?

"What's the cause of all the ruckus upstairs?" the second voice asked.

"They have quite a party going on up there," the girl said.

Instant confusion struck. Connor was afraid he'd been hit harder on the head than he'd first thought. The girl sounded like Charlotte. Exactly like his Charlotte.

"Must be a real rout," said the first voice.

"Harby sent me down to invite you up," she said.

Connor strained, listening to every subtlety in her voice. Whoever she was, she was lying, but fairly convincingly. Impossible or not, she sounded just as much like Charlotte as before. Connor could hear her stepping closer to the men. He nearly cursed aloud. The woman had no idea what scum she was dealing with.

"That's generous of him," said the first man. "But now that you're here, we might just have our own party. You should have worn something a little more festive."

"Our own party?" she said. "What a good idea." From the sound of her voice she'd moved even closer to the men. Connor worked madly at the ropes. The strands were loosening and he'd be free soon, but he still had the canvas and the binding on his legs to deal with. But when he freed his hands, he'd be able to move faster.

"Why don't we untie him and let him join us?" she suggested.

Connor went still again, knowing that all three pairs of eyes would be turned on him. The girl was leading the men down some path.

"Careful, Charlotte," he muttered to himself. He didn't know how she could possibly be there, but she was. He'd never forgive himself if anything happened to her. He had no clue what could have brought her to the cellar of a brothel. But she had the right idea. Bless her misguided, studious, little heroine's heart. Charlotte had mettle.

"Now, puss, don't go getting yerself into business that ain't none of yer affair," the second man said. "Come here and sit on my lap and show me yer assets. You ain't dressed much like one of Molly's girls."

"I've just started work," she said. "Is this better?"

Connor heard a brief scuffle. He struggled with the ropes once more. It pulled free. His arms were free.

"Now ain't that better sitting on me knee?" the second man continued. "Let me do those buttons."

"Yes, but I just wanted to see what he looks like," she insisted. "Who is he, anyway? Is he truly the Scots fighter like Mr. Harby said?"

"Aye, that's who it is," the first man said.

"Show me," she persisted. "I never seen a boxer up close. I mean, he's so still over there it's enough to make a girl think he's dead."

Have care, Connor wanted to warn her again. He squeezed his eyes shut, blocking any image of her sitting on the man's knee, with the bastard's hands all over her. But he was going to kill him.

"He ain't dead and he's too dangerous to toy with," said the second man. "Besides, what's wrong with our company?"

"Why, nothing at all," she said sweetly. "I still think one of you should go see what Mr. Harby wanted. I hear that gent can get ugly when he's angry."

"Harby wanted something?" the first man asked, mild alarm in his voice. "Why didn't ye say so?"

"He said to send one of you up," she said. "That's what I tried to do, but you wanted to have your own party."

"Well, maybe I'd better go, then," said the first man.

Connor heard the man rise, cross the cellar, and start up the stairs. Smart girl. Now he and Charlotte only had to deal with one guard. Slowly, to avoid attracting attention, he began to pull the edge of the canvas free of the rope that held it fast around him.

Charlotte jumped up from the black-haired man's knee and forced herself not to pull closed the bodice he'd just unbuttoned. She stood between him and Connor, facing the man and allowing him to leer at her breasts straining against her muslin shift.

"Aw, come here, puss," the man said. "Don't get shy on me now."

Charlotte smiled at him coyly, or at least in what she thought was a coy fashion. She'd seen the canvas move. She'd glimpsed the edge of it pulling up from beneath the ropes wound around Connor's knees. She knew he was alive and trying to free himself. Only she didn't know how to help, except to keep the guard's attention on herself.

"So what sort of card game were you playing?" she asked, lamely longing to distract him from leering at her nearly bare breasts. She knew nothing about cards, though Cassie had urged her to learn whist.

"The cards be damned," the man said, leaning closer and reaching for her waist.

Reluctantly Charlotte allowed him to pull her to stand between his legs. He squeezed her waist with cruel hands and nuzzled her breasts with a scratchy, bearded face. She closed her eyes against the disgusting sensations. His hot, fetid breath sent shivers of revulsion through her.

"My, aren't you a fast worker," she said, speaking loudly for Connor's benefit so he would know his guard was occupied.

The man began to tug at her skirt, and Charlotte squelched the urge to run.

Canvas rustled behind her. She didn't dare look over her shoulder to observe Connor's progress. Desperate to block any further sound he made, she clapped her hands over the man's ears.

"I'd rather have your tongue there," the man murmured, as she toyed with his lobes. He pulled Charlotte so close that she could feel intimate details of his swollen male anatomy against her thigh. "You know, flick it in and out real fast."

The sound of ripping fabric reached Charlotte. She laughed to cover the noise, leaned closer to tempt him with her cleavage, and fondled the man's ears. "Not just yet," she whispered. "Let's save that for later."

Behind her she could hear soft leather scraping the stone floor and she prayed Connor was gaining his feet.

"Then how about a kiss, puss?"

Before Charlotte could resist, the man grabbed a handful of her hair and pulled her down toward his mouth.

She shoved her hands against his shoulders pushing him away with all her might. But he wound his other hand in her hair and his grip tightened, drawing her closer to his face. She gasped from the pain shooting through her scalp. What was taking Connor so blasted long?

"No more games, love," the guard warned in a low voice and opened his wet lips to kiss her.

Straining against the fist wound in her hair, Charlotte managed to turn her cheek to his mouth.

Then he started and yelped in pain. Yet his hold on her hair remained fast.

"Get your mouth off her, you bastard." Connor's voice was no more than a deadly hiss so near Charlotte's neck she could feel the warmth of his breath. "And release her now or I'll break your arm."

THIRTY-NINE

From the corner of her eye, Charlotte saw the black-haired man's eyes widen in surprise, then they narrowed. Angry red stained his face. As he glared at Connor, over Charlotte's shoulder, his grip on her tresses tightened. She bit back a cry of pain.

"Let go of me, Scotsman, or I'll break her neck," the man growled and clutched at the other side of Charlotte's head.

The pain shot down her neck. Charlotte bit her lip. Enough was enough. With as much thrust as she could manage, she jammed her knee where it would hurt most—a trick Janet had suggested.

The man roared. His grip fell away, instantly. His eyes flew wide open. His ugly mouth mimed a silent 'Ow' as he clutched himself and dropped off the stool.

Charlotte ducked out of his reach and stared in horror at the man rolling on the floor in agony. As she rubbed her sore scalp, she noted all color had drained from his face. He seemed incapable of making any intelligible sound. "What have I done? I knew that was a sensitive place, but I—"

"Now you know why Broughton's Rule number seven forbids blows below the belt," Connor said, grabbing Charlotte's arm and drawing her away from the injured guard.

"But I didn't mean to—" Charlotte protested. "Oh, he's suffering so."

"I'll put him out of his misery for you," Connor said, hauling the man up by his collar with one hand. The moaning guard staggered and struggled and tried to swing at Connor. With his free hand Connor landed a solid punch to the man's jaw. When he released the guard, he dropped to the floor like a dead man.

Charlotte gasped, astonished by Connor's cold, heartless revenge.

"He'll feel better when he comes around," Connor promised.

He grabbed Charlotte's arm and started for the stairs. She hurried along behind him as fast as she could, tugging her bodice closed and fretting about the man on the cellar floor.

At the top of the second flight of stairs Connor stopped so abruptly that Charlotte stepped on his heels. "Harby."

Charlotte peeked around Connor to see the tall, slender man with a raspberry birthmark on his chin. His shirt was hanging open, one button held his trousers about his waist, and his feet were bare.

The moment he recognized Connor, he turned to run, but Connor was faster. He caught Harby by the seat. With a quick, powerful movement he threw the slender man against the wall and choked him with his forearm against his throat.

Charlotte forgot about her unfastened bodice. "Connor, you're going to hurt him!"

"That's the idea," Connor growled in Harby's face. "I have a couple of questions for you, friend."

"I don't know anything," Harby choked out, his eyes round with fear. "I can't help it if you can't hold your ale."

"You drugged me and I saw you do it," Connor said between bared teeth. "But that's not what I want to know about. Where's Forbes? Is he here?"

"I'd send you his way if I could," Harby gasped, his terror evidence enough to lend truth to his words.

"But you received orders from him?" Connor demanded, his face hard and cold with anger.

"But always verbally through a messenger sent by his business agent," Harby insisted. "I called on the agent once and he claimed the marquis had never left Edinburgh."

"That's a lie," Connor snarled. "He was here. I saw him a month ago at the opera. He's been here—he's behind this."

Pinned helplessly against the wall, Harby could barely shake his head. "I don't know anything about that."

"Connor, let the officials take care of him," Charlotte urged, tugging on Connor's steely arm. Harby's face was rapidly turning from red to blue. Though Connor appeared amazingly cool, Charlotte could feel the anger radiating from him. She was afraid that in his present state Connor might actually murder the young man.

Connor ignored her. "Where's Grady?"

"Don't know," Harby muttered, his eyes rolling back in his head.

"Connor, that's enough," Charlotte said, yanking on his arm again. "Here's Tony."

"Connor? Thank God Charlotte found you?" Tony strode toward them, taking something from his pocket. "You've caught the man I was looking for myself. Hold him right there."

In a flash, Tony stuffed what appeared to be a deck of cards into Harby's trouser pocket. Then he called back over his shoulder, "Magistrate, here he is. The man I said cheated me."

He turned back to Charlotte and Connor. "Do up those buttons, cousin, and both of you get out of here before anyone recognizes you."

"Forbes?" Connor asked. He looked beyond Tony toward the drawing room, where order was being restored by blue-uniformed officers. "I suppose he's too smart to be on the scene."

"Listen, Connor, there's nothing you can do about Forbes now," Tony said. "The important thing is for you to get out of here before anyone finds out what happened. We want the newspaper writers to see you on your way to the fight. Erik is around back with the curricle. Take Charlotte and Cassie with you."

Cassie came scurrying down the hall, a frown on her face. "I think I've had enough adventure for now," she muttered as she passed them and headed for the back door.

Charlotte linked her arm through Connor's and drew him back toward the door.

"Do you feel like fighting?" she asked, displeased with the color of his complexion and the bruise on his brow.

"I feel like hell and as mad as a wounded boar," Connor muttered as they made their way along the winding hall at the back of the brothel. "But I'll fight. And I'll win."

Erik was there at the back door just as planned. Relief washed over his face when he saw them emerge. "Connor. No more drinking without me."

"Not before a fight," Connor agreed as he helped Charlotte and Cassie crowd into the curricle.

First light glimmered in the east as Erik pulled the curricle to a halt down the street from the St. John townhouse.

"Your father is going to want an explanation," Connor said.

Charlotte shook her head. "Horton will let us in the servants' entrance. Papa will probably never know."

"I should hope not," Cassie muttered. "I don't want to have to explain this. I'll go scratch at Horton's window."

"You go on to your lodgings and the fight," Charlotte said, suddenly depressed by the thought of finding Connor at last, then saying good-bye again so soon. Every time they said farewell it was more difficult.

Connor pulled her back into the shadows cast by the street lamp. "You'll be there, won't you?" he asked with a movement of his hand, as if he wanted to touch Charlotte's hair but thought better of it. "My lady rescuer. You know, you didn't have to flirt with that blackguard that outrageously."

"I did what I thought had to be done," Charlotte said, annoyed and offended that he should criticize her efforts on his behalf.

Connor seized her hands and brought them to his mouth. "And I am grateful. When this is all over you'll tell me how you did it and I won't raise one objection to anything. I promise."

"Connor, this doesn't change how I feel about your fighting,"

Charlotte warned. "I just couldn't let Forbes win without you having a chance at your heart's desire."

"I know it doesn't change anything." Connor kissed her knuckles again and gazed into her face as if he wanted to say something more.

"And I never expected you to give up what you wanted," Charlotte said. His lips on her hands were beginning to stir the weakness in Charlotte's knees.

"My lady rescuer," Connor whispered, his head bowed over their hands. "Thank you for coming to my aid. Give me a kiss for luck, kitten."

Charlotte kissed him, a quick and sweet kiss, their hands still clasped between them.

"Connor?" Erik called from the driver's seat of the curricle. "Time is short."

Connor muttered a curse. "We must leave things unsaid again, kitten."

"I wish you good luck," Charlotte said.

He released her hands slowly, reluctantly. "Think of me during the fight," he called as he climbed into the curricle.

"I will." Charlotte waved in return, knowing there would be little else that she would be able to think of.

"Ye donna feel ready for a fight to me," Erik said as he worked on the muscles of Connor's shoulders. "Yer stiff."

Erik was right, Connor thought as he sat hunched on the stool outside the fight ring, his elbows on his knees, his head between his hands. He felt sluggish and tired and still dazed from the drug that Harby had put in his ale. He'd had no restful sleep in the last twenty-four hours and no time to warm up with a bit of sparring like he usually did before a fight. The only good thing about his condition was his empty stomach. It was always best to climb into the ring without food in your gullet. "Aye—as angry as I am, Erik, I'm not ready to fight."

"Ye'll warm up after the first round," Erik reassured him, moving his efforts to Connor's right shoulder.

The day had turned bright and breezy, just as it had promised at dawn when he'd bade Charlotte farewell. The heath was already covered with men and women on foot, horseback, or in vehicles of all descriptions. Vendors roamed, crying out their wares and looking to turn a profit.

The crowd was a noisy lot, the type to be quick to voice their preferences. Connor scanned them warily. Men and women from all walks of life, gaily dressed, with money to wager. He saw coins and bills exchanged between betting men, avarice shining in their eyes and greed curling their lips. Every last soul was eager for the fight to begin. They'd soon make their impatience known with loud shouts. Offended by their mood, he turned away.

"There be a lot of money riding on this fight," Erik said.

"I know." Connor had never deluded himself about the wagers placed on his fights. Of course, that was where the purse money came from when it was all said and done. The purse money was why he was a prizefighter. But today, in his dispirited mood, wagering seemed to taint the noble art.

Erik continued to work Connor's taut muscles. "Ward looks bright-eyed and fit."

"Yeah, but smaller than I expected," Connor said, taking the measure of his opponent, who was dancing in the opposite corner. Ward's black hair lay close to his pate. He had a large nose and a cleft in the middle of a prominent chin. Standing under six feet tall, he was a powerfully built man, well-muscled about the shoulders and chest. His fans cheered him on as he paced along the boundaries of his corner. Connor rubbed a hand across his face. It was going to be a tough fight.

"Donna underestimate a small fighter like Jem Ward," Erik warned. "His reputation has suffered because he threw that fight a few years ago. He's bound to be eager to prove himself against all newcomers. And Forbes is backing him."

"After Charlotte's performance last night at the brothel, I'm not underestimating anybody," Connor vowed, shaking his aching head. "That's a loser's mistake. But have you seen *him?*"

"He won't be here," Erik said. "Lord Linirk knows better than to show his mug around here. But he's waiting someplace to hear the outcome, you can wager your reputation on that."

Connor nodded, certain that Erik was right about the dark marquis. Ramsay never walked onto the stage where he was pulling the most strings. Defeating Jem Ward was the best thing Connor could do to spite Forbes.

A quick survey of the spectators revealed some friendly faces. Tony was there. Loyal, energetic Tony, who'd been arrested in the melee at Molly Driscoll's and later bailed out of jail by his father. He stood up in the landau and waved. And the Earl and Countess of Seacombe were there with their son.

Connor even glimpsed Cassie with Dudley, sitting in the landau with Tony and the Derringtons. Gents from Gentleman Jack's salon and others who'd followed him from fight to fight were there, too. But he saw no sign of Charlotte anywhere. Not that he'd really expected to see her. She'd been honest about her feelings and he could hold nothing against her for being true to her sensibilities.

"The referee is in the ring," Erik said, giving Connor a final pat on the back. "Let's go. We've got a championship to win."

The referee walked to the center of the ring, raising his arms in the air to draw the audience's attention.

Connor rose from the stool, preparing himself mentally to climb into the ring. Luck would have to be with him if he was going to win. He'd fight his best; he always did. There wasn't anything he could do about the disadvantages the kidnapping had imposed on him. Tenderly he unwrapped Charlotte's handkerchief from around his right hand and tied it to the belt of his kilt. He climbed through the ropes and walked to the center of the ring to shake hands with his opponent, Jem Ward, the prizefighting champion of England.

They took each other's measure in the first round, blocking, parrying, slipping in, then hitting on the retreat. There was also a goodly amount of feinting and evading. The impatient crowd scoffed at the maneuvers.

Moving in the ring neither improved Connor's reaction time nor rid him of his sluggishness. The swiftness seemed gone from his blows and his feet dragged on the canvas. As he and Ward danced around the ring, Connor read an eagerness to prove himself in Ward's dark eyes. The ugly, derisive calls from the spectators had put Ward on notice. He was ready to show the world that he deserved to be the champion. Obviously, if he had to pound Connor into the canvas to demonstrate it, the champ was determined to do just that.

At every feint or duck, the spectators reacted with calls of scorn. By the third round it was clear to Connor—and to Ward, too—that their jeering audience wanted bloody entertainment. The crowd wasn't after fun or humor, contest or stamina; they wanted bruises and broken bones.

The thought soured Connor's mood. He could give them that. His practiced eye caught a hole in Ward's defenses and he launched a doubler punch at the champion's middle.

Ward grunted, bent over, and staggered backward. The crowd roared its approval. Connor's fist ached from the contact with Ward's solid midsection. Connor grinned, pleased with his performance, relieved that he could still box.

Ward circled him more warily. Connor knew he had to sharpen his guard. Ward was on his mettle now. Suddenly the champion moved in and popped a blow under Connor's defensive block. It connected with Connor's jaw. His head snapped to the side. He tasted blood.

The crowd's approval rang in his ear, ugly and growling. But the match was underway at last. The joy of it thrummed through Connor's blood. He wouldn't think anymore; he'd just fight. The blows and punches came fast and furious then. The din of the crowd ebbed and flowed with the flurry of blows.

By the break at the end of round ten, Erik was almost as ecstatic as the crowd. Connor had the champion in retreat. Erik hovered over Connor with a wet towel. "You've got him on the run, lad. Keep at it. He'll be down in another round or two. You've split his lip and the crowd is crying for more blood."

"What if I don't feel like giving them blood?" Connor asked, the first symptoms of exhaustion beginning to steal over him. Ward was a hell of a decent fighter. Connor's doubts about the fight and why he was facing the champion returned.

"Then maybe you'd like to take a look at who be in the Earl of Seacombe's landau," Erik said, pointing off to the side of the ring. "Go ahead, turn around and take a look at the Derrington carriage. I saw her at the beginning of the last round."

Connor turned, his mind too muddled to imagine what Erik was babbling about. It took him a moment to locate the carriage again. But when he did, he snapped immediately out from under the numbing effects of the fight.

There, next to Lady Dorian, sat Charlotte, dressed in pearl gray, her complexion pale and her china-blue eyes wide.

"Charlotte?" Connor murmured, hardly believing she was real.

When she saw him looking at her, she smiled an uncertain smile that tugged at his heart. Connor blinked, but she was still there and he knew all that he needed to know—she loved him.

FORTY

"Donna ye want to impress yer lady?" Erik asked, dropping the wet towel over Connor's head and giving his head a vigorous rub. "Go out there and level Ward."

Connor cursed Erik's words. His sparring partner's cold towel rub and Charlotte's presence stirred his determination once more. "Charlotte isn't as simple as you think."

"Aye, well, beat this bloke who thinks he's the champion of England," Erik said, "and I'll wager ye can have her or any lady in the crowd ye takes a fancy to."

The referee called the beginning of the next round and Connor charged into the ring, ready to do battle. Charlotte was here. Luck was with him. He summoned all his strength and stamina into one directed force.

The next round passed quickly, with Ward desperately throwing everything back at him, blow for blow, dancing in and retreating just as quickly. Connor had passed the first dizzying, painful part of the match and was numb to most of the blows. Sweat trickled down into his eyes, blinding him, but his mind was clear and his reactions good, if not improving. Erik was right; he could defeat Ward and everything would be his.

With each round now, Ward seemed to be weakening, but he wasn't out of commission by any means. He parried and punched for every one of Connor's strikes. But a moment came at last, another one of those split seconds when the champion's defenses were down. Connor caught him on the jaw. Ward dropped like a dead man.

The crowd went wild. Connor danced to the far end of the ring while the referee counted off time. Ward struggled to his knees. His seconds came to his aid, dragging him to his feet. The crowd taunted the fallen champion. The cruel fickleness of the spectators angered Connor.

He glanced around at the myriad faces suddenly so clear to him in their ugliness, contorted and twisted as they called for Connor to bring defeat down on Ward. Money changed hands. Odds changed again. How quick they all were to lose faith. How eager to see one man fall and another rise for their own pleasure and profit.

When Connor looked back across the ring, he saw Ward on his feet once more, weaving as he was released by his seconds. But he was soon circling Connor once again. The spectators' voices roared in Connor's ears. Their shouted slurs rang harsh and sadistic. Their bloodlust extinguished the joy Connor had always taken in a good fight, in a contest well met, in a brawl well fought, in the exhilaration of physical release.

Ward threw a punch. Connor ducked. His swiftness was back. His instincts were sharp. He parried with a swing to Ward's ribs. The champion groaned. He tottered on his feet for a moment. The spectators cheered at the prospect of seeing the great fighter go down. But Ward managed to retreat, favoring his side. They danced around each other once more. Ward's exhaustion was evident to all at last.

Connor's feet were strong under him now and he'd caught his second wind. The hand that had connected with Ward's ribs ached, but he could go the distance. He could win. He knew it as surely as he felt the roughness of the canvas beneath the soles of his shoes. He could give the crowd everything their greedy, blood-thirsty hearts desired.

But his heart said no.

The answer came in a sharp flash of clarity, without pain or regret. Sheer anger smouldered in Connor's gut. He wasn't going to bash anyone into the canvas just to please the cowardly, ruthless faces he saw in the swarming crowd. He did not want money earned from another's pleasure in seeing a man beaten to a pulp. And Glen Gray would never matter as much as Charlotte. The promise of property was never why he fought a fight, not really.

He could give the crowd what they wanted.

Connor lowered his guard just a fraction, only enough for an experienced fighter like Ward to notice. Ward's next blow found the opening and struck Connor in the side of the head.

Pain flashed up his jaw and wrenched down his neck. He staggered backward, barely able to stay on his feet. But the punch changed nothing of what he knew of his heart now. He was no prizefighter. Slaking the spectators' savage tastes gave him no pleasure. He only prayed that Charlotte would not be disappointed in him.

Connor brought himself around and ducked the next blow, but caught a third, Ward's mean upper left punch. He blocked another thrust by the champion, then took a follow-up blow in the gut. The wind whooshed out of him, but he kept fighting. The crowd clamored for more. Just before he knew the referee would call the end of the round, Connor rallied and threw himself at Ward. They exchanged blows in rapid-fire succession. Ward's next four punches rendered Connor nearly senseless.

At the end of the round he staggered toward his corner, discovering the canvas seeming amazingly close to his face. When he came to, his cheek pressed against the grimy fabric, Erik was shaking him by his tender jaw.

"Come around, man," Erik urged.

As soon as Connor blinked his eyes open, Erik started in on him. "Have ye gone daft, walking into Ward's punches like ye did? Ye have got to win this fight."

The referee called the beginning of the round. When Connor didn't get up, the official began to count the seconds.

Erik grabbed Connor's arm and pulled him off the canvas.

Dazed, but well aware of what he was doing, Connor climbed to his feet with Eric's help just before the end of the count.

"Now protect yerself," Erik ordered, shoving him toward the center of the ring. Connor resisted.

"Don't you pull me up off the canvas again," Connor growled softly so only Erik could hear. The dark-haired Scot's mouth went slack in surprise.

Then Connor turned back to finish the fight with Ward.

Charlotte saw Connor go down. She chewed on her lip and held her tears back as best she could. Silently she counted off the seconds along with the referee. She whispered a prayer as she watched Erik trying to revive Connor. *Please don't let him be hurt. Please don't let him be hurt.*

By the beginning of the next round, Connor was back on his feet once more, unsteady, but his fists up in position to ward off the champion's blows. Charlotte could hardly watch the match. She stared down at her hands in her lap, only glancing up when Tony or Aunt Dorian cheered or groaned. She hadn't come to see the fight. She'd come because she couldn't bear to linger in the house not knowing how Connor fared. She'd come because she could not stay away.

Victory or defeat meant nothing to her. She wanted to know that he was alive and uninjured. She was here because he'd asked her to come. If he thought her presence brought him luck, then she would gladly let him believe that.

But none of that made watching him being beaten by another fighter any easier. She knew better than anyone the disadvantage under which he was fighting—lack of rest and the lingering side effects of the drug.

"Are you all right, dear?" Aunt Dorian asked, touching Charlotte's hands.

Charlotte nodded though she didn't feel all right and she and Cassie exchanged glances of understanding.

"I don't think it's going to last much longer," Tony said.

"What do you mean?" Charlotte asked, looking up at her cousin.

Tony shook his head cryptically.

The spectators roared. Everyone in the landau jumped to their feet. The crowd began to chant Ward's name.

Charlotte rose slowly and elbowed the others aside so she could see. In the middle of the ring Connor lay flat on his back. His eyes were closed and blood ran from his nose. Charlotte's heart ceased to beat and she covered her mouth to stop a scream of dismay from escaping her.

Erik was leaning over him, speaking rapidly into his ear. The referee counted down the time, the seconds ticking past with the rise and fall of his official arm. Connor did not move.

Charlotte's knees went weak. Tony's arm was suddenly around her waist. He gently tried to guide her back to her seat, but she refused. She had to see the count finish. Seven. Eight. Nine. She had to see Connor move.

"It always looks worse than it is," Tony reminded her.

But the thought offered no comfort. Connor still hadn't moved. The referee's declaration of Jem Ward as the victor was drowned in the shouts of the crowd as he lifted the champion's arms into the air.

Charlotte jumped from the landau. She started off toward the ring alone, but she heard Aunt Dorian. "Go with her, Tony."

Soon Tony was at her side. The crowd thronged around them, congratulating each other on their wagers. But Charlotte and Tony forged their way toward Connor. By the time they reached his corner of the ring, Jem Ward had been lifted up on someone's shoulder and carried off. Erik and Connor, the defeated, had been left behind.

Charlotte scrambled through the ropes without regard for her gown and threw herself down on the canvas next to Connor. She touched his battered face, brushing her fingertips along his brow and longing for him to open his eyes. Blood trickled from his nose. A bruise was swelling on his arm. But when she touched his chest to reassure herself, it was rising and falling with deep, regular breathing—a good sign, Charlotte thought.

"He threw it," Erik kept repeating and shaking his head. "He threw the fight. He's never done that before. Never."

"I don't care what he's done," Charlotte snapped. "Give me that towel."

Tenderly, she cleaned Connor's face. "Has he ever been out like this before?"

"I've never seen him do nothing like this," Erik said, his voice full of astonishment—and disgust. "He could have been carried out of this ring as the champion just like Ward. He was throwing some of his best blows, but he let himself be beat."

Charlotte ignored Erik. "Connor? Sweetheart?"

Suddenly Erik seized her arm, his fingers biting into her flesh. "It was ye he did this for, didna he?"

Startled, Charlotte stared at Erik and tried to pull free of his painful grip.

Tony bent over them and grabbed Erik's wrist. "Release my cousin."

Erik glared at Tony, the bitter anger in his eyes frightening Charlotte. Finally the dark-haired Scot pulled away. "I donna know what you said to him, what promises you made to turn his head from his goal, but they'd better make up for everything he's lost because of you."

Erik rose to his feet, his anger and frustration shimmering around him like a light. "If ye want him, save him yerself then."

He spat out an unintelligible curse and disappeared into the crowd.

"Where's he going?" Charlotte asked, astonished that Erik wouldn't help Connor.

"I don't know," Tony said with a shrug. "May be he lost a big wager on the fight. Or he thinks this is like losing a battle in the feud."

Charlotte shook her head. She understood that Erik's disappointment must be great. But Connor's condition of was more importance. She bent over the man on the canvas, softly repeating his name, praying for him to open his eyes and grin at her.

Tony knelt across from her. "Come on, old chap, I don't want to have to carry you up those blasted stairs to your lodging again."

"Wake up, Connor," Charlotte pleaded. Her heart leaped when he squeezed her hand in response. His sable lashes began to flutter and he groaned.

"He's coming around," she said, breathless with relief.

"I'll get the landau," Tony volunteered.

Charlotte's face came into focus slowly, but Connor recognized her presence instantly by the soft touch of her hand on his cheek. He tried to offer her a smile of reassurance. But every part of him ached, tight and swollen from blow after punishing blow. He couldn't be sure which muscles worked and which didn't. He was probably make a ghastly face. "I'm glad you came, kitten. I have something to tell you."

"But Connor, why?" Charlotte begged. "Why did you lose?"

"Did I lose?" he asked, vaguely aware that he was lying on the canvas. All he really knew was that Charlotte was peering down at him with tears in her eyes. He had something important to tell her, but he didn't want to make her weep. "I lost, didn't I?"

"Resoundingly, sweetheart." A smile seemed about to appear on her face, then it crumbled into a tragic frown. "Why? Connor, you could have been champion. You could have had what you wanted."

"I remember now, the crowd," Connor muttered, his eyes falling shut again. "I wasn't going to give that bloody, depraved crowd the satisfaction. Can you understand that?"

Charlotte nodded, then added, "Not really. Well, perhaps I do, but Connor. The toll on you—"

She was weeping now. He could feel the wetness of her tears on his cheek.

"Don't cry," Connor implored. He managed to raise his hand to the back of her head and pull her down against his shoulder as the darkness began to gather around him again. Swirling and churning. But the silk of her hair felt so good against his skin. Her scent filled the air. He summoned what strength he had left to fight back the shadows. He had to tell her the truth he'd become certain of today, the truth that he could share with her at last. "Don't cry, kitten. I have something wonderful to tell you. Promise you won't cry. I love you, kitten. Do you hear me? I should have told you before. I love you."

His weakness was so complete he couldn't open his eyes to see her face. But he'd said the words he should have spoken long ago. "Do you hear me?"

"Yes, I hear you, Connor," Charlotte whispered. "I hear you, sweetheart."

Connor, smiled satisfied he'd done all that he could do, then he sighed and surrendered to the darkness.

FORTY-ONE

Connor came awake suddenly, aware that there was someone hovering over him who usually wasn't there. He opened his eyes and stared up into Charlotte's kittenish eyes. Her oval face came into immediate focus, her hair piled loosely on her head and a questioning smile on her lips. She looked absolutely delicious.

"Am I dreaming?" he asked without bothering to move.

"Only if you dream with your eyes open," she said, her smile broadening in a fashion that made Connor take a deep breath and struggle to sit up.

He was in his lodgings and the morning sun was pouring through the windows. "How'd you get me back here?"

"Tony and I brought you back and you've been sleeping about twelve hours," Charlotte said, rising from the bed and moving to the table. She returned with a plate of cheese, fruit, and bread. She sat down again and offered him a slice of apple. "Hungry?"

"Famished." Connor seized the food, feeling surprisingly clear-headed, light-hearted, and thoroughly starved. "How long have you been here?"

"Since we brought you back," Charlotte said. "Cassie is covering for me."

Still, something was strange, Connor thought. "And where's Erik?"

Charlotte frowned and refused to look at him. "Erik was ver

unhappy about the outcome of the fight. He left right afterward and we haven't seen him since."

"I'm not surprised," Connor said, disappointed. He'd known Erik was not going to like his decision. "Don't worry about him. He worked as hard as I did to get a chance to challenge the champion and the loss was hard for him. He'll turn up when he's got his frustration out of his system."

"And you?" Charlotte asked, her head tilted to the side as she spoke. "You're not disappointed about losing? Do you remember what you said while you were lying in the ring?"

"Aye, I remember," Connor said, the memory of the fight amazingly clear in his head.

When Charlotte started to open her mouth, Connor immediately put his finger to her lips. They were warm and soft and a shiver of pleasure banished his aches and pains. "And I meant every word of it. But I didn't get the chance to tell you that I knew why you came to the fight."

Charlotte glanced up at him, bewilderment in her eyes. "I came because you asked me to. Because you said if I could do it for Cassie, I could do it for you."

Connor shook his head and touched her cheek. "You were there because you wanted to tell me that you love me."

Charlotte's mouth dropped open and a furrow formed between her brows. "You're very sure of yourself."

Connor noted that she didn't deny what he'd said.

"So now's the time to say it," he urged, grinning at her. He could tell she didn't like him pressing her, but he remained undeterred. "Tell me again. I need to hear it, kitten."

"I'll tell you what you need," Charlotte said, bent over the food. "You smell like a stableboy who's been cleaning stalls and you need to wash up. I wiped you down some when Tony and Uncle Nicholas brought you in, but—"

"Yes, I see I'm in the same clothes I fought in," Connor admitted, looking down at his wrinkled kilt and bare chest. He eyed Charlotte more closely, a bit troubled by her resistance. "I suppose a confession of love does deserve the honor of a clean shirt and a shave."

Charlotte stood with the plate of food in hand. "Well, don't count on any confessions, but I do suggest that you clean up."

"I think I might need help," Connor said, recalling how well she responded to his pleas the last time he was hurt.

"I'll pour the hot water," Charlotte said, walking away from the bed.

Connor swung his legs over the edge. By the time he was on his feet, he was glad to find that he felt better than he expected. But for Charlotte's sake, it was time to groan. "Ooooh."

Charlotte whirled around. "Are you all right?"

Connor bent over and rubbed his back as if he were an old man with aching bones. "Could I lean on you to get over to the basin?"

Charlotte dropped the plate on the table and rushed across the room to come to his aid. With all the self-discipline he could muster, Connor kept the grin of pleasure from his face as he dropped his arm over her shoulder and she slipped hers around his waist. She smelled delightful and felt small and soft, yet strong enough to bear up in the circle of his arm. Funny how he'd misjudged her strength—and her courage. But her soft, generous heart had never been in question.

"How's that?" she asked, peering up at him as they slowly made their way across the room.

"Better, much better," Connor said, limping along. "I'm glad you stayed."

"Well, I want to be of help," Charlotte said, "but don't expect this visit to turn out like the other."

"Oh?" Connor stopped before the washbasin. "That's disappointing. Is it because I lack a black eye?"

"No." Charlotte retrieved the hot water from the fire and poured it into the basin and replaced the kettle before she turned to him. "It's because of Glen Gray and you know it. I've had all night to give this a lot of thought."

Connor stared at the steaming water and cursed his luck. He

should have forgone the urge to sleep and pressed for her confession in the ring while her heart was on her sleeve and she could refuse him nothing. "You're going to think us to death, aren't you, Charlotte? Tell me, what did you discover in your intellectualizing?"

"That this attraction is infatuation," Charlotte said, standing just beyond his reach as if she were determined to avoid his touch. "A flirtation. Call it what you will, but we're so different. It can't be true love, Connor. It can't be. You want a strong woman like Janet. I want an intellectual man like Edward."

"Really? Like Edward?"

"Well, not exactly," Charlotte admitted, looking away. "But you know what I mean."

Connor sighed, troubled by her reluctance to accept what seemed so plain to him now. He was going to have to prove to her again how right they were together. "I can't raise my arm, Charlotte. And my hands hurt. Will you help me wash?"

FORTY-TWO

To Connor's dismay, Charlotte stiffened upon hearing his request.

"You are here to help, aren't you?" Connor challenged, his impatience growing. "Why be missish now? We've spent the night together once. Are you sorry about that?"

"It was an impetuous thing to do," Charlotte said, meeting his gaze without embarrassment.

Connor would have liked a more enthusiastic answer, but he was sure she didn't regret their first night together. He couldn't hold back his grin as he held out a washcloth and a piece of soap toward her. "And 'twas impetuous going into that brothel. Impetuous and very unintellectual and courageous. Come help me, kitten."

With that invitation she stepped closer, a small smile of admission on her lips. She began to wash his back. He talked her into gently scrubbing his ribs, his arms, his chest.

When he began to unfasten his kilt, Charlotte paused, then handed him the washcloth. "I think you can manage from here without me."

"I don't know." Connor fumbled with the slippery soap and the dripping wet cloth. They hung in the air for an impossible moment, then dropped onto Charlotte's shoulder. Her bodice was immediately soaked.

"Connor, how could you do that?" Charlotte asked.

"You can't wear those damp clothes," Connor said as apologetically as he could manage while admiring the way the damp fabric already clung to her fragile collarbone and the fullness of her breast. "I think you'd better take that off and let it dry."

"Connor? You did that on purpose," Charlotte accused, more annoyance in her voice than outrage.

"I told you my arm hurt." Connor shrugged. "It's all right, you know. I've seen you in your shift before. Need help with the buttons?"

"I thought your arm hurt," Charlotte snapped, turning away to remove her dripping bodice.

"Aye, that's right," Connor said, looking down at his perfectly good arm and flexing his hand, which did ache a bit. "I'll finish my washing up and then you can give me a shave."

"I don't know anything about shaving," Charlotte protested as she shrugged out of her bodice.

Connor figured he didn't mind what kind of shave he got. It'd be worth it to have her leaning over him with no more than the sheer silk of a shift between him and Charlotte's breasts.

Charlotte turned her back as she handed him fresh clothes when he'd finished washing. She didn't exactly regret that she'd come to stay with him after the fight this time. Someone had to see to him with Erik taking off as he'd done. She had promised herself that she wouldn't be weak as she'd been before, even if he had declared his love. But he was being impossible.

As soon as he was dressed and ready for his shave, they pulled the table close to the sunlight. Connor sat down and lifted his chin as if he was sitting in a barber chair.

Charlotte hesitated. "I have no experience. Maybe we should send for Tony to do this."

"Oh, no, I trust you," Connor said, his face upturned so that his dark stubble gleamed in the sunlight. "Just do the steps I told you. First a warm towel, then the soap, then the razor."

Charlotte touched his beard tentatively, amazed at how prickly it felt. "I'll do my best."

She carefully followed the steps, quite forgetting how close she was to him and how little she was wearing. Now that he was dressed in a shirt open at his throat and a clean dress kilt, she felt safer with him—until she'd shaved the last lather from his jaw. She felt him nuzzle the bare underside of her arm.

"What are you doing?" she squeaked. His touch and the feel of his warm breath against so protected a place shocked her.

She looked down into his face to see that he was breathing unsteadily.

"It's confession time, Charlotte," Connor whispered, encircling her waist with his hands and bringing her down onto his lap. "Tell me you love me as much as I love you, or I'll carry you to my bed and have my way with you."

"You've already done that," Charlotte said, resisting his embrace. Despite her defiance, he pulled her easily into the familiar comfort of his lap. "If this is about Glen Gray—"

He rubbed her back, the warmth of his hands soaking through the silk. He kissed her neck lightly. The sensation was exquisite, but she couldn't allow herself to be distracted.

"Papa would never settle property on Cassandra and me like that," Charlotte said, hurrying on to say all that Connor had to know. "If you profess love for me, it has to be because you love me, not because of what my dowry might or might not bring. And you know I'm not like Janet."

"This has never been about Glen Gray, Charlotte," Connor said, nibbling his way down along her collarbone. "This is not about what your father owns or about Janet. It's about the woman I glimpsed hiding behind her sister's name the first day we met. You found her and so did I."

"Connor?" was all Charlotte could say as he scooped her breast toward his descending mouth. Through the silk he sucked on her budding nipple, his tongue teasing the most sensitive point until she cried out in ecstasy. Pleasure tugged deep inside her.

"Hmm, delicious." He moved to her other breast while his fingers stroked the nipple he'd just left.

"Connor?" She moved her hips against his thighs where she could feel the hard length of his sex.

He gave a low moan and stroked one hand down her body and beneath her knees and rose from the chair, lifting her in his arms. "Let's seal our betrothal in my bed."

"Betrothal?" Charlotte murmured as she wrapped her arms around his neck. "Connor, don't toy with me."

"Never. I've given up fighting," Connor said as he carried her across the room toward his bed. "Though I won't make any promises about a brawl now and then, for fun. But you have to give me something for my sacrifice, kitten. All I ask is your promise to wed me."

"Connor, if you're doing this because—" Charlotte began.

"But I'll admit Kinleith Castle is not the Foundling Shelter," Connor said as he lowered her onto the bed and began to slip her skirts and petticoats down from her waist. "But there's a library that needs someone to buy books for it and families that could use an encouraging word and the example of a strong lady of the manor."

"No fighting?" Charlotte repeated.

"I'll save my strength for our marriage bed and our children," Connor said, tugging at her shift. The moment her belly was bare, he lowered his head and kissed her stomach. "Say yes," Connor urged, stroking the tender skin of her middle with his chin. "Tell me you love me and say yes."

But Charlotte's world had plunged into a wordless existence made only of sweet, fierce sensations.

His hands stroked the insides of her thighs, entreating them to separate, though without threat or impatience. With his tongue, he bathed her navel.

When he kissed the cluster of red curls between her thighs, she cried out again. She could hardly believe the sweet, melting intimacy that spread through her when his tongue, soft and agile, began to explore her. He kissed her intimately, until she thrashed her head on the pillow, the pleasure too intense to tolerate, but too thrilling to give up. Her body quickened with each stroke.

Connor spoke to her softly and rose above her, pressing into her gently. This time her body yearned for the hard length of him, needing to know once more the joy of him buried snugly inside her.

Poised over her, he kissed her eyelids. "Say it, Charlotte. Tell me you love me and you'll go to Scotland with me. Trust your heart. You, Charlotte. Not Cassie's sister. Not Edward's muse. Not Davis St. John's daughter. You, Charlotte. Say you love me."

"This isn't fair, Connor," she panted without opening her eyes. Every fiber of her body strained to feel him inside her. She could bear no more emotions, no added tumult.

"I know," he said, his body still but his lips moving against her ear. "If it makes you feel better, I'm as tortured at this moment as you are. Say it, Charlotte."

She ached to entwine her body and soul with this man's. To deny that fact would be to deny herself, and she would not do that again. "Yes, Connor, yes, I love you."

He kissed her ever so lightly and began to move inside her, stroking her, the rhythm increasing, the pleasure racing through her body and into her veins until it broke over her in a wave of joy.

She cried out. Connor breathed her name against her lips.

As Charlotte sank back into the world again, she knew she had done the right thing in trusting her heart. She loved and was loved in return. Connor rolled onto his side and drew her close to him. Lovingly, she rubbed her nose against his solid chest, inhaled his scent, and sighed with contentment. Her life was changed forever, and whatever happened from now on, she would never masquerade as anyone but herself again.

FORTY-THREE

The day of Charlotte's engagement breakfast dawned perfect. The sky was a seamless blue and the sunshine warm and radiant but not too fierce—just right for a garden party. A soft breeze fluttered the white tablecloths and carried the scent of roses across the green. Nearly everyone on the St. Johns's guest list had accepted the invitation and the garden was soon full. To the sweet strains of violins and cellos, the ladies paraded out in pastel muslins crowned with wide hats and ribbons. The gentlemen strolled about in linen frock coats and tall top hats. The sound of laughter filled the air. Every detail was perfect.

The very perfection of it annoyed Cassandra.

She crumpled her handkerchief in her fist as she watched Connor hover over Charlotte near the food table. Tenderness filled his eyes as he handed his bride-to-be a flute of champagne. Adoration glowed in Charlotte's smile as she took the stem and looked up into Connor's face. Cassie's irritation deepened. It wasn't fair. They looked so utterly, blissfully happy that she could hardly bear to look at them.

She turned away, angry and ashamed of herself. Just what exactly was unfair about the situation wasn't clear to Cassie. Her vexation was silly and petty, she knew, and she didn't like finding such meanness in herself. But there it was, nettling her like a knotted stitch in her undergarment.

"Here, love," Dudley said, thrusting a flute of champagne at Cassie. He was beautifully dressed in a Skeffington brown sarcenet coat, a Spanish blue and yellow striped waistcoat, buff trousers, and brown boots. Dudley's ensemble was the perfect complement for her jonquil yellow garden dress and straw hat. If nothing else, her fiancé knew what to wear. She had managed to teach him that during their courtship. But the knowledge did nothing to soothe her vexation.

He leaned closer. "Why the frown, my dear? Is it because your sister and Kinleith make such an odd looking couple? Kinleith so big and coarse in that kilt and your sister, so delicate and refined."

"I think they make a perfectly lovely couple," Cassie snapped, aware that privately she agreed with Dudley. But she was feeling so contrary that if he'd pronounced them lovely, she would have called them odd. "And I shall frown if I like and when I like, thank you."

Cassie knew part of her annoyance came from the knowledge that she was losing her sister. But she and Charlotte had known all along they would be parted. They had vowed they would stay close, even when they lived in their own houses. But neither had counted on the emotional distance a man could put between them.

She'd not noticed much change between her and Charlotte when Dudley had come into the picture. But when Connor had appeared on the scene, Charlotte had become preoccupied with him and then with his cousin's orphanage. The confidences she'd shared with Cassie had become fewer and fewer. Cassie had found herself without a confidant. While Charlotte had Connor to share her deepest thoughts, Cassie had only Dudley.

She glanced at her fiancé who was discussing a new racehorse he'd bought with Archibald Smithfield. Dudley only wanted to hear her witticisms and gossip, not her observations or questions about life. No, she could not share all her thoughts with him. How often she'd longed for Charlotte's ear in the last two weeks, but Charlotte was preoccupied with Connor. Cassie knew this separation was bound to come, but did it have to be so complete?

The smile fell from Dudley's face. "Of course, they make a lovely couple, my dear. I'm sorry. Is something wrong?"

"No, nothing is wrong," Cassie muttered as nearly mystified as Dudley appeared to be about what was troubling her. "Everything is just perfect."

"Yes, I say, your mother does always put on the most smashing affairs," Dudley agreed, sipping from his champagne glass and surveying the garden. He leaned closer. "And absolutely everyone has turned out. Isn't that the Duke and Duchess of Fincham over there? The gift table is absolutely heaped with gifts. Just like at our engagement party. Remember our day?"

"I remember," Cassie said, avoiding his gaze once more. The memory of their engagement breakfast brought little pleasure to her. Not that it hadn't been a splendid occasion. Every detail from the hothouse flowers, oranges, and pineapples had been flawless, just as every party her mother undertook was. Cassie had been perfectly happy at the time. In fact, she'd been elated. She was making a good marriage, with a viscount whom she'd made over into the sensation of the season and whom was on his way to being an earl. She was the envy of every eligible girl in Town. The social world was at her feet.

But now as she watched Charlotte with Connor, she could feel doubt wiggling into her heart. What was the tantalizing mystery she saw in the soft looks they exchanged, in the manner in which they touched so casually, yet so expressly? What truth lay in the invisible cocoon of happiness that separated—protected—them from all the others at the breakfast? What was the truth that Charlotte and Connor seemed to share that Cassie knew she and Dudley had never experienced?

Cassie glanced at Dudley. He was brushing some invisible lint off his lapel. Dudley, Viscount of Monksleigh, was a handsome man with hazel eyes and brown hair and a round good-natured face. He was well-enough educated and heir to a prosperous earldom. Just like Charlotte, Cassie was destined to join the ranks of the aristocracy. She would be a countess. But none of that had anything to do with the mysterious void she sensed in herself—and in Dudley.

What was it then? Cassie wondered, turning her scrutiny on her twin sister. Charlotte must have felt her stare, for she turned, smiled, and waved to her sister. Half-heartedly Cassie returned the greeting.

Dudley leaned closer once more. "I say, you're not envious of all the attention your sister is getting, are you?"

"What?" The word exploded from Cassandra's mouth. Then she pressed her lips together in exasperation—and denial. The man could be absolutely idiotic. "Envious! I certainly am not envious of my sister. What on earth would ever make you say such a thing?"

Dudley gave a nervous laugh and stepped back. "Just the way you were looking at her as if you thought she'd gotten something that you haven't a chance at. Though I can't imagine what that would be."

"Nor can I." Cassandra tossed down the last of her champagne.

Suddenly a commotion at the side entrance into the garden silenced the string quartet. Cassie caught the quick movement of her father and mother moving toward the noise. Uncle Nicholas and Aunt Dorian followed close behind. Other heads turned in the direction, also curious.

"Who is it?" Dudley asked, peering over surrounding heads.

"I don't know," Cassie said, standing on tiptoe to get a better view. Her irritation scattered before the prospect of some deliciously scandalous scene occurring. "Can you see anything?"

"I do believe I see the Marquis of Linirk's livery colors," Dudley said as he continued to watch.

"Lord Linirk?" Cassie breathed the name in surprise. "He wouldn't dare come here without an invitation."

"I don't believe it's him, just a footman and some retainer or other." Dudley reached for Cassie's elbow. "Your father seems to be motioning toward us."

"Well, let's see what he wants," Cassie said moving through

the crowd toward the terrace where she could see her father standing with a footman and another man she'd never seen before.

As she approached she saw Connor and Charlotte join her
father. Erik followed them. The Scots retainer had reappeared
two days after the fight, contrite and humble. The loss had been
too much for him he explained and begged for forgiveness for
his weakness in the face of the defeat.

When they were all gathered around Papa and the new guest,
Papa made introductions.

"Kinleith. Charlotte, this is Graham, steward and foster
brother to the Marquis of Linirk," Papa said, more ill-at-ease in
making introductions than Cassie had ever seen her father.
"Graham, my daughter Miss Charlotte St. John who is betrothed to Connor McKensie, Earl of Kinleith."

Graham performed a curt bow in Charlotte's direction.

Cassie snapped opened her fan to remind Papa of her presence.

"Oh, yes, and this is my daughter Miss Cassandra St. John
and her fiancé, Dudley Moncreff, Viscount of Monksleigh,"
Papa added.

Linirk's retainer turned to Cassandra and studied her for a
long moment before offering her a slower, more graceful bow
of respect. "I'm honored, Miss St. John and Lord Monksleigh."

Cassandra curtsied, wondering why she merited such scrutiny.

"It seems the Marquis of Linirk has sent engagement gifts
to you both." Papa tugged uncomfortably at his cravat.

"How kind," Cassie said, smiling at the stranger wearing a
dark coat over tartan trousers. He had short bushy brown hair,
a strong brow, and keen gray eyes. There was no mistaking that
he was a Scotsman like his lord.

Charlotte glared at the man, the happy glow gone from her
complexion. Behind her, Connor frowned, his face cold and
forbidding. He drew Charlotte closer to his side. They'd made
it plain to everyone in the family after Connor's loss of the fight
that they held Linirk responsible for Connor's kidnapping
though nothing could be proved.

But Cassie studied this new Scotsman, her curiosity overcoming her dour mood.

"What's this all about, Graham?" Connor demanded. "Ramsay Forbes never gives without expecting some return for his generosity."

Graham frowned at Connor's ill-mannered comment. " 'Tis about his lordship paying his respects to the happy couple on this day of celebration of your coming nuptials."

"I'm certain Lord Linirk is but offering a token of goodwill," Papa explained, obviously trying to keep the confrontation from becoming a scene.

"Humph." Connor folded his muscular arms across his chest.

Cassandra bounced impatiently on the balls of her feet. Clearly Graham had brought gifts. She loved gifts and was eager to see them, even if they were from a stranger. "Pray, continue Mr. Graham."

Graham eyed her eagerness with a frown of disapproval every bit as deep as the one he'd cast Connor.

Offended, Cassandra shot him a rebellious glare.

"As I was saying," Graham continued, turning toward Charlotte, "Lord Linirk sends gifts to honor the occasion of your engagement to be married. For you, Miss Charlotte St. John, he sends this pair of love birds."

With a flourish one of the footmen stepped forward, whipping a silk, fringed cloth off an elaborately gilt bird cage. The guests gathered around gasped in admiration of the gift. Upon being unveiled the pair of love birds inside began to bill and coo. Not unlike Charlotte and Connor's behavior earlier, thought Cassie.

"How fitting," she said, not particularly impressed by the gift. Exotic pets were not difficult to come by for a marquis, but she was too polite to disparage the gift before others. "Aren't they lovely, Charlotte?"

"Yes, indeed," Charlotte said, coolly admiring the birds. "Please convey my thanks to Lord Linirk, Mr. Graham."

Breakfast guests applauded politely. Charlotte motioned to a St. John footman to take the bird cage away.

Then Graham turned toward her. Once again, his eagle-eyed scrutiny brought her up short. She glared back at him, feeling more than a bit offended by his frank regard.

"And for you, Miss Cassandra St. John, his lordship sends his deepest regrets that he did not honor you at the time of your engagement to Lord Monksleigh."

"His lordship is too thoughtful," Mama said, casting Cassie a warning glance.

"Yes, indeed, very thoughtful," Cassandra echoed, humbled by her mother's rare disapproval. She wondered seriously for the first time why Lord Linirk should choose this occasion to take notice of her.

"He sends you and Lord Monksleigh this belated but sincere token of his respect and his best wishes for a future of happiness and joy," Graham said.

Graham gestured to the other footman, who turned to the doorway, then reappeared leading a sleek, elegant black dog. "This is a Nairn hound."

"Ooh," uttered Dudley, his eyes grown wide and his voice filled with awe. "A true Nairn hound?"

"Aye," Graham said with a nod. "The best hunting dog, retriever, or companion to be found in the world."

A hunting dog? What a strange gift, Cassandra thought. But then it was just what Dudley would love. What was that saying? You could take the lad out of the country, but not the country out of the lad. And a hunting dog was the sort of thing a Scotsman would judge a valued gift.

"But Nairns are near priceless," Dudley said, staring at the dog. "I mean you can hardly find a chap who will part with his Nairn hound."

Graham inclined his head respectfully. "My lord was reluctant to give up Tophet, but he felt that the lovely daughter of Davis St. John and her betrothed deserved nothing less than the very best."

A mutt? Granted, a mutt with a fine heritage, but a mutt

nonetheless. Cassie forced a smile to her lips. "How very thoughtful of Lord Linirk."

Graham took the dog's leash and led the animal toward Cassie. With long-legged grace the pointed-nose hound politely heeled on its leash until it stood before Cassie and looked up into her face with liquid black eyes.

Cassie softened under the gentle admiration she saw in the dog's gaze. She glanced at the end of the leash that Graham offered to her. "What did you say its name is?"

"Tophet," Graham said.

"What a strange name," Charlotte said from Cassie's side. "Isn't that another name for Hades."

"Undoubtedly the animal's black color served as inspiration," Graham explained with an inclination of his head. "Tophet is trained to go anywhere with you, Miss St. John," the retainer added, patiently holding the leash out to her. "Or he will hunt for you, if you like. Or he will fight. He is trained to kill. But most importantly, he will protect you."

At a gesture from Graham, another Linirk footman hurried forward with a scroll of parchment and handed it to Dudley. "Here are the dog's bloodlines."

Dudley unrolled the scroll and studied the tree of names, his excitement clearly growing as he read through the hound's lineage. "Damned fine lines here. Sorry, Cassie. But this is smashing. I know blokes who'd give every last crown of their fortunes for a Nairn hound."

Cassie stared at the dog once more in disbelief. Fortunes, indeed. It was only a hound. A hound so large its spine was hip high on her. Soft fine black curls edged its long ears, the back of its legs, and the long comely tail. She was willing to grant that it was a very handsome hound, but only a hound.

Tophet's tail began to wag slowly as he perceived that Cassie was studying him.

"Sit," commanded Graham.

Tophet sat at her feet and cocked his head endearingly to look up at Cassie.

Graham offered the dog's leash to Cassandra once again. "Please accept this gift from Lord Linirk."

She looked down into those dark doggy eyes which seemed to seek her attention and approval. With a sigh, her resistance collapsed. She accepted the leash from Graham.

Tophet watched the exchange. When Cassie's hands closed around the leather, his tail beat the grass enthusiastically.

Graham bowed. "My lord will be very pleased."

"Please give him my thanks and appreciation," Cassandra said, unable to take her gaze from the dog's friendly face.

"Yes, do give Lord Linirk our gratitude," Dudley echoed, circling the dog and obviously aware that he'd just been delivered a goldmine in canine form.

"I shall convey your sentiments," Graham said, giving them each a bow, then taking his leave.

Papa reached for the leash. "I'll have the animal put in the kennel."

"No, no," Cassie said. "No, he seems well-behaved. Why not let him stay as long as he minds his manners? Charlotte has her love birds on the terrace."

Papa frowned. "As you like. It's just that—"

"Just what, Papa?" Cassie asked. "That a dog is an odd gift? I quite agree, but it is such an agreeable dog."

"Linirk is a very strange man," Connor warned.

"Well, I think his eccentricity is our good fortune." Dudley grinned from ear to ear as if he'd just gotten the best of a bargain. "I can hardly wait to take the mutt to the country for a bit of shooting. Archibald has invited me down to his country place next week. I say, Archie, over here. Come have a closer look at this dog."

For the next half hour Dudley and his friends admired the newly acquired Nairn hound. Cassie allowed the fuss, amused to see grown men so completely convinced that a dog could perform some kind of hunting magic.

A footman brought a chair for her and another brought her a flute of champagne. She settled down, smiling at Tophet who with another wag of his tail seemed to return her interest. The commotion over his head seemed of no concern to him. He stationed himself at Cassie's feet, gazing up at her.

"Shall we be friends, Tophet?" Cassie asked, accepting the dog's cue and ignoring the men.

Tophet's tail beat faster. Gently the hound laid his chin on Cassie's knee and looked up at her as if he was enraptured. With a smile Cassie surrendered to the urge to stroke his head. Tophet blinked with each touch of her hands, seeming to soak up her warmth. His head was sleek and silky and he continued to allow his chin to rest on her knee, his ears perked toward her as she petted him.

"I say, he doesn't look very ferocious the way he is allowing Miss St. John to pet him as if he was a lapdog," Archibald said. "Do you really think he has what it takes in the field?"

"That just shows his good breeding and training," Dudley said as if he'd suddenly become an expert on hunting dogs. For the first time he reached down to pet Tophet.

Instantly the dog's ears flattened and his tail went still. A threatening snarl hissed through the dog's teeth. Tophet never moved his head, but his eyes flickered warningly in Dudley's direction.

"I don't think he likes you," Cassie said, perverse pride coursing through her. She bit her lip to prevent a smile from coming to her lips.

"I just surprised him," Dudley explained, apparently embarrassed in front of his friends. "Hey there, boy, I'm going to give you a little pat then take you around to see some other folks. Maybe we'll snatch a treat from the table."

Once again Dudley stretched his hand toward the black hound. This time, Tophet growled. The rumble rolled forth from deep in his muscular chest, deeper and more menacing than any snarl. His black upper lip curled back exposing pink, healthy gums and exceedingly long, glistening fangs. But his head never left Cassie's lap.

"Dudley, stop," Cassie warned, working to keep a smile from

her lips. Tophet was making his preferences known in no uncertain terms. Though she'd never admit it to anyone—except
Charlotte—sometimes she didn't care to have Dudley put his
hands on her either.

"Right," Dudley said, standing back and reappraising the dog
as though seeing it for the first time. "Maybe your father is
right. The mutt should be in the kennel."

"No, I find him quite agreeable." Cassie said, growing fonder
of Tophet's company by the minute. He was a lovely companion.

"Well, as you say, my dear," Dudley said doubtfully. "I think
I'll join the croquet game."

"Yes, you do that," Cassie said, content to sit with Tophet at
her feet.

As Dudley strolled away, Tophet leaned affectionately against
Cassie's leg. She sipped her champagne and stroked the dog's
head again. He already seemed to understand her better than
Dudley probably ever would. Tophet was a lovely gift. Someday
she would have to thank the Marquis of Linirk personally for
his thoughtfulness.

Connor lingered behind the tree, a bit light-headed from ump-
teen glasses of champagne and tired of the formal socializing.
He and Charlotte had been separated in the crush of the party
and he was longing for a few moments alone with her. Finally
she left her conversation with a throng of women and drifted
toward him.

Quick as lightning Connor slipped an arm around her waist
and drew her behind the tree, out of sight of the prying eyes.
She gave a small cry of surprise, then came willing into his
arms and smiled up at him.

"Are you happy?" he asked, wanting to hear her confess her
contentment one more time. He couldn't hear the sound of pleasure in her voice too often.

"I'm happier than I've ever been," Charlotte said. "But I
can't help but wonder about those gifts from Lord Ramsay.

Connor frowned. "Think nothing of it. No doubt he's up to some game, but he won't get anywhere with it. People are wise to his game. They won't be fool enough to fall for his tactics."

"But a black dog for Cassie and Dudley?" Charlotte asked. "The love birds are nice and appropriate, though I'm not certain I will ever be able to be fond of them, considering who they come from. But a dog for Cassie?"

Connor shook his head. He laid his finger on Charlotte's lips. "Let's not talk about Linirk today. I resent that he even dared to send his man here. This is our day to announce to the world that we will soon be husband and wife. The Earl and Countess of Kinleith."

"Yes, no matter what is to come," Charlotte agreed with love shining in her face. "Husband and wife. Kiss me, my husband-to-be."

Connor gladly obeyed, moving his lips over hers. The contact filled his head with her familiar scent. He drew her close and tasted her greedily. Her body pressed immodestly against his sent warmth racing through him and set his body to aching.

"Oh," Charlotte sighed against his chin. "There's a poem about this."

"About what?" Connor murmured thinking surely no legitimate poet had been so indiscreet as to write about the things a kiss could do to a man's body—and his head.

"A kiss." Charlotte began to recite, her eyes closed as if she floated in some far off euphoria. "The greatest bliss is in a kiss—"

Connor chuckled. "No it isn't. You know better than that. I know you do."

Charlotte opened her eyes and blushed. "Connor, you are no gentleman." She laughed at him shyly.

"I know exactly who and what I am," Connor said, thankful Charlotte had come into his life and changed it forever. "I'm the luckiest man in the world."

ABOUT THE AUTHOR

Linda Madl started her fiction-writing career in St. Louis, Missouri. She and her family now live in the Flint Hills area of Kansas. As author of seven historical romances, including *The Scotsman's Lady* from Zebra Books, Linda loves hearing from readers. You may write to her c/o Zebra Books. For a response, please include a self-addressed stamped envelope.

BOOK YOUR PLACE ON OUR WEBSITE AND MAKE THE READING CONNECTION!

We've created a customized website just for our very special readers, where you can get the inside scoop on everything that's going on with Zebra, Pinnacle and Kensington books.

When you come online, you'll have the exciting opportunity to:

• View covers of upcoming books

• Read sample chapters

• Learn about our future publishing schedule (listed by publication month *and author*)

• Find out when your favorite authors will be visiting a city near you

• Search for and order backlist books from our online catalog

• Check out author bios and background information

• Send e-mail to your favorite authors

• Meet the Kensington staff online

• Join us in weekly chats with authors, readers and other guests

• Get writing guidelines

• AND MUCH MORE!

Visit our website at
http://www.zebrabooks.com